LOVE IN THE *After*

Nicole Bazley

To anyone who has ever suffered loss, in whatever form.

I see you!

Authors Note

Love In The After is a romance novel etched from real life narratives. Themes reflect realities that many people face in their own personal journey. The story explores sensitive topics like death of a spouse and miscarriage, written from a place of deep understanding through my personal experiences.

I understand that these subjects can be triggering for some readers. If you feel this is something that might affect you, please visit my website for a more detailed list of content and trigger warnings.

Reader discretion is advised.

1

Hannah

Knock knock, knock knock.

"Mum, someone's at the door."

"I heard it. Be there in a second." I wipe my hands over the floral tea towel that is already stained with greasy finger marks. It hangs over my shoulder while I finish dinner prep. Chucking it on the kitchen bench next to a bowl of haphazardly chopped vegetables I have been trying to make resemble a salad.

I glance at my watch. It's 5:45 PM. Callum should have been home by now.

I have been rushing around like a headless chicken trying to scrape together something other than beans on toast for dinner. Not that Callum would ever complain. In all our years together, he has never made a comment about coming home from work to a messy house or an uncooked dinner. He never blanched at having to make dinner for everyone. He would walk through the door, step over the obstacle course of toys that littered the hallway, kiss me on the cheek and get stuck in. I've been especially grateful for this since returning to work after having kids.

I know he is not going to care if he has to wait half an hour for the chips to cook. Or if the chicken is dry. Or that the lettuce is slightly wilted because I didn't get a chance to run to the shop for fresh salad ingredients.

The knocking starts again. It's not rushed or loud, but it makes my pulse quicken. Like clockwork, Callum calls when he leaves work to check in and ask if I need him to pull into the shops for anything.

I tap my phone on the way out of the kitchen. No missed calls. My body heats slightly with panic. He would have called if he was running late. He knows how hectic the after-school rush can be, between picking up the kids, sports, dinner, unpacking school bags, washing lunch boxes and doing homework. It's usually a chaotic mess.

I walk towards the door, half expecting to see my mother-in-law. She often pops around at this time, usually with some form of family gossip. The knock comes again. It's not followed by my mother-in-law's voice. The way she always announces herself with a, "It's me," after knocking.

My skin prickles as I open the door and make contact with the sombre faces of two police officers. I don't notice much more about them at first, my eyes instantly darting to their cruiser that shadows them. Right where Callum's car should be. The lights aren't flashing, and I don't hear sirens. Trying to focus back on the officers in front of me, I glance between them. Sorrow seeps into their glassy eyes, lips downturned in practised sympathy. It tells me everything I need to know.

This isn't good news.

The female officer takes a tentative step forward, her hands clasped behind her back, deep blue eyes dipped low. "Ma'am." She clears her throat. "Are you Hannah Grace?" I nod. Fast, sharp movements as the blood drains from my face. "We have some news about your husband."

The room fades away as my heart pounds in my chest. "I'm so sorry to tell you this." The faint smell of chicken burning registers in the back of my mind, but I'm too numb to care as the officer continues to speak. My brain only processes fragments. "There was an accident."

My legs seem unable to hold my weight.

"They did everything they could."

I feel them give out.

"I'm so sorry for your loss."

I'm steadied by firm hands, guiding me towards the lounge and helping me to sit.

Noah breaks from his homework spread across the kitchen table. He walks into the room and sits next to me, placing his small hand over my own. I look into his eyes. Eyes that are all too like his fathers.

Ethan's Minecraft block tower topples over. The sound of magnetic blocks chiming snaps my eyes to him as he moves from the rug on the floor to the other side of me. Confusion paints his smaller features. Liam appears in the hallway, having come out of his room to see what all the commotion is, no doubt.

I feel like I can't breathe. My chest is being crushed by the weight of the officer's words. Cramps pull at my stomach. The flickering flames from the electric fireplace that sit under the TV dance and swirl through my blurred vision. Making me feel like I'm in a real-life mirage, the room warps around me, anchored only by the warmth of Ethan's body next to me and the feel of Noah's hand on mine.

The female officer hands me a glass of water that I had not noticed she went to retrieve. My mouth is dry, but my throat feels too closed off to even swallow.

There are no tears.

I know they'll come.

The other officer who has barely spoken asks me if there's someone they can call for me, but my brain can't function. I can't put words together in my mind to respond. It's spinning. A cyclone of thoughts, feelings and emotions.

Noah squeezes my hand, and the sensation brings me back to the present. He is a mini version of his father. The same thick dark hair, light green eyes and defined straight nose. Every time I look at my eldest son, I'm reminded of Callum.

Although it's Liam, our middle child, that has his dad's personality and sense of humour. He's smart and blunt. So it's no surprise he is the one to break the silence. "What's happening?"

How do I answer that? How can I possibly tell them what happened?

How do I tell my three children that their dad, the man they idolise, isn't coming home?

Not tonight.

Not ever.

2

Hit me with it
Clark

The doctor calls my name from the waiting area. "Clark, come on through."

He isn't my usual doctor or the specialist that Cherie and I have been seeing. When they rang to tell me that they had my test results, I couldn't wait. I needed to hear them as soon as possible. They squeezed me in with whoever was free. I was in my car ten minutes later headed straight to the clinic. Between the rush of packing up the job I was working on, notifying the staff that I was headed out and getting here as quickly as I could, I didn't have a chance to tell Cherie they called. I'll fill her in as soon as I get the results.

I follow the doctor down the light green hallway, passing a few signs about vaccinations and skin checks. He stands aside to make way to his exam room. The worn black leather squeaks as I sit down. I grip my hands to my thighs, desperately trying to stop the nervous bouncing of my legs.

"Hit me with it, Doc." The suspense is killing me.

Cherie and I have been trying to get pregnant for over a year. A month ago, we saw our doctor to find out why it wasn't happening. A few fertility specialists' appointments, a blood test and sperm sample later, and here I am. Both of our blood work had come back with no issues. This is the results of my sperm sample.

The doctor removes his glasses to rub his hands over his face, before settling them back on the bridge of his long nose. "We look for a few things that can contribute to infertility." His monotone voice grates on my nerves. Like this news isn't the single most important thing to me.

"I know, they explained all this when I did the samples. What do mine say?" I press.

He glances down to his computer screen and then back to me. I can tell it isn't good news by the way he is stalling, and the sympathetic look that blankets his face.

My leg starts bouncing uncontrollably again.

"Your sperm count is low."

"What does that mean?"

"Well, we may see infertility in any sperm count under fifteen million sperm per ejaculation. Your sperm count was recorded at six million. Then we look at their health. In simple terms, we want them swimming forward."

What the hell does all that mean? "Mine don't swim forward?"

"Yours looked fine in that regard; forty-three percent swimming with progressive motility, which is good."

It feels like someone has taken a baseball bat to my stomach, the wind completely knocked out of me. "There just ain't enough?"

"Exactly. Look, normally the specialist would give you these results and be able to talk you through it all. I know you were eager to hear the results, but we have booked you in with the specialist next week. They will be able to advise you of the next steps."

I nod. If I open my mouth, I don't trust that it won't be a scream that comes out. Nothing makes a man feel more emasculated than hearing that he is the reason his partner can't have kids.

How am I going to tell Cherie about this?

The doctor gives me some other information about my test results; I barely hear a word of it. I drag myself from the room, my crushed soul following behind me and an appointment card clutched in my fist.

Sitting in my truck in our driveway, my hands twist around the leather of the steering wheel. I try to steady my rapid breathing. All Cherie has wanted is a baby. To be honest, it's all I've wanted for a long time as well. Now because of me, it most likely isn't possible.

My pulse races and my feet feel heavy as I trudge up the few steps lined with flowers to our wooden patio, fumbling with the little silver key before I push the front door open.

I hear a high-pitched squeal and my already racing heart skips a beat. My keys clang on the tiled floor as I run towards the bathroom. Cherie rounds the corner and jumps straight into my arms.

"Clark, Clark, Clark!" Each squeal of my name reaches a higher octave before she hands me a white stick with a pink lid.

I know exactly what this is.

I'm sure we have kept the pregnancy test companies afloat this last year, each one coming back negative. I know what a negative looks like.

I risk a glance down. Two distinct lines, not one.

It's positive.

No doubt about it.

We are pregnant.

3

Fuck you tyre

Hannah

*B*ANG!

The sound rings out around me, loud enough to be heard over the blaring music, and my cats so called 'singing'.

Fuck! That doesn't sound good.

A loud thud follows. I try to steady the car without over correcting, as my mind ticks over. When was the last time I checked the tyre pressure? Or the tyres in general for that matter. Don't mechanics do that in regular services? I don't recall them bringing anything up when I went for my last one. When was that, though? I sift through my memories, trying to recall.

I bought this car second hand from a dealership two years ago. Short of its services, I haven't done a damn thing to it. That was always Callum's job. I mean, I know how to change a flat, pump the tyres, check and refill the oil and coolant. But all of that became things my husband took care of. I never used to put fuel in my own car. I remember I called Callum my fuel fairy. He would take the car without me realising and fuel it up.

I never realised how much those little gestures made a difference to my life, until suddenly they were gone.

I push the large red button to put my hazard lights on. One hand instinctively reaches for the ring that lays heavy around my neck, as I try to direct the car as close to the edge of the road as I can. It's one hundred and ten along Forrest Highway, cars flashing by in blinks as I slow.

Each side of the road is dense with tall, thick trees. Lush green shrubs and fallen branches create ground cover, making a place to pull over safely nearly impossible. There is a turnoff not too far ahead, which seems like a far safer option, so I make the left-hand turn. The street is dead. No other cars and no houses to be seen for kilometres. Just rotten wooden poles with barbed wire fences making way to green fields with cattle crazing.

Finding a flat section of dirt, I pull over. The ground is littered with leaves, twigs and rocks, before a slope drops down to a thicker part of the forest that isn't fenced. I climb out of my Toyota Fortuner. I haven't had to change the car's tyres yet, but I know the spare is under the boot. Opening the door, I find the little side compartment, assuming this is where the tools are kept that I'll need.

Bingo.

I squat to look under the car, checking the exact location of the spare, and instantly regret my decision to wear a short sundress. The soft cotton material rides up, almost flashing my ass to a herd of cows, as I assess how to get the spare out. The brown tropical leaves and burnt orange sun pattern scrunch together as I bend.

I bought this dress specifically for this kid-free trip. If I'm not in gym clothes, I'm covered in some form of mess from the absolute carnage my three boys create. A two-night kid free weekend down south seemed like the perfect opportunity to splurge on some new clothes. But damn, it's going to be hard to change a tyre in a short dress, and I don't want to get it dirty. I'm supposed to be meeting a group of friends at The Long Pour in Yallingup for lunch. I really don't feel like rocking up covered in tyre grease and dirt.

I fling open my suitcase and start rummaging through it. Ahhh, why have I packed eight dresses for a weekend trip? My towel hangs from my beach bag. That will work. A quick glance around reveals nothing but farm animals and trees swaying, so I quickly slip my dress over my head and chuck on the hooded towel.

My post breastfeeding boobs are small enough to not warrant a bra. Plus, my dress had such beautiful, beaded shoe-string straps, I didn't want to ruin the aesthetics. I'm also far too old to live in rib-constricting shit like a strapless bra. Comfort and free nips all the way.

However, those decisions have now left me in a black lace thong with a hooded towel gaping open at the sides.

Whatever, no one is around. Let's just get this tyre changed.

I connect the long poles and thread them into the hole in the boot to loosen the tyre from the recess. It lowers down to the ground on a chain. Squatting again, I disconnect the tyre from the chain and wheel it around to the front left. I wipe my already dirty hands right across the hot pink material of the towel. Shit, this is annoying.

I put the tyre iron over the first nut and get to work. Well, for exactly the one point three seconds that it takes me to realise that I am never getting these wheel nuts off. I push down on the tyre iron with every ounce of strength I have.

I'm a physical therapist. I strength train four days a week, so I consider myself strong. But this thing isn't budging. Like not even a millimetre. Putting one foot on the tyre iron, I try to push down with all my body weight. My cute, buckled slides, ironically, slide right off the slippery metal.

Damn thing.

I'm glad that I bought a million different outfits. I find my Docs in my suitcase and chuck them on, not bothering to tie the laces. Then, I try the standing approach again. Only this time, I put two feet on and bounce, holding onto the bonnet of the car as I do.

It moves. Shit, yesss.

I loosen the nut but leave it on, then try the next one by hand. Holy hell, this one is just as bad. I place a foot on it and stomp. It budges. *Yes.* I repeat the process for the third nut. This one comes off more easily than the last.

All right, two more and I am on my way to a pizza and a margarita.

Placing the tyre iron on the fourth nut, I try with just my hands first, hoping it will be easy. No such luck. It doesn't budge. Stomping on it with one foot doesn't do a damn thing either. I put two feet on and bounce.

Shit, still nothing.

What the hell?

I check the time and realise I have been at this for over fifteen minutes already. Slumping down on the dusty floor, little pebble rocks pinch my bare ass. I give myself a mental pep talk.

"Come on, bitch, you can do this. It is just a tyre. Stop sulking and get it done." I am aware I look mildly crazy; slumped on the ground in a towel screaming into the forest.

I suck it up and stand, ready to try again. Connecting the tyre iron, I stomp a few more times before my foot slides off and I smash my knee on the side of the car.

"AHHHHH FUCK YOU TYRE!" I scream, yanking the tyre iron off the wheel nut and throwing it into the forest. Sucking in a few deep breaths, I calm myself down. "You can do this."

I will not be defeated by a flat tyre.

Marching down the little hill, I search for the resting place of the tyre iron.

I can do this.

I am hungry

And I want a margarita.

4

The man or the bear

Clark

I am dying to take a piss. It feels like I have been driving forever. This stretch of road is pretty dense, with thick trees lining either side of the double lane highway. I haven't been this far south before. It's beautiful.

A turn off up ahead to the left seems like a safe option to do my business. I don't particularly feel like getting hit by a car with my dick in my hand.

I make the left-hand turn down the dead street, noting a car parked on the side of the road. The driver doesn't appear to be in the car, but it looks like it has a flat. Going far enough past them to have some privacy, I find a flat spot to pull over, quickly do my business, and then I'm on my way. As I drive back past the parked car, I see the jack and spare out, but no sign of the driver.

Damn, I'm already running late for lunch. But I am also not the type of man to leave someone stranded on the side of the road. Being a mechanic, I could change a tyre in my sleep.

Letting out a breath, I pull over and start to cross the road towards the car. Then I see her, stomping out of the bush, clutching a tyre iron and mumbling to herself. She is wearing a hot pink...Is that a poncho? And big black boots.

"Hey." I make sure I'm loud enough for her to hear me. "Do you need a hand?"

She jumps out of her skin, letting out a little shriek as she slips down the hill, almost toppling over. I slowly make my way closer. The tyre iron drops from her hands as she moves to clutch the towel around her waist.

Now that I'm close enough, I see it's a hooded towel. It also becomes blatantly clear that she has not much on underneath, as I get a glimpse of her bare tanned skin through the sides.

She carefully bends to grab the tyre iron, still clutching her towel with one hand, and makes it back to the top of the hill. "Shit, you can't just sneak up on a girl in the middle of the woods like that."

"Sorry," I chuckle, bringing my hands up, as if I'm under arrest. "I come in peace, I swear."

She takes a step to the side, getting closer to her car. I don't know what else I can say to tell her I am not a threat. I suppose I'm well above average height, and I've been hitting the gym hard this last year. Not a heap else to do with my time. But I can understand why she would be cautious with my sudden presence.

Keeping my hands near my face, I take a step back to show her...I actually don't know what I'm trying to show her.

Her eyes roam over me, but she doesn't move away again.

"I'm the man, not the bear." I drop my hands. "You're safe, I promise."

She lets out a laugh. The kind of laugh that makes her whole body shake. I try not to scan my eyes down as her hands loosen on the towel, revealing more smooth skin.

"You mean you are the bear," she corrects.

"Huh? No, I just mean I'm not going to hurt you."

"Yeah, so you are the bear, not the man." She is still laughing uncontrollably.

Okay, if I'm totally honest, I have no clue what that saying means.

I try not to smile at her laughing but damn it's hard. It's intoxicating, and she is drop-dead gorgeous. Even in a poncho towel and boots.

"I actually don't really know what that saying means." I slide my hands into my pockets, trying to appear cooler than I am.

"It means that most women, if alone in the woods, would rather encounter a bear than a man."

"What! Why? Bears are savage."

"People wouldn't question you if you told them a bear attacked you, nor would they ask what you were wearing. And generally, a bear is going to mind its own business and only attack if it feels threatened."

"Okay, then I suppose I am the bear." I take a tentative step closer to her, aware I'm still standing in the middle of the road.

"But you're not just minding your business, are you?" A playful smile tugs at the corner of her lips.

Chuckling, I slowly move closer. "I'm a mechanic, and I saw your flat. Just wanted to see if you need a hand?"

Her head tilts as she looks down at the flat tyre then back at me, almost like she had forgotten what she was doing on the side of the road. Then her shoulders sag. "Oh my gosh, honestly, I would love a hand. I've been stuck here for like"—she checks her watch—"almost half an hour and I cannot for the life of me get these last two nuts off."

"May I?" I gesture towards the tyre iron she is still wielding like a weapon. She nods, so I move in, tentatively taking it from her hand. I crouch next to the tyre.

"Honestly, it took me forever to get the first three off. I had to put boots on and jump on the tyre iron. They were on so tight."

"So you're saying this isn't your normal attire?"

That infectious laugh starts again.

"No, I swear I had on a hot little sundress and slides, but I didn't want to get grease on them."

"Fair call." I twist the tyre iron. Shit, it is on tight. I have a rattle gun in my car. I could go and get it, but there is a small, cocky part of me that wants to see if I can do it by hand. Especially because she is standing right by me, watching with sea glass green eyes. Every time I glance sideways, I get a view of her toned legs and torso.

I swallow and try to focus on keeping my eyes on the task at hand. I crank the tyre iron harder this time, desperately trying not to look like I'm straining.

It budges.

Slowly...

Then it eases off.

"You're kidding me." She makes a sarcastic huff. "How did you do that so easily?"

"You must have loosened it for me." I playfully wink up at her.

Fuck, what am I doing? That was so cheesy.

"Mmmhmm, sure I did," she says behind a smirk.

I move to the next nut. This one is just as tight, but I manage to get it off.

"Want me to change it over for you?" I start jacking the car up.

"No, it's fine. I can manage from here. You look like you're dressed so nice. I don't want you to get dirty."

I feel the heat of a blush as it works its way up my collar. She thinks I'm dressed nicely?

"I don't mind, honestly. Besides, I wouldn't want you to get dirty either." I smile up at her.

What the actual fuck am I doing? Am I flirting? I don't flirt. I mean, I'm an okay looking guy.

I think.

I've been on some dating sites since my marriage imploded. I haven't found it hard to find women. I just don't let them get too close to me these days.

"I'm already filthy," she says. My eyes snap to hers. Is she flirting back? She isn't blushing, so she must just mean it literally. Her towel already has a smear of grease, and it also covers her hands.

"I honestly don't mind. It will take me less than five minutes."

"Okay, if you're sure you don't mind. I'd really appreciate it."

I pull the flat off and chuck the new one on for her.

"Where are you headed?" I ask as I hand-screw the nuts back on.

"Bear, remember?" She's chuckling again.

"I'm not trying to stalk you, just that you should only drive eighty kilometres an hour on this spare. You're on a freeway that is one hundred and ten and you are at least an hour from any form of civilisation."

"Oh shit, I hadn't thought of that. I'm actually headed to Yallingup, then back to Dunsborough. I'm down for a friend's wedding."

"You definitely want to get it changed over to a proper tyre then. I have a mate in Bunbury; I'll call him up and see if he can get you sorted. That way, you only have to get to the next town."

Her eyes light up. "Really? That would be amazing. Thank you."

"I'm also down here for a wedding in Dunsborough. Wonder if we are at the same one."

"Who's your bride and groom?" She eyes me sceptically.

"Olivia and Rowan." I glance up at her, trying not to notice how she no longer holds her towel closed.

"No way, same. At Driftwood Estate," she says, tone laced with shock.

"Yeah, staying down here for the whole weekend."

"I'm here for the weekend as well. Thought I'd make the most of the babysitters. How do you know Rowan and Olivia?"

She follows me as I place her flat into the boot of her car and pack away the jack and tyre iron. She takes a seat on the edge of her boot, making her towel ride up over her legs.

It's hard to avert my gaze as I lean back against the boot. "He was one of the first people I met when I moved here almost eighteen months ago. I fixed his car and we stayed friends. What about you?" I ask curiously.

"My husband and Olivia's ex-husband used to be friends. So that's how we originally met, hell, almost twenty years ago now.

When they divorced, he moved overseas and we stayed good friends with Olivia, and now Rowan, as well."

Did she just say husband? My eyes trace to her delicate fingers. No ring. But she mentioned babysitters, so she has kids.

"Wow, so you've known her for a long time, then. And your husband, is he meeting you down here?" I try to throw that last bit in as nonchalantly as I possibly can. Wiping my palms on my dark blue shorts, I try to hide the fact that being so close to her is making me sweat.

I'm not looking for a relationship—my ex made sure I'm too messed up for that—but I can't ignore how gorgeous she is.

She shifts uncomfortably. "Uhhh, well, no. I mean...he's dead. So no, just me."

I choke on a cough. Did I just hear that right?

She smirks before a little chuckle escapes her lips.

Is she actually laughing at that?

"Sorry," she says as her expression softens. "Laughing is a bit of a coping mechanism. I never really know how to chuck that into conversation."

"I'm so sorry." I don't really know what else to say.

"Thanks. It's been three years now, so I'm actually okay. For the most part, anyway. Things like this can be rough, though." She twists a piece of stray cotton fraying on her towel.

"Like getting a flat?" I gesture to the tyre behind us. It was probably a job her husband would have done.

She laughs again. "No, the tyre is fine. It's the weekend that will be hard. To be at a wedding surrounded by love and married couples when you are solo is a tad depressing. They probably put me at the table with all the other widows who are over the age of eighty. My dancing choices are going to be Albert with the fake hip or Calvin in the wheelchair." She yanks the stray piece of cotton free from the towel.

"If it makes you feel any better, if there is a table for forty-two-year-old losers, whose ex-wife had an affair, fell pregnant and tried to convince him it was his, then left him for the other dude...well, that's where I'll be."

"What the fuck? That bitch," she blurts out, turning to look at me, horror pulling on her face. "I'm sorry, I shouldn't call your ex-wife a bitch, but damn, that's harsh. I'm so sorry she did that to you." Her face softens, and I can see the genuine emotion behind her pretty eyes. It's not pity, like most people give me. There is a level of understanding there. Someone who has felt the pain of loss herself.

"I mean, personally, I call her Satan, but bitch works as well." I don't know what possessed me to spill my depressing life like this on the side of the road to a stranger, but it's too late to retract it now.

"How did you find out?" she asks.

I debate answering this question—it's something I haven't really talked about. Something I've barely even dealt with.

I glance down at my feet, kicking a few rocks, watching the sand swirl around them. "We were trying for kids for a long time. We were doing initial fertility testing to start IVF." I pause, choking on the next part. She is staring at me with the kindest green eyes. Something in me breaks and I want to keep talking. "I had just finished at the doctors, where he in no uncertain terms told me it would be a miracle if I managed to get someone pregnant as is. Low count, apparently."

A hand flies to her mouth to stop the gasp that escapes, like she knows exactly what is coming.

I'm shocked that I'm even talking about this with a stranger.

"What? Your sperm count is low?" She somehow effortlessly finds the words I struggle to say. She doesn't seem to match my modesty in talking about this kind of thing. Her eyes are wide, and her hand goes back to her lips.

"Yeah, really low. They wanted me to go back to see the specialist for more testing and treatment options. But when I got home, Cherie told me she was pregnant."

"Holy hell, so what did you do?" she asks.

"It took me a while. I was caught up in the excitement of it, but then eventually, I confronted her. She swore black and blue that I had to be the father. But I could see it on her face. Long story short, she eventually came clean. She got her happy ending, and I got..." I mull over what to say. I wanted kids so badly. To have it within reach and then ripped away felt worse than her having an affair.

"You got a broken heart," she finishes, the words holding so much sympathy. I look back down at the ground. "You had something you sounded like you really wanted, then you had it taken from you. I understand that heartbreak."

"Thanks. I'm sorry, too, about your husband. I can't imagine what that felt like. How did he die?"

"Car accident. Drunk driver ran a red light." Her face falls like she is in physical pain just talking about it.

I don't ask any further questions.

Something in me wants to reach out and hold her hand but I refrain. "Well, I promise I won't let Calvin in the wheelchair near you. Or any of the other widows for that matter. I'll dance with you." I swear I catch a glint in her eye when I say that.

She smiles across at me, then looks down at her watch. "Shit, we better move or we are going to miss dinner, as well as lunch."

"Let me call my mate to let him know we're on our way." I pull my phone from my pocket to give him a call.

"Can you text me where I am headed? I'll give you my number."

"Sure." I pass my phone to her. She types in her number, then passes it back to me. I jump into maps to find my mate's workshop. I drop a pin and send it to her number.

"I'll just get changed and then I'll meet you there." She turns to grab her dress that is placed over her suitcase.

"No worries. You have my number, so just call me if you have any issues on the way. Remember, you can only go eighty. I'll hang back a bit as well, just in case."

"Thanks," she says with a genuine smile.

I cross the road back to my car, fighting the urge to glance back at her, knowing she may be slipping the towel off and her dress back on.

Once behind the wheel, I risk a side glance. She is clearly waiting for me to leave to get changed. I shake my head, not really believing the coincidence of it all or the conversation I just had with this stranger on the side of the road.

I just told a smoking hot woman that I'm infertile and that my ex-wife had an affair.

Jesus, something is wrong with me.

5

Margaritas, Tacos and Sex

Hannah

What the actual fuckety fuck just happened?

Our eyes meet as he drives past, and I swear my knees actually give out a little. I'm not normally a nervous person.

No man since my husband has given me butterflies.

My late husband.

I have to get better at saying that.

We just spoke about the literal worst parts of our lives, and I don't even know his name. He told me he is infertile, for fuck's sake, and I didn't even think to ask him what his name was. What an idiot.

I grab my phone and quickly bring up his text.

HANNAH: Thank you so much. I'm Hannah, by the way.

I hit send. He is driving, so I don't hold out hope for a reply. I try the best I can to wipe the grease from my hands on my towel, before changing back into my sundress and sandals. My phone pings right as I make it back into my car.

MYSTERY MAN: No problem, Hannah. See you soon. I'm Clark.

Clark. His name is Clark.

Hmm, suits him.

I ask Siri to dial my sister. It barely rings through the Bluetooth speakers before I hear the familiar chime of her voice.

"Your kids are fine, Hannah. Go have fun," she says before I have time to open my mouth with a hello.

Her kids are eighteen and twenty now, so she agreed to stay at my place and watch my three boys while I take this much-needed weekend vaycay.

"Thanks, Kate, but no, I have other news. You will never guess what just happened to me."

"OH MY GOSH, tell me," she all but squeals. Her voice echoes around me in the confines of the car.

"I got a flat tyre, and I'm on the side of the road in nothing but a G-string and a towel changing it—"

"Why are you in a towel with no other clothes?" Kate questions.

"Because I didn't want to get my pretty dress dirty. Anyway, that's beside the point..."

"Get to the point."

"I'm trying, if you would shut the fuck up for a minute."

"Okay, go."

"I'm changing the tyre..."

"In nothing but a towel, right?"

"KATE!"

"Okay, okay, sorry. Go, go, go."

"I'm changing my tyre, and this guy pulls over to help me."

"Oh my Gosh, did you just bang someone on the side of the road? You dirty little stop out."

"What the fuck, NO. Kate, shut up."

"Okay, sorry, go on...The guy."

"Kate, he is sooo damn hot. Imagine Jensen Ackles and Charlie Hunnam had a love child."

"Stop it, Dean Winchester."

"Yes. Yes Dean. Like he had these hazel eyes, but they were aqua and caramel and yellow, and like blondish, sandy hair. He was just so sweet, Kate. He changed my tyre and somehow, we got talking..."

The bitch cuts me off again.

"Hang on, I thought you weren't into blonds."

"I am when they look like that."

"Thought you were giving up on the dating thing?"

"Yes, I thought the same, but then I saw him and my vagina had other plans."

She cracks up laughing, and I can't help but follow.

My sister is my best friend. I literally would not have survived these last three years without her. Come to think of it, I would not have survived motherhood at all without her. She has been there for me through it all.

"Did you get his number?" Kate asks after we calm ourselves down from our laughing fit.

"I'll raise you one."

"Thought you didn't screw him on the side of the road?"

"Stop, NO. We're at the same wedding. We're like, in the same circle. He is driving to his mate's tyre shop right now to help me get a new tyre fitted."

"No way." She screams again and my ears ring.

"Yes way."

I tell her the entire story in great detail, going over our conversation word for word. She listens intently, adding little playful jabs and 'shut ups' along the way. Then we say our goodbyes, and she tells me she will call me with the boys when she picks them up from school.

It's a Friday and the majority of my friends have taken the day off to come down early and make the most of the weekend, hence why we booked lunch. A lunch we are probably not making it to.

I glance down at my watch. It's already a quarter past eleven. Everyone will arrive around twelve, and I'm still over an hour and half drive away. Plus, a tyre change.

The rest of the drive is uneventful. I have my maps up on my phone and follow along, making sure I stay under eighty. I crank my music, singing along to my random playlist. Jessie Murphy's 'Heartbroken' comes on and I belt it out, completely out of tune.

It's a slow old drive, and I get beeped at more than twice. Assholes.

It takes forever to hit Bunbury, but the tyre shop is easy to find. I see Clark as I pull into the car park. One foot is bent against the tyre with his back leaning on his car. I park and he pushes off the passenger side door to come and meet me, opening my door before I get the chance.

"Been a while since someone has done that for me," I say, giving him a smile as I slide out of my seat.

I notice his eyes slowly scan my body, pausing briefly on the chain around my neck that houses my wedding ring close to my heart. "I never know if it's something women want any more."

"I think most women still like it." We move towards the shop doors. "Pull out a chair, give me your jacket, open doors, all the chivalry," I add.

"I went on a date once where a girl got really annoyed at me." He pulls the front glass door of the shop open, stands to the side and gestures me through first.

"What?" I say in shock.

"Yeah. She told me I was undermining her independence."

I scoff. "Well, I like it. I can do a lot by myself, so it's nice to not have to every now and then."

He gives me a nod as we make our way through. "Noted."

The coolness of the air conditioner hits my bare shoulders, making me shiver. The small reception area is clean and tidy. It looks freshly painted, but you can't mistake the distinct smell of oil that seems to be embedded in the furniture.

Clark's mate is already walking through from the garage to greet us. They slap a handshake that ends in a manly hug with pats on the back. Clark introduces the man as Jake, and he extends a hand for me to shake as I explain what happened. Jake asks a few questions and then heads off to fix my tyre.

Clark moves us towards the back wall where there is a worn brown leather couch with two matching armchairs.

"You honestly don't have to wait with me. I feel bad that you're going to miss lunch," I say, mindless grabbing a magazine with a jacked-up truck on it off the low coffee table.

"I don't mind."

"Well, I appreciate the company. Besides, if you didn't stop to help me, I'd probably still be in a towel stranded on the side of the road." I try to stifle a laugh.

"I'll be honest, you did look slightly unhinged when I pulled up." He leans closer to me. Close enough to feel the warmth of his breath on my bare skin. "And I have to say, I do prefer the hot sundress," he says, mimicking my words I had used to describe my outfit earlier.

I'm not normally one to feel shy. I rarely get embarrassed, and I'm quite outspoken in how I feel and what I want. But I think a large part of that has come from being in a very secure marriage for years.

Suddenly, I feel my cheeks grow pink at his words. At his closeness. At how his large, corded arm skims mine. I lick my bottom lip, hyper aware of how he is watching me.

I mean, it is what I want, isn't it? Callum has been gone for three years. It's not a long time when you consider we were together for seventeen. It's not a long time at all when I think about starting a new relationship or remarrying. But that is not what I want.

It is a hell of a long time when no one has touched you. Told you that you are beautiful or opened a car door for you. It is a long ass time to not feel the hands of another person tracing up and down your body, leaving goosebumps as they go. It's a long time to not have felt someone's lips on yours. Not to have felt the warmth of someone else's body next to you.

I miss Callum in every way possible. I miss having someone to talk to and tell stories to. To parent with and live life with. To laugh with.

But fuck me, do I miss intimacy.

I don't think I will ever be able to replace what Callum was to me and our kids. But casual sex, surely I can find that. Someone to do fun shit with every now and then. Someone who is kind and respectful but doesn't want it all.

Okay, maybe that is going to be hard to find. Let's just stick to sex for now.

I feel the butterflies flapping and dancing around in my stomach and my, well...my vagina.

"I'm just glad someone appreciates the effort I put into my outfits. You'd have to be the first in a long time." There is a hint of snark to my comment, thinking about the asshats that I have met since Callum.

"Somehow, I doubt that very much," he comments.

"Oh no, trust me. Have you been on Tinder lately? Fucking nightmare fuel, I tell you."

He laughs at me. "Ohhh, please do tell."

"No way. I'm not going to bore a stranger with my tragic dating life."

"Come on, I just poured my heart out to you on the side of the road. Cheating, conning ex, baby to another man. Remember?" His tone is playful, but I hear the undertone of hurt that laces his voice.

He is not over what happened to him. But, I mean, neither am I. So, I guess this is a match made in heaven. The playful flirting feels good. Really good.

"They are long, depressing stories."

"More depressing than your husband dying?" Clark nudges me gently with his shoulder. A comment like that would offend most people. But I find it refreshing.

So many people walk on eggshells around me about Callum. But I long to talk about him. Seventeen years. Almost half of my life and all my adult memories involve him. It's hard not to talk about him. But talking about dead people makes others uncomfortable. Usually, anyway. So, I lean into comments like this. I'm not put off. It's refreshing that he isn't afraid to bring it up. Maybe he isn't put off by me talking about him, either.

"I was with Callum since I was twenty. We had a great relationship. I mean nothing is perfect. He left the toilet seat up like every other guy. But we basically grew into adulthood together. When he passed, I thought I was going to die along with him." I twirl the ring at my neck absentmindedly around my finger, deciding to hold off on telling him how my heart just didn't beat right without him. How my soul seeped from my body when those officers left our house.

"How did you survive?" he asks, almost like he is trying to gain insight on how to survive his own pain.

"I had three little kids to carry on for. They were only six, ten and eleven. I threw myself into the kids and my business. I needed to be able to provide for them. Before I knew it, years had passed, and I had not even looked sideways at anyone of the opposite sex."

I pause to take a breath, aware he didn't ask for my entire tragic life story and was probably praying for the flirty banter to come back. But when I glance at him, he is watching me intensely, following along with compassion.

I keep talking.

"It wasn't until earlier this year that I kind of felt ready to get back out there and date, and the thing is, I actually don't want..." I wonder how honest I should be with him. I'm aware that there is a shit tonne of men out there who don't like women to be too outspoken and open when it comes to sex.

But I'm not one to hold back on what I think.

"To be honest, I don't really want to date. I don't have time for a relationship. I'm not looking for a father figure for my kids. I just want to get laid."

Clark chokes on a cough as his eyes shoot to mine.

I smirk back at him and carry on. "It's different for women. Well, for me anyway. Even if it's just sex, I still need there to be a level of mutual respect and trust. I feel like that is lacking with everyone I tried to meet, especially when I say I just want something casual."

He nods, following along. But I don't miss the way he rubs his palms up and down his shorts. It's also hard to miss how they stretch over his muscly legs.

"My sister helped me join Tinder. She warned me about my profile bio, but I wanted to be honest. I didn't want to say I want a relationship when I don't. But the moment you write down that you are just after casual sex, they think you are a cheap whore and that they don't have to put a single bit of effort in."

I can see this conversation has Clark slightly flustered. Little clusters of a blush keep creeping up his neck. But I carry on.

"I went on this one date, and I suggested La Vida Tacos in Northbridge."

"That place is the best," he cuts me off, speaking for the first time in a while.

"I know right. Margaritas and tacos, like can you think of a better combo?"

"No, I really can't."

"Exactly. Now, I'm a widow with three boys. I live in gym clothes and am surrounded by mess. I don't get out much. So,

I went all out. I bought a new dress, new underwear, and not the cheap kind."

His brows raise and I see his hand grip his thighs a little.

"I got a Brazilian wax for fuck's sake. Do you know how much that hurts?"

His brows almost hit his hairline now, and he stifles a laugh. "Nope, really don't."

"Well, it's a lot, let me tell you. I got my kids a babysitter. I spent forever getting dressed. I'm looking fine as hell."

He smirks at me. "I can imagine."

"I drive an hour out of my way. And I'm waiting at this restaurant excited for margaritas, tacos and sex."

"Okay, there's a better combo," he says behind a laugh.

"No, you're absolutely right. So much better."

Clark nods in approval with a smile across his face. "So then what happens?" he asks.

"Seven comes and goes."

"He did *not* stand you up?"

"Oh no, it's worse."

"Worse?" he says in horror.

"Yeah. I'm waiting, it's now ten past seven and I get a text from him saying he is running late. He tells me his Uber cancelled on him and he's trying to order another one."

"Why didn't he just drive?"

"Well see, you would think that, wouldn't you? But he tells me he's had a few drinks. It's now twenty past, and the server comes to tell me they can only reserve the table for an hour and a half. I text him, asking how far away he is."

"Oh no."

"Oh no is correct. He tells me that the second Uber is fifteen minutes away and he has tried to call a taxi with no luck. Now I'm pissed, but I'm also hungry and horny."

Clark starts laughing again as he runs a hand through his short hair. Shit, it's hot and my train of thought gets lost in the movement. "This guy sounds like a dick."

"Oh, it gets worse."

"What! How?"

"Hold on, cowboy," I say, playfully nudging him, not missing the buzz of electricity that hums between us. "Because I am a nice person and generally see the good in people, I decided to offer to pick him up. Thought I would go get him and then we can come back in and roll the dice on the restaurant having walk-in tables."

"You didn't."

"Oh, I did. I know, so stupid. He jumps at the offer and that should have been all the red flags I needed. I pull up to his place and there are like fifteen cars on the front lawn."

"Nooo."

"Okay, that's an exaggeration. It was more like five, but still. Now, some dude who looks about twelve opens the door."

He raises a brow. "Exaggeration again?"

"I'm forty, so everyone under the age of twenty-five looks twelve to me."

He nods. "No, no, you've got a point."

"Anyway, he goes to get Cam, my date, who comes to the door looking sloshed and reeking of alcohol. He asks if I want to come in and have a drink and meet his friends."

"You DID NOT go in, did you?"

"Are you fucking mad!"

"What did you do?"

"Told him I was just going to grab my bag from the car and then I high tailed it out of there. Proceeded to cry into the big mac I got for dinner on the drive home."

"What the hell," Clark says, scrubbing a hand down his face. "Did you talk to him again?"

"No. I blocked him on everything and deleted Tinder for a while."

"You went back on again?"

"Yeah, about a month later. My sister convinced me to change my profile. But the moment you say you are a widow with three kids, men instantly seem to think I'm some gold digger looking for a sugar daddy or a new dad for my kids. I don't want any of that. I just want a Daddy, if you know what I mean."

He looks sideways at me, chuckling. I notice the red start to rise up his neck again. I know that I'm acting like a horny teenager, but I'm past the point of caring what people think of me.

Honestly, a hot, dirty weekend with this random guy at a wedding sounds like exactly what I need. The thought of actually moving on with someone else makes me feel physically ill, but I can't deny the fact that I'm lonely and miss sex.

Clark is hot as sin, damaged enough to not want a relationship, but not so damaged that he is an asshole. I mean, from what I can tell, anyway.

"Did you go on any other dates?" he asks with curiosity.

"Yeah, one more and then I gave up for good."

"So that ended badly as well, huh?"

"So fucking bad."

"Worse than the first?"

"Hmmm, kinda."

"Do tell."

"Okay," I say, getting the recollection of the events clear in my mind. "We decided to go for a drink in the city. I got all dressed up again. New dress, nice lingerie."

He cuts me off. "Tell me more about this Brazilian wax thing."

I start laughing and nudge his side. The connection creates heat low in my stomach. I see the embarrassment creeping into his face, almost like he wished he could take it back.

I don't want him to. I'm loving this flirting. Weirdly, I'm also loving watching him sweat from this conversation. I don't share his bashfulness with this topic.

"Yes, I absolutely got another wax, and it was just as painful."

"Please tell me he actually showed up this time."

"Well, yes, so I mean props to him. We got a drink and started chatting and the conversation was okay. Then it got to eight and I was starving, so I suggested we go get something to eat. I could kind of tell he just wanted to go home and get it on, but I needed more."

"What do you mean?" Clark asks quizzically.

I pause, wondering how in depth to go with my feelings here. I have already talked about losing my husband and waxing my vagina, so why stop with the oversharing now?

"I guess for men, they can turn it on and off easier. They're more visual so it doesn't seem to take much."

"To be turned on?" he asks, furrowing his brow. His hand rubs the back of his neck as he tries to follow my train of thought.

"Yeah, like for women, the risk is higher. I need to feel comfortable. To trust before I just go back to his house." Clark nods his head, following along. "I just wanted to go to dinner and flirt over a game of fucking mini golf. I wanted to actually have a night out first. Maybe I'm asking for too much but..."

"No, I don't think you are."

"Well, we start walking through Northbridge trying to find somewhere to eat. I suggest this amazing smelling Korean BBQ place we walk past. Nope, he doesn't really like Korean food."

"Okay," he says, huffing a laugh.

"We keep walking, and I suggest about three other places that he also shoots down for whatever reason. It's 8:30 PM now, so I am starving." I pause, glancing sideways at Clark. He has a huge smile on his face, and his hazel eyes are alight with humour. "I'm glad you find this so amusing."

"Sorry. Go on."

"Hungry Jacks."

"Hungry Jacks what?" he repeats.

"Hungry Jacks, that's where he wants to go for dinner." Clark breaks out in a full-on belly laugh now. "Nooo, I'm not even joking. And I'm not snobby. I don't mind Hungry Jacks. I'll eat it, no worries. But I'm wearing a two-hundred-dollar dress with Honey Birdette underneath for goodness sake."

"I have no clue what that is."

"It's very nice, expensive underwear. I know I'm starting to sound materialistic, but honestly, I'm not. It was just that I put so much effort into everything for the date. The sitter, the outfit, how I looked, driving an hour out of my way. I was so disappointed to be sitting my ass in a plastic stool at hungry jacks when we had all these amazing restaurants around us that I never get an opportunity to go to."

"I get it, you wanted to be wined and dined."

I raise my hands and give a shrug. "Yeah. A little, I guess. It would have been nice. I give so much to my kids and my business, I just wanted a fun night out. I wanted to get dressed up and sit at a nice restaurant with good conversation and beat someone at time crisis, have some good sex and then come home. Is that too much to ask for?"

He folds his lips together, holding back a laugh. "Kinda sounds like the perfect date to me."

"Right! Anyway, I gave him some slack. I thought maybe he didn't have a heap of money. He also has three kids and is paying child support, so I didn't expect him to pay for anything. But I had not even finished chewing my last mouthful before he hit me with the, 'Let's go back to my place.' It honestly pissed me off. I was all for casual sex, but it made me feel so used. Which I get is stupid because that kind of was the whole point. But...I just...I said no."

"How'd he take it?"

"Like an asshole. Told me I was a cock tease and stormed off."

"Dick."

"Jokes on him, because he left half his milkshake."

Clark spits out a laugh, and we both start cracking up, right as Jake comes out from the back entrance of the garage with a smile and my keys.

"She's good to go." He passes the keys back to me as I stand and start to head towards the counter to pay. Clark heads in the opposite direction, making his way to the door to hold it open, waiting for me.

"How much do I owe you?" I ask.

Jake glances towards Clark and then back to me. "Take it up with Clark. He said to add it to his tab."

I jerk my head towards him in shock. Clark rubs the back of his neck, looking somewhat embarrassed. His head tilts down to the ground but his hazel eyes flick up, looking through his eyelashes at me.

I hate that he has paid for this. I'm not angry, but for the last few years, I have had to do everything myself. Rely on myself. Callum's life insurance had paid off our mortgage on the house we had only just finished building. Plus, it had allowed me to buy the car outright. But everything else we had saved was quickly eaten up by the months on end that I wasn't working.

I was trying to claw my way out of the deep depths of hell that losing him had created. After that, everything had fallen squarely on my shoulders. The responsibility to make enough money to pay for all the bills, three growing boys' appetites and almost thirty thousand dollars a year in private school fees.

I was so used to fending for myself now that this gesture was making me feel...well, a little incompetent for some reason. I didn't want him to pity or feel sorry for me, but rather view me as the strong, independent women I have had to become by circumstance. Opening a door or buying a drink was one thing, but tyres are expensive.

I swallow my feelings before I let them ruin a good thing. I will pay him back. Maybe that was his intention all along. Just to make it easier for Jake.

No harm done.

I pass through the door that Clark holds open for me, hoping he didn't see the quick shift in my mood.

6

It's just casual flirting

Clark

Crap, I messed up. I can tell. I wasn't thinking.

When I rang Jake on the drive here, I told him to chuck Hannah's bill on my tab. I'm picky with the jobs I take in my business, and I only work odd hours here and there. I haven't bothered getting accounts with suppliers set up. Instead, I use one of my prior employees, who now has a very successful mobile business, to get the parts and tools I need. It's easy and convenient. Jake wasn't going to charge me for the time it took to change the tyre over.

I could organise with Hannah at a later stage to do a tyre rotation and alignment, which it probably needed. I wasn't planning on asking for the money back. I'm not short of a penny, as it is just me and a few animals. No kids, no partner. So I don't need much.

I didn't miss the subtle change on her face when Jake told her that I had sorted it. Now I'm panicking that I have messed this all up by undermining her independence, or something like that.

I let out a breath as I follow her to her car.

Hannah unlocks it and I pull the door open. "Thank you for organising that, but I don't like that you paid. You have to tell me how much it cost so I can pay you back."

I meet her eyes. Her honesty is refreshing. I swear my ex would have stewed on it for days without me knowing what was wrong, then she would have blown up at me later over stacking the dishwasher 'incorrectly' or something else completely unimportant.

"I'm sorry," I say, feeling stupid as hell. "I wasn't really thinking. I just told Jake to chuck it on my tab because I often buy parts off him for my own business. It will be wholesale cost, anyway."

"Oh, okay," she says, a very slight look of embarrassment washing over her cheeks, as if she read the situation wrong. She hadn't. I had no intention of asking her to pay me back. "Can you give me your bank details and tell me how much? I'll transfer it to you."

"No worries." I hold the car door open as she jumps into the seat.

Shutting the door, she winds the window down to say goodbye. "I guess I'll see you at the winery. It will be nice to actually go the speed limit and not have people pulling finger signs at me the whole way."

I laugh at her sarcasm. "Yeah, that would have sucked. I'll see you soon."

With that, the window goes up, and I head back to my ute to head to lunch.

I almost miss the turn off for the winery. Thick forest trees and vast paddocks line each side of the road, leaving a small margin of error. The red pebble driveway sneaks up on me fast. I turn into the bumpy entry way for the winery, and it opens to a larger car park.

Hannah was behind me for a while, but somewhere along the hour and twenty-minute scenic drive, she had fallen back. As expected, we are late. I imagine everyone is already into their food by now. I should have just gone straight to the accommodation.

My stomach twists with anxiety as I rub my palms along my thighs. I don't love crowds at the best of times. Walking in with Hannah, everyone is going to want to know what happened and how we met. It's going to be awkward.

Locking my car, I decide to just go inside. Maybe we will avoid some questions if we walk in separately.

Ahh, that will be rude.

Anxiety won't let me take another step, but it doesn't want me to stay either. I lean against my car and try to calm my nerves. I see Hannah pull in, far slower than me, obviously expecting the turn off. There aren't many spots left, so I make my way over to where I see her parking.

Shit! What am I doing? She doesn't need me to hold her damn hand into the place. Stop being such an awkward weirdo.

My feet won't stop moving towards her, though.

Hannah steps out of the car and holy hell she looks good in that dress. "Thanks for waiting for me."

My anxiety fades the moment she smiles at me and is replaced with another primal instinct far stronger.

"No worries." Okay, I made the right call in waiting. Just breathe.

"This is going to be awkward," she laughs, saying so easily exactly what I was thinking. "Our friends are going to want to know how we randomly met on the side of the road and are now late to lunch."

I hide how nervous I feel with a little chuckle. Although she says that this will be awkward, she doesn't seem to show a single ounce of anxiety over it. Instead, she struts up to the doors with a smile on her face and her head held high, her blonde hair swinging behind her.

I try to match her energy. If she ain't worried, then there is no reason I should be.

Opening the door for her, we walk through. We're hit with the smell of pizza and the clinking of glasses. Heavy shoes on raw wooded floorboards as wait staff bustle around, laughter and conversations follow behind them. No one is manning the dark wooden front desk, so we walk past it, heading out the open glass bifold doors and down the vintage red brick steps. Hannah spots our group first. They have taken up the entirety of the long table in the middle of the grass, bench seats lining both sides under an open pergola wrapped with vines.

Without an ounce of hesitation, she walks towards the group as I follow at her side. I have only lived in Mandurah for a little over a year. I don't know a heap of people. I've attended a few group things since I met Rowan and Olivia, so I've met a handful of this group, but not everyone.

My skin crawls, a sensation Hannah doesn't seem to share as she confidently walks up to the group, announcing her arrival.

"You're here," one of the girls I haven't met yet squeals as she jumps from the white-wash wooden bench seat to give Hannah a hug.

"Yay, we were worried," another says, standing.

They all seem to follow suit, making their way over to greet us. Rowan and I clap a hand that ends in a bro hug. A few of the other guys I have met before do the same.

Rowan then turns to the entire group. "Guys, for those that haven't met yet, this is Clark."

We all say our hello's before I find an empty seat. Hannah is deep in conversation with a handful of the girls as a waiter brings out two armfuls of plates and starts placing them down in front of people. The girls start taking their seats again and Hannah makes her way over to me, leaning over to grab a menu off the table. Her long hair falls forward and brushes over my shoulder. Shit, it smells good. It has me wanting to bury my face in it.

She stands back up, reading the menu, and I have a feeling she knew exactly what she was doing. She is flirting with me.

I think!

"You hungry?" she asks, handing me the menu to look over.

"Starving."

"Everything sounds so good. I can't decide."

"Are you opposed to sharing food?" I ask with bated breath. Cherie hated sharing food, even if it was tapas style, which is meant to be shared.

I didn't have high hopes for her answer, but I agree that this menu is good and there is too much I want to try.

She smiles at me. "I'm down with that. You pick two and I'll pick two. Anything you hate or can't have?"

Well shit, that was easy. "I'm good with everything. You?"

"Same. I think I want the sliders and arancini balls. I've had them here before and they are amazing."

"They were at the top of my list, too. I'll get the potato roasties and woodfired chicken pieces."

"Perfect. I'll go order." Hannah turns to walk away, but I'm already standing to go with her. Hell if I'm letting her order and pay for my lunch while I sit here. That is not the type of man I am.

We walk across the grass and weave our way through the busy outdoor tables, and back up the steps to the bar area.

"This place is nice," I say, trying to distract myself from how close she is standing to me and how good her tan skin looks against the maroon of her dress.

"Have you ever been here before?" she asks.

"No, first time. I've only been in Western Australia for a little over a year."

"What made you move here after your divorce? Assuming you divorced the adulterous devil," Hannah says with a smirk.

"Oh yeah, definitely divorced, and I don't really know. I had an old employee who moved here and loved it. Seemed like a good idea at the time."

"And now?" She pauses. "Still a good idea?"

"It's a pretty great lifestyle here. I feel like I get the best of both worlds. The town is big enough not to feel isolated, but I live a bit further out. I have property so I'm not in the hustle of it all. It's a beautiful town."

She nods along while I talk. The line moves quickly, and we are at the front of the rustic bar before I know it. I order the food and drinks. I see Hannah getting her card out to pay, but I'm already tapping before she gets a chance.

"Well add that to my tab of what I owe you," she laughs.

"It's fine." I'm the type of man who likes to spoil a woman. I like to pay for everything. But I am mindful that despite the insane chemistry that buzzes between us like a live wire and the flirty banter, this isn't a date.

We take our number and drinks and make our way back to the table. The conversation flows around us. We have to talk loud over the kids playing in the nature playground behind us, and the helicopter taking people for joy rides over the fields of grape vines that line the property.

We end up retelling the story of how we met as we sit next to each other. The bare skin of her thigh rests against my own, heating my body from the inside out. I don't know if it's intentional or just the space restriction, either way, I'll take it. I find myself shifting to be closer, almost unintentional, like a magnetic pull.

I have had a handful of dates and hook ups after Cherie, but I have never felt this much spark. Hannah has me crawling out of my skin to touch her. My hands itch and I have to grip my thighs to stop them reaching for hers.

The food arriving offers the distraction I need, and we both start digging in. I pass Hannah a slider on a serviette, and she stabs an arancini ball with a fork, dipping it in the creamy sauce and passing it over to me.

"You guys look like a married couple already," Jason comments, eliciting a few laughs from around the table.

My cheeks heat and I instinctively draw away from her, creating a tiny bit of space that wasn't there before.

I have no desire to marry again. In all honesty, the dramatic ending of my prior marriage messed me up more than I'll ever admit. I've been honest with everyone I've seen since. I have no desire for a long-term relationship. The thought of giving myself over to someone like that again, leaving myself open to have my heart ripped from my chest, is enough to give me hives.

I'm a good man, I know that. I don't use women or treat them like crap. I would never have acted the way those men did to Hannah on her dates. But I am always upfront and honest with what I want. Although, that has backfired a few times. In my experience, women say they are okay with casual but they, in fact, are not.

"Can't two old, depressed people just enjoy some casual flirting, Jason? Leave us alone," Hannah playfully snipes at him with not an ounce of embarrassment in her body language. I can't help but huff a bit of a laugh, and the rest of the group joins in.

"Okay, okay, we'll leave you alone," Jason says as the conversation picks back up.

After eating, we don't get much more of a chance to chat just the two of us, but the group conversations flow. Eventually the girls pair off, and everyone seems to chop and change seats. It's three by the time we decide to head back to the resort to check in.

"Are you heading to the group dinner tonight?" I ask, catching up to Hannah as we walk back to our cars. The whole group has a booking at a restaurant in Dunsborough, so we have a bus picking everyone up at seven.

"Yeah, absolutely. It will be fun."

"A few people were talking about heading to the beach for the arvo before dinner. Are you keen?" I try to hide the hope in my voice.

"Yeah, I am dying for a swim, and I bought my paddle board."

"I've never been on one of those." Our fingers brush as we both reach for her door handle at the same time, a jolt of electricity humming through me at the subtle contact.

"Come meet me down there and I'll take you out. It's fun."

Hannah in bathers? I'm definitely in. "Sounds good."

She drops her hand, allowing me to open her car door, before she slides into the seat. I have a feeling this is going to be a fun weekend.

7

Salt and Sunshine

Hannah

I make it to the resort and check in. There are quite a few of us. I stop to chat to some of my girlfriends in the lobby, making a plan for the afternoon and discussing what we are wearing for the dinner and the wedding.

I don't get to chat to Clark, but I feel him—a faint hum of electricity between us. Every now and then our eyes meet across the room. I don't see him leave, but when I don't spot him in the lobby, I decide to head to my room and get down to the beach.

I don't want to seem like a desperate housewife, but I'm dying to see him without his shirt on.

My paddle board is a pump up one and it comes folded in a bag. I easily carry it as I make my way down the wooden steps framed by wire fence line. The golden sand is warm under my bare feet as I hit the beach. The dunes are covered with pink pigface and yellow wattle shrubs.

I spot Liz and Leah with their partners, small waves lapping at their ankles as they talk. Then I see him.

HOLY CRAP.

This isn't fair. I'm not a self-conscious person. Actually, quite the opposite, but one look at his broad, strong shoulders and firm abs has my nerves failing. That mean-girl voice in my head tells me that he probably goes for far younger women.

Looking at Clark shirtless, walking towards me, the muscles in his body rippling with each movement, his strong jawline and bright kind eyes, has me realising that he would definitely not have a problem getting them.

"Hey," I say as I chuck the board bag and my towel down on the sand, swallowing my insecurities.

"Hey," he says back. We stand there stupidly smiling at each other for a brief moment. Me, not really able to peel my eyes from the hard V line sprinkled with light hair that leads down to his shorts.

"Do you need a hand with this?" He leans down to unzip the paddle board bag.

"It's pretty easy, just have to connect the pump. It doesn't take too long."

Clark unfolds the board while I clip together the two ends of the paddle. Connecting it all, he starts pushing down on the hand pump to inflate the board. The flexing of his arms has my body feeling all kinds of crazy things that I have not felt in a very long time.

"Jesus Christ," I mutter under my breath, not realising the words left my mouth.

"What? Am I doing it wrong?" He stops working the pump and looks at me shyly. Warmness spreads up his neck.

"Oh no, very right. Please don't stop."

The confidence returns to his features as he laughs at me but averts his eyes from mine to look down at the board. I stand there watching him like an absolute creep, but seriously, I could not look away even if I wanted to. He is like a solar eclipse. Too hot to stare directly at. It is hurting my eyes, but I can't seem to stop.

Before I lose my nerve and head back to my room all together, I undo the buttons to my cotton throw over shirt and let it drop to the ground, leaving me standing there in a deep green bikini with golden seashells painted across the material.

His eyes slowly trail up my body, taking me in, stalling briefly at my boobs before meeting my eyes. "Jesus Christ yourself." His eyes flutter back down my body before he disconnects the pump and picks up the board.

We make our way to the water, standing in the shallows.

"Are we going on at the same time?" He moves around the board, holding it in place.

"Yeah, why not?"

Clark tilts his head at me as if saying, *how the hell are we doing that?* "Okay, where do you want me?" he asks with a playful smile on his lips.

"On your knees."

His smirk widens and goddamn it's hot as hell. "Yes, ma'am," he responds, tone playful as he kneels on the board.

"Turn around." I make a circle gesture with my hands, showing him that I want him in front me but facing out. He complies and I steady the board as I push it out a little deeper.

My pulse quickens as I place a hand on the warm golden skin of his shoulder, using him to prop myself up on the board. I move my legs out wider, giving me better balance with the added weight of a second person.

"You good?" He tilts his head around to look back at me. My body tingles with how close he is.

"Let's go." I start to paddle us out deeper. He stays on his knees in front of me, and I have to lift the paddle around him every time I need to change sides.

He doesn't seem to mind being splashed, and the view looking down at his broad, muscular shoulders with water droplets coating them is doing all sorts of things to me. Tiny freckles are scattered faintly across the skin there, so subtle you wouldn't notice them unless you were this close. The same delicate dusting speckles his nose and cheeks, which only seems to mirror the shyness and playfulness of his personality.

It's alluring and so damn sexy.

The water is crystal clear and flat, so I head out deeper, away from where most of our friends are swimming.

He turns to look up at me again. "You're good at this."

"Do you want a go?" I ask.

"At paddling?" he smirks. "Sure. How do we swap?"

"Okay, stand up."

He places a hand on the board to balance it and slowly rises. The board wobbles slightly at the movement.

"Now what?" he asks.

"Spread your legs." He starts laughing at me. I playfully slap his back. "Just do it. I'm going to crawl through your legs, okay, and then you can step back."

"Gotcha." He moves his legs slightly wider as I pass him the paddle.

He is quite a tall guy, and I'm below average height, so it isn't hard for me to drop down and crawl through his legs. Except I don't stay on my knees. I stand up. My back is so close to him that I can feel his breath on my neck, and it makes the tiny hairs stand.

Clark starts to paddle on one side, and we basically move in a circle.

"You have to change sides so we go straight."

"I know, but I can't get around you."

I step back closer to him and feel his body heat against my back. He circles his arms around me so he can swap sides with the paddle in front. This would be far easier if I kneel like he did, or if I stayed behind him, but I'd be absolutely lying if I said this wasn't way hotter.

I think he agrees.

The feel of his hard body so close to mine, not quite touching, has every hair standing on end, as if reaching out to him.

We paddle around a little bit like this. His breath on my neck and arms wrapped around me makes my skin itch to be touched by him.

"Any more tragic dating stories?" Clark asks over seagulls squawking and the distant chatter from our friends.

"Nope, that was enough to scare me off Tinder for life. At this point, I've basically just accepted a life of celibacy. What about you? You got any tragic dating stories?"

"What, my wife having a baby with another man wasn't enough for you?" His tone is playful, but I can sense the hurt behind the sarcasm.

"You haven't dated since?" I ask, not out of jealousy or even trying to pry. Just interested to know. He is such a good-looking guy, and at this age, that body is rare. I really doubt he has trouble getting women. But he seems to be shy and reserved. I really think if I wasn't the one driving the flirting it wouldn't be happening.

He looks at me like he is unsure of how to proceed. Maybe he just isn't that into me. I try to push that feeling aside.

"You can be honest, Clark. I am not a judgemental person."

He lets out a breath and stops paddling. "I don't want to date. Not seriously, anyway. I'm kind of in the same boat as you. I don't want to get married again, but I do like having company every now and then."

"So, you also just want to get laid."

"Yeah, but in my experience when women say that, they don't mean it. Not for the long term, anyway." He pauses. "No offence."

"None taken. How so, though?"

"I'm not an asshole. At least I don't think I am."

"That's exactly what an asshole would say." I playfully nudge him with my elbow.

"Well, I've never treated someone the way your dates treated you. Quite the opposite, really. I always tell them upfront that I'm not interested in a long-term relationship, but I do like going out. I like being a gentleman. I pay for dinners, and I pull out chairs and give jackets and call when I say I am going to."

"I'm failing to see the problem here."

"Well, the last girl I was seeing told me that I led her on. Not as kindly as that, either. I said that I had been clear from the beginning, and she told me that she thought because of the way I treated her that I had changed my mind."

"Ahhh, I see," I say as I turn my head towards him.

"See what?" He genuinely looks confused.

"Ever heard the saying 'actions speak louder than words'? You were telling her one thing, but your actions were telling her another."

"So what? I'm supposed to be more of a dick? More like the guys you went on dates with?"

"To be fair, I never actually got my dates. I got stale HJ's and beer breath. But no, you shouldn't change who you are or treat women worse."

"I don't know how I could have been clearer with her. I hate that I hurt her."

"How long were you seeing her for?"

"Four months."

"How old was she?" I turn my head again to look at him and see that blush creep up his neck again.

"Why does that matter?"

That response instantly confirms my thoughts. She was young.

"Ohhh. What, twenty-five?"

He says nothing.

"Younger?" I ask, eyes wide.

"NOO."

"She was twenty-five, wasn't she?"

"Okay, she was twenty-seven," he fesses up.

I laugh. "Are you picking young women because you know you will have nothing substantial in common with them? That way you don't risk developing feelings but subconsciously they are at the perfect age to have your babies. Which is what you really want, isn't it?"

"What the hell!" he laughs. "Are you psychoanalysing me?"

"I have had many years of therapy," I jokingly say. Although, it's the absolute truth. "You know, you're not too old to still have kids. If that's what you want," I say more seriously.

He lets out a breath. "I know."

"You have options: surrogates, donors, adoption, foster."

"I've wanted nothing more than to be a dad for a very long time, but the thought of doing it all alone...I'm sure you can testify to how hard that is."

"You're right, it's the hardest thing I've ever had to do."

"I've let that want go. I've accepted I won't have children, but I fully hear what you said earlier about missing company. It's been hard to find people who are after the same things as you. I didn't think I was intentionally going for younger women, but it just worked out that way."

"Well, I feel you. It's not easy to find someone who wants the same things," I snipe.

"Tell me exactly what you're looking for. What you want. No-holds-barred." His face turns slightly more serious.

"What I want? No-holds-barred," I repeat, thinking it over.

"Yeah, dream situation," Clark says.

I slowly turn around on the paddle board to face him. Luckily there is no tide or waves, or we would be halfway out to sea by now. Instead, our paddle board has swayed gently back and forth while we have been chatting, and every now and then Clark has put the paddle in to turn us around.

"Okay, here goes. Don't be offended," I add for good measure.

"I won't."

"Big dick, kind heart, savage in bed, chivalrous out. Good sense of humour but not immature. Doesn't want to live in my pocket but keen to do fun shit. Understands I will never stop loving my husband and that my kids will always come first," I spit it out like a rap, holding in a laugh, but I'm deadly serious.

His eyes are wide, and a smirk plays at his lips.

"Is that too much to ask for? It is, I know. A girl can dream though, right? Your turn."

"No way, this is a trap."

"Ohh, come on. No-holds-barred, remember? Hit me with it."

Clark shakes his head. "Absolutely not. Nope, no way."

"Come on. Blunt truth, perfect situation. Let's go."

He runs his hand through his hair. "Okay," he chuckles. "Here goes. Nice tits, thick ass, has her own money, kind, doesn't try to change me, must love horses," he spits it in the same rap as me.

I look at him in shock. His face falls, panic washing over his features. He thinks he has offended me. His panic morphs into confusion.

"You like horses?"

"I have horses."

My voice breaks with excitement. "You *have* horses."

"Mmmhum." He still looks a little confused.

"I love horses. I did this equine therapy thing after Callum died. It seemed weird but it was awesome. Then I started riding and I've been going on trail rides ever since."

He scratches his head, looking down. "Shit, I thought I had offended you for a moment there."

"Yeah, well, I definitely don't have good tits. They are barely a B cup, and they are slightly saggy after breastfeeding three kids, but I mean...my ass is kind of thick, so I have to take the wins where I can get them."

"Your..." he clears his throat, "tits look pretty damn good from where I'm standing. Ass, too."

"Well, you haven't seen me naked yet."

Clark raises an eyebrow at my very presumptuous comment. "Yet."

Yes, yet.

He is so goddamn fine and this flirting all day is killing me. I figure it's too late to act coy now, especially seeing as though when we first met, I was wearing nothing but a G-string and a towel.

"Well, you can't go comparing me to your twenty-seven-year-olds. I've had three children, remember? I have a c-section scar and stretch marks," I say playfully.

Clark takes a small step closer to me on the board. "I have a feeling you're in a league of your own."

My body instinctively moves towards him, and his hand gently lands on my hip as he pulls me closer. Tilting his head down toward me, I feel his breath on my cheek as his lips move towards mine...right as a boat comes flying past us, way closer and faster than necessary, or legal, for that matter. Asshole.

The paddle board starts to wobble from the waves, rocking from side to side. With both of us on it, we lose our balance and start to fall. Strong arms wrap around me as Clark twists my body on top of his. He hits the water first. We both go under, and I feel his grip loosen on me. He gently pushes me back to the surface.

We are both laughing as we break the water. I grab the edge of the board, and he places his arms around me, one hand on either side. I turn around, treading water facing him, placing my elbows up and shifting my weight to get out of the water slightly. He moves in closer to me. Somehow, he looks even hotter all wet like this. Water drips from his short hair and the brightness of the sun makes his hazel eyes glow golden.

"I'm sorry. I got your hair wet." He tucks a stray wet stand behind my ear.

"You think I give a shit about my hair right now?" I know most girls would, and I get it. I did just wash it this morning. But right now, with the way he is staring at me, and how I'm enclosed in his arms, my hair could be on fire and I wouldn't give a shit.

Let. It. Burn.

"I'd really like to kiss you right about now." Clark's eyes bore into me. Our legs are both kicking, treading water, and I feel his brush against mine every now and then.

"I feel like it would be rude not to at this point."

A big smile breaks across his face and then he leans in. He is gentle and soft; his hands don't touch me. They stay on the board at my sides. His body moves closer to mine, and I can't help but wrap my legs around his waist. Our lips meet and his tongue finds my own. I am done for.

This is the first kiss.

The first time another set of lips have touched mine since Callum. A pang of guilt laps at me like the small waves around us, but I push it away. This is what I've wanted. I shut my mind down and let my body lead.

Right now, my body wants to rip his shorts off and fuck him right here in the water.

"Hey, love birds, we're headed back to the hotel."

Clark breaks the kiss, turning slightly to see Rowan and Olivia waving goodbye to us at the shore. Most of the others look like they have left already.

I wave a hand at them, but I want more. More of that kiss, and more of him.

"You taste like salt and sunshine." His voice is gravely in my ear, and I can't help but grind into him, still wrapped around him like a koala.

"My signature scent." It takes every ounce of will power to uncurl my legs from his waist. I turn to pull myself up on the board, when his strong hand finds my ass and pushes me up the rest of the way.

"We better head back and start getting ready for dinner," I say. But I really don't want to. I want to take him back to my room and miss dinner all together.

I realise I'm now being that horny asshat from my date that couldn't even let me finish my meal, but the way I want this man is killing me. I haven't met anyone I feel so insanely attracted to since Callum. To be honest, I've barely seen another man that I thought even remotely stacked up in the looks department.

Clark looks completely different, light to Callum's dark, but the attraction between us is pure fire and it's burning me alive.

By the way he just kissed me and the bulge I could feel in his shorts, I'd say he feels the same.

Clark nods.

Staying in the water, he swims by the board and I half wonder if it's so he doesn't have to get out with a giant hard-on. The thought makes me laugh, but at the same time, insanely turned on.

We make it to the shore, and he carries the board. We're the last ones left at the beach.

I wonder if our friends saw us making out in the water?

I decide I don't care. I deserve this after three years of celibacy. Leave me be.

8

That Kiss

Hannah

I'm still high from the taste of his lips. The feel of him between my legs. The way he held me to his chest as we hit the water.

I dry off from my shower and apply my moisturiser. The sensation of rubbing it into my body only reminds me of how good it felt to have someone's hands on me again.

Damn, I want more. I knew I missed sex, but I didn't realise just how much I was craving this kind of touch until Clark kissed me. I know I barely know this man, but I can't see how or why someone would have had an affair on him. I'm a girl's girl through and through, and I'm generally always going to side with them. From what he has told me so far, and by what I have seen, I'm finding it hard to find a reason to side with Cherie.

I rub some product in my hands, running them through my damp hair and scrunching it up so it can dry naturally without being too frizzy. I used to hate my curly hair. Pre kids, I would never have left it like this. However, time doesn't work the same with children. You are sucked into a vortex where everything spins and moves five times faster. I just don't have time to worry about it now; I've been forced to love it natural.

I've never been one for a heap of makeup, mainly because I grew up before the era of contouring. I then had small children right as it was taking off, so I literally have no clue what I'm doing and don't have the time to learn. I admire the girls who manage to do a full face of glam makeup. I would have no clue where to even start, and honestly, my patience wouldn't allow it. Although, I'm at the age where maybe I need more.

But fuck it.

I apply some tinted moisturiser, blush and bronzer. Then I put on eyeliner, mascara and a nude lipstick. It's not all that different to how I looked earlier. It's my go to and takes me all of five minutes to complete.

I slip into my dress. The buttery soft material clings to my body, flowing down to the floor. I chuck on a pair of sandals and stand in front of the mirror, watching the moody charcoal fabric flow with my movements.

Panic rises in me at the thought of seeing Clark again. Questions roll through my mind. Will he be thinking I'm a giant slut after I all but dry humped him in public?

Shit.

Will he tell his friends? Say he has it in the bag?

Visions of me walking into the foyer and all eyes turning to me swirl. Did they see us kiss?

Waves of nausea and anxiety wash over me as I slump down onto the soft mattress. I'm a forty-year-old mother of three for Christ's sake. I should not be acting like this. What was I thinking?

Clark is a random guy I met on the side of the road earlier today. I barely know him. Embarrassment encases me. I don't know why I feel so ashamed now that the heat of the moment is gone. Why should I?

I'm a grown woman, and we both consented to that kiss. He didn't push me away. I, for one, want more. I know what my intentions are, and I want to sleep with him. Is that why I feel so nervous?

I know it can be different for men. People find out he had a weekend fling with a stranger, and he will get high fives and pats on the back. It's the women who get called a desperate slut with no self-respect. 'Where were her kids?' and 'How irresponsible'. The worst part is, it's usually by other women.

I take a deep breath. I'm with my closest friends. Friends I've had for years. Friends who have been there for me through thick and thin. They are not going to judge me.

I dial my sister so she can solidify the track my thoughts are on, and to check in on my kids now that guilt has found me.

"We were just about to call you. How is it?"

"Are the kids there?" I ask before I dive into my tangent.

"They're outside playing basketball with the neighbours."

I sigh in relief. "I'm a giant slut."

Why am I even calling myself that?

"OMG, you slept with the tyre guy, didn't you! How was it?"

"No, not yet. We kissed and I basically dry humped him at the beach in front of all our friends. Oh, my gosh, I want it so badly. Why am I such a ho?"

"Hannah," Kate says with sympathy. "You are the furthest thing from a ho. What's your body count? Like two?"

I laugh, "It's three." I had only slept with two people before Callum and no one since.

"Do you know what, it wouldn't matter if it were three hundred. You're allowed to like what you like and do what you want. If others don't like it, then that's on them."

"You're right. See, that's why I needed to call you."

She laughs. "Oh, my God, I knew you had an exhibitionist kink. You were always into weird shit."

"I definitely do not have an exhibitionist kink. It was one public kiss and some grinding. And I'm not into weird shit."

"Remember when we helped you move house and you had like three boxes of weird sex toys and costumes." Kate starts uncontrollably laughing. Callum and I did enjoy our sex life, especially before kids. "You had those weird bar spreaders."

I smile, remembering the last time we used them. "Hey, I like what I like."

She laughs so hard she snorts. "Who am I to judge? People are into all kinds of wild shit. I'm glad you met someone. I hope he matches your freak. You know, Sierra has a friend whose parents are swingers."

My eyes widen. "Really, who?"

"Her best friend Mia's parents, Alyssa and Alrick. Probably just a rumour, but who knows."

"No way! That's wild." Sierra is my sister's oldest child. She is twenty, and her and her best friend Mia are planning on travelling together next year after they turn twenty-one.

"They're lovely people. I have no clue what's true, and I don't care. The point is, let your freak flag fly, girl. Go for it. Who is anyone to judge you?"

"Thanks, Kate." I smile. "I knew there was a reason I always call you. You never fail to pep me up. Can I talk to the boys real quick?"

"Nooo, they don't even care that you're gone. We went to the shops after school and got all the good snacks that you never let them have. They told me they want to come live with me now."

"Ha-ha, Kate. You better not be giving them Cheetos because those things are full of crap."

"Cheetos, the super cheesy Doritos, M&Ms, Skittles. All the things."

"You are only punishing yourself, Kate. Those things make my boys wild. You've never been in the trenches with three boys who are all absolutely crazy. Godspeed to you, sis."

She laughs at me. "I'll go get them."

I hear her open the door and yell out to them. Then balls bouncing, getting closer and closer, before I hear Noah's voice. "Hey, Mum. Are you having fun?"

We chat back and forth for a bit, talking about his day. He then puts his brother Liam on. Then Ethan. I chat to them all and then say goodbye before hanging up.

Shit, the bus will be here in five minutes.

Okay, time to suck it up.

I enter the bar area and spot Clark straight away. He looks incredible in cream chinos and a dark blue button up shirt. He looks up from the bar where he is chatting with one of the guys and my irrational fears melt into the floor. He smiles and gives me a head nod in acknowledgement.

My whole body comes alive with the sexy movement. Olivia, Gabby and Jess come up to me, and we start chatting about dinner and the weekend plans, and how excited Olivia is for tomorrow.

I join in on the conversation, but my mind is solely focused on Clark. My eyes can't help but find him at the bar. A margarita is placed in front of him by the waiter. He grabs it in one hand, his beer in the other, and makes his way over to me.

"I didn't want to interrupt, but I got you this," he says as he hands me the drink.

"Thank you."

"I can't do anything about the tacos but the other two in the trio, I can help with." He winks at me and heads back to the bar, leaving me with my cocktail and a tingling between my legs at the earlier conversation of tacos, margaritas and sex.

The girls chuckle and pull me in. I realise we are all forty or above, but when we get together like this, it is still like we are teenagers, giggling at the most inappropriate things and talking way too dirty.

"You two look so hot together," Gabby says, nudging me.

"Spill! I saw you making out in the water," Jess adds.

Olivia just stares at me wide eyed with a giant smile on her face.

"I'll never tell," I tease.

"Ohhh, come on," Jess hounds, grabbing my arm.

"It's been three years since I've been with someone. If anyone is allowed to get laid this weekend, it's me."

Olivia hugs me, squeezing me close. "I'm so happy for you."

"And your vagina," Jess adds around a laugh.

"She has definitely woken up, that's for sure." I take a long sip of my cocktail, loving the saltiness on my tongue.

I was afraid of Clark being the one to tell everyone and now I'm blabbing about it. Oh well. I can't help that he makes me feel like a giddy teenager with a crush.

More of the girls join our group and we loudly laugh and chat about absolutely nothing of importance. Until Rowan announces that we have to head out. We finish our drinks and make our way to the bus. We are headed to Cabana, which is about a fifteen-minute dive. The group files in, us girls all choosing to sit together down the back of the bus while the boys group together further up. The chatter is constant between smaller groups, and everyone is buzzing.

We arrive at the restaurant and are led out the back to the garden bar. Twinkling lights and vines form coverage over a dark wooden frame, with black wooden tables and moody velvet green chairs, creating a sexy but elegant vibe. It quite honestly is suiting my mood.

Everyone is next to their significant other. Clark and I are literally the only two single people in our group of friends. So, it makes sense that we sit together. Clark pulls a chair out for me, and I take a seat. We order rounds of drinks and garlic bread, and the conversations pick back up.

The dinner goes fast. My chair rests as close as I can get to Clark, and I occasionally brush my leg against his, feeling electricity run up my veins every single time. I wonder if he feels it, too.

I notice his hand that rests on his thigh inches closer and closer to mine as dinner progresses. First a pinky grazes the side of my leg over my dress. Then two fingers. I push my leg into him to give him the consent he might need. And eventually his whole hand rests there, gently rubbing small circles with his thumb over the thin satin material.

Fuck, it feels good. My skin tingles, craving his touch. The fire that little make out session has lit inside of me has me feeling a little sex crazed. It's all I can think about.

It's loud in here, so every time we speak, I have to lean close to him. I place my own hand on his thigh as I do. I feel his grip on me tighten as I get closer, making sure I let him get a good view down my dress as I lean in.

I'm interrupted by my phone buzzing in my bag. Spotting its Noah, I excuse myself and head back through the restaurant and down the hall to the toilets where it's quieter. I talk to the kids for a bit, them all just wanting to say goodnight again.

I'm headed back to the group, staring down at my phone, when I hit a solid mass. Gentle hands grip me as I'm walked backwards and pressed against the dark green walls. I look up and lock eyes with Clark, alight with passion, probably mirroring my own.

He places a hand next to my head on the hallway wall and leans down close to me. His warm breath sending chills down my spine as he whispers in my ear, "I can't stop thinking about that kiss."

I breathe heavily. "Neither can I."

He closes the distance between us, his lips finding my collarbone as he kisses gently, slowly moving up my neck. Clark moves closer and I arch into him. His knee works its way between my thighs as he pushes closer still. I can't help but grind into it.

I inch across to the accessible restroom door that I see only a few steps to our left. Pushing back on it, I grip his shirt at his chest and yank him in with me. Clark pauses for a minute, a little shell shocked, but I don't give him time to overthink it. I pull him close to me, kissing him desperately. He catches on fast, and his hands grip my ass as he pushes me back into the cool tiled wall. Our kisses are feverish as my hands find their way under his shirt and roam his body.

I can't get enough. It's hot and heavy. Fast and frantic.

Our mouths clash together as his body pushes me harder into the wall. The pressure of his thick thigh between my legs has me almost screaming. I start unbuttoning his shirt and he slides one strap of my dress over my shoulder.

The door swings open, followed by: "Shit, I'm sorry."

Fuck. I completely forgot where we even were, let alone remembered to lock the door.

Clark moves his body slightly to make sure my exposed nipple isn't on display as I pull the strap back over my shoulder and straighten my dress out.

"Sorry, we're going," he says as he starts to button up his shirt and then adjust himself in his pants, before turning around and leading me out the room.

A young man on crutches stands back, allowing us to exit with a very amused look on his face. "Sorry to interrupt. I can probably use the other bathroom if you want to continue," he says around a knowing smirk.

"We're good. It was a dress...umm...emergency," I fumble over the words as I sheepishly follow behind Clark, trying to shield my body from anyone else who may have seen or heard what we were just doing.

We round the corner, and Clark pulls me into his arms in a hug. I laugh into his chest. "Well, that was interesting. I'm going to need a minute before I go back out there, but you have to go. He isn't going to go down with the feeling of you in my arms like this."

I laugh again, peeling myself from his embrace that feels a little too comfortable. "Okay, I'll see you out there." I turn to leave but he grips my hand and pulls me back into him.

He looks down at me, then tucks a stray bit of hair behind my ear. "Beautiful." Clark leans in to place a kiss on my forehead, and my heart rate picks back up. I break away before we end up back in the bathroom.

Sitting down at the table, Jess asks me if the kids are all okay.

"Yeah, they just wanted to say goodnight." Not a complete lie.

Clark makes it back a minute later, just like nothing happened. But I notice how the bulge in his pants doesn't completely disappear for the rest of the night.

Dinner goes quickly. Some get dessert and more drinks, and we all chat until the bus is ready to take us home. It's not too late, but with the wedding tomorrow, we are all eager to get back.

Clark walks by my side, his pinky finger finding mine before he grabs my hand, our fingers interlocking. "This okay?" he asks, motioning down to it.

"I must admit, it feels kind of nice."

We sit together on the bus, and he casually throws an arm over my shoulder, pulling me into him.

"I never asked you what you do for work?" he asks. "I remember you said you have your own business."

We have been around each other all day. We talked about our worst losses and heartbreaks but hadn't really spoken about this stuff.

I tell him about my business and how I'm a physical therapist. I opened up my own little gym from home to work out of. It keeps me busy.

He listens intently, asking questions as I go. It feels easy and comfortable.

Clark tells me how he used to own multiple mechanical workshops—eight to be exact—in different locations across Sydney. He tells me how he started from one small workshop and built them up. How he was so busy and stressed in the end that coming here and selling everything was like taking a breath he didn't realise he had been holding.

He also tells me how he made a heap of money when he sold it all. Half went to Cherie in the divorce because he just wanted to be done with it as fast as possible.

My heart breaks for him as I listen to his story.

He moved here and now just does mobile jobs when he wants. He tells me how he wanted to create more balance. Not that what she did was fair, but I wonder if this influenced her decision to have an affair. Was he always working and never around? I don't voice that, though. An affair is never justified in my opinion.

We get back to the resort, and everyone says their goodbyes as we all head off in different directions. Clark walks me back to my room.

"I had fun tonight," he says, leaning down to kiss me gently.

"I've had a pretty awesome day, if I'm honest," I say, chuckling. I'm spent and so ready for bed, as much as there is a huge part of me that so desperately wants to invite him in and finish what we started.

The heat of the moment has passed, giving way to something deeper. The conversation on the bus ride home. The comfortable way I fit in his arms.

Quite honestly, it scares me.

It has taken me so long to get used to being alone, especially sleeping by myself. Don't get me wrong, I'd sell a body part to have Callum back in my bed. But Clark isn't Callum.

Despite our insane chemistry, I'm not sure if I'm ready to have him sleep in my bed. And I know that is where this will lead to if I invite him in. I'm happy to go to sleep alone. I hope he doesn't think that's rude of me or that I've led him on.

Before I can start explaining the inner workings of all my tangled mind, he speaks. "Goodnight, Hannah."

"Goodnight, Clark."

He turns to walk away, and I turn to open my door.

Holy shit.

What a turn of events.

9

Passion inside the void
Hannah

I chop my pillow, trying to get it comfortable, before giving up and throwing it across the room. Rolling over, I find a cold spot on the mattress in this massive bed that I'm alone in, then I grab another pillow to assault.

I punch this one, trying to get it softer. When that doesn't work, I give up, shoving it out the way to roll over onto my stomach. My arm flails around and hits the side table while trying to find my phone. Ouch.

It's still dark outside, but not the darkness of night. Soft hues of pink and grey illuminate the edges of the window, telling me that sunrise isn't that far off.

Finding my phone, I check the time. The stark brightness of it burns my retinas as it lights up the room. 5:27 AM. I grunt. It makes sense that my body clock wakes me up at this time. It's around the time my alarm is set for every morning, allowing me to get up and get a workout or run in before the kids wake.

There was a long period of time where that wasn't in the realm of possibilities. I would have been waking at this unholy time feeding or resettling a wakeful baby or toddler.

I'm not sure why I punish myself now by getting up to exercise when I could be sleeping until seven like my kids. Deep down, I know I love it. The pain, the determination. Pushing yourself to do hard things. The adrenaline of exercise is addictive.

However, I wasn't planning on exercising over the weekend. Instead, I was supposed to be sleeping in, reading books, sunbaking and thinking of absolutely no one but myself.

Except now all I can think about is Clark. The sexy curve of his smile, the way his lips felt when they met mine, and how strong his hands held my body, somehow dominating but gentle at the same time.

I wish I had asked him to stay the night. I regret watching him walk away. We could be wrapped in each other's arms right now or doing other activities that sound more fun than tossing and turning and punching my pillows to a pulp.

Loneliness pulls at all sides of me. It's a feeling I have grown accustomed to. A dull ache, always present.

A void.

Clark kissing me had set off a grenade of passion inside that void. It now burns my insides in the best possible way. It needs more. It makes laying here alone feel infinitely worse.

I run my hands along the expanse of the bed. The space that is made for another body. The sheets feel ice cold under my fingers.

I throw the blanket off and sit up. I take a few deep breaths as my fingers find my necklace. Twirling the cool metal around my finger, I head to my suitcase. Of course I bought exercise gear. I live in activewear, so they are staple pieces of my wardrobe. But I definitely overpacked.

My frustration wrestles with the tight, soft material as I slide them up my thighs and hips, adding a sports bra and oversized tee with my sneakers. I pull my hair into a low pony and chuck my cap on. Deciding that if I can't sleep or have wild sex, then a run might clear my mind.

Placing my headphones in, I select my running playlist. It is a real mixed bag of jams. One minute you are slanging drugs and committing drive-bys' with 2Pac, and the next you're making love with the tailgate down in the pines with Sam Hunt. DMX to Cher Lloyd, Yelawolf to Ellie Golding, Rise Against to Rihanna. I really never know what I'm going to get. I have no idea how this playlist came to be. I've just added songs to it over the years, and it is my go-to mix to run to.

I decide to run along the beach. The soft glow of morning light peeks over the trees, illuminating the water and sand. Fast walking the first kilometre as a warmup, I then pick up the pace before settling into a rhythm. It's quarter past six by the time I get back to the beach in front of the resort.

I slow to a walk to cool down. I see his silhouette moving towards me, his long legs eating the distance between us. His shirt clings to his broad chest with sweat. Clark slows to a walk as he gets closer, and we both pull our headphones from our ears.

"You run?" I ask.

"Yeah. I only started when I moved here. I'm slow, but it clears my head."

"I know the feeling. Why are you up so early?" I ask.

He shrugs. "I couldn't sleep. You?"

"Same." I turn around to walk in the direction he was headed, back to the resort. We fall into step with each other.

"How far do you run?" I ask.

"Only five kilometres. You?"

"Six. I was going to go get a coffee. You want to join me?"

"Sounds good."

We make our way back down the path to the resort and through to the restaurant where they serve breakfast. A comfortable silence falls over us as our heart rates settle back to normal. His arm brushes mine every now and then, and the feeling has the same effect as last night. My body is drawn to him, coming alight with the slightest touch.

Both grabbing water from the complimentary water station, we then go and order our coffees at the front counter and find a place to sit.

"What are the boys up to today before the wedding?" I ask as the waitress places our cups down at the table.

"We are playing golf. The bus is picking us up at eight, then lunch and back here to get ready for the ceremony. What about the girls?"

I glance down at my watch. "The bridal party will already be in hair and makeup. But the rest of us are going to brunch and then going to get our nails done before coming back here to get ready."

Clark glances down at my fingers that wrap around my mug. I never normally do my nails. Honestly, I can't stand having them long. Although, I do love the pretty colours, but I just never bother to go regularly enough. They end up chipping and peeling and looking worse than just leaving them natural.

"Nails, huh," he says in a playful tone.

"Yeah, thinking of bright red."

"Nice." He chuckles. "Do you like them long?"

"Nope. I literally can't do anything when they are long. Like I can't even flush the toilet."

"You use your knuckles."

"What! How do you know that?"

Clark gives me a slightly sheepish grin. "Cherie. She always had them long," he says with a slight undertone.

"You don't like them?" I can sense there's more to the story here. I don't want to pry but I also have no issue with him talking about his ex.

He stares at me over his mug of coffee as he takes a sip. His hazel eyes are bright. "I have no issue with the nails. It doesn't bother me either way, to be honest. It was just...sometimes it felt like she cared more about that stuff than anything else."

I nod, following along. "How so?"

His eyes stare into mine, like he is conflicted about how much to say. "Just little things. It seems silly but..." He lets out a breath.

"You can tell me," I urge, voice gentle.

"I'm going to sound like an asshole."

"I don't think you're an asshole."

"Well, outside of these things costing us a fortune, she was always so worried about them. She didn't want to sweat cos it would ruin her lashes, didn't want to swim at the beach because the sand and water would ruin her fake tan. She didn't want to get her head wet in the pool because the chlorine would ruin her hair extensions."

I listen intently. I want to interject that if that's what made her happy, why did it matter to him if she sat on the sidelines? But I bite my tongue and let him continue.

"It didn't hugely bother me at the time. Although sometimes I did wish she would let loose and just have some fun with me. But once we ended, I realised just how different we actually were."

"I'm sorry," I say. However, I have no clue what for. Just the situation, I suppose. I can tell he is still hurt over it all. Angry at her for cheating, sad for losing something he wanted so badly, frustrated that he didn't see the differences in them sooner.

"Moving to a property, having the animals and being so close to the beach and the slower lifestyle has made me happier. She would have hated it here."

I reach across and grab his hand that is resting on the table. I don't want to judge Cherie based on things he tells me. I know there can be different truths. Both living within the same relationship but seeing things so very differently. Everybody shows and feels love in a different way.

I know they have those love language tests you can do now. 'Are you an act of service kind of person?' Feeling love by the small actions someone does every day or by grand gestures. Like the way Callum used to make my morning coffee every day. 'Do you feel love by physical touch?' Like the way Callum used to always play with my hair while I drove. The thing is, I don't think people fit into one box. They might sway more towards one than the other, but we need all these things to feel loved, seen and appreciated.

I really believe the pendulum swings with different seasons of life.

I love physical touch. I love intimacy. I love having an arm slung over my shoulder while we are walking or being pulled

in

for a hug. But let me tell you. During the deep dark depths of parenting small children, the cycle where they are breastfeeding, sleep on you and need to be endlessly in your arms, and where they cling at your feet with every task, I wanted nothing more than to be left alone. Physical touch by one more person, even my husband, felt like my skin was crawling. There was a time I was so exhausted that the thought of having another set of fingers near me made me recoil.

The thing that got us through changes in seasons like this was good communication. Being able to explain what I needed and having a partner open to listening. Not just hearing but actually listening, and vice versa.

Who knows what Clark's relationship was like behind closed doors. Maybe he didn't listen. Maybe he was never around. My instinct is to always side with the girl, but the more I hear, the more I dislike Cherie. And nothing could explain away or excuse having an affair, falling pregnant and then lying to your husband about it.

The very thought makes me angry deep within my bones.

Clark squeezes my hand that rests near my coffee cup. The gesture sends warmth through my veins and butterflies to my stomach.

"Is that your wedding ring?" he asks, nodding towards my other hand that has subconsciously made its way to the ring around my neck.

I drop it to my lap. I go to remove my other hand from his, but he doesn't let go.

"You don't have to stop. It obviously makes you feel closer to him."

"I don't even realise I'm touching it half the time, if I'm honest. I only took it off my finger late last year."

Clark looks at me with the most intense hazel eyes. "I'm sorry," is all he says as he squeezes my hand. I turn it and our fingers interlock. Then we sit in comfortable silence, finishing our coffee, and letting the soft morning light and mutual connection of loss coat us.

More people start to filter in for their breakfast, so we decide to head back to our rooms to get ready for the day.

Clark pulls me in as we stand, kissing my forehead. "I'm glad I met you," he whispers.

"Me too."

I'm left wondering how he could ever be the villain in someone's story.

10

Crack the champagne

Hannah

"Hannah, your music choice is insane," Liz says as she presses skip on Pantera's 'Walk'.

I stifle a laugh. My general Spotify playlist is no less messy than my running mix. "I actually think Ethan added that."

"Your nine-year-old likes Pantera?" Leah chimes in, popping her head through the front seats from her spot in the back.

The bride, her sister Izzy, Jess and Gabby are in the bridal party and are having nails, hair and makeup done at the resort, with the bride and groom's mothers and the groom's sister and sister-in-law staying with the wedding party. That leaves Liz, Leah, Kelly and I from our friend group. We decided to head into Busselton to have brunch and get our nails done.

We are piled in my car. Liz is in the passenger seat, and Leah and Kelly are in the back. I have no clue how half these songs made it onto my playlist, but I enjoy most music, so I'll happily scream along to the words.

"Jeez this song is no better," Liz says as she grabs my phone. Keith Urban's 'You'll Think of Me' shuts down and makes way for Gracie Abrams's 'That's So True'.

"There, Hot Hits Australia. Can't go wrong." She places my phone back in the centre console.

It doesn't take long for us to get into Busselton, and we file into the cafe for brunch.

"You and Clark are hitting it off," Kelly says.

I'm still not overly ready to talk about it with the girls, but it's been pretty obvious—too much to deny—and they are my best friends. They are all going to find out at some stage.

"He's really sweet. We've...I don't know, just been filling a void we both have."

"Filling something," Liz chuckles, elbowing me in the side.

"You are as bad as my sister. Honestly, I'm not ready to date or be in any kind of relationship and neither is he. So, it's a perfect fit. We both just want casual, easy, fun."

Thankfully the waiter interrupts to take our orders. I breathe a sigh of relief, hoping we can change the subject.

I'm not so lucky.

"Do you think it's a good idea? I mean he's kinda in our friend group now, being close to Rowan and all. You're going to see him again. What if it ends awkwardly?" Leah makes a face that looks like she is in pain.

Leah is my most serious friend. She's the organiser of the group and generally has the most practical, realistic advice. She is the one telling us to drink water when we take it too far on a girl's night out. She is the person who pre-orders the Uber so we aren't left stranded. She was the one who made the reservations for our nails and brunch. Our group would be lost without her. As much as she is probably right, it's not what I want to hear right now.

I want to enjoy this free-falling feeling of being wanted and desired again. I want to bathe in a post orgasmic glow and just switch off to the reality that I know is waiting for me come Monday. Back to a house to clean, three kids to cook for, a business to run and a husband that is dead, leaving me to brunt the full force of this life alone.

Just for a weekend, I don't want to feel every single year of my age. I don't want to think about my clients and if I have enough booked in for the week to cover all my expenses and keep my kids in private school. I don't want to think about their weekend sports or social calendars, or if I forgot to move the client I had booked over a school assembly where Noah will now be getting a certificate. That all the boys need new shoes and where I'm coming up with the four hundred dollars that's going to cost me. I spent it on this weekend vacation.

I internally chuckle, although it's not funny. They do all need new shoes. And I didn't need that new bikini.

Nope, I don't want to think of any of that. I want to be irresponsible and carefree, just for a weekend. I want to have hot sex with a man I barely know in inappropriate places. I want to feel wanted and just have someone take care of me for one night.

Why can't Leah just let me have this?

I start to explain but I really can't be bothered. Honestly, if it all turns to shit, well, I'll deal with it then. No point stressing over something that hasn't happened yet.

"I know. I'm old enough to know this is probably not the greatest idea. But honestly, this is the first time since Callum that I have felt a desire to be with someone else sexually. I'm just enjoying what it is at face value for now." I pause, sipping my coffee that the waiter had quietly delivered. She looks apologetically at me.

"I didn't mean to be so harsh. I just don't want you to get hurt," Leah says.

"I know. I don't want to get hurt either. We've talked a bit about what we want. I think we are both okay with this just being a weekend thing. We don't have to put any other pressure on it beyond that."

"I think it's awesome. Get that D, girl," Liz says, cheering me with her coffee.

"Look, Monday I'm back to work, parenting, household duties, eat, sleep, repeat. Don't get me wrong, I love my life and my family, but this...is exactly the escape I need. I just need to feel something. Something other than responsibilities, okay?"

"I get it. I'm happy you found that in Clark. He seems like a really nice guy," Leah says as our food is bought out and placed down.

"Thanks." I waste no time shovelling a forkful of eggs benedict into my mouth.

We eat the rest of our meal over talks of our kids and life, then we make our way to get our nails done. I opt for shellac in a deep red, happy to be sinking into the massage chair and thinking of nothing for the next hour.

It's just after lunch when we make it back to the resort. We collectively decide to get ready together and drag our stuff into James and Leah's room. The boys are still playing golf and will most likely roll on in at 2:30 and be ready by 2:45 PM.

Leah cracks some champagne while Liz cranks some music. We start slowly getting ready together and dancing around the room like we are back in our early twenties.

This weekend has already been exactly what my soul needed.

11

Clark

e've taken our shoes off and made our way onto the beach for the ceremony. There are a few rows of white wooden chairs decorated with flowers that no one wants to be the first to sit on.

A few of us boys stand at the back chatting and waiting for all the guests to arrive. Really, I'm just waiting for her.

With the implosion of my own marriage in such a dramatic fashion, I was dreading coming to this wedding. One chance encounter on the side of the road and suddenly all that has changed.

I'm happy for my friend to get married. I don't want to rain on their parade with my marriage grinch bullshit. Having met Hannah, I feel like I may just be able to have some fun tonight.

I spot her walking down with a few of the girls. She looks incredible. I wouldn't even know where to start to explain her dress. All I know is it has a long slit up the side that shows enough thigh to make my mouth go dry and my knees feel a little weak.

I clear my throat, trying to get a grip of myself before my reaction to seeing her starts to show through my pants. I give her a head nod in acknowledgement as she makes her way over to me.

"How was golf?" she asks.

"It was...golf." She chuckles at my response. "No, it was fun. It was good to hang out with the guys."

"I've actually never played golf. I mean, I am exceptional at mini golf," she quips.

"Is that so?" I tease.

"Oh yeah, I'm undefeated. Although I do have an inkling that Callum used to sometimes let me win."

I laugh, as that sounds exactly like something I would do. "How was your brunch and nails?"

"Really good, actually. I opted for a deep red." She holds her hand up and wiggles her fingers to show me.

"They match your lips." My eyes float to her painted deep red lips and all I can think about is biting them between my teeth. Everything about Hannah has me feeling like a desperate teenager. Like I'm hitting all the firsts again.

I had been happy with my sex life with Cherie, but I wouldn't exactly call it exciting or experimental. Since Cherie, I have been with a few women, but it has never felt like this. I don't remember ever wanting someone this badly. My body feels like it's in physical pain standing this close to her. The way her dress hugs her firm ass, the way I can see the slight peak of her nipple though the material.

I take a deep breath, trying to clear my head. The thoughts of her body on mine as I kissed her in the bathroom last night torment me. How it took every ounce of strength I possessed to kiss her forehead and walk away from her when we said goodnight.

I focus on the bride and groom and try not to get lost in the way her body skims mine. The ceremony goes faster than I anticipated, which suited me just fine. They opted for a simple monitum, and their vows were beautiful but quick.

Hannah and I stood side by side before we all piled into a group photo. The photographer had to climb a ladder that seemed to come out of nowhere to be able to get us all in the shot.

The rest of the wedding goes just as fast. All the normal train of events. The entrance, the dinner, the speeches, the cutting of the cake, the first dance. Luckily, Rowan and Olivia had placed Hannah and I at the same table. Part of me wonders if we didn't meet on the side of the road, would we have been pushed together at some point anyway—our friend's way of setting up the only single people at this wedding. Well, besides Hannah's predictions of the elderly and the children.

The night has progressed; people are making their way to the dance floor after the couple's first dance. Hannah and I have spent the entirety of the night with back-and-forth flirty banter and general chit chat about our lives. It feels comfortable to ask her to dance with me now. Plus, I did promise her that I wouldn't leave her stranded when the slow songs came on.

The Boyce Avenue cover of 'Teenage Dream' plays, and I place my hand out to Hannah. A sexy smile splits her lips, her red lipstick somehow still intact as she places her delicate hand in mine.

My heart is pounding like a jackhammer in my chest as I lead us to the dance floor. I hate that she makes me this nervous. I try not to falter or let it show as I pull her body close to mine. I have been wondering what my hands would feel like over her body through this soft clingy material all damn night.

I suddenly feel like a kid back at his high school ball. Afraid to go too low with my hands. Afraid to get too close. I gently place one hand on the small of her back as I hold her other hand in mine.

I don't know how to dance properly, and to be honest, I feel awkward as hell right now. But the dance floor is packed, and everyone is focused on their own partners. There is no room to do anything fancy like try to spin her or lean her back and kiss her stupid like I want to. Instead, we move slowly, side stepping for a few beats. Removing her hand from mine, she wraps her arms around my neck and pulls herself tighter to me.

I breathe her in. She smells sweet, delicate and florally. It's a total contrast to her confident and strong persona.

I love it.

I place my now free hand on her upper back. Her dress is low, leaving her skin exposed. I drag my thumb back and forth over the bare skin, not missing the way goosebumps rise in my wake.

We dance like this, swaying to the music in each other's arms for the rest of the song. Then the DJ does a complete one-eighty and plays Daryl Braithwaite's 'Horses'.

It has three quarters of the crowd dispersing back to their tables or to the bar. The remaining quarter, which seems to consist of our friend group, start holding fake microphones and doing dramatic serenades to the person next to them. Hannah is no exception. She doesn't seem to give a shit if people are watching and is happily laughing and dancing like a lunatic with her friends.

I stand back with a group of the guys chatting, but I can't seem to pry my eyes from her. The hypnotic way her hips move as the dress clings to her. The muscles in her back as she throws her arms around. The movement of her lips as she sings along to the song, now pretending to ride an imaginary horse.

I can't help but laugh, but not because she looks ridiculous. Quite the opposite. Somehow, she makes those dance moves look sexy. Her carefree confidence has me hook, line and sinker.

Before I know it, they are ringing the 'last call' bell. I follow Hannah to the bar. She is sipping a glass of water.

"Where to from here?" I ask as I place my empty beer glass on the bar.

She raises a brow. "Oh, you think I'm going home with you, do you?"

"A guy can dream, right?"

She chuckles. "Want to go for a walk on the beach?" She has a mischievous sparkle in her eyes, and my pulse quickens at what she might be thinking.

"Sure."

I give her my elbow for her to link her arm through, and she grabs her bag. We make our way around to a few of the groups that are still standing strong and say our goodbyes, before heading to the path that leads to the beach.

It's a beautiful night. The air is fresh but there isn't a single breeze. The ocean is still and quiet, and the sky is full of stars, creating enough glow to light our way. Hannah stops where the paved footpath ends to make way for the sand path.

Realising she needs to take her heels off to be able to walk on the soft sand, I drop to one knee, trailing my palm to her ankle. She steadies herself with a hand on my shoulder as I place her foot on my knee. With deft movements, I undo the dainty straps of her heels and slide them off, before placing her foot back in the cool sand. I repeat the process with her other foot.

"Just leave them here. We can get them on the way back," she says.

"Okay." I kick my own shoes off and place hers next to mine in the sand. I doubt anyone is running around stealing shoes at midnight at this resort.

Taking her hand, we make our way down to the water's edge. The moon is low and a few moored boats rock in the gentle waves just past the shoreline.

"Well, that wasn't nearly as bad as I was anticipating," Hannah says as we walk along the shore.

"Agreed. I'm glad I met you. I feel like PTSD from my own wedding would have taken over if I didn't have your crazy dance moves distracting me."

"My dance moves are phenomenal. I saw you watching me."

"They were captivating, that's for sure. I especially liked the ones during that Pony song."

She spits out a laugh. "Well, Genuine's 'Pony' will turn any girl into a slut- dropping whore."

Now I laugh, too. That's not quite how I would have described her dancing, but she definitely knows how to move, that's for sure. It has me thinking how she would move in bed. On top of me.

"Well, I couldn't keep my eyes off you on that dance floor."

"Good, because your eyes aren't all I want on me." She stops walking and turns her body towards me.

Holy hell, I've never had beach sex, and I have a feeling I'm about to experience it. I'm not mad about it.

Not at all.

My hand finds her face, and I cup her cheek before leaning down to kiss her. She presses up into me, kissing me back. I am done for. My hands find her hips as I pull her close. She breaks contact, and my lips follow her, trying to chase the feeling. But she is already turning, grabbing my hand.

"Come with me."

Seriously, how could I not?

Hannah pulls me up towards the dunes and I blindly follow. Finding a space where there is some coverage by foliage and higher sand dunes, she turns me so I'm facing the water. She then pushes my chest till I'm sat in the sand. Hannah lifts her dress and straddles me, knees on either side of my thighs. Her dress bunches around her hips, the slit showing a glimpse of black lace underneath.

Her fingers work down the buttons on my shirt, and I do nothing but stare at her. Leaning back, placing my hands in the sand to allow space for her to work, I take her in. She slips my shirt off my shoulders, and I shuffle to lift my hands to allow it off my arms. She smirks at me, admiring my abs. Abs that took way too long to show, but the gym has become a therapy for me over the last year.

I lean in, placing my hands on her hips again as I kiss over her collarbone, across her neck and over to her other shoulder, sliding the thin strap of her dress down to give me better access to her body. The material falls on one side, exposing the top of her breasts. I follow the line of the material with my mouth, kissing it as I slide it further and further down. Then I do the same thing on the other side until she is bare to me. My mouth finds her nipple, and I slowly flick it with my tongue as my mouth gently sucks. Hannah lets out a sigh and relaxes into my touch.

Her hands roam my back and neck, before making their way to the button of my pants. She moves down a bit so she can get to the zip, sliding it down before standing. I shuffle the remainder of my clothes off. The sand is most likely going to be a pain. Right now, I couldn't care. Cover me in it, as long as she sits back down on me.

Damn, she looks amazing, standing in front of me. She slips the dress off and steps out of it, leaving her in nothing but a black lacy G-string. The moon illuminates her skin. It has my whole body heating. Then she hooks her fingers in the sides of her G-string and slides them down. My breath catches and I lick my bottom lip as my hands reach for her, pulling her down to straddle me again. It's almost painful having her pussy so close to me without being inside her.

I'm throbbing at the thought of it.

I lean in and kiss her, running my hands through her hair and spreading my fingers, before gripping a handful of it and pulling back gently. She moans into my mouth, kissing me harder. Then she pulls away.

"Fuck, did you bring any condoms by any chance?" she asks.

"Shit, no, I forgot. I have some in my room." My cock is so hard it feels like it could burst. But I'm not about to make her do anything she isn't comfortable with. "I can lay you down and make you scream with my head between those sexy thighs of yours."

Hannah is slowly grinding her hips on me. I can feel her wetness already coating me as she slides her pussy lips up and down the base of my cock. A cock that is painfully throbbing to slide into her.

She kisses me again, playfully biting my bottom lip and moaning.

"Have you ever been tested?" she asks between kisses.

"Yeah, a couple months ago. Haven't been with anyone since. I was clean." I don't bother asking her. She had already told me that she hasn't been with anyone since her now past husband.

My thoughts start to spiral. Cherie was cheating on me. Did Hannah ever cheat on her husband? I refrain from asking the question. It would only kill the mood. Everything I have learnt about her so far doesn't give me the impression that she would cheat. But she reads my mind.

"I've never been tested, but I haven't been with anyone since Callum. I was always faithful and so was he."

"I believe you."

"Same," she says as she wraps her hand around my cock and raises slightly before sliding down onto me. I don't have time to interject. And I don't want to. I let her lead.

The feeling is euphoric, and my hands have a mind of their own as they grip her hips, pulling her further down.

My mind knows better, though.

"I want you so desperately, here and now, more than anything. But if you want a condom, I will happily carry you all the way back to your villa right now. There is no pressure here." But she slowly starts to roll her hips, and the movement has me already gasping for air.

"You're clean and you can't get me pregnant. I don't want to go anywhere."

That's all the permission I need.

I lay back, allowing her to ride me while my hands grip her hips, helping her get the friction she wants.

"Sorry," Hannah says, leaning down close to my face. "I didn't mean to bring up the…" I know exactly what she is about to say. The fact that I can't have children.

I stop her with a kiss, gripping her behind the neck and pulling her into me. "Don't be. Not right now. I ain't worried about that."

Our bodies move in sync, the moon above her making her skin glow. Everything about her is so damn sexy. The way she moves, the way she kisses, and her moans.

She rolls her hips slowly as I thrust into her from below. I let her lead, mindful that this is the first time she has been with someone since her husband. But she feels so fucking good, and I can feel my restraint starting to crack. Electricity runs through my veins. I've never wanted to love harder.

Her head falls back as she rocks on me, starting to move faster. I grip her hips, slamming up into her, over and over again as our movements turn more frantic.

"Clark," Hannah moans my name, and it takes every ounce of strength I have to stay this gentle with her. I pull her down onto my chest, kissing her as she moans into my mouth.

She pants my name again, breaking from our kiss and burying her head in my shoulder as we cling to each other. My arms wrap around her, pulling her deeper into me with each thrust. Hannah bites down on my shoulder as she lets go. I follow her over the edge, breaths heavy and ragged as she collapses onto me.

It's settled. I'm definitely a fan of beach sex.

Sand and all.

12

Guilt and Betrayal

I feel his heavy arm draped over me, and his steady breath on my neck. He radiates heat, warming me everywhere our bodies meet. I float into the feeling.

Home.

I roll over to cuddle further into his embrace. I want to feel his beard tickling my face. Feel his hands and how his fingers would join the dots of my freckles on my shoulder.

I wrap my arm around his body. It feels different. Nuzzling further into his neck, I breathe him in, but it smells different. My heart rate spikes as I lean my face up, searching for the familiar feeling of his beard. Panic makes my breath catch as my eyes shoot open.

"Hey, hey, are you okay?" Moving his arm off me, Clark gives me space as I lean back, staring into a face I wasn't expecting.

"I'm fine, I just…" I choke on the words. Desperately trying to steady my rapid breathing, I move off the bed. "I just need to go to the bathroom." I don't bother to cover up as I make my way across the room.

Fuck.

I knew having him stay the night was a bad idea. I'm obviously not ready to do this. It's too soon. It's too much. In my sleepy, slightly hungover daze, I felt the body heat of him and his arm on me. Suddenly I had lost the last three years of my life, and I was back in bed with my husband.

Callum.

I couldn't hide my initial panic. They are so starkly different. In looks, in personality. Everything.

I pull myself together behind the comfort of the closed door of the bathroom, but I know he felt the shift. Clark had walked me back to my room last night and I had asked him to come in. It felt good to lay in his arms and fall asleep wrapped up in him.

I don't know what happened to me this morning. Maybe it was the lack of sleep. It was after two in the morning by the time we made it back to my room. Maybe it was all the champagne. My head does feel fuzzy.

I drink from the tap, washing away the taste of last night, and stare at myself in the mirror. Gripping the chain around my neck and holding the ring, it burns in my palm, hot with guilt and betrayal.

I have to go back out there and explain to Clark what the fuck just happened to me.

After splashing water on my face and brushing my teeth, I decide it's time to face the music. Feeling a little self-conscious that I'm completely naked, I throw the bath robe that is hanging on the back of the door over me and suck in a deep breath.

He is still laying down but pushes himself up onto his elbow as I open the door. His defined chest and abs flex with the movement. His short hair is a little ruffled. It is unfair how guys wake up still looking so damn good.

"Are you okay?" Clark asks again.

I make my way back to the bed and throw some pillows up by the headboard so I can lean back on them, careful not to knock the large beautiful wooden framed picture of Eagle Bay that hangs over us. "I freaked out a bit. Sorry."

"You don't have to apologise."

I feel like such an asshole. This man has been so badly hurt by a woman that he loved. We had an amazing night together and now I'm about to tell him that I woke up and thought I was in the arms of another man.

My brain spins with the thoughts. I'm not someone to lie. But I also want to have some tact in how I tell him my feelings. I know we said we were both okay with it just being casual, but I had always said that even if it was just sex, there still needs to be respect. So, I don't want to lie to him about it.

"Honestly, in my slightly hungover, half-asleep state, I felt arms around me, and it felt a little too familiar." I pause, gauging his reaction. Clark's face holds nothing but sympathy. "For the briefest of moments, it felt like I was back in bed with Callum. When I woke up properly and realised where I was, it was just an initial shock. That's all." I lean my head back on the giant pillow head rest I had created. "I'm sorry," I add.

"I already said you don't have to be sorry. I can't imagine what that would have felt like." His kind reaction leaves me relieved. He takes my hand. Most men would have had their ego so badly wounded that it would have enticed an angry comment or they would have up and left altogether. "I understand it's different for you. He didn't betray you or break your heart. You didn't fall out of love or have a fight." He reaches for the chain around my neck and toys with the ring. "He was there and you were happy, and then he was gone. I understand you still love him."

"That actually sums it up perfectly. I don't think I will ever stop loving him, because there was no closure. No end to our relationship. We were happy. I was in love. Like actually in love. Not just where you co-exist and co-parent under the same roof. No, we still loved each other." I choke on the words, but his hand finds mine, giving me gentle reassurance. "Then he was just gone."

"Would it be easier if I left? Let you process what you're feeling alone?"

I laugh. "How are you so sweet after what I just told you?"

Clark props himself up further to look at me. "Look, I'm not going to lie and say it didn't wound my ego a little. But I also understand. I get it. You have made it clear from the beginning that Callum was your everything. I know what this is. If you want to be alone, I'm okay with that. If you want to talk about it, I'm okay with that too."

"I don't want you to go, and I definitely don't regret last night. It was amazing. I know I have said this before but fuck me Cherie was an idiot to ever let you go. You deserved so much better, Clark."

"Well, you didn't deserve the cards you were dealt, either. We are both just doing the best with what we have."

"Well, I guess we have each other for a little bit longer. My check out isn't till two."

He stands and starts putting his clothes from last night back on. My heart cracks thinking I have hurt him. Annoyed at myself that I've ruined exactly what I had been looking for.

"I'll go grab us coffees and we can go for a swim. Nothing clears your head like cool saltwater."

I smile up at him, grateful for the moment of space he is giving me to collect my thoughts but insanely grateful that after what just happened, he isn't put off and running for the hills. "A swim sounds so good right about now."

Clark buttons up his shirt and somehow the movement is just as sexy as it was coming off. "I'll be back."

With that, he leaves. I make my way to the bathroom, thinking I have fucked this up royally. He had said that in his experience, women say they want casual but don't mean it and I just proved him right.

The moment we slept together, I went and made it all weird. I mentally kick myself as I get into the shower, hoping the scalding hot water will cleanse away the last half hour and we can start fresh.

He is knocking on my door twenty minutes later, looking completely unholy in a tight white tee and board shorts, with a towel slung over his shoulder and a coffee in each hand.

I let the liquid gold awaken my soul as it courses through my veins. "You remembered my order." I'm surprised he was paying enough attention to me yesterday when I ordered my latte with a half a shot of hazelnut. It's strong and extra hot, just how I like it.

"I pay attention." He smirks as he sips his own.

We make our way down to the beach, slumping in the sand. Side by side, my leg touches his as we sip our coffee in comfortable silence. I let the crashing of the waves and birds chirping wash over us.

"Despite my freak out, I am happy you are here. It feels nice to have some adult company," I say after I have finished my coffee and can feel the slight zap of energy it has given me.

"I'm glad you're here, too. It's been a long time since I had as much fun as I did last night," Clark responds.

"You don't get out much?" I ask.

"Not really." He turns his head to look at me. Light stubble coats his jaw now. It somehow makes him look even hotter and rougher around the edges.

"That is why I haven't seen you at any of the other friend catch ups." I'm wondering how he is such good friends with Rowan, but I haven't seen him at any of the other things we have all been at over the last year.

"I went to a quiz night a couple months ago," he says.

"The nineties one?" I remember the girls messaging about that. "I was sick that weekend. What about James' fortieth birthday? We went to that dart place in the city."

"Yeah, I was meant to go but my nephew had his eighteenth birthday that same weekend, so I went back to Sydney for that. The Comedy Night?" he asks.

"Couldn't get a sitter."

"So we've been just missing each other for the last year?"

"Seems like it."

"One flat tyre was all it took," Clark adds with a smile.

"I still need to pay you back for that."

"Probably want to do an alignment and rotation for the tyres. I can sort that out for you when we get back to Mandurah."

"I'd appreciate that."

"Should we go for a swim?" He motions to the clear water. It's slightly windier today but the water is fairly calm, protected by the little cove of rocks to the left that create a barrier from stronger winds.

We wade out into the fresh water. I half expect him to splash me or tackle me. Maybe close the distance between us and kiss me senseless. Memories of us in the water just yesterday flood my brain, making my skin heat despite the cool water.

I find this sweet, respectful Clark so endearing. But I'd be lying if I said I didn't crave that rougher, dominating Clark that kissed me in the hallway at the restaurant. The one that shoved me back against the tiled wall and let me grind myself on his knee between my thighs.

I want that Clark back.

He was right, though. The instant my head submerges under the water, the slight pang of a headache dissipates along with the residual guilt.

We head back to the shore, and I know exactly what I want to spend the rest of the day doing. I just hope he is on board.

13

Just the normal way

Clark

The water was exactly what I needed. I felt awful about Hannah's momentary freak out this morning, not knowing if she wanted me to stay or go. I can't be mad at her over it, though. I mean, it stung a little, but I get it. She has made it clear what she wants—all this can be—and I'm okay with that. I want the same things she does, and I have my own trauma from my ex to deal with.

As much as I've wanted the flirty banter and hot passion from yesterday back, I'm reluctant to initiate anything until I know she is okay. I know that last night was the first time she has had sex with anyone since her late husband. I haven't missed the way her hand instinctively finds the ring around her neck every time she talks about him. Maybe she needs more time to process all of this. In the meantime, good company and salt water is fine with me.

However, watching her ass move in front of me as we walk the path back to the resort has my heart racing and my dick pulsing.

I chuck my towel over the little wooden balcony that sits in front of her villa as she unlocks the door. Stepping through, I nervously follow her.

Fuck, I want her so bad. I want to throw her on the bed and tear that tiny bikini that covers too much from her body. But the things she has said to me about respect still play in my mind. I'm hoping she doesn't regret the sex we had last night now it is the stark daylight.

Hannah pauses just inside the door, smiling at me. She slowly drops her towel to the floor, leaving her in nothing but her bikini. The look on her face tells me she wants this.

So I decide to man up and throw caution to the wind. She did, after all, invite me back here. And now she stands half naked biting her bottom lip looking at me. Fuck, I want to remove it from her teeth and bite down on it with my own.

I shake my head at the thought. Cherie hated any form of rougher sex. But Hannah said she likes a savage in the bedroom. Did she mean that or was she just flirting?

I gently grip her hand, pushing her back against the door. She's a fair bit shorter than me, but I lean down, pressing my body to hers before I kiss her. Her lips are salty and the feeling of her under me has me instantly hard. My hands cup her face, and she leans into it as she kisses me back.

I break from the kiss, moving my mouth to her ear as I suck on her lobe. Her breath catches and the noise has my already hard dick twitching.

"Did you mean what you said yesterday on the paddle board?" I whisper in her ear.

"About what?" she asks breathlessly.

"About wanting a savage in the bedroom?"

"Every word." She tilts her head to look at me and our eyes meet. Her playful side is gone, and her eyes look like pure porn. My confidence falters.

"What does that look like exactly?" I'm curious. I hate that I'm thinking about this right now when this goddess is standing in front of me half naked. But Cherie was a light's off, missionary girl. Hannah's confidence has me so turned on but also a little terrified.

"Give me your hand," she says, not breaking eye contact. She brings it up to her delicate neck and places my hand on her throat. I curl my fingers but don't apply any pressure. "Now squeeze," she instructs, voice husky.

Fuck me! I've never done this before, but I can't say that it doesn't turn me all the fucking way on. After being thrown from a relationship that left me feeling completely emasculated, the feeling of having some form of control is making me harder than iron. Even though, deep down, I know Hannah is the one with all the power. She would only have to utter one word and I would stop. Still, the illusion of power feels good.

"Like this?" I softly close my grip around her neck.

"Tighter." There isn't an ounce of second guessing in her voice. I love that she knows exactly what she wants and isn't afraid to speak it.

"I don't want to hurt you."

"I'll tell you if it's too much," she says confidently.

I work with my hands all day, every day. My grip strength would make a vice look weak. We did one of those grip strength tests at some men's health day I went to at the gym. Mine was one hundred and thirty-nine pounds. I had no clue what that meant but the lady said it was off her chart and she hadn't seen someone get that number before.

I feel like if I use even a quarter of my strength on her, I'm going to crush her windpipe.

"You won't be able to speak if it's too much." I'm not trying to threaten her, but I don't miss the way her eyes glint with want at my words. Like she is turned on by pain or fear. I'm intrigued and also slightly feral at the idea.

I close my grip around her throat, and her eyes roll to the back of her head as she lets out a little breath.

Fuck!

I instantly let go, running a hand through my hair. Flashes of the one time I slapped Cherie's ass during sex and she started crying tear through my mind. She told me I was disrespectful and then didn't speak to me for over a week.

"I'm sorry. Too much?" I take a step back to give her space, wanting her to feel safe. But she doesn't falter. Hannah folds her bottom lip between her teeth again.

"No," she breathes. "That was perfect."

Well shit. I guess I'm going for it.

I close the distance between us, wrapping my hand around her throat again and pushing her back towards the door. I lean down and take her mouth with my own.

Hard.

She moans into me.

"You like it rough?" I question, voice tight.

She gives me a *mmmhum*. My mind starts racing with all the things I've wanted to try but never been able to.

"Do you like being tied up?" I ask, taking a chance.

"Yes," she pants.

I break the kiss and step back. Her body moves forward to follow mine, but I place a hand on her stomach and push her back towards the door.

"Stay," I tell her.

"Yes, sir." The cheeky way she says that almost makes me unable to walk away. But I have an idea.

I walk towards the bed where I saw her robe earlier. Grabbing the waist tie, I pull it free. Hannah is right where I told her to stay, leaning against the door. Her body is to die for. She is still in her bathers and her long wet hair looks wild around her face.

She smiles when she sees me coming towards her with the tie. I'd love to know what's going through her mind. I wonder if she can tell I've never done this before?

"What are you doing?" Her voice is sexy and playful. Curious, but not worried.

"Do you trust me?"

She nods.

I reach for her hands. "May I?"

She willingly lets me take them and I start tying knots.

"This is a Highwaymen's hitch knot. But I've added an extra bight," I explain to her. I use this knot all the time for the horses. It's easy and releases fast.

I fasten the knot around both her wrists and then a knot to the end of the tie. Pulling her arms up over head, I open the front door and chuck the knotted end over it, creating an anchor when the door is shut. People on the outside will be able to see it, but I don't give a shit about that right now.

The way Hannah is smiling at me and licking her lips has my hands shaking in anticipation. I place the tail of the added bight in her mouth. "If you pull down with your weight on the tie or if you pull that tail end up towards your hands, it's going to make the knot tighter around your wrists. If you pull this tail down,"

I motion to the one in her mouth, "it will all come undone. Okay?"

I want her to know she is safe, that she can get out of it at any time, but also give her what she clearly wants. I stand back, admiring her. Her hands stretched up high over her head, the tail in her mouth. I move back in, placing kisses over her collarbone and down to her tits. I pull the strings of her bathers around her neck, and it comes undone. The little triangle pieces fall away.

A whimper escapes her lips. I kiss over her tits. I can see the faintest stretch marks running down them. Is this what she was worried about? They look perfect to me. Sucking her nipple into my mouth, I gently bite down and pull away with it between my teeth. She hisses and pushes her chest out to follow me, but I push her back to the door with a hand on her stomach. I let the nipple go, afraid I've gone too far.

"Clark, that feels so good." She likes the pain.

The feedback spurs me on. I kiss down her stomach to just above her bikini line. Pulling it down slightly, I see her c-section scar. I trail my tongue over the raised skin. I pull at the side string of her bather bottoms, and they fall away, revealing her smooth pussy.

Fuck me!

Hair, no hair, I wouldn't have cared either way. But I have to admit that when I bring my face between her legs and lick up her slit, the soft, smooth, salty skin feels and tastes so fucking good.

I move slowly and gently, but she is pushing her hips into my face, begging for more. I comply. I lick up and suck her clit into my mouth, pushing down to create a bit of pressure. Hannah grinds into me with her hips. I lift her leg, helping her to place it over my shoulder. Then I run a finger through her wetness, sliding it into her pussy. She arches her back and lets out a moan.

I add a second finger, moving them in and out, deep but slow, while I lick and suck her clit. She wraps her other leg around me now. I'm completely supporting her weight with my shoulders, with the tie holding her to the door.

She grinds herself into me, and I take that as a hint that she wants more. She did say she wants 'savage in the bedroom'. I move my fingers hard and fast, twisting and stretching her out while I suck and roll her clit in my mouth, letting her grind into me.

Fuck it's hot.

Watching her squirm and buck on my face while I pound her with my fingers. She is breathing heavily and moaning, letting her weight pull down on the tie while I support her. She has long since dropped the tail from her mouth, trusting me completely.

"Clark, I'm going to come."

I add a third finger, going harder, and her head hits the door. Her hips push her into me further as her legs tighten around me. I can barely breath, but fuck me, I'd die before I stopped if it meant she would come on my face like this.

"OH.MY.FUCKING.GOD," Hannah screams as her body shakes. Then she goes weightless. "Holy hell," she cries.

I grip her ass as I stand, allowing her to slide down my body, wrapping her legs around my waist. Gripping the tail of the bight I made, I pull down to release her hands. She flops forward, draping her head on my shoulders as her arms fall by her sides.

Walking her over to the bed, she clings to me. Without warning, I throw her onto the mattress, not overly hard, but she lets out a little yelp. Her eyes light up and a smile dances across her face. Propping herself up on her elbows, she watches as I crawl over the top of her, hovering there for a moment.

I want to kiss her so desperately. I want her to taste herself on my lips. I have no clue why the thought of that turns me on so much. But again, my ex has me second guessing my instincts.

I hate that she is crossing my mind right now. It's not so much her, but just the flashbacks of things she used to do. Like instantly spitting and brushing her teeth after head, like I was the grossest thing she has ever tasted. She would never kiss me after I had been down there, either.

Hannah must see my reservations, because she pushes herself up to meet me. The moment our lips touch, I devour her, letting go of any second-guessing. Her hand finds my chest, pushing me back to lay on the mattress so she can straddle me. I lay down on the soft bed as her tongue starts a trail down my chest until she meets the top of my shorts. Pulling them down, she frees my cock.

Her eyes light up. "Damn." She leans back, trailing her tongue across her bottom lip.

"Big enough for you?" I'm no slouch in the size department. I mean, I don't spend a heap of time looking at other men's cocks to compare, but I've been told I'm big. Guess I had to make up for the fact that I'm shooting blanks.

Hannah licks up my shaft as her hand wraps around the base. I grip a handful of her hair as her hot, wet mouth takes me in. She bobs her head up and down, moving her hand at the same time, gripping me tight. I fist her hair harder and start controlling her movements slightly. I'm trying not to be too rough but fuck me it feels so good.

She looks up at me through her lashes, and I swear I'm about to come from just the sight of her. I try my best to think of mundane shit as her mouth works me over. I don't know if I'll be able to go again if I blow now. And I really want to feel my cock sliding into her pussy.

I pull her head up by her hair, and she meets my eyes. She licks her lips, smiling. Like she loves the taste of me. It makes my heart flutter and my cock twitch.

It also gives me the confidence to do what I do next.

I lean up, grab her, and flip her around onto her stomach, yanking her hips up in line with mine as I move behind her. Her ass is so fucking perfect and I'm itching to slap her round cheeks. Fuck, it's like all the control I ever had has slipped. I've become feral with how badly I need her.

I'm about to ask if this is okay, when she pushes back into me, turning her head to watch. My hard cock is lined up perfectly and she doesn't give me a second to think. I sink into her, and it feels like ecstasy. She arches her back and moans, letting me push deeper.

"Fuck, hang on," Hannah says as she pulls forward.

Did I hurt her for real? Shit. Has she changed her mind?

I pull out completely. "Are you okay?"

"More than okay. I want you so bad." She shifts to grip a pillow that she shoves under her hips to help prop herself up, then she pushes back into me.

"Better. Now fuck me like you mean it," she says, smirking. I was half expecting her to ask to turn the lights off or move to have me on top, because that's how most of my sexual encounters have gone in the last eighteen months. Well, really my whole life, if I'm honest.

At this stage, if she wanted me to put on a straw skirt and do the hula, I would, if it meant I got to slide back into her. But Hannah doesn't seem to have an ounce of confidence issues. Or if she does, she isn't letting it show. The openness is making me crazy with want.

I grip my dick with one hand, her hip with the other, and I slam back into her. A low rumble escapes my chest. I move slowly to begin with, then I take what she said at face value and fuck her like I mean it. I grip both her hips hard and pound into her. She meets every thrust, panting and moaning.

I push down on her back, so her chest and face hit the mattress. Hannah turns her head to the side, biting her bottom lip in between moans as I fuck her.

Jesus Christ, I'm so close already.

I lean over her slightly, wrapping a hand around her waist to find her clit. I start rubbing my hand over it, pushing down on her lower back to add pressure. I feel her muscles tighten, gripping me, and it almost makes me lose my shit right there. Her hands are gripping the bed sheets, and she is panting hard.

I take my hand off her lower back and lean down to her, nibbling her ear lobe and wrapping my arm around her to pinch her nipple. She bucks underneath me, pushing her hips down into my hand still working her clit.

"Fuck, Clark. Fuck, I'm—I'm—"

She starts screaming my name, and it's my undoing.

"Come for me, baby," I whisper in her ear, pinching her nipple harder.

I feel her clamp down on me.

"I'm coming. Fuck me harder." It's nothing but a breathless plea.

I take my hands from her clit and nipple and grip her hips like a vice. Lifting her ass up off the bed to meet me, I savagely pound into her.

She is screaming profanities mixed with my name as her hands fist the mattress and the feedback sends me over the edge. I come undone in quite possibly the best orgasm I've ever had.

I collapse down next to her, and she rolls to her side to face me.

"That"—*pant*—"was"—*pant*—"amazing"—*pant*. Hannah lets out a deep breath. "Like I knew I missed sex but seriously."

"Glad to be of service," I say, pulling her into me. She nuzzles into my chest, smelling so good. Like salt and vanilla.

"I've never had sex like that before. I had no idea what I've been missing out on," I say.

"How have you been having sex your whole life then?"

"Just the normal way." The lust filled haze that had me feral is fading and I'm back to being shy and kind of awkward, especially next to Hannah who is so sure of herself.

"Wait, what's the normal way?" she says with a tone of playful teasing.

"Cherie wasn't very adventurous. Like mood lighting and romantic, slow, me on top type stuff." I internally kick myself the moment the words leave my mouth. Why would I bring my ex up when I am naked with another woman?

What the fuck is wrong with me?

Hannah doesn't even flinch.

"Is that how you've always had sex?" I ask.

She laughs at me. "Callum and I were quite adventurous. We loved trying new things. Role play, props, toys. Definitely haven't done it all but there isn't a heap we didn't try."

I'm intrigued. "What's your favourite thing you've tried?" I ask, just gaining insight.

"I love being submissive. Not full BDSM, but I love when you take control and when you're rough. I love dressing up. It's so fun." She relaxes her head on my chest as I roll onto my back. "What about you? What's something you have always wanted to try?" she asks.

To be honest, I hadn't given it a heap of thought. Well, there is one thing, but I feel too awkward to share right now.

"I dunno, really," I answer, somewhat honestly. "I'm a lingerie man. I love sexy lingerie on a woman."

"Good to know." Hannah sighs. "This is so good. I miss my kids, but I really don't want to go home."

"I'm not ready for this to end either," I add.

"The weekend or this sex?"

"Both, if I'm honest." I want to ask if I can see her again. But she beats me to it.

"Would you want to do this again? The sex, I mean."

Fuck yes. Call me anytime. I refrain from acting too desperate. "Yeah, I'd love to. I could take you horse riding one day if you wanted."

Dickhead. She wants sex, not a date. Why are you asking this?

"Really!" Hannah turns her head to look up at me, excitement washing over her face. "I would love that. I miss riding. It's been hard to get the trail ride dates to line up with weekend sports."

"Yeah, it would be nice to have someone to ride with."

We make rough plans to contact each other when we get home. Hannah peels herself from my arms to go and get in the shower.

"I'll get out of your hair." I'm unsure if she is going to be offended at me leaving right away. I'm not trying to bail out, but I have to pack and get my shit out of the room. My checkout is eleven and I'm cutting that close.

"I'll see you in a bit," she yells from the shower, seemingly not giving a fuck if I stay or go.

I chuck on my shorts and open the shower door. She is all smooth and shiny from the body wash, and it smells like coconut and something else sweet. I lean in to grip her waist and pull her towards me, kissing her forehead. "I will come back once I check out if you want."

She nods, and then I leave.

Shit, was that the mixed messages she was talking about? Should I have just left? But I've never wanted to stay more.

14

A spark reignited

Hannah

The drive home is uneventful. I replay the weekend events over in my head. The entire weekend was amazing. Two nights away with no one to care for but myself, catching up with my friends, and witnessing one of my best friends get married after everything she went through with a brutal divorce.

Despite that, I can't help but to keep coming back to my time with Clark. His hazel eyes dance in my mind like a kaleidoscope. My skin still tingles from his touch earlier today, and my lips feel swollen from his kisses. I stare down at my wrist, a light rope burn from the tie he used brands the skin. It makes me all too aware of the emptiness I now feel in my heart.

Is it better to not know what you are missing out on, than to feel the passion and connection briefly, only for it to leave you feeling emptier when it ends?

My heart throbs at the loss. I'm aware Clark isn't Callum, and what we had over the weekend can't compare to the years of marriage, raising babies and all the memories.

Closing the car door on the weekend, the feeling of loss and loneliness is amplified. The comfort of my own home doesn't quell the feelings.

I drag my suitcase through my spotless house. The wooden floorboards are shiny and there isn't a toy out of place. I knew Kate would clean. She always does. I bet my washing is all up to date as well. I chuck my suitcase in my room, running my fingers over my freshly made bed. It's the same treatment I had for months after Callum passed.

It's definitely not lost on me how lucky I am to have my sister and my parents so close. Callum's family, too. We were close to them all.

The months that followed his death, they wrapped me in cotton wool and carried me through the worst of it. The thing with time, though, is that it doesn't stop moving just because you are stuck in a loop. Eventually, everyone had to continue with their own lives. They had their own washing and kids to care for, and meals to cook. Slowly but surely, the village I had surrounding me dwindled until the sting of loneliness was all too painful again.

Day by day, I clawed my way through for my children. I was happy and doing well. Thriving even. I thought I had been ready, not for a relationship but for something. Only now, the ache of emptiness echoes through my bones.

I walk back out to my empty house. There's no indent on the couch in Callum's favourite spot. Instead, he sits in a pile of ashes on a shelf in the lounge room. His ring rests atop of the urn. I twirl the matching pair around my neck. If this is what it is going to feel like to have something else end, I don't know that I want it to even begin.

I don't have time to unpack because I have to head to get the kids from school shortly. They are old enough to catch the bus, but after losing their dad, I'm grateful to be able to schedule clients around them. I love that I can be there for drop offs, pick ups, and all the events in between.

It's a twenty-minute drive to the school, but I left a little too late and now the kiss and drop line is insane. I'm not even in the car park, and the traffic is backed all the way out to the road. At this rate, it will be faster to park on the curb and walk to collect the kids from the pick up line. The zen from the weekend is leaching from my body as the minutes tick by without us moving an inch.

I turn my music up and try to relax.

The line moves slowly, and finally I see my boys. They stand together under the little shed waiting area. Their smiling faces instantly ease all my stress. I feel the loss and pent-up frustration leave my body.

Noah sees me first and directs the younger boys down the path towards the car. We then spend the car drive home chatting about the weekend and how much they loved having Auntie Kate there with them. Apparently, no curfew and unlimited snacks made her the clear favourite. I fake being mad at her lack of ability to follow my rules, but I'm so grateful for her help.

The rest of the afternoon and night flies by, unpacking school bags and washing lunch boxes. Washing, cooking dinner and helping the boys with homework. By the time the boys head to bed at eight-thirty, I'm well and truly spent.

The bliss of the weekend has completely left my body, and while I love my life, it is back to hustle, hustle, hustle. I clean up the remnants of the dinner dishes and wipe down the kitchen bench, before finally making it to my room to crawl into bed. I've barely had a chance to look at my phone all afternoon.

Now, my thumb hovers over Clark's last message on my phone. Locking it and chucking it on the bed, I climb in and grab my book. I make it through one page before the pull to pick it up again wins out. I head back to my messages, click on his name and start typing.

HANNAH: I had a fantastic weekend. Thank you.

I hit the backspace button and wipe the message from the screen. With a sigh, I chuck the phone back on the bed and pick up my book. I reread the same page as none of it sunk in. Bringing my thumb up to my lips, I nibble on my nail.

I don't know why I'm being so ridiculous. I'm a forty-year-old woman with three children. I do not need to be nervous to send a damn message. I just had a dirty weekend with this guy and let him tie me up against a door for crying out loud. Why am I acting like a love-struck teenager now?

We both knew the score. We both said we didn't want anything serious, and I meant every word of that. So why does it matter if I send him a quick message saying I had a great time?

If I'm being honest, I felt alive again with Clark. A spark I had not felt in years was reignited. I felt comfortable, confident and myself again. I want more of that. I want to see him again. I also don't want him to feel like I'm using him. But if he feels the same then maybe it is mutually beneficial for us to just carry on with a little bit of casual, respectful fun.

I grab my phone and open the messages again.

> HANNAH: Thanks for a great weekend. I know we are both busy but if you ever want to catch up again, message me.

I quickly hit send before I can chicken out and then go back to my book. My phone lights up with a reply almost instantly.

15

Loose, lace and see-through

Clark

I pull into my driveway and see Vin's car parked up by the house. He was coming by twice a day to feed the animals and make sure everything was okay. I've known the guy since he was just fifteen years old. He had a pretty rough start. Dipshit drunk for a dad. I always knew there was more to his story while he was working for me, but he kept his cards close to his chest. He moved over here to be with his childhood girlfriend and has made a good life for himself.

Vin gives me a head nod when he spots me while refilling the troughs of water for the horses. Banjo, my kelpie, spots me and comes bounding over to the car. His black and white tail wags so fast it is a blur.

I scratch him behind the ears, and he pushes his snout into me further. "Good boy. Did you miss me?" He nuzzles further into my hand.

I rescued him from a pound as soon as I arrived in town. I needed the distraction. He is a good running buddy and has been a lifesaver to my mental health over the last year and a bit, providing much needed company.

I make my way over to Vin with Banjo on my heels. He places the hose in the trough and shakes my hand. "Hey, mate. How was the weekend?"

"Was surprisingly good. How was everything back here?"

"No issues. I'm doing the arvo feeds early as I have clients all afternoon, so wasn't sure when I was going to get a chance to head back here."

I grab the hose out as the trough fills, and we start making our way back to the barn to shut the water off and clean up. "No worries. I appreciate you coming out to help."

"After all you have done for me, feeding your animals was the least I could do." We make it back to the barn and I shut the water off. "Your chickens are laying like crazy. I've put all the eggs in the kitchen. Horses have fresh water and hay for the night, and I've already fed Banjo and Pam so don't let them fool you into a second dinner."

I nod, searching for Pam. She is probably taking up residence in Banjo's dog kennel. She quite often kicks him out. We head over to the house, and sure enough, she comes bounding out, head and horns first.

I bought this place when I moved here and have been slowly doing it up. It's a small kit home that was built in the eighties, with old slate flooring and outdated wood panelling on the walls inside. The ensuite bathroom was added on but never kitted out. It's small but it sits on five acres of land and has a massive workshop just off to the side of the house that I have all my tools set up in. It also has a large barn further out the back for horses and a chicken coop off to the side.

I love that it is far enough out of town to feel rural but close enough to not be driving for days to get to a store. It's situated just across the main highway and only takes me twenty minutes to get into the centre of town. It's a hell of a nice change from the hustle of having multiple mechanic businesses across numerous busy towns.

"Take some eggs for you and Scarlet." I start placing the eggs in a spare egg carton I have on top of the fridge.

"Thanks," Vin says with a nod. "I better get going. I have to head home quickly and then be over to the other side of town for a job."

"No worries, thanks again." I walk him out to his car, and we shake hands in a goodbye before he heads off.

Home and with nothing else to do but think about the weekend, I pull my phone out. I head straight to the messages and start typing.

I go to press send and then pause. What the fuck, man? I sound like a fifteen-year-old with a crush. We said this was just casual sex. No need for me to try to make it awkward now.

I really want to see Hannah again.

I delete the message and decide to unpack my suitcase. I chuck on a load of washing then pace the house. There is a shit load I could be doing. After building out the ensuite, extending the master bedroom and adding a walk-in robe, I redid the kitchen—old brick and raw timber with deep blue cupboards. It probably isn't for everyone, but I love it.

Cherie was obsessed with ultra-modern, clean, crisp and white. Everything goddamn white. I didn't hate it, but it wasn't my taste. It has been fun having full creative control over this place and not having to ask anyone for permission or swallow my own wants to keep someone else happy.

I'm currently renovating the second bathroom. Not sure why when no one uses it, but I figure for the sake of resale—if that time ever comes—having two bathrooms is a selling point. I'm in the process of pulling the old tiles up and gutting it. So, I could always get stuck into that to help take my mind off things.

I love hard work. Even though I can afford to pay someone else to do the renovations and probably have had the house completely overhauled by now, I have loved doing the work myself. There is something therapeutic and healing about working with my hands. Pulling things apart only to fix them back up and make it better. I love seeing something I have built from scratch come together.

I head to the bathroom and evaluate the state of it, then decide to go for a ride instead. Vin is great with the animals, but he wouldn't have ridden the horses, and I know that Salt and Pepper will be chomping at the bit to get out. I change into jeans and a flannel and head back out to the barn.

"Salt, Pepper," I yell, inwardly cringing at the names. I do every time I call them. They came with the property. I didn't care to find the full story but there was some shit with the prior owners. They were in trouble with the tax man. Dodgy dealings with a business, apparently, and wanted a quick sale. So, the house came as is, meaning fully furnished with a coop full of chickens, two horses and a pretty savage goat—Pam. I never bothered to change their names. It suits them. One is white with light grey flecks, and the other is black with grey flecks. They all seemed happy with their names. Except Pam. She didn't seem happy about anything, and I spent the best part of six months getting rammed by her every time I walked outside.

Trust me, if you have ever been rammed by a goat, it hurts.

The horses come bolting over to greet me and proceed to follow me back into the barn. I make quick work of tacking them up and lead them both back out. Chucking on my Akubra, I jump on Salt. Ponying Pepper, we make our way to the back side of my property.

The ride will give me time to think. Or to stop thinking. Stop thinking about a certain someone.

The ride doesn't work.

The fresh air and birds chirping left my mind clear to think of nothing but Hannah. Her soft tan skin, the way she smelt, the feel of her thighs when they shook around my head as I made her come on my tongue.

Damn, I'm too old to play games. If I want to see her again, I should just message. That's exactly what I plan to do. I just need to think of the right thing to say first. Luckily, I don't have to. Like most of the weekend, she makes the first move. I was hovering over the send button on a pretty lame message when her text came through.

HANNAH: Thanks for a great weekend. I know we are both busy but if you ever want to catch up again, message me.

CLARK: I had a great time, too. Glad I met you. I meant what I said about taking you riding. Let me know when you are free and I can take you out.

I hit send before I have the time to overthink it.

She responds straight away.

HANNAH: I'd love that. My weekends are insane with kids sports and running them around, but I keep Thursdays as an admin day for my business. I could come after school drop. If that day ever works for you?

I check my calendar. I have two bookings for mechanic work on Thursday this week, but I'll change them. No way am I turning her down. I don't know when I'll get another chance.

CLARK: I'm free this Thursday. Come around after you drop the kids and we can go for a ride.

HANNAH: Really! This Thur. I'd love that. I can be there for 9. Want me to bring you a coffee?

CLARK: I just bought a new machine. I'll make you one here.

HANNAH: I'm fussy with my coffee.

CLARK: Triple shot, extra large, extra hot, lots of foam, and half shot of hazelnut. I recall.

HANNAH: You have hazelnut flavour at your house?

CLARK: I got you covered.

HANNAH: Lol, okay. See you Thur.

CLARK: See you Thur. Hope getting back to reality didn't hit too hard.

HANNAH: My sister left my house immaculate and left a full meal for us all. So it wasn't too bad. Although, I haven't braved unpacking my suitcase yet. Future Hannah's problem.

CLARK: Don't want to brag, but I already did mine. Washed and currently on the line.

HANNAH: WHAT! You hang your washing out on the line?

CLARK: Yeah, you don't?

HANNAH: No, I'm washing for four people. If I hung everything on the line, I might as well move my mattress under the clothesline. If it can't go in the dryer or needs ironing, it doesn't belong in my house.

CLARK: No wonder all your clothes were so tight.

HANNAH: You weren't complaining
about that on the weekend.

CLARK: Thinking back to how amazing
your ass looked in those dresses, definitely still not complaining.

HANNAH: I'll be sure to wear something
t ght on Thursday then.

CLARK: I don't mind loose if it's lace and
see-through.

HANNAH: Get my coffee right and I will
reward you with something lace.

I don't know why I was so nervous to text Hannah. The moment the texts started flowing, the conversation slipped straight
back to what it was like to talk to her in person.

The texts didn't stop. Back and forth when we can. About
nothing and everything at the same time. Back and forth with
flirting and witty quips, and general chit chat about our days.

By the time Thursday rolls around, I'm so pent up with my
need for her, I feel like I could burst.

16

Gravity and collagen are against me

Hannah

The week has flown by. Work has been busy. My days were packed with back to back clients from the moment I got home at nine to the moment I left to collect the kids at around two-thirty.

The kids' schedules are insane. Basketball training for all three kids across three different afternoons. Noah also does jujitsu on Wednesday afternoons. Then three basketball games have me at the courts all day on Saturday. Which leaves Sunday for running the kids around to catch up with friends, cleaning and grocery shopping and maybe...maybe if I'm lucky, five minutes to sit in peace or catch up with a friend myself.

The good thing about my kids now at this age is that I can leave them at home for short periods of time. It was almost impossible to have any semblance of a life when they were all little. Even loading them all in the car to head to the shops for essentials would have rivalled mission impossible. Thank goodness for click and collect and online shopping. Most mornings I'm up at five-thirty to get my own workout in and quickly check my schedule for the day. Then it's time to help the kids make breakfast and lunches for school, and get ready.

The anticipation for today has been building in me all week. I feel butterflies as I get dressed, which is a feeling I'm entirely not used to at all. It doesn't help that I have something planned for Clark.

I mean, dressing up in sexy lingerie isn't new for me. I used to do this type of thing all the time. But Callum was my husband. I knew him and what he liked. I felt comfortable and confident with him.

Clark, I barely know. Will he think I'm a complete freak, a giant slut, or a weirdo? God, what if it is just embarrassing and awkward?

I stare at myself in the mirror. I look good.

I think.

I mean, I have things I don't love. I stare at my slightly lopsided boobs that no longer sit where they used to. The faint stretch marks that line them. Nipples that are slightly bigger than they used to be from breastfeeding children. The raised pink line of my c-section scar. My thass—that little roll where your thigh meets your ass, that no matter how many squats you do it never goes away.

I exercise regularly and I eat really well, but I'm also forty and have grown and birthed children. Gravity and collagen are against me. Nothing is where it used to be. I never used to feel conscious about these things, but I was happily married to a man who worshipped me. Clark didn't seem to judge or even notice the things I see every day. These things about my body are sometimes all I see.

Sucking in a deep breath, I put on the set I had intended to wear—a black bra that pushes my boobs up to astronomical heights, complete with three thin buckle straps that lay over the top of my now round boobs. Three thin strips of material sit on each side of my hips and track down to make a V, meeting at a tiny scrap of material that covers my intimate parts. The G-string at the back leaves my ass bare. A black buckle up garter set wraps around my upper thighs with thin straps that run down to connect into my stay up sheer black stockings.

The kicker…I bought a bondage kit to go with it. Forrest green leather and buckle wrist cuffs with a matching collar, and gold metal loops attach to each with a chain, creating a leash.

It looks sexy and I feel amazing, but my stomach tightens with a mix of nerves and guilt. I toy with my ring before mentally reminding myself I have nothing to feel guilty for.

I remove the bondage kit, garter belts and stockings, and chuck them in my bag. Then I get dressed in my standard attire of a work shirt and tights. I pack a trench coat and a pair of jeans, tee and boots to ride in. Then I head out the door.

The kids are already waiting.

Noah is standing impatiently at the kitchen bench. "What took you so long?"

"Muuumm, we've been ready for ages," Ethan adds in a particularly whiny tone.

I walk past them, grabbing a banana from the fruit bowl. "Mum has needs too, you know, boys."

They follow me towards the door to the garage, and we all pile into the car. Dropping them off is far easier than picking them up. The kiss and drop line moves smoothly and they are at an age where I'm now a giant embarrassment to them. Lingering too long is absolutely cringe, or so I am told. They all basically drop and roll out the car, eager for me to not be seen.

I shamelessly wave, winding my window down to yell, "BYE. I LOVE YOU!" as I leave, laughing to myself.

Mum mode has well and truly left my body as I drive out to Clark's house. He lives about fifteen minutes from the school, and it's a nice drive out of town with minimal traffic. I follow my maps from the address he had given me, and when I see I am getting close, I pull over to the side of the road to get ready.

Sliding my driver's seat back as far as it will go, I slip my tights down and slide my stay up stocking on. The velvety material glides up my smooth legs, and I would be lying if the cheekiness of all of this did not ignite a fire deep within me.

I'm shaking as I buckle up the garters and attach the little straps. Then I add the wrist cuffs and collar. I decide to leave the chains off for him. I place my heels on and then wrap myself in my big trench coat, tying it across my stomach to conceal everything.

Fuck, I hope he doesn't already have the horses ready to go. If that's the case, this is going to be awkward. My skin is crawling with anticipation and nerves. I steady my breathing and find some inner confidence to just do it.

I love doing things like this. This is exactly what has been missing from my life for years. The fun, the excitement, the thrill. Not to mention the good sex. I mean lots has been missing from my life since Callum, but none of them are easy to replace.

This though...

This I can do.

This seems to have fallen in my lap with a simple flat tyre, and I'm going to take full advantage of it until the very end. Hopefully Clark is on board. I mean, our flirty banter seems to show me he is.

I put the car back in drive and pull back out onto the road. I'm on his long street. There aren't many houses, and I see what must be his driveway coming up. Two vintage red brick pillars on either side, with a white wooden gate across the middle. The fence line is white painted wooden pillars with three rungs of wire running through them. I see the number in large gold metal on the brick and the gate is open, ready for me to enter.

I turn down the limestone driveway and head towards the house. The drive is long, and the house sits up high on a little hill. A large wrap around patio with wide steps lead down to a perfectly manicured lawn.

Pulling up in front of the garage, I see a black and white dog come bounding towards the car. Followed by... Is that a goat?

Clark walks out the door and damn he looks better than I remember. My heart rate spikes. He stands at the top of the steps with one hand in his pocket before following his animals down towards my car.

I exhale loudly.

Show time.

Making sure my coat is secured and not giving anything away, I open the car door and step out. His eyes meet mine then slowly scan down my body to my heels. They look so out of place on this rural property. Sinking into the compact limestone, I steady myself to start to walk towards him. He closes the distance between us in long strides and leans in to hug me. His dog and goat nudge into my legs, sniffing excitedly.

"Pam, Banjo, leave her alone." The dog complies, moving to Clark's side and calms, but the goat completely ignores the request and carries on butting its head into my leg.

Ouch.

He grabs its collar and gently directs it away. Deciding I'm not worthy of more exploration, the goat—Pam, I assume—moves over to the lawn.

"Sorry about them. Banjo is a sweetheart, but don't turn your back on Pam. She's a savage." Clark wraps his large arms around me and kisses me gently on the cheek.

"Hi," I say as I lean into his warm body. God, he smells good.

"I'm glad you came. Interesting choice of footwear, though."

I chuckle. "I have something else in mind first."

His eyes darken with lust as he leans back slightly to look at me. I fold my bottom lip between my teeth as he takes a step back, smirking.

His hand reaches out for me to take. "Okay, officially intrigued."

Placing my hand in his, I let him lead me up the steps. Banjo bounds off, and Pam has moved on to better things and is over on the far side of the lawn happily munching away.

As soon as the door shuts behind him, I reach my hand into the trench pocket and pull out the chains. Sliding the coat off my shoulders, it pools on the ground at my feet. If I thought I saw lust in his eyes before, well now they are on fire with heat. The way his hungry eyes scan my body and take in my outfit makes my core swirl.

He lets out a strangled huff. "Holy shit."

I can see the effect my body and intentions are having on him instantly. His tight jeans grow tighter around the groin area as he swells. I move my eyes from it and back up to his face.

I love his shyness and how he has been so respectful. I love that he has waited for clear consent and for me to lead. But I'd be lying if I said I didn't want him to lose control. To wrap his hands around my throat. To throw me over the back of the couch and rip this expensive G-string right off my body.

I wait a beat, just to see what he will do before I make my next move.

Clark stands, breathing heavily. He works to swallow as his Adam's apple bobs. I step closer to him, reaching my hand out with the chains, directing him to take them. This seems to be the permission he must have needed, because handing him the chains snaps him out of his trance. His expression shifts from the lustful, shy, good guy, to something hungrier.

Predatorial.

My body almost wants to take a step back as he stalks forward with the chains in his hand. He snaps his free hand out and it finds my throat, almost like he read my mind. He squeezes over the collar and breathing becomes difficult, but it makes my body feel alight. It hums. Tingles move from the heat of his hand around my throat, all the way down to between my legs.

His hand with the chains moves up, shifting his grip on my throat to clip the trigger snap hook to the ring at the front of the collar. I lick my lips in anticipation.

Fuck this is hot.

I fight the urge to take control. I want to see what he does, and I do love being submissive.

He tugs the chain attached to my collar and I move forward slightly in response. This makes him smile. Tilting his head to the side, Clark pauses for a moment as he runs his other hand over his jaw. He then turns around and pulls the chain as he walks.

I have no choice but to follow behind, pulled by the collar. He leads me only a few steps before stopping and turning me around so my back is towards him. Grabbing me gently by the chin from behind, he drags his hand to my throat, then plays with the collar, spinning it so the clip and chain are at the back. Clark runs his knuckles down my spine with one hand while the other finds mine. Pulling it behind me, he clips the other smaller chain to my wrist cuff and then to my garter belt around my thigh. Moving to the other arm, he pulls it behind my back, repeating the process. My hands are now secured to my thighs by smaller chains.

I turn my head, looking at him over my shoulder, but his eyes are roaming my body. Placing a flat palm between my shoulder blades, he pushes down. With my hands secured at my sides, I have no way to stop myself, but this was exactly what I wanted. I fold over the back of the couch, my face hitting the cushions on the front side, ass in the air.

Clark tugs back slightly on the collar and my neck lifts. I twist to look up at him. He is standing there like a dark angel, contemplating his next move. I'm not going to give him any direction, though.

His hand finds my ass, and he smooths over the bare skin gently. Then he brings his hand up and slaps it down hard across my ass cheek, before gently rubbing over the stinging area straight after. I moan into the couch. I love the mix of brutal strength with sensual caresses.

It's something new for me.

It's like he is conflicted between two sides of himself. A side that wants to lose control, take what he wants, and be rough and dominating. And a side that wants to please, to be sweet and affectionate. I love that he is both.

"You like that." It isn't a question. He says it like a statement, giving me a chance to tell him to stop if I don't.

"Yes," I moan, pushing my ass higher in the air. He slaps it again, then gently massages the stinging area. I clench my thighs together and pull against the chains at my wrist. He repeats the process over and over.

I can't explain why the mix of pleasure and pain, of complete submission, makes me feel this way. But I'm about to come right here, right now.

He drops to his knees and slowly pulls my G-string down as far it will go, meeting the garter belt at my things. Spreading me, he runs his tongue along my pussy lips up to my ass. My breath catches in my throat, and I push back as he slides a finger into me.

I can feel how wet I am already. The anticipation of this, the dressing up, the submission, and the way he is giving me exactly what I want. It's like he is in my head.

He adds a second finger as he licks up my thigh and around his fingers, moving up to my ass and back. I haven't said a word, but he reads my body. Bringing me right to the edge and then slowing and changing up what he is doing. He repeats the process until I feel like I'm hanging over a cliff. I've been close to coming too many times to count, only to be brought back each time.

By the time Clark stands, dropping his pants and sliding painstakingly slow into me, I basically come undone right then and there. I arch my back, lifting my ass higher, trying to push back into him. He lets go of the neck chain and grabs the chains at my sides. There is just enough for him to grab, and he yanks them back further, using them as leverage to pound into me harder.

Picking up the pace, thrusting hard and fast, he yanks me back as he pushes deeper, holding both chains in one hand. My undoing is when he slaps my ass again with his free hand.

I can't hold in my scream as I come. I try to muffle it into the pillows, but I swear I hear birds take flight from how earth-shattering this feels.

My body slumps over the couch, going limp for a moment as I come down from this high.

17

She came to ride something, and it most likely wasn't a horse

Clark

I can't even find the words to explain what I'm feeling right now. I had Hannah's coffee made, sitting on the kitchen counter turning ice cold, and I was in my riding jeans.

The moment she stepped out of that car, and I caught a whiff of her sweet perfume and saw her outfit, my dick was twitching. I knew she was up to something. The coat cinched her in at the waist and the heels were a dead giveaway that she came here to ride something. But it most likely wasn't a horse.

I wasn't about to be presumptuous. I was happy to just take Salt and Pepper out for a ride and have some company. But hell, who was I to say no to a rerun of the weekend? The sex we had has been on a loop in my mind since I said goodbye.

Hannah gives me the sexiest little smile when I question her shoe choice, and I know I'm in for something. And she did not disappoint.

I swear the shy considerate man I am is held underwater when she is naked in front of me. The best part? She has been open about how she likes it. I would be mad to not deliver. So when she drops her coat, showing off her amazing body, highlighted by a black and gold buckle lingerie set, and hands me some chains, I know exactly what she wants.

Bending her over the couch and slapping her fine ass has me so wound up. I see how hot she is for it. Hannah is moaning and burying her face in the pillow, arching her back and pushing back into me.

Panting hard.

I edge her, smirking to myself as I finger fuck and lick her. I feel her clench and tighten up every time she is close, so I back right off, changing the tempo or removing my fingers.

Her frustrated breathy moans make me twitch every single time. By the time I slide into her, she is dripping and I lose any semblance of control. I'm no longer sweet, thoughtful, shy Clark. I savagely pound into her, yanking her wrists behind her back. The iota of control I have left is used to not yank her shoulders out of her socket.

I slap her ass and she comes hard. I feel her body stiffen, muscles gripping me. It almost sends me over the edge, but I'm not done yet. I let her come down, and she melts into the couch, going limp. I slap her ass again to wake her up.

I let go of her wrist and undo the clips, releasing her hands. Hannah slowly moves them to her front and stretches them out.

"Rub your clit," I demand, and she obeys. Moving her hand underneath her to find her clit, she rubs it as I fuck her from behind.

"That's it. Good girl," I growl. I want to slap myself across the face for saying that. I don't know where it came from, but the way her body reacts to the words has me thinking maybe she likes a bit of praise with her torture.

She sucks in a breath, and I feel her muscles tighten around my hard cock again. I decide to test it more. I've never been one to talk a lot during sex, but I have never been with someone so responsive to my touch, my words, and the way I move. It's intoxicating. I've never felt so in sync and attuned to someone.

"Your pussy feels so fucking good. I love how well you take it, baby."

I'm so close that I swear my brain is short circuiting because the words that are coming out of my mouth are not me. I don't know who this person is, but it isn't Clark. I cannot be held accountable for what this woman does to me.

I don't have time to overthink it. With every sentence, I hear her gasp and clench. Like the words alone would send her spiralling.

"Clark," she pleads. I don't know what for. To stop. To keep going. To go harder. My name rolling off her tongue sends shivers down my spine, and I feel my balls tighten. I'm about to come, but fuck I need her there with me.

I reach forward, sliding my hand up through her hair, grabbing a fistful of it and gently pulling back. She moans my name again. I lick up the side of her neck, not sweetly or gently. Landing at her earlobe, I suck and then bite down. She gasps and I feel her tighten again.

I hold back my own release the best I can, trying to keep pace as I whisper in her ear, "Are you gonna be my good girl and come for me? Or will I have to slap your ass again like the little slut I know you are?"

You did not just say that. My head and body are at war. My mind's telling me that was so wrong. *You can't call her a slut or talk about hitting her.* But it's like my brain and body are not even connected anymore.

My dick has taken the steering wheel, and he is sending everyone insane. It's like that scene in Wolf of Wall Street when Jordan Belfort does that big speech where he starts shouting.

I ain't leaving.

I ain't fucking leaving.

My dick brain has been awakened by this confident sexy woman, and it won't leave quietly. I don't think I've ever felt harder in my life. Something about saying those words out loud has me spiralling.

There would not be a single thing I could do to hold it back. Fuck.

I feel like I've never come so hard. Thank God I feel her clench.

"I'll be your good girl, Clark." Her body convulses as she pants and comes with me.

My brain chooses now to take back the reins from my dick, and he is shocked at what we just did. My eyes track down to her red and swollen ass from how I had slapped her raw.

I'm mindful of how long she has been bent over in this position. Grabbing her by the shoulders, I gently help pull her up. Her legs are wobbly as she tries to find her feet, and she flicks her shoes off.

I kneel on one knee and undo the garter buckles from her thighs. Her skin is red and marked. I go to slide her underwear back up her legs when I see my release dripping from her.

Sliding my knuckle up her inner thigh over the cum, I drag it back up her legs to her pussy. Scooping it up, I push two fingers back into her. I have no idea what possess me to do it. Maybe some deep primal instinct to reproduce. Something I know I will never get the chance to do.

I glance up at her, slightly embarrassed by my forwardness. But I'm filled with confidence and my ego triples in size when I see her flushed face smiling back down at me. She is biting her bottom lip, like what I just did somehow turned her on even more.

I slide her underwear back into place and stand. Placing my hand gently on the collar, I unbuckle it and let it fall to the floor. Her neck is also slightly marked. I trace my fingers softly along the visible red marks on her throat.

"I'm sorry," I say, shaking my head and running my hands down her sides to her ass, and over the red swollen hand prints I have left on her body. "Did I hurt you?" I place soft kisses across her neckline.

Hannah leans her head back, giving me better access to her neck. "In the best possible way," she pants breathlessly.

"Are you okay? I got a bit carried away. You just looked so damn good and…" I'm not even able to compute what just happened to me. Hannah is so much more together than I am. She doesn't seem embarrassed or shy about what we just did.

"Clark, I didn't put on a collar and hand you chains to be cuddled. That was exactly what I wanted, and I loved every minute of it." She leans close to me, whispering in my ear, "I like being your slutty little good girl."

And shit. I'm hard again.

But she is already walking away from me.

"Can I use the bathroom?"

I point past her to my bedroom. "It's just through there. I'll remake your coffee. It will be stone cold by now."

"Thank you." She disappears into the bedroom. "Would you mind also grabbing my bag out of the car? Can't exactly go horse riding naked," she yells from the room.

"Yes, ma'am."

I'm still smiling ear to ear as I make my way to her car, grab her bags and deliver them to her in the bathroom, before heading back to the kitchen to make us new coffees.

18

Orgasms, coffee and cowboys

Hannah

I walk out of the bedroom in jeans, a long sleeve dark grey button up and boots. Clark hands me my coffee and leans in, placing a soft kiss to my cheek. The sweet gesture is at odds with the way he just bent me over, slapped my ass and called me a slut. This is what I like about Clark, though. I get the feeling he has never treated a woman like this.

I see him struggling with the internal conflict. One side of him likes what he is doing to me, while the other is unsure of how I will react or if he is taking it too far.

The thing is, if a man is respectful and kind in other aspects of my life, I feel safe and confident enough to ask for what I really enjoy in the bedroom. I've long ago quit questioning why I like the things I like. And I like being submissive. I like a man who is rough and dominating in the bedroom.

I bring the mug to my mouth and take a long sip. It's perfect, exactly how I like it. "This is great, thank you."

"No worries," he says, smiling at me, sipping his own.

I gesture to his strong black coffee. "That's disgusting. I don't know how you drink it like that."

"Could say the same about that sugar syrup you put in yours. How do you drink it so sweet?" he chuckles, as I basically have another orgasm over how good the coffee is.

"Did you taste my coffee?" I squint my eyes at him. He nods. "Did you purposely go and buy me hazelnut syrup?"

"I was doing the shopping anyway, so it didn't hurt to add that in."

"Thank you."

"No worries." Clark takes a long sip of his coffee and pulls out a kitchen stool to sit.

"So how did you end up out here with horses, a goat and a dog?"

"You know the young kid that worked with me I was telling you about?"

"The one that went to jail?" I say, placing my half-finished coffee on the table.

"Yeah. When he got out, he moved over here. Came to find his childhood girlfriend and ended up staying here. We had kept in contact while he was away and when he got out, I helped him out a bit. So when shit hit the fan with Cherie, he told me to head over." He pauses to take another sip of his coffee, and I move around to sit on the stool next to him.

Before I get a chance to sit, he pushes back on his seat and pulls me in front of him. Grabbing my waist, he lifts me to sit up on the kitchen bench in front of him, his hands resting gently on my thighs.

"He had started up a mobile mechanic business that was thriving, so he needed the help from someone he trusted. I moved over and worked with him for a bit. He had a client that was a real estate agent. So, when I was looking for a place, he told me about this farm.

Apparently, the owners were in some kind of trouble with a business they had. Owed a tonne of super to employees and tax. House and all assets were repossessed, and it was up for a set date sale.

The animals were supposed to go to pounds and rescue places. So, I just said I would take it as is. Animals and all." Clark pauses, gauging my reaction.

"That's crazy. So you had never had animals before?" I bring my mug back to my lips and peer at him over the rim.

"Not really. We had a cat, but that was it. Suddenly I had a coop full of chickens, a goat and two horses. Then I adopted Banjo to add to the troops. There is even a duck somewhere that comes and goes. I've named it Henry."

I almost spit out my mouthful laughing. "Henry the duck. Pam the goat. Banjo, and what are the horses' names?"

"Salt and Pepper."

"Salt and Pepper," I repeat, choking on my coffee this time as I try to stifle my laugh.

He scratches his head, before moving his hand straight back to my thigh. "Yeah, I think their kids named them. It'll make sense when you see them."

"So you'd never ridden a horse before moving out here?" I place my now finished coffee down to the side and move my hands to his shoulders.

"Nope, but all the gear was here, and the horses are both really relaxed. To be honest, it was therapeutic riding. But you probably know that. You said you had done equine therapy after Callum passed?"

"Yeah, I started a grief counselling group thing after he passed, and I met a lady there who had tried it. She said she had done this therapy, said it was mostly for special needs. People with ASD, ADHD or other Sensory Processing Disorders. We went out and we would brush the horses and look after them, and then we started riding them around the property and eventually started trail rides. But she was right. It was therapeutic being out in the fresh air and away from the hustle of life. It was quiet and peaceful and I loved it."

He is watching me intensely. His hazel eyes swirling, greens and blues and golds.

"How long did you do it for?" Clark asks.

"About a year, but it just got really hard with the kids. Once life settled back into our new normal and the help died down, it just got too hard. They only did trail rides on weekends, and between three kids playing sports and having social lives, I could never find the time."

He raises a hand and tucks a stray piece of hair that has fallen loose behind my ear. The pad of his thumb lingers on my skin. "I'm sorry."

"Don't be. I'm here now about to ride again. I'm excited."

"Shall we?" He rises from his stool, standing between my legs. Stepping back and moving the stool out the way, he then reaches out a hand for me to grab. I jump down off the counter, and he makes his way to the fridge, grabbing a soft Yeti cooler. "Snacks." He holds up the cooler as we walk towards the back door. "Grab your drink bottle," Clark adds, stopping by the back sliding door. He grabs an Akubra off a hook.

"If you put that thing on, I swear to God we are not making it horse riding." The image of him in a cowboy hat may just send me past the point of no return.

"Oh, you like the cowboy look do ya?" Clark deliberately moves at a painfully slow speed as he places the hat atop his head in that dead sexy one-handed way cowboys do. He tips the front down slightly, and I swear I almost come again just from the sight of it.

I swat his arm playfully on my way past him.

"I have a spare one for you if you like." He moves back inside and disappears for a moment, before returning with a second hat that is slightly lighter and more worn. It is also smaller. "This is my old one. I stupidly chucked it in the wash and it shrunk a little, made it a bit misshapen, but I reckon you will pull it off." He places it on my head, standing impossibly close. I feel his breath on my cheek as he pulls it down at the side to fit my head.

"Perfect." The word is barely a whisper. His eyes linger intensely on me.

We move down towards the barn, and Clark calls for the horses. I understand instantly why they are called Salt and Pepper. The horses follow us along the fence line all the way to the barn, where we tack them up. Clark has a saddle bag for Salt that he places our drink bottles in, along with the small cooler.

We hop on and make our way along the edge of the fence line. Birds chirp, carrying on the soft breeze, and the gentle sway of the horse as they amble along the sand are the reason why I loved the trail rides so much. The added benefit of having a sexy cowboy leading the way may just make this ride absolute perfection.

We head up a small hill along the fence line of his property, and Clark dismounts to open a gate. He leads Salt through, and I follow on Pepper. He closes the gate behind him and mounts his horse effortlessly, turning the simple motion into something jaw droppingly sexy.

Making our way down the path, there's a dip that leads past another gate. A hard to miss sign attached to the fence says: 'Private Property. Trespassers will be prosecuted.' There is a second sign that looks homemade with spray paint. 'Trespassers run the risk of being shot.'

"We're not going onto that property, are we?" I can already see we are by the way he is leading the horses right to the gate.

Clark simply smiles at me. "Didn't take you for a rule follower."

"I like to bend the rules, not break them. And I definitely do not feel like getting shot."

"Never mind Earl. He is a grumpy old bastard, but he isn't going to shoot us. He knows me." He slides off Salt again and moves to open the gate, leading us through. "It's just to deter kids who come on their motorbikes. They scare the cattle."

"Okay?" I reluctantly lead Pepper through the gate. Clark shuts it behind us, before jumping back onto Salt. "Does he really have a gun?"

"Yes. We all have rifles out here." Clark says 'out here' like we are in the wild west and not a mere twenty minutes from a large suburban town.

"What do you need a gun for?"

"Mostly kangaroos. They break the fence line and scare the sheep. Foxes and feral cats, too. They attack the sheep, and break into the chicken coops and attack the chickens. And scare the dogs and horses."

I pause, taking it all in. I've never seen a gun in person before. In the movies, yeah, but in real life, no. It's not something I'm used to or even comfortable with.

He senses my apprehension. "You don't like that."

"Not sure how I feel about it, if I'm honest. Suppose I'm just not used to it."

"Fair enough. There are pretty strict rules to be able to get one. We have licenses and they are kept in safes."

"Do you eat any of the animals after you kill them?"

"Yep, especially the kangaroos. I use it to make the dog's food, jerky, and once made a kangaroo stew."

"Guess it tastes just like chicken."

He throws back his head, laughing. "It tastes nothing like chicken. It's kind of like beef, only a stronger flavour. Has to be cooked right, otherwise it's terribly gamey. I'll cook you some one day."

I laugh. "Only if we don't get shot today."

"No one's getting shot. I promise you."

We continue to ride through the property, making it safely out the other side and down along a rivers edge. The water is shallow and the ground full of clay as our horses trudge through. It's absolutely beautiful. Trees sway gently in the breeze with the backdrop of birds singing, soft waves lapping at the horses' heels as they find their rhythm.

Clark and I settle into steady conversation. Our topics range from light and breezy, laughing and flirting, to deep and meaningful, talking about our pasts and pain. We move away from the river and back into the bush, making our way around property lines.

"There is a nice place up here where we can stop for lunch if you like." Clark gestures just up ahead where the bush clears out to a large grass opening.

"Is this another property where we run the risk of getting shot? Because I don't feel like a side of bullets with my snacks."

He chuckles at me but directs us through, then pulls his horse up to dismount. "You will not be shot, I can guarantee." He moves closer to my side and reaches a hand up for me to grab to help me off. Gripping the reins, I swing my leg over Pepper. Clark reaches up, gripping my ass to help guide me down. I turn and we stand with our toes touching. He is so close I can feel his breath, face tilting slightly down to kiss me. Pepper swings his head around and nudges him in the side, forcing him back a step.

Clark pats the horse's snout. "Okay, okay, no kissing in front of the horses." Salt is happily grazing on the longer bits of grass in the field. Clark opens the little saddle bag and pulls out our drink bottles and cooler. "Want to sit?" he asks.

"Sure." I move to sit down on the grass, and he comes to sit beside me, opening the cooler and pulling out two of the most gourmet rolls I have ever seen.

"Did you make these?" Surprise etches my voice, making it slightly higher than I intended.

He nods. "It's just a sandwich."

"It's on a sourdough roll; that's not just a sandwich. Is that three different meats in there? And what is that?" I say playfully as I unwrap the plastic wrapping and pull out a softish, pink looking onion ring.

"That's a quick pickle." His mouth is already half full.

"What the fuck is a quick pickle?" I take my own bite, and all thoughts of quick pickles float out of my mind. "Ohhh, my GOD. This is delicious!" The flavours explode in in my mouth and form a dance party on my tongue. Salty cured meats, nutty sweetness of Swiss cheese, the tanginess of the quick pickles. Crunchy fresh lettuce mixed with creamy mayo.

Clark smirks sideways at me. He looks insanely gorgeous in that damn hat. "They are just onions, but I soak them in vinegar. They're good, right." It's not a question.

I nod enthusiastically. There is too much food in my mouth to form a sentence.

We mostly eat in silence, enjoying the sounds of the horses munching and the birds chirping.

"Thank you, that roll was amazing. You really didn't have to make me lunch."

"It was nothing," Clark says as he starts collecting the rubbish.

It wasn't nothing. Not to me.

I'm not normally someone who is lost for words, but I'm finding it hard to say what I really feel. Clark and I have been open and honest with our discussions so far. No topic has really been off the table for us. I mean, I just let this man put a collar on me and bend me over his couch.

All day, every day, for the last three years I have done nothing but care for others. Making dinners, shopping, cooking, cleaning, planning, organising. It's crazy to think I'm that exhausted that the kind act of a man making me a sandwich has me wanting to cry, but it does.

"It's not nothing. It feels really nice to not be the one making lunches for everybody else. So thank you for thinking of it."

"Anytime." He stands and reaches a hand down for me, pulling me up to my feet. Then he starts packing up the cooler.

The rest of the ride is beautiful, and by the time we make our way back to his property, it's 2 PM and I'm well and truly spent.

19

the ride or the RIDE

Hannah

> HANNAH: I had an amazing day today. My ass is so sore. Thank you.

CLARK: Sorry, I didn't mean to be so rough. I had a great day, too.

> HANNAH: I mean from the horse ride all day haha! My thighs and butt are killing me. But that other part was also fun. So, as I said, thank you.

CLARK: No worries, happy to do it again. Anytime.

> HANNAH: The ride or the RIDE?

CLARK: Both…

Am I trying sexting? I chuckle to myself. It's ten-thirty at night and it's the first chance I've had to sit down at my computer. I usually dedicate Thursdays as an admin day. A day to catch up on all the client notes and programming, then all the other aspects of business life that no one ever tells you about but that take up a considerable amount of time. Like social media posting, creating content, invoices and reconciling accounts, advertising. The list goes on.

The mental load of running a business is insane, and I know my brain will not be able to turn off until I have a large part of what I missed today done. Sometimes I think it would be easier to just go get a job with someone else. Get a weekly pay check, holidays and sick days. But I also know the reality of that just wouldn't work for my family. I'm all the boys have now. I love that I can schedule my clients around them. They only have one parent, and I get to be there for school drop offs and pick ups, assemblies, sports carnivals, Mother's Day stalls and every single thing in between. I would never have this type of flexibility if I worked for someone else. If this means sitting up to midnight to get it all done, then that is what I will do.

I mean, today was worth it in every way possible.

HANNAH: My schedule is insane, so it may be few and far between. Sorry. But I would love to do both again.

CLARK: Don't apologise, I understand. I'm happy to be your late-night booty call whenever you like.

HANNAH: You would drive here in the middle of the night for that?

CLARK: Considering I can't get the image of you standing there in a collar and handcuffs out of my fucking head, yeah, pretty sure I would drive across the country in the middle of the night for just a taste.

HANNAH: My kids are here.

CLARK: I can be quiet.

HANNAH: I think I have proven that I cannot, in fact, be quiet.

CLARK: Then I'll tie you up and put a gag in your mouth.

Holy hell… That last text causes a tingle up my spine and well…in other places, too. I clench my thighs together. The thought of his words make me feel hot. I want to tell him to come over right now, but I barely know this man.

I feel safe with him, but I'm not sure how I feel about having him in my house while my kids are just down the hall. Nothing Clark has done thus far has left any questions of his character, but still. It doesn't sit right with me. But this flirting is driving me wild. I decide to roll with it.

HANNAH: Then what would you do?

CLARK: Hmm, I'd cut your clothes from your body and fuck you right there on the floor.

HANNAH: That doesn't sound very quiet.

CLARK: You're gagged, remember?

Damn, I don't want this to stop.

HANNAH: I like the sound of that.

CLARK: Me too. Say the words and I will be there.

I want to say, *Now! Come NOW!* But I don't want to seem like a sex crazed lunatic and the stress of catching up on this work mixed with the exhaustion of the day is swirling through me.

So, I change the subject.

HANNAH: Why are you up so late anyway?

CLARK: Couldn't get to sleep. You?

HANNAH: Trying to catch up on work. Worth it though.

We continue to text back and forth about nothing in particular for a solid two hours while I work. My eyes are well and truly falling out of my head when I finally say good night.

My body is exhausted, and it doesn't take long for sleep to find me. I decided to change my alarm from five-thirty to six-thirty and skip my morning workout.

My body needs the rest after today.

20

Keeps getting better and better
Clark

Hannah and I have been texting nonstop, but I haven't seen her since our horse ride. I know her life is hectic with solo parenting and running a business, so I don't push her to catch up. I'd love to take her out for a night. But...I also know that we said from the very beginning that we didn't want to date. Hannah has made it clear that she just wants casual and easy, so I'm trying not to put any pressure on her. While casual is fine with me, I can't deny that Hannah has consumed every waking minute of my thoughts for the past week.

If I'm honest, my dreams, too.

The image of her bent over my couch runs through my mind at least a hundred times a day. God, I want to see her again. It's Friday afternoon and I know she has kids' sports most nights. I open up our message threads and start typing.

It's as if she had the exact same thought.

Before I hit send, a message pops up from her.

HANNAH: So my two older boys were having sleepovers tonight and Ethan and I were going to just hang. But now he wants to go to a friend's house as well. So, I'm all alone for the night. You free? Want to come around?

I want to ask her if she wants to go out instead. If I could take her out. For dinner, a movie, a drink. But I also know she doesn't seem to get a heap of down time. Hannah didn't have an issue with our friends seeing us together when we were down south, but now we are in our hometown, where the kids have friends and go to school. Where Callum's family live.

Hannah has talked about them and how close she still is with them all. She may not want to go out and be seen with another man. I also know Hannah is pretty straight up. She just says what she thinks and if she wanted to go out, she would have said that. But she said: "Do you want to come around?"

So, I go with it.

CLARK: Tell me when and where. I'll be there.

HANNAH: I have to go home and pack Ethan a bag and then drop him at his friend's house. I can text you when I'm home. Probably around six. We can just order takeout if you are okay with that?

CLARK: Sounds good. Just text me your address.

She sends a message with her address. The anticipation is already building within me. Then I get an idea.

I have just finished packing a bag with the supplies I need when my phone lights up with a text.

HANNAH: On my way home now. Head around whenever.

I almost strain a muscle running to the car. Like an absolute pussy-whipped fool.

I fly out the gate, tearing down the road to her place.

I get another text as my map shows I'm about five minutes away.

HANNAH: Just in the shower, but I put a
key under the mat. Feel free to come in
and join me…

My car reads the text out through Bluetooth and my foot automatically hits the accelerator a little harder. The traffic isn't bad, but I'm mindful that the built-up streets want me to drive fifty. I growl under the restraint it takes to go the speed limit.

I arrive at Hannah's place and find the key under the mat, just as she said it would be. My hand hovers over the door, wanting to knock. It feels wrong just going inside. But she wouldn't have told me to use the key and join her if she didn't mean it.

I unlock the door, stepping inside and taking it all in. It's a beautiful house, right near the beach in a really nice area of town. I stand in the entry hall and spot what is clearly her bedroom just off to my left. Big double doors. A large bed, perfectly made with a million throw pillows. A bench sits at the foot—whitewash, old looking carved wood. With…you guessed it, more throw pillows. Towards the back of the room is an entry way to what looks like a large walk-in wardrobe. I hear the running water coming from behind it.

Moving back out of the bedroom, I walk through the entry-way and into the main area of the house. There is a step down into a sunken lounge room just to my right. A TV hangs on the back wall above an electric fireplace, and just past the lounge, back up the step, is the kitchen. A large wooden bench table sits in front of the kitchen counter. Glass windows are nestled behind it, looking out to the back yard.

I place the wine I bought in the fridge and put my bags on the bench seat. Taking out what I need, I sit down on the seat and wait for her. I'm not waiting long before she comes out of the room, dressed casually in a pair of tights and a tank top. The tights cling to her body, showing off her perfect ass, and I can see she doesn't have a bra on. Her nipples peek through the light material of her top.

Shit, I'm hard already.

Hannah stops dead in her tracks when she sees me and lets out a little squeal of fear. Her eyes snap to mine as recognition dawns on her pretty face. She lets out a breath and her shoulders relax. "Shit you scared me."

God, I'm an idiot. I didn't want to scare her. I thought it would be hot, her finding me sitting here with rope in my hands, only now I'm terrified that I've crossed a fucking line. I should have just text her that I was here and waited.

Shit, shit, shit.

Before I can apologise, she smirks at me. Her eyes fall to my lap, noticing the rope I have draped across it. She licks her lips and I relax. Okay, maybe I haven't fucked it up yet.

I wanted to surprise her and turn her on, not scare her half to death.

"Sorry, I didn't mean to scare you." I stand and stalk closer to her.

"You didn't want to join me in the shower?"

"I have a better idea." I move closer to her, our bodies almost touching.

"Oh, yeah?"

"May I?" I say, as I trail my fingers down her arms. Hannah takes a little step back as I grab her hands in my own and I turn them palms up with her wrists together so I can tie them up.

I'm terrified that this plan is going to end badly. Terrified she isn't going to like what I do. But I've committed now. Gotta see it through.

"Behind your back." I slowly turn her around and she moves her hands willingly behind her back, which tells me all I really need to know. She loves this kind of thing.

But what if I take it too far?

Fuck, don't chicken out now.

I spent the better part of an hour after she called looking up bondage positions. I settled on this as it looked far less complicated than most of the others.

I tie Hannah's hands together behind her back, making sure to leave a decent amount of length between them. She can just rest them at her sides now, which will make it easier for what I have planned next.

I turn her back around. She's smiling at me, her eyes alight with lust. I can tell she is down for whatever I have planned next.

Grabbing her hand, I lead her down the little step into the lounge room. It will be softer for her on the plush carpet than on the wood floorboards.

"On your knees."

Hannah curls a brow at me in amusement and bites her bottom lip. "Yes, sir," she says as she drops to her knees in front of me, hands tied. The words make my cock twitch.

Grabbing one of the many pillows off the couch, I place it in front of her. Then I push her forward onto it, careful not to let her face smack the floor as she has no hands to help her, and assist her body until she is lying face down over the pillow. I roughly grip her hips and hike them up, bringing her onto her knees with her ass in the air and her chest and face on the pillow. Slipping the rope over her ass, so that her hands are down by her ankles, I now tie her hands and her ankles together.

I lean back on my knees, admiring my work. Not bad for a first try.

Hannah turns her head to look sideways at me. "You look pretty pleased with yourself there," she says, smiling. She's not at all intimidated at being tied up on the floor with her ass in the air.

I stand and move around to her side. Squatting down, I place a gentle kiss on her cheek. I want her to know she is safe. While this definitely is turning me all the way on, I hate the thought of actually hurting her. "If it gets too much, let me know straight away, okay?"

She nods, and I reach into my pocket for phase two of my plan. Shit.

This is the part I'm worried about. That I'm taking it too far. But again, I've committed now. I'm going with it.

I pull out my pocket knife, and her eyes go wide.

"What is that?" Hannah asks. She doesn't look scared, just more so amused.

"I told you I was going to cut your clothes off with a knife," I say around a dark chuckle, mimicking what I sent to her via text the other night.

She starts to laugh, and her body vibrates with the minimal movement she can make. She can't lower her hips, straighten her legs or move her arms. I tried to leave some wiggle room for her, but she looks like she can barely move an inch.

"Do you trust me?' I ask as I move back behind her.

"Yes," she breaths.

I pop open the blade and place the backside against her skin. She sucks in a breath as I slide the cool metal up her calf and under her tights. I sharpened this thing to within an inch of its life before I came, so it slices through the thin material like soft butter.

I move up her calf, the material peeling away as I go. When I get to her knee, I pull the tights out slightly so I don't get too close to the curve of the back of her knees and risk nicking her skin. My hands are surprisingly steady as I move up the back of her thigh and over her round ass to her hips. The material falls away, leaving one side of her ass exposed.

Hannah lightly chuckles, but I see her body shiver as I place the back side of the knife on her lower back. I hope that was a shiver of pleasure and not fear.

Knowing what I know about Hannah so far, she would speak up if she didn't like what I was doing.

I make quick work of her top. It falls off her body, leaving her bare back exposed. I run the back side of the little knife down her skin, watching as goosebumps trail it. I follow them with little kisses as I move down to her other leg, repeating the process with the other side of her tights. When I reach her hips, the black material falls to the floor, leaving her in nothing but a G-string. I flick the knife under the thin band around her hips and one side falls away. I move to the other side and repeat, and the small amount of material drops to the floor.

Picking it up, I scrunch it into a ball and place the knife back into my jeans, deciding not to tempt fate any further. I grip her chin hard, and our eyes meet. She can see exactly what I'm asking.

She opens her mouth, and I shove her underwear in. It's a small amount of material—she could push it out or even talk around it if she really wanted to. She is already immobile, so I don't want to take away any chance she has of telling me to stop.

I did tell her I would tie her up and gag her, though.

I move back behind her. Fuck, I don't think I've ever been harder in my life. I say that every time, but this just keeps getting better and better.

I don't know why this turns me on so much, but it fucking does. Maybe just how confident Hannah is. How trusting. How much I can see she is enjoying it by the glint in her eye and the smile on her face. The way she keeps getting little shivers racking down her body even though it is in no way cold in here.

I hadn't thought much further than this in my plan. I figured instinct would just take over.

21

You are safe with me
Hannah

oly hell, this is the hottest thing I think I've ever done.

Clark seems so shy. He almost seems shocked by some of the things we have done thus far. And for some reason that coyness is such a turn on. His words are confident and his movements assertive, but I can tell he is nervous as hell by the slight wash of pink that creeps up his neck. His skin is tanned so you would miss it if you weren't watching carefully.

I notice it every time. It starts at his collar, just below his shirt, and moves up his neck to his cheeks. Like he is so unsure if what he is doing is okay.

This though? This is most definitely okay.

A fucking pocket knife.

Now, I have never done that. Or rather, had that done to me. The way he pushed me to the ground. So dominating yet so careful, making sure that I didn't face plant and knock out my teeth with my hands secured behind my back.

The ropes are tight but not in a painful way. I can tell he has left me some room to move. The way he just shoved my panties in my mouth has my pussy clenching and I swear it is dripping from how wet I feel.

Damn, he has barely even touched me.

I move my hips slightly. The anticipation of what is about to come is killing me. Clark moves back behind me and my breath stills, waiting for what is next. I pinch my lips together between my teeth.

His hand slowly trails over my ass and down between my legs. His fingers, feather-light, spreads my wetness around. I feel him move closer to me and lower his face between my thighs. He spreads my feet as far apart as they will go. And then I feel his tongue on me, licking slowly up from my clit to my ass and back down.

He's holding back.

I push my hips into him, moaning into the pillow.

He pulls away slightly, his breath warming my skin, sending tingles all over my body. I'm so turned on I feel like I will burst if he doesn't fuck me soon.

"Please," I moan around the gag, pushing my hips back further, trying to urge him back to me.

He lets out a low dark chuckle. "I thought I was teaching you how to be quiet, Hannah."

Fuck me. The way he says my name.

He moves to stand, and I hear him fiddle with his belt and zip. His pants drop to the floor, and he steps out of them. His shirt hits the floor near my face next. Kneeling behind me, I feel him at my entrance. He swipes his hard, thick head through my wetness.

"Is this what you want, Hannah?"

He plays with my entrance, sliding his tip into me before pulling it out again. I push back as much as I can, trying to force him deeper, but he grips my hips, holding me still. He repeats the process, letting the tip enter me, stretching me to the point of teasing and then pulling away.

I moan his name, but it's barely coherent. His belt that I didn't even realise he was holding slaps across my ass. It's not hard but I wasn't expecting it. I jolt forward, gasping. The soft sting of it warms my core.

"I told you to be quiet, Hannah."

I can't help myself. "Clark."

The belt slaps me again.

"Hush, baby. Every sound you make will get you a slap."

I whimper into my own panties. But my body pushes back into him, liking the burn. Another chuckle rumbles in his chest as he thrusts into me. Hard. I have no ability to move but I don't need to. He grips my hips like a vice with one big strong hand. The other probably wielding that damn belt.

His hips pound into me with each hard thrust. I'm thankful for the pillow under my chest and face, otherwise, I swear I would have carpet burn from the ferocity of his movements. Honestly, I wouldn't have cared if the carpet burnt a hole right through my cheek. It would be so worth it.

"You like that, baby. Is this what you want?" His tone is deep and husky.

I fucking love this side of him.

"Yes, yes, yes," I moan around the gag. But it just earns me three fast little slaps with the belt across my ass. One for each word. The sensation has that coil deep inside of me tightening. I clench around him.

"Be a good girl and come quietly for me, Hannah."

Holy shit.

As if on cue, I explode around him, my body shaking and quivering with the after waves. His pace doesn't slow. A few more hard, deep thrusts and his death grip on my hips tightens even more with his own release. I feel him pulse inside of me.

Every time we do this, I don't think the orgasms can get better, and every time, they somehow do.

I'm a boneless heap on the floor of my living room, and I swear I have dripped a mix of our cum on the plush carpet. I make a mental note to spot clean it before the kids come home tomorrow.

Clark pulls the knife back from his pants and cuts the ropes, helping me to bring my hands out in front. My muscles are strained from being tied up for so long, but my body vibrates with the euphoric post orgasmic feeling. It hums with the electricity that is between us.

I have had plenty of good sex in my life, but the sexual chemistry between Clark and I is undeniable. I never want this sex to end.

He rubs the tender marks around my ankles and then pulls me up to stand. Lifting me into his arms in a wedding carry, he moves towards my bedroom. He walks through the room and into the walk-in robe. Two sections are off to each side. Past those, it opens up to my ensuite. He spots the large claw bath. It was a splurge purchase, and cost way too much for how often I actually get the chance to use it, but it is beyond beautiful. Four shiny black claws lead up to black porcelain with a roll top white lip, flowing into a large deep white porcelain tub.

Clark places me in the tub before turning on the water, finding a good temperature, and then puts the plug in. I lay back and relax as the warm water starts to rise over my perfectly aching body.

"Bubbles?" he asks.

"Under the sink."

He moves to the cupboards and pulls out my spare bottle of body wash. Squeezing the milk and honey liquid under the fall of water, it starts to bubble up, spreading around the bath. Clark steps into the bath at the opposite end, so we are facing each other. Grabbing my ankles, he gently rubs over the red irritated burns from the friction of the rope.

I can't help but laugh. "Where the fuck did that all come from?"

"No clue."

"So, you've never cut someone's clothes off with a pocket knife, hog tied them and railed them from behind?"

He lets out a chesty laugh, choking on it as it leaves. "Nope, definitely a first." He smiles shyly at me, and I see a blush start to creep over his cheeks again. "I don't know what comes over me, but I'm like a horny animal who can't control his urges around you."

"Well, I loved it."

He rubs his hand over his mouth and chin. "I was terrified I was going to completely freak you out."

"I feel safe with you, Clark. I love these crazy things when I feel safe enough to explore them."

"You are safe with me. I've never had sex like this, so this is a whole new world for me."

"Are these things you've always wanted to try?" I ask. Just curious, really. I have never really been shy to talk about or experiment with sex.

He hums in thought. "I mean, the knife thing, I hadn't thought about that before. Being dominant, rough? Yeah. But I knew it wasn't what Cherie liked, and I was okay with that." He pauses. "Sorry, I don't mean to bring her up."

"I don't mind." And I mean it.

It doesn't bother me when he talks about her. I still love my late husband with all my heart. But I can honestly say when I am with Clark, especially when he is fucking me the way he just did, I'm not thinking about a single other thing but him. His presence, dominance and kind-hearted nature consumes me. Engulfs me. It wraps me up so completely that I have no space to feel anything else except him. To be in the moment with him.

If he feels even a fraction of the chemistry between us that I do, then I don't think he is thinking about Cherie while we are together.

"What else do you want to try?" I ask.

He looks at me sceptically, tilting his head to the side. His hand moves back to his jaw, running over the stubble there.

"Clark you literally just cut my clothes off my tied-up body with a knife. I think you can tell me what you want to try. I might be into it."

"Fuck, I'm sorry about that. I hope they weren't expensive."

I let out a little squeak. "I mean they were Lululemon, so yeah, kind of expensive."

He blushes again. "Shit, I am so sorry. I will buy you a new set. The underwear too."

"Clark, I would pay you to do that to me again. I don't give two shits about the tights."

He pulls on my ankles that he has been gently massaging the entire time, sliding my legs over his so I am almost straddling him. He cups my cheek as his lips meet mine in a slow soft kiss. It feels intimate and romantic in this giant tub with bubbles and the sweet scent of honey wafting around us.

Pulling away slightly, his lips find my collarbone, before making their way up my neck to my ear. He sucks lightly on my earlobe before whispering, almost like he is too afraid to say the words out loud, or he can't look me in the eye when he says them, "Anal."

I pull away, trying to get him to look at me. He lets out a little cough and rubs his large hand over the back of his neck, averting my gaze.

"You've never done anal?" He shakes his head, looking up through his brow at me. Embarrassment covers his manly features. "Clark, why are you so shy? Especially after what we just did."

"I don't know. I just haven't really talked about these things with a partner before. Sex was always kind of vanilla. And I mean I'm not complaining, great flavour. I loved it. But this...this is..." He tilts his head to the side, trying to hide a smile.

"I mean, I haven't done anal in a long time, but I remember enjoying it. I'm happy to do that with you."

Lust blown eyes snap to mine. "You are?"

"Absolutely."

"I...I—" He goes to speak, but a stutter comes out.

"Let's try it."

"Okay." Clark clears his throat. "Cool." He goes back to laying kisses all over my body.

This guy is so fucking adorable.

22

Stepping up to the plate

Clark

Hannah understandably doesn't want to introduce me to her kids, so we savour the time we get. The weeks fly by and the little moments we steal replay through my mind on a carousel. The time she rang me on her lunch break, and I broke far too many traffic laws than I care to admit to get to her. I pinned her down on a workout bench and took her while watching the two of us move in front of her ceiling to floor length mirror. The smooth lines of her body, and the way she moved, watching her muscles tense and relax under my touch. The mirror allowed me to see it in ways I had not before.

My brain is unable to forget, reliving it at least once a day. The 'admin days' that she bails on to come and ride through nature with me. Hannah's face lights up with wonder every time she sees a giant open field. I would load the horses up in the float and drive us to places that I know have vast open lush green fields for us to gallop through.

I must say that she is right, though. You come alive on the top of a horse as it gallops at full speed across the open land, the wind in your hair.

The odd afternoon where her kids go to their sports with friends' parents. We headed to the beach to relive our first kiss surrounded by sand, salt and sunshine.

The nights she would text me past eleven to tell me that her kids are finally asleep. She left a key out and I snuck into her bed to do unholy things to her. She always kicked me out before the sun rose so that her kids wouldn't find a strange man cuddled up to their mum.

Hannah has me three sheets to the wind without a single drink. I'm infatuated with her, and I don't think she even realises it. It's not just the sex. It's everything. She is smart, hard-working and so down to earth. When she laughs, her whole body shakes, and when she really gets going, she snorts, which only makes her laugh harder. She is passionate and such a great mother, which somehow makes me fall even harder.

Lately I see her in everything I do. The way the hay looks spread across the floor when I'm feeding the horses. The soft honey colour reminds me of the darker strands that run through her blonde hair when it is sprawled across my chest.

The fucking green in the threads of the horse blankets reminds me of the green in her eyes. How they start darker on the outside and fade into the lightest shade of green around the irises, almost glowing in the sun. Like sea glass.

The sweet smell of the molasse tub reminds me of her honey smelling body wash.

I want more time with her. Truth be told, I want more.

I want to take her out on a date. I want to let her get dressed up and take her to that Mexican restaurant in the city that she keeps talking about. The one the other deadbeat failed to make it to. I want to see her dancing under flashing lights, and beat her at mini golf because I know she is competitive and I want to see her get flustered.

I've almost broached the subject multiple times. Typed the text only to hit the back button and watch the words disappear. I know that she doesn't want a relationship. I know she doesn't want serious. No expectations. I know she has enough to think about, and I want to make things as easy for her as possible.

So, I've let it be.

However, now she is sitting on my kitchen bench with her hair tousled and face flushed.

I don't think I will ever get sick of this woman.

"I have to go. I have so much work to catch up on before it's time to go get the kids."

I move back between her thighs. The mixture of our release is running down her open legs. I trail my finger up the inside of her thigh, scooping it up and sliding it back inside her pussy. Hannah moans and arches her back. I don't know why I'm so obsessed with having my cum inside of her. I obviously have a breeding kink I never knew about, but she lets me have my moment and I'm glad for it.

"Let me take you out. Get dressed up and I will take you to that Mexican place you always talk about."

She shoots up, her eyes alight. "La Vida Tacos?"

I nod, still playing with her pussy. I can't seem to drag my eyes or fingers away from it.

"I would love that. When?" Her voice is breathless, and I'm sure I could get her there again if she had the time.

"When can you get sitters?"

"I'll try for this weekend." *Pant*. "I'll let you know later." *Pant*.

I chuckle. I love the little noises she makes. I love how responsive she is to my touch. How she doesn't shy away from being spread out like this in broad daylight, with every inch of her on display. Her confidence bleeds into me. I'm sure there would be men who would find it intimidating, but it has the opposite effect on me. It builds me up. I come alive, feeling more like the man I used to be than what I have in a long time. My own self-doubt and fears fade, and I want to match her energy in every way. I know she likes me dominating and assertive. I have no issues stepping up to that plate. I welcome the challenge.

I circle her clit, adding pressure, and she arches into my touch.

"I really do have to go." Hannah makes no move to get off my kitchen bench, so I place a palm to her belly and lay her out even more, not letting up until she is crying around my fingers one last time.

23

Why can't this be love?

Clark

I run my hand along the tops of my thighs, trying to steady my breathing in the car before I go to knock on Hannah's door. I'm nervous as hell. I've had this woman in every compromising position I can think of over the course of the last couple of months, but this feels different.

We were clear in the beginning that this was just casual. Just respectful sex and companionship to fill a need, a void. We have both spoken at length about our feelings and I know that she doesn't think she has the ability to ever move on from Callum. We agreed that this was a no strings attached and no pressure situation. However, we also agreed that we wouldn't sleep with other people. I showed her the STD test I had done to put her mind at ease, and I meant it when I said I wouldn't sleep with anyone else. I am a man of my word.

If I am being completely honest with myself, things are changing for me. I find myself thinking of her more often than not, wanting to be in her orbit, but I'm evolved enough to not push her. She doesn't need that after all she has overcome.

She needs a hard dick and someone to make her laugh. So that's exactly what I'll be.

Her kids are staying the night between friends and her sister's place. So, I have gone all out for her. I want to give her the dates she never got with the other losers. I laugh thinking about how much they missed out on. If only they knew what a dime she was. While I'm not glad that she was hurt by those experiences, I am glad that they fumbled.

I won't.

Hannah opens the door before I get a chance to knock. Damn, she is beautiful. Her hair is down and curled in big loose waves, and her green eyes sparkle under the porch light, framed by her thick lashes. Soft pink lips, so fucking kissable.

I pull her towards me, giving her a kiss on the forehead. I've learnt over the years you don't kiss women on the lips when their lipstick is that perfect. They get mad at that shit.

"You look stunning." Light wash jeans with rips in the knees sit high on her hips, hugging her ass in the most delicious way. A low-cut black silk singlet allows me to see the points of her nipple through the thin material.

It has an instant effect on my cock, and I suck in a breath, composing myself. I don't want to ruin her right here by the front door before she gets a chance to have a margarita and a taco.

"I'll grab your bags." I have told her that we are staying up in the city, but I haven't told her where. I booked the Crown Towers. A premier suite. We don't need all the space, but I wanted the big tub overlooking the vast city views. I booked her a spa package as well for tomorrow morning after a buffet breakfast. It's three hours long and I have no clue what takes that amount of time. When I rang, that is what they recommended. Dinner tonight is at the Mexican place she loves, followed by a game of mini golf.

I have probably gone well and truly overboard, but I really wanted to make it special for her. I know she isn't the type to splurge on herself and she doesn't get the chance to get out much. Hannah is down to earth and low maintenance from what I can tell. Her nails are always left natural, and no fake lashes or tattoo eyebrows. She doesn't seem to be at different appointments for hair or massages, so I really hope I haven't fucked up thinking she will like this.

Surely every woman likes a spa day.

Right?

Right?

Shit!

I swallow the fear and grab her overnight bag.

Hannah locks the door, and we make our way to the car.

"Does the 'driver pick the music, passenger shuts their cake hole?'" she asks, sliding into the passenger seat with a cheeky grin across her features.

"Are you quoting Supernatural to me?"

She chuckles. "I love that show."

I can't help but smile at her.

"You can choose the music." I start the car and back out onto the street.

She wastes no time connecting her phone to my Bluetooth and selects a playlist. A country song starts playing through the speakers. I'm more of an old school rock and roll kind of guy. Rolling stones, Van Halen, and Guns n' Roses.

She hums and sings gently, knowing every lyric. I find myself smiling and humming along even though I have never heard a single song before.

"What music do you like?" Hannah asks as the song fades out and there is a brief moment of silence before the next one kicks in.

"I like the old school rock and roll." I glance sideways to see her reaction. She smiles then tinkers with her phone.

Van Halen's 'Why can't this be love' comes on and she cranks it up.

"Like this?" The keyboard riff kicks in, and the beat drops as she starts gently head banging, before belting out, "Whoa, here it comes," with zero shame for the fact that she is completely out of tune.

An uncontrollable laugh spills from my mouth as I try my hardest to concentrate on getting us to our destination alive. I'm slightly in awe of this woman. She talks about her hang ups, but I see none of them. Her energy is contagious, and I start to sing along with her. Hannah knows every word, and we end up holding our fists like microphones and belting out the song.

She leans across the centre console, getting close to the side of my face, singing, "Whoa, it's got what it takes, so tell me why can't this be love."

I turn my head, trying to keep one eye on the road as I volley back at her, "You want it straight from the heart, hey, tell me why can't this be love."

We both end up in fits of laughter, and I can't recall a time I have ever felt so happy.

The rest of the drive follows the same suit, chatting between song riffs.

It's perfect.

By the time we pull into the towers, my cheeks hurt from how much I have been smiling and laughing. Her eyes light up when I pull into the valet, and a little gasp escapes her lips. "We're staying here?"

"Mmmhum."

There's that gasp again. The one that makes me want to kiss her mouth and bury myself in her.

"I've always wanted to come here." Hannah is already trying to unbuckle herself to get out the door.

I come to a stop and rush to her side of the car so I can open her door, but ever the independent women, she is already out by the time I make it there. The valet comes over, and I grab the bags off the back seat, before handing him my keys for him to park the car.

Placing a hand on the small of her back, I lead her inside where I check in. I have already paid upfront to avoid her chipping in; I know that she isn't going to be happy about that.

The concierge gives me the key card, and we opt to just carry our own bags up. I only have one small duffel bag, and I'm slightly shocked that so does Hannah. I was expecting more.

I easily grab both the bags in one hand so that I have one free to hold hers and lead us towards the lifts. We make it to the fourteenth floor.

Hannah squeals again as we enter the room. The entry way opens up to a large studio. A king size bed sits against the back wall overlooking the city below. She completely ignores the basket of wrapped goodies sitting on the bed that I organised for us for later—champagne, chocolates, massage oils and candles. She heads straight through to the bathroom that sits off to the side.

"Ohhhh, look at this." She is already climbing into the giant free-standing bathtub that is situated right in front of sweeping floor to ceiling windows that overlook the city.

I climb in behind her, wrapping an arm over her chest and pulling her back to me. Her back sits flush to my chest and I kiss up her neck.

"This, right here, was the whole reason I wanted this room," I whisper in her ear.

"It's so perfect."

"Later though, because dinner is at seven." I look down at my watch. It's already six-thirty. We left late so she could watch her kid's basketball games.

I stand, stepping out of the empty tub, and give her my hand to help her step over the high lip. We make our way out of the towers and order an Uber to the restaurant.

I can see why Hannah raved about the place. The bar is lined floor to ceiling, wall to wall with different types of tequila. Its dark and electric and they have added clear panels on the floor, giving you a view to the underground cellars.

We shared guac and freshly made corn chips with a selection of tacos—pulled pork and slaw, and fish with chipola mayo. We sipped on margaritas from spicy salt rimmed glasses.

Good company and conversation.

Bright flashing lights and loud music assault my senses as we enter the indoor mini golf centre after dinner. A giant clown face with its tongue making a ramp leading up to its mouth starts off the course of eighteen holes. Each hole is bright and unique—a mini medieval castle and a dinosaur with a mouth that opens and shuts to try and stop your ball.

Hannah glows under the flashing lights. Her tight jeans make her ass look too good to concentrate fully, but I don't take it easy on her. Most girls, I probably would have. Played it sweet and let them win. But I know that Hannah is competitive and I want to see her get flustered.

She put up a good fight and there were a few points where I started to sweat. But when she got stuck in an alcove after a giant ferris wheel knocked her ball out, I knew I had her. It all went downhill for her from there and I couldn't help but rib her for it. I love this playful side of her, and trust me, she gives as good as she gets.

We make it back to the hotel, buzzing from too many cocktails. Her dainty feet slip out of shoes the moment we enter the room, and her top follows. Her hips sway as she makes her way through to the bathroom, shuffling her jeans down her thighs as she goes.

I grab our gift basket that she has barely noticed, taking no time to rip the cellophane wrapping from the goodies. I grab the champagne bottle, peeling the wrapping and popping the cork as I follow her.

Turning to face me, Hannah stands naked, her soft skin shadowed by the inky night sky and city lights behind her. I start the faucet of the bath and add the plug so it can fill.

She wraps her hand around the neck of the champagne bottle, her eyes never leaving mine, mischief dancing in them. I watch in awe as her lips wrap around the bottle to take a mouthful, then she kneels in front of me. I undo my belt and let my pants and briefs fall to the floor. My shirt comes off next.

Her pretty green eyes stare up at me as she takes another mouthful of champagne before wrapping her full lips around my cock. It bubbles and pops, the champagne still chilled from its time in the fridge prior to being packaged up. It warms slowly as her mouth takes me deeper.

I let out a low groan. "Fuck, Hannah."

She takes another swig before sliding her mouth back over my length. I run my fingers through her hair, gripping a handful as I control her movements. Her eyes are glued to mine as she slides her wet mouth up and down my cock. I pull her off and she passes the champagne bottle up to me. I take my own mouthful before pulling her head back by her hair so she is angled up at me. I tip the bottle and let a small amount of liquid run into her mouth.

She sticks her tongue out to meet it and holds it in her mouth before sucking me back into her.

I take another mouthful, this time spitting it from my mouth as it drops down to hers. I have no idea what possesses me to do it. Something about her on her knees in front of me, and the night sky behind her with the buzz of the alcohol in my veins. Her eyes sparkle as she takes every drop, licking her lips before taking me in her hot mouth again.

The bath fills as she works her mouth up and down my hard cock. God, it feels good. I wanna fuck her face till I come down her throat. But I have other plans.

I pull her back by her hair, then bend down and scoop her up. Her naked body straddles mine, still clutching the bottle. I carry her to the bed. Laying her back, I pour the bubbly gold liquid over her stomach. It pools at her belly button and runs down her hip. I lap at it, sucking it off her body. Taking another mouthful, I suck her nipple into my mouth. Hannah arches her back and moans my name.

My cock instantly grows harder at the sound.

I grab the candle from the gift pack. I brought my own lighter, knowing that the hotel probably wasn't going to give me one. Lighting a candle in here probably goes against some form of safety code, but I don't give a shit right now.

I light the candle and let some of the wax melt, allowing it to pool in the centre. Her lust blown eyes watch me intensely. I move slow so she can see what I'm about to do, giving her plenty of opportunity to say no, before angling the candle and letting the hot wax drip on her skin.

She gasps.

More wax pools and I tip it over her tits. The hot wax solidifies slightly as it connects with her body.

Taking another mouthful of champagne, I suck her clit into my mouth. She lets out a little cry and arches her back. Candle in one hand and bottle in the other, I alternate between hot and cold, using my mouth to tease her.

By the time I carry her back into the bathtub that was near overflowing, Hannah is a begging mess. We sink into the warm water. My back is to the city views so she can watch the night sky while she rides my cock.

Straddling me, she rocks her hips, taking me deep. It's romantic and intimate and far slower than we normally fuck. But I love it just the same. Maybe even more.

It's perfect. She is perfect.

Except she doesn't want this permanently.

Fuck, I'm in trouble.

All my talk of 'in my experience the women never really mean casual' has blown up in my face. Now it's me that apparently can't do casual.

I want her.

I want more.

24

Surprise its perimenopause
Hannah

"Hey, it's me," I all but yell into the speaker, wondering why it took Kate so long to answer the damn phone.

"Hey, how are you. What's up?" my sister asks. But I don't have time for pleasantries. I'm in between clients. The weeks have been so busy.

Clark and I have managed to squeeze in rendezvous at least once a week, and the sex has never been better. It's honestly the perfect situationship. I'm too old to use that word but it's what I hear the younger ones call it.

I don't really know how else to explain what this is between us. We get along great. There are always good conversations. We text back and forth most days. A video or phone chat in between. And...well, some very steamy sex catch ups.

Our conversations range from deep and meaningful—life before we met. About his relationship. About mine. About the kids—to light and easy. Flirting and banter. It's quite honestly the perfect set up for the stage of life I am in. There is no pressure to catch up. No unmet expectations. Just two consenting adults filling a void.

I've filled Kate in on all the details. She has always been my go-to. My sister and best friend. But this isn't about Clark.

Looking at the time on my watch, I realise I don't have much time to chit chat. I get straight to the point of my call. "Have you gone through menopause?" I ask.

"Menopause? How old do you think I am?"

"Perimenopause," I counter. "It can start in your mid-thirties."

She lets out a laugh. "What the fuck is perimenopause?"

"It's pre-menopause. It's like the same as menopause but it's a pre-thing."

"What are you even talking about?" She emphasises *what*.

"It's the same symptoms, I think, but you do it pre...I don't know," I huff, feeling exasperated.

"I have no clue what you're talking about. But no, I have not gone through menopause or perimenopause. Why?"

"I've been feeling really weird lately. Like my boobs are sore as hell and I've been having hot flushes. Remember Mum used to get hot flushes all the time when she was going through menopause."

"Oh, my God, yes. Shame, I remember we were so horrible to her as teenagers. I actually feel awful now that I'm a mum of young adults. They're mean."

A laugh slips out unintentionally.

"No, it's not funny. They can be real assholes," she adds.

"No, I believe you, it's not funny. And yeah, so sad about Mum. We should really apologise to her."

"We should," Kate adds.

"Anyway, back to me. I'm having these weird hot flushes. My periods are off. My last one was really light, almost just spotting. I'm having weird cramps and I don't know, I just...I'm so fucking tired all the time."

"You have three kids and a business, Hannah, of course you're goddamn tired."

"This feels different. It's not busy tired. I feel dead on my feet. I'm exhausted. My brain is all foggy. I've got no patience or energy."

Kate's voice softens, "Maybe make a doctor's appointment. They can take your blood and check all your hormone levels. Maybe your iron is low."

I nod in agreement, even though she can't see me through the phone. "Yeah, that's a good idea actually. I'll try to get in. I've got to go, my next client just arrived. I will call you later, okay?"

"Okay, love you. Bye."

"Ditto, bitch. Bye." I hang up, staring at my phone. I can see my client walking through the side gate to come through to my home clinic. After her, it's straight to school pick up, after school sports, then the dinner rush.

I make myself a promise to call the doctor's office to make an appointment on my drive to school or while I wait in the kiss and drop line.

My alarm goes off at 5:30 AM and I swat at my bedside table, trying to shut it up. Normally I get up and get a workout in, then I sort through my emails and check my schedule over coffee. I then get the kids up at seven to get out the door by eight, but I just can't seem to summon the energy. My hand connects with my phone, and I hit the snooze button. I repeat this process in ten-minute intervals for the next hour, mentally berating myself for not just changing the alarm to six-thirty when I first grabbed it.

Rolling out of bed, I take lazy steps to the coffee machine, checking my emails on my phone as the beans grid. A text pops up from Kate.

KATE: How did you go with the doctor?

Fuck! I forgot all about making the appointment. I got stuck on a call to my bank trying to sort a charge I didn't recognise on the way to school. Turns out it was a wholesaler I had ordered some Therabands from. They had just used a really weird eftpos tag. It took up most of the drive to school.

In the pick up line, I ordered Noah new school shoes that he has desperately been needing and I have been putting off. By the time I had done that, the kids were piling in the car through loud conversations about who likes who and what the weekend plans are. We didn't walk through the door until after six-thirty, and then it was a mad rush to scrape together some semblance of a healthy dinner. The boys helped me clean up after dinner, and then I tackled the pile of laundry. It had been threatening to overflow and could probably kill someone with its monstrous size.

I crawled into bed at nine-thirty, watched one episode of Grey's Anatomy and passed out.

I set myself an alarm to go off at eight-thirty. My doctor's surgery always keeps on the day appointments available, but you have to ring at opening time. If you are three seconds past eight-thirty, you miss out.

I have just finished dropping the kids when the alarm goes off. I immediately pull over and make the call, managing to get an appointment at midday. I go over the symptoms with my doctor, and she gives me a referral to go for a blood test to check my iron and thyroid levels. There is a clinic next to the surgery, so I head in and take a number to just get it out of the way.

I walk out with a cotton wool ball sticky taped to the inside of my elbow with precisely ten minutes to get home, eat and be ready for my next client of the day.

Two days later, I'm sitting in front of the same doctor, over-thinking with all the worst-case scenarios.

Do I have cancer?

They don't call you back into the office to tell you that all is peachy. They only force you to make an appointment for results when they have news to deliver. Usually bad.

I tried to pry it from them on the phone, but the receptionist only knew that the doctor wanted an appointment.

Panic bubbles away inside of me. There is a lump in my throat that I cannot swallow no matter how hard I try. My stomach feels like it's filled with lead.

The doctor sits down at her desk and smiles warmly at me. "Okay, we've got your results back, Hannah. You are not peri-menopausal. You're pregnant."

The lead in my stomach drops and the lump in my throat threatens to spew out bile. "W-what," I stutter. "I can't be." The words leave harsher than I intend.

"The test is very clear. HCG levels are just over one hundred and twelve thousand. Could be between eight to ten weeks but we will know more when we do a dating scan."

"No. This…I can't be pregnant. How? I've had a period." My mind rakes back over my last period. It was spotty but it was definitely there. And eight to ten weeks? I was sure I had a period before that as well.

"Sometimes you can still get some bleeding or spotting with implantation. It's not completely uncommon for women to have some bleeding during their first trimester. The blood test shows you are definitely pregnant. Let's get you an appointment with our OB Dr Ellis and we can organise a dating scan."

My shoulders slump and my chest feels heavy. My mouth hangs open but nothing spills from it. She must sense the shock on my face.

"This doesn't seem like it was planned. Are you okay?" she asks kindly.

"My husband's dead." I don't know why I say that. It has no relevance in this conversation. My fingers wrap around the ring that sits over my chest.

"I am so sorry to hear that." Her eyes soften. "That is a lot to deal with all at once."

She understandably thinks he passed recently. I can't be bothered to correct her. My head is swirling.

"Okay," is all that manages to spill from my lips. I sit stunned as she leaves the room, advising that she is going to find the obstetrician and see if she can make some time for me straight away. She must be able to feel the stress emanating from me in waves.

I think I leave my body because the next thing I know, I'm lying on that horrid paper that crunches with every breath as the OB squirts cold gel onto my lower stomach.

I am stunned silent as she moves the doppler over my lower abdomen.

"There's your baby," she coos.

Holy shit. My body feels like it is vibrating. A hollow pit forms in my stomach as I squeeze my eyes shut, trying not to look at the screen. But I'm not fast enough. I know instantly that I'm past ten weeks.

I have been through this before. Three times to be exact. That is not a tadpole. There are no arm and leg nubs. That is a full baby I glanced. A head that looks way too big for its tiny little body, and arms tucked up with hands squished by its face, knees tucked in. This is a fully formed baby.

"I'm just going to do the measurements now." She silently moves the doppler around, holding it in certain spots and clicking away on her machine. I force myself to a different place in my mind.

"Okay, by the measurements, I would say you're about twelve weeks. Everything looks good. Would you like me to print a picture for you?"

I want to scream, "NOOOO," but my head subconsciously moves to nod. I still can't bring myself to open my eyes. She snaps the picture and moves the doppler back to the holder, before giving me some paper towels to wipe away the gel.

I fold my tights back up and sit. Moving off the bed and back to the chair in front of her, she hands me the grainy black and white image of my baby.

The OB starts talking but nothing she is saying is computing in my scrambled brain. Something about the next steps. Some other blood tests we can do for genetic disorders, and information about finding out the gender. I don't hear a thing. It has sounded like I'm underwater from the moment the doctor uttered the word *pregnant*.

"What if I don't want this baby?" The words tumble from my mouth, too heavy to hold on my tongue any longer.

She stops her sentence and looks up at me. They are trained not to judge. They see all walks of life and are experienced in handling all different types of people and topics. I'm sure she has dealt with abortions before. But I don't miss the slight wash of sadness that blankets her petite features. She composes herself fast.

"You do have some other options. You can abort the pregnancy up to twenty-three weeks here in Western Australia. I can sign off on the abortion and put you in contact with a clinic." She pauses, allowing me time to catch up. "Unfortunately, there are none here in Mandurah, but there are few in the city area. Your other option is adoption. I can put you in contact with the Department of Communities. They will advise you of the steps from there."

I nod, bringing my hand up to my mouth to stop myself from saying anything else.

Abortion.

Adoption.

I had never considered these things with my others.

But now?

I'm forty years old with three children, a dead husband and a fuck buddy. I cannot have another child.

My mind flashes to Clark, replaying the conversations we have had over the last few months. He wanted nothing more than to have a child. He still wants to have children. Jesus, he thinks he is infertile. He told me he had a low sperm count. So low that getting someone pregnant was impossible. His ex lied to him about her baby being his. He is never going to believe that this is his baby.

Panic washes over me at the conversations I now have to have with him.

My kids.

Goddamn. My kids. They don't even know about Clark.

"Can I just ask s-something?" I stutter.

"Of course." Dr Ellis' kind eyes put me at ease a little.

"If someone had a low sperm count, can that improve or change over time?"

She takes a beat to think of her next words but stays professional. "It depends. Without knowing all the details, yes, a low sperm count can be improved with a healthier diet, more exercise and less stress. There are multiple factors, but it can be possible."

"The father of this baby... Umm... My husband died three years ago. I already have three children. I really...I...I have been having a fling, I suppose, for lack of a better word. But he told me he was infertile. His sperm count was too low. Could that have changed?"

She does well to keep up with my scattered sentences. "Like I said, it really depends, without knowing his background. In general terms, possibly."

Well it must have changed because I have not been with anyone else and I am definitely pregnant. There is no other option here. We had not been using condoms, and I really didn't feel like catching chlamydia. So we had agreed that we would not sleep with anyone else. At least while whatever this is between us is going on.

"Is there a way to do a paternity test while I'm pregnant?"

Her face falls slightly again but it is subtle. Ever the professional, she forges on, answering all my questions. "Yes, absolutely. I just need to see him, and I can write a referral for a blood test. We then match that to the blood we already have of yours. It can tell us with accuracy if that person is the father.

"Okay, thank you."

I drag my feet from the doctors office with an appointment made for Clark for tomorrow, clutching the tiny picture of our baby in my hands.

My body feels heavy, and I languish with every step I take towards the car, knowing the conversation I have to have next.

25

Tiny threads of grief
Hannah

My phone thuds as I slam it down too hard on my desk. Shit. I pick it up to inspect that nothing is cracked. It's the third time I've done it. Each time the force is a little harder.

My hand itches to call Kate. She is my best friend, and I need someone to talk to about this.

I try to slow my breathing. I inhale deep, feeling my rib cage move and expand, letting the air fill every part of my body. Then I blow out in an audible exhale, pushing until every last breath is expelled.

Repeat.

I do this five times and feel marginally better.

Younger me would have hit the dial button within three point two seconds of walking out of that doctor's office. But I'm an adult. This is Clark's baby and he deserves to know before anyone else. But it doesn't stop my body instinctively wanting to call Kate, though.

My mind is so conflicted. I know that I don't want this baby. I know that logistically, financially, practically, it isn't smart. But the thought of aborting at this stage feels gut-wrenching. I also know that Clark will want this child. He has made it clear that he wants kids. He had all but given up on the idea, which is going to make this conversation even harder. I have to be honest with him.

I bypass Kate's name and send a text to Clark. I try to keep it casual and simple, so he doesn't suspect anything. He deserves to hear this in person.

> HANNAH: Hey, you free this arvo?

He replies instantly.

> CLARK: Can be. What you thinking?

> HANNAH: Kids are going to sport with friends' parents today so I can head around after my last client. Four-ish?

> CLARK: See your fine ass then.

Normally we would text back and forth throughout the day, or have a phone call here and there, but I try not to prolong the conversation. I feel guilty enough with the fact that I haven't told him yet.

I can't even begin to process the feelings that bubble in me over how to tell him that I don't want this baby. He isn't going to agree, and I don't know how we are going to work this out. I know it's my body, and it should be my choice since I am the one that has to grow it. Birth it. No matter how good the man, the majority of the pressure is going to be on me.

Technically, I don't need him to have the abortion. He doesn't need to know. I could make the appointment and he would be none the wiser. But that goes against every fibre of my being. I would never be able to live with myself. Especially when I know the type of man Clark is. If he had been some deadbeat asshole one night stand I didn't speak to again, maybe this wouldn't feel as hard.

Tears well in my eyes. I vividly remember growing my three sons. I remember their births and the newborn smell. I remember the elated feeling of them being placed on my chest. The first feed. Now that I have seen this baby in my belly, I'm not sure I can go through with saying goodbye to it. However, I painfully remember the hardships, too. The pain, the pregnancy aches, the horrific morning sickness, the birth trauma, the sleepless nights, the colic, and the toddler stage. I just don't think I can go back to that.

And Clark and I are...what? We're not dating. Not official, or married. We get along well, we have a great connection and discussions, but we have not had to deal with any hardships of life together.

Do I like him? Yeah. The sex is great. I can't deny that the chemistry is off the charts. I can't say I don't love being in his company. That I don't feel my heart rate pick up and breath quicken every time I see him.

But is it enough to raise a baby together?

Either way, I know that I have to tell him. We made this baby together and we have to come to a decision together. I know that Clark is a good man, we just need to hash this out.

"Hey," Clark says as he rushes towards me, pulling me into a hungry kiss. I can't help but kiss him back. My body melts into him and the need to be close to him makes me forget what I came here to say. "God, I missed you." His breath warms my neck as he hums the words over my skin, leaving kisses as he goes. His hands find the back of my shirt and start to pull it up.

Shit!

"Clark, wait." I pull back and his eyes find mine. "I need to talk to you first."

He takes a step back. A flash of fear washes over his gorgeous features, like he knows what's coming.

He has no clue.

"It's not what you think. Well, I don't know. Maybe it is. I don't know. Just...just sit down, okay?"

"Do you want me to make you a drink? Coffee?" He moves towards the kitchen bench.

"I'm okay for now. I just need to get this out."

"Okay," he says tentatively. "You're scaring me a little bit." It is hidden behind a soft chuckle, but I can hear the fear in his voice.

"I'm scaring myself, to be honest." A nervous laugh escapes. "I'm just going to come out and say it, okay?"

"Hit me with it," is all he says as he sits on the stool at the kitchen bench.

"I'm pregnant." I probably could have softened the blow a little, but I am not one to beat around the bush.

He reels back. His hand moves to his jaw, running across the stubble there.

I let out a sigh, folding my bottom lip between my teeth. "I know what you're thinking. That I've been sleeping with other men."

I see his face falling. He probably had a conversation very similar to this with his ex, and I know how much that broke him. But this baby is his. There is not a doubt in my mind. I have not been with another man since my husband.

Only Clark.

There is no possibility that it's anyone else's baby. I know that, but he doesn't.

"I know what you're thinking, Clark. That you can't have kids. This isn't yours. But I promise you, it is."

His jaw pops open, his mouth hanging clear with an un-readable expression written all over his face. Shock? Confusion? Frustration? Maybe even a little bit of anger. In his eyes, definite-ly. They give him away. They look dark, stormy.

He lets out a low, chesty rumble.

I've never really seen him like this before. I desperately try to swallow the lump that has not left my throat since I found out.

"I know for certain that it's yours, Clark. I have not been with anyone else. Not since Callum. Only you. I know we never..." I pause to catch my breath. "This was always just casual and fun, but I told you I wasn't sleeping with anyone else and I meant it."

I pause, thinking of what a giant slut I've acted like with Clark. I've let him tie me up, slap my ass, choke me, cut my clothes off with a knife. Fuck, he probably believes the absolute worst of me right now.

"I went three years without touching another soul. I was faithful to my husband for seventeen years." I emphasise the *seventeen* to really drive it home. I'm not the unfaithful, dishonest kind. "I wouldn't lie to you. It's yours and I know that you probably find that hard to believe. I spoke to the doctor and there's a test you can do. It's a simple blood test. They already have my blood work. It'll tell you with accuracy. They can test something in the blood. I don't know how it works but I booked you an appointment tomorrow to go get the referral."

He says nothing, just stares at me.

"Look, the doctor did say lifestyle changes, diet, exercise and less stress can increase your sperm count. You said yourself that you were low. But you never followed up. You never had more testing. You never went through the process. Maybe there were things you could have done to increase your count. Maybe the changes over the last year have made a difference. I don't know. But what I do know with absolute certainty is this baby is yours. If you need to do the blood test, I'm okay with that. If you need that peace of mind, it's a quick and easy test."

He still says nothing. His face is frozen, jaw clenched.

The panic in me makes me keep talking. "Okay? Well, I'm going to let you process that. When you are ready, we need to talk about what we do."

"What do you mean?" He's quick to reply to that. He steps towards me. Almost protectively, he reaches a hand out to my belly. It's barely there. I'm only twelve weeks.

"I mean—" I pause. How do I say this? "This is hard to say, Clark, but"—I swallow hard—"I don't know that I want this baby."

"What are you saying?" His voice is harsh and rough, laced with gravel.

"I mean, I'm forty years old. I'm a widow. I have three children already. I cannot go back to kids in nappies and breastfeeding. How...how would I even do that? I don't have a fifth room in my house for another child. I need a crib and pram and all the other shit that comes with a baby. It's also the financial impact on me. I am solely responsible for three children. I can't provide for them when I can't work. How am I going to work when I'm thirty-five weeks pregnant and can barely get off the couch?"

He moves closer to me still, his hand itching to touch my belly. I step back.

"How am I going to work to provide for them when I'm up all night with a little baby while I'm breastfeeding? Logistically it just doesn't work. And—" I'm well aware I'm rambling. Unloading on him. My voice softens. It's hard to speak the truth, but I have to be honest with him. "It's not what I want. I don't want any more children."

"Hannah." His voice is soft, pleading. He steps towards me again, reaching forward, as if drawn to me. I don't move this time. "Are you saying you want to get an...abortion?" He chokes on the last word.

I play it over in my head. "No, I really don't, but I do at the same time. I'm so conflicted. The thought of aborting this baby...I mean, I saw the ultrasound. It's got little arms and legs. A strong heartbeat. How could I? But how can I raise it?" The tears I have been holding at bay spill over my lashes. "I don't know how to explain the conflicting feelings in my mind, but I just know I cannot go through with having another child. It will change my life so much and I finally, *finally*, started to get my life back, Clark. Having a baby...it puts pressure on even a great relationship. My life at the moment is so full. I don't know how I would fit in another child." I'm rambling again, the words tumbling from my mouth without full control. My brain feels so scattered.

Clark is motionless, just listening, but I don't miss the tick in his defined jaw. His hands clenched at his sides. But mostly the fear in his eyes.

"And we..." I motion between us with my hands. "We are not even—I mean, what are we? What's going to happen when the baby is up all night feeding? I had help the first time around. I could feed, and Callum would be there getting me a snack or a drink or settling the other children. He would get up early so that

I could sleep in. Take the baby so that I could catch a nap, or settle them when I needed a longer shower or just a break. How is this going to work?"

My shoulders sag, and I pinch my eyes closed, trying to slow the fall of tears. But it doesn't work. "It's the mental load of it as well. The planning, the coordinating. Four children. I can't do that." I throw my hands in the air in defeat. His eyes haven't left me, but he still doesn't speak. So, I fill the silence. All my tangled thoughts fall from my mouth. "The financial impact alone. I would be starting from scratch. Cot, pram, clothes, toys, nappies, car seats, and if I'm not working, I cannot provide for my kids. It's just me, Clark! How am I supposed to work enough to provide for three kids with a new baby? The school fees alone. I... I—"

"Hannah, don't do this to me."

I squint my eyes at him, my brain trying to catch up to the fact that Clark has finally spoken.

"Hannah, I'm in love with you," he blurts out, stepping towards me.

My mouth falls open. I'm speechless. Did he just say what I think he did?

"I want this baby. I want you. I'll do whatever it takes. I don't care about the cost. I'll buy you a new house. Seven bedrooms if you want them. Fuck, I'll pay to expand your house. Add a second story, more rooms. I don't fucking care what it costs me.

You need a bigger car? Car seats? It's yours. I'll buy everything. I'll support you while you're off work. Fuck, Hannah! If you never want to work again, then fine. Don't. You, this baby—I haven't met your boys yet, but them too. I want all of you, Hannah."

The ground beneath me feels like it gives way and my stomach drops.

He moves closer again and I step back.

I can see the sorrow in his eyes. "I'm sorry to just drop that on you. I know that you probably don't feel the same. I know it's different for you. You still love Callum. I get it. I was giving you space. Waiting for the right time to talk to you more about... us."

Truth is, I really care about Clark. He is perfect. He's smoking hot, fucks like an animal, is kind, funny and genuine. In another life, I would have loved him. But my heart belongs to another man. I can't just forget about my life with Callum. Raise a baby with another man. What about my current children? I can never have them thinking that what their dad and I had wasn't everything to me. That I was just willing to replace him and start a new family.

"Hannah, I understand if this isn't what you want—us—and if you don't feel the same, but we can work this out. I'll move closer. Hell, I'll live in a tent in the back yard. We can get walkie talkies. Every time the baby wakes, I'll come in. I'll be there for everything. I can support you. Whatever you want. Just don't take this from me. Please."

Tears well in his eyes but they don't fall.

"It's your body. I'm not stupid or naive enough to think that the majority of the load isn't going to fall on you. I get it. You go through the attachment to that baby as it grows. The pain of labour and childbirth and all of that. I get it. I really do. But I want this! I will do whatever it takes, please. *Please.*"

Somehow between the words he has moved close enough to touch me. His hand finds my lower belly. It feels good on my body. Safe and comfortable. Clark looks down at me and there is a part of me that wants to be happy about this. I want to loosen the grip that loss and grief have tight around my throat and let myself feel all the things this beautiful man wants to give me.

But I just can't. I feel its tug. A deep internal pull that I don't think I will ever be free off. It's woven through my bones. Tiny threads. So small you miss them individually. But all together, they have a hold on me so strong that I am powerless.

I go to speak and nothing but a muffled squeak comes out.

"I'll take them, then," he says, gently rubbing his hand across my belly. "I will adopt them. Legally. Or however it works. Sign the baby over at birth. I will take them."

"W-what," I stutter.

"Hannah, I know you're not ready to move on yet. But if you really don't want us, or this baby...I want them. I'll take my baby. I don't care what I have to do. I have the financial means. I don't need to work. I own my house, my car. I have the space. I can set up a room. Let me have my baby. I cannot lose…” The word catches in his throat. I'm sure he went to say another baby, but the first was never really his to begin with. I see the pain in his eyes at the realisation. I swear I see the moment his heart shatters all over again, forced to relive those painful memories.

“I can't do that, Clark.” The thought of growing this baby for nine months and then handing it over to someone else, even if he is the father… There's no way. I can't feel this baby inside of me, be attached to them, and go through labour and birth, to what, just hand them over?

“What would happen then? I would just pretend I don't have another child out there in the world. We're going to live in the same town and I'm going to be walking around and spot you with your child. And what? Just pretend that's not my baby, too. There's no fucking way I could do that. What would I tell my kids?”

He rears back from me and his hands return to fists at his side. “This is your kid, Hannah. Your kid. And what, you can just kill it and then carry on with your life like nothing happened?”

“It's not that simple, Clark.”

“It is to me. I thought this was not an option. I didn't think that this was something I would ever have. Now you're telling me this baby is mine and I'm looking at you, I'm believing it and I want it. You CANNOT DO THIS. Please. You can't.”

He's choking on the words, pleading, begging. His eyes are filled with tears threatening to spill, but he's holding them back, trying to keep it together, but only just.

I don't quite have the same resolve as my chunky tears have not stopped rolling down my cheeks.

"It's so complicated. My kids don't even know you exist. How am I supposed to tell my three boys that I'm having a baby to another man? They loved their dad. How do I tell them that I'm starting a family with another man? I can't just move you in and start pretending that the seventeen years I had with Callum didn't happen. They don't know you. Now you're going to live with us. Raise a baby with me."

He rubs his hand over his jaw, and I hear the stubble scratching. "I'll buy the house next door or across the road. We will get a baby monitor that reaches. I won't live with you. I'll just move closer. I'll give you your space, but I'll be there. To support you. To raise this baby. Every whimper, every cry, every need. I'll be there."

He steps forward again, grabbing my hand in his. My heart cracks wide open. I remember back to what it felt like to tell Callum that I was pregnant for the first time. Even the second and third. The same reaction on his face—joy, happiness. How excited we were picking names, buying furniture and talking about what it would be like. I don't feel any of that excitement now.

I feel fear and anxiety. I'm sad that Clark doesn't get that moment of joy. That I have tainted his happiness with my own dread.

Whether Clark accepts it or not, whether he knows the true ins and outs of it or not, having a baby is hard fucking work. In reality, the majority of it falls on the woman. He could decide halfway through my pregnancy that this is not what he wants and take off. What am I supposed to do then? He could be six months into having a newborn and decide it's too fucking hard. He could bail.

I suppose women could do that too, but I would never. I know deep down that I would never. I have only known Clark for four months. I don't know him well enough to say with absolute certainty that it would be the same for him. That no matter what, he will stand by this child. By me.

I step back from him, releasing our hands. "This is a lot. I wanted to tell you straight away; it's your baby too and we need to make this decision together. I would never do anything without talking to you first. But I have to be honest about my feelings, Clark." The tears start rolling again, an uncontrollable force streaming down my cheeks, painting my shirt. "It breaks my heart to say that out loud because I know how beautiful children can be. But I also know the reality of it. Even with a great partner, I'm working my ass off providing for my kids."

"Hannah, I told you I'll pay for whatever you need."

"It's not the point, Clark. I've been on my own for three years. Now, all of a sudden, I will have to ask permission every time I need to buy nappies or something for the baby."

"I'll give you a bank card. I'll set you up with your own account. I'll give it all to you. I don't care. I don't think you realise the extent of my feelings here, Hannah. I don't just want this baby. I'm in love with you. I want it all. I want to meet your boys. I want to raise this baby with you. I know you're not ready to hear all that." He lets out a nervous laugh, like it just split from him without thought. He rubs his hand across the back of his neck. "Just promise me you won't make any decisions without me." He moves back into me and swipes the pads of his thumb across my cheeks, wiping the tears from my streaked face.

"I would never do that. I only got the results today and I texted you straight away. I wanted to tell you in person." I pull the little folded thermo picture out of the side pocket of my tights. "Here, this is our baby."

Clark takes the paper and the tears he has held at bay break. One single drop trails past his lashes and down his cheek. He sniffs, stopping the rest from spilling but doesn't wipe the stray away.

"Your appointment tomorrow is at ten. I'll text you the details."

"Hannah, I believe you. I don't need the test."

"I want you to do it. I know without a slither of doubt. But if there is even an iota of question about it for you, I want you to have that piece of mind. Especially if we—" I swallow hard, fighting the itch to reach for the ring around my neck in comfort. "If we have this baby, I need you to know. I can't have you ever second guess it."

Clark nods, but his eyes don't leave the black and white picture. "Thank you."

"I'm going to go. I just need to process all of this." I motion towards the picture.

His eyes still haven't left it, but he nods.

I turn and leave, and he follows me to the door with his eyes still fixed on his baby.

Clark reaches out and grabs my arm gently before I pass the threshold of his door. "Can I—" He pauses, finally breaking to look away from the picture to me. "Can I call or text? Just to check in. I know you need your space, but...would that be okay?"

"Yeah, that would be okay."

He smiles, and before I know it, his free hand has made its way back to my belly. He nods and then drops it as I turn to leave.

I feel even more confused.

He loves me!

Do I love him?

26

Slithers of doubt

Clark

My knee uncontrollably bounces, shaking the entire row of uncomfortable plastic chairs in the doctor's office. The elderly lady three seats down glances sideways at me in annoyance, but I can't seem to stop.

I've been sitting here for twenty minutes, and I've almost walked out about five times. The doctor is running late. As always. I don't have the patience to wait any longer.

I believe Hannah, but...there it is a BUT. A tiny slither of doubt that I can't seem to shake. A *what if.*

I never would have thought Cherie was cheating on me. We were married. Trying for kids and building a future. When I came home after finding out it was me that was the problem, I wanted so badly to believe that it was a miracle. That the baby was mine. I did believe it. The ecstatic feeling. The moment she shoved that little test in my hands, I forgot everything the doctor had just said.

We celebrated and planned, and it wasn't until three days later that the doctor's voice started ringing in my head. Like a tick burying under the skin. The *what ifs* came. When I told Cherie about the test, she swore it was a miracle. But I couldn't let it lie. She eventually came clean.

The soul crushing feeling when she hit me with the truth is something that I will never forget.

I packed my shit that same night.

I made a call to my business lawyer on the way to a hotel. She put me in touch with a divorce attorney, and I started the process the next day. The only conversation I had with Cherie after that was about the division of assets.

Being with Hannah over these last few months has opened my eyes to all the ways Cherie and I were so wrong for each other. I believe Hannah. This is the miracle I always wanted. But I need to know. I need to know without a shadow of doubt.

I'm grateful that Hannah made this appointment. I would have been too terrified to offend her to ever ask. The fact that she did this for me speaks volumes for the woman she is. Despite all her own turmoil that I know she is feeling, she still thought about what I would feel and need.

It's clear she always puts the needs of others first. I could see it in her face when she was telling me she didn't want our baby. She will keep it, but it isn't what she wants. She will do it for me. I could tell by her words, her body language, and the way she gave me the photo of our little baby.

Can I live with myself knowing I'm pushing her into this? Am I pushing her into it? This is a life altering decision. It's not like this is a purchase we can return. A piercing she can take out. A tattoo she can remove or a bad decision that may haunt us for a few weeks and then blow over.

Having a child is forever. Well, it is to me. I meant every word I said to her. They were not fake promises. But maybe the emotionally charged situation got the better of me. I laid it on a bit thick.

I may not know exactly what it takes to raise a baby by myself, but I would be willing to learn. I would give anything to have the chance to learn. I have the means. I don't think Hannah knows exactly how much money I have. I mean, I'm not driving around in a Lamborghini or living in a lavish mansion. I was never one to care too much about materialistic things. I have enough. If I wanted to, I wouldn't ever have to work again.

I had built my mechanic business up over a number of years. In the end, I had eight stores across neighbouring towns. I ended up taking a sweet deal from a massive franchise who had been wanting to buy me out of the market for years.

After the divorce, I couldn't care to argue and just wanted shit done as fast as possible. Cherie and I split everything pretty much down the middle. I walked away with around two million. Smart investments in crypto have seen that skyrocket and now my bank account sits relatively untouched well into seven figures.

I owe nothing on my property or car, and I have no other debts or need to spend exorbitant amounts of money. I work enough to pay the incoming bills and groceries, fuel and spending, and keep the animals well looked after.

Nothing I said to Hannah was empty promises. I have the means and am willing to deliver on all of it.

I meant what I said when I told her I loved her. I think I knew it the moment we spent the first weekend together. But I knew the score. I don't want to force myself on her, so I have given her space. I should have found a more romantic way to tell her I loved her. However, I couldn't let her think that I'm only saying it now because she is pregnant.

I want this baby. I want her. I want her family, and I want this life. This life I thought I would never be able to have.

I don't want her to feel boxed into a corner. Whilst I don't have experience in it, I know that post natal anxiety and depression are serious issues, and I don't want this baby to be what breaks her after she has already risen from so much grief.

But abortion...I think women should have the choice. But when one of the parents desperately wants the baby, not to mention has the means to offer not just financial security but unconditional love, I don't know if I could support it.

I slide down in my chair and rest my head against the cold hard plastic, closing my eyes briefly before I hear the doctor call my name.

Finally.

We chat briefly and she offers to give me a referral to another clinic if I would like to have my sperm count rechecked for the future. I decline and leave with the referral for the blood test.

I don't need to know what changed. I don't need to know any of the specifics. All I need to know is that I'm going to be a father.

I make my way next door and take a number. It isn't busy, and I'm in and out before I know it. I rip the sticky tape from my arm the moment I walk out the glass doors. I want to head straight to Hannah's. I want to see her. To talk to her more calmly than what we did yesterday. To tell her I meant what I said. That I am in love with her. Tell her that I believe her.

I take out the little black and white picture. I have been carrying it in my pocket since yesterday.

Pulling out my phone with my other hand, I flick a text to Hannah.

> CLARK: Just finished at the docs. Should have the results in a couple of days. Whilst I appreciate you setting this up for me, I want you to know I believe you. Can I see you?

I sit in my car staring at the three little dots that pop up and then disappear. I wait ten minutes before I decide to just head home. My head is a mess. I just pray that she isn't the type of woman that would do something behind my back. It's not lost on me that she doesn't need my consent to abort. She could do it and I would be none the wiser.

I get home and move to my shed, pulling open the garage door and ripping the blanket off the car. I bought her years ago. She was the only thing I bought with me when I moved. The only thing from my old life I kept.

When Cherie and I decided to start a family, I bought her. I had visions of me and my kids fixing her up, and showing them how to build an engine. I had somewhat channelled that energy into Vin, but he had wanted to do his own car. It had been great showing him the ropes and seeing it take shape.

I always imagined I would get that with my own kids one day.

Even with the diagnosis of infertile, I held hope. I had kept this car. Paid the cost to have her put on a truck and sent over. Now she sits in my shed under a blanket collecting dust.

I decide to walk around and examine what needs to be done. She is a 1967 Shelby GT500. She isn't in awful shape but for the beauty of this car, it's a damn shame to not see her perfect. All the interior is still original, but the leather seats are ripped and worn, needing to be refurbished.

The Wimbledon white paint is faded, and small rust spots sit down by the door frames. The car had been converted from left hand drive to right hand drive when it was first imported to Australia. I have no clue when. The original 428 block won't start. The cylinder heads, intake manifold and exhaust manifold will all need to be rebuilt. I just haven't been able to bring myself to start.

I decide now is as good a time as any. I'm going to be a father. I hope!

27

Watching him, watching me
Hannah

I'm not ignoring Clark. I have packed my day so full that I don't get a chance to think about anything. Working for myself means I'm in control of my bookings. Normally I leave myself some room to breathe. Fifteen minutes between clients to properly type up their notes, go get a snack or a drink, and use the bathroom.

I spent yesterday afternoon texting clients to move them all forward, squeezing in a couple more from my waitlist with the space I created. I don't want to have time to think about this baby, about the fact that I'm already pretty much in the second trimester, or that I didn't have crippling morning sickness with this one like I did with Noah and Ethan.

I see Clark's message pop up and I quickly go to reply, but my client comes through the door into my little gym space. I chuck my phone back into the draw and give them my undivided attention.

I then forget all about the text. It isn't until I sit down in bed to watch TV later that night, grabbing my phone to check my social media and what I've missed throughout the day, that I remember.

Shit!

> HANNAH: I am so sorry. I wasn't ignoring you. Just a very busy day. I'm glad you did the test.

His reply is instant. Like he has been waiting with bated breath all day.

> CLARK: No worries. How are you feeling?

> HANNAH: Tired, anxious, terrified.

> HANNAH: I'm okay, just trying to process all my feelings. It's a lot. Sorry if you feel like I blew you off.

CLARK: No need to apologise. I understand. Hope you are in bed and not working.

HANNAH: Overbearing dad already. Yes,
am in bed. I was about to watch Bones.

Shit, I should not have said that. Yesterday I told him I didn't want this baby and today I am calling him a dad.

My head is a mess. Now the adrenaline from the day has died down, I'm left with nothing to distract me. I can feel the tears pricking at my eyes again.

CLARK: How dare you!

A smile splits my face, and I let out a sigh of relief that he isn't going to broach the subject.

HANNAH: Sorry, I am desperate to know
what happens. FaceTime me.

My phone lights up instantly with a call from him. We have been watching Bones together. It's possibly weird but it has also been the highlight of my day some days. With my kids and work, it's impossible for us to see each other all the time. I can't even remember how it started. I think we were Facetiming and the TV was on in the background. We started chatting about TV shows we liked, and next thing I knew we both settled on watching Bones together.

We call each other and literally just hold the phone. We make sure we press play at the same time but there is always an echo that has us laughing. Then we usually sit in silence watching the other watch Bones, making running commentary as we go. We have made it to season two and we are right in the thick of the plot with the gravedigger. I'm dying to know what happens, so yes, I was going to cheat and watch without him.

I answer my phone and God it is good to see him. The last memory I have of him was me leaving him clutching the small photo of our baby. Heartbreak etched into his features after what I had just confessed to him.

I snuggle down into the bed and hold my phone up.

"Episode nine. You ready?" I say.

"On three."

"One, two, three." We both hit play and the 'previously on bones' starts playing.

"Skip," I yell.

He laughs.

"One, two, three." We both hit skip and the episode starts to play.

We are silent for a while, just watching the plot unfold. It's an on the edge of your seat episode. We make comments back and forth about who we think the gravedigger is and if Booth is going to get to Bones in time.

"Obviously she can't die. There are a million seasons of this show. They are not going to kill her off in season two," I say.

"You're right but what about Hodgins? They could kill him off," Clark responds.

"No, they would never. I'm googling it."

"What, Hannah. DO NOT GOOGLE IT."

"The suspense is killing me. I just need to know."

"Just watch the show."

"Absolutely not. I'm googling it." I move the call to the top corner of my screen and bring up Google.

Clark yells down the phone, "Hannah, you listen to me. Put the phone down."

"Nope. Ohh, thank God," I gasp.

"You looked, didn't you?"

"Sorry, I couldn't help it, but now I can relax and finish the episode without this crushing anxiety."

He laughs at me but doesn't ask me to tell him. We finish the episode and start the next, following the same process.

I don't think I make it through the second episode before I fall asleep still clutching my phone in my hands, watching him watch me while we both watch TV.

I wake to the sound of my kids clanging around in the kitchen with my dead phone still gripped in my hand.

28

A second great love story
Hannah

The next day follows the same suit. I cram in as many clients as I can, and by the time we all walk back in the door at six-thirty, I'm absolutely shattered. I grabbed take away for all of us on the way home because I didn't have the energy or mental capacity to make dinner.

Clark and I text back and forth, avoiding the elephant in the room. Or rather the baby in my belly.

I am itching to talk to Kate. I need my family right now, more than anything.

Once the kids' bags are unpacked, lunch boxes are washed, a load of washing is on, and the kids are happy and relaxing, I shoot Kate a text.

> HANNAH: Can you pop round for a bit? I need a chat.

I don't elaborate.

KATE: Absolutely. I'll bring wine. Be there
in ten.

Again, I don't bother to tell her that I can't have the wine. She will know soon enough.

Kate only lives a ten-minute drive away. My kids are fourteen, twelve and nine, so I feel okay leaving them at home for a couple hours on the weekend while I do shopping or run errands. I don't feel as comfortable at night leaving them. I also know that the second I leave, Liam will just jump straight on his Xbox, and I have already called time on that for the evening. Otherwise, he will sit up till midnight playing. Kate's kids are young adults, so she can come to me tonight.

Kate knocks on the door dead on twelve minutes later with a bottle of wine in one hand. She is wearing a giant woollen poncho and big fluffy Uggs.

"Come in." I move to the side to let her through the doors.

"I'll pour, you talk."

"I can't have that," I say, motioning to the bottle she is holding up like a prize.

Her jaw drops and her eyes go wide. "Ohhhh shit!" she mouths softly so the boys sitting in the lounge room don't hear. "Guess it isn't perimenopause."

I just shake my head and lead her through the house. "Boys, we are in my gym. Unless someone is on fire, do not disturb us," I say as we walk past.

"What if someone breaks in?" Liam counters, being a total smart ass.

"Are you on fire?" I quip.

"What if the house is on fire, but it's just a little fire? Like I try to make toast and the toaster catches alight," Liam adds.

"Again, are *you* on fire?" I articulate each word slowly.

"What if Liam gets on his Xbox?" Noah chips in now.

"OMG, boys, just leave us alone for a few minutes. OKAY."

I hear a choir of "yes, mum" as they start laughing. Little shits. They knew exactly what they were doing.

Kate and I head out to my little studio gym out the back, and I unlock the door.

"Spill," Kate says as we sit on the chairs I have for clients.

"He said he was infertile. Low sperm count. When shit hit the fan with his ex, he never did more testing. I guess it changed. His lifestyle is so different now. He eats better and is way less stressed. He had multiple businesses back in Sydney. He is exercising and doesn't drink. All those factors apparently can increase sperm count."

I have told Kate pretty much everything about Clark. She has been the person I would call after each time I saw him. She knows all about what we talk about and our sex life. At this stage, she pretty much knows Clark as well as I do. I don't need to elaborate. She is already covered.

"How far along?"

"Twelve weeks."

"Shit. Have you told him?"

"Yeah, it was the first thing I did."

"How did he take it?"

"I ruined the moment by telling him that I don't want the baby."

Her face softens and she reaches a hand out to me, placing it on my knee. I wipe a tear from my cheek that has escaped.

"He wants kids so badly. He offered to take sole custody if I don't want the baby. Basically begged me to keep it. Said he would buy the house next door or live in a tent out the back so he can be here for me and the baby."

All she says is, "Wow." I think she is still processing everything I am saying.

"He told me he loves me."

Now her face falls even more, eyes bulging in shock.

"What did you say?" she asks.

"I said nothing. Said that I needed space."

"Shit, Hannah. Do you love him?"

It's a question I have been asking myself since the words left his lips. I run my fingers through my hair, letting out a small breath as they automatically find their way to my ring. I twist my finger around the chain, tears pooling in my eyes again.

I ignore the question altogether.

"I can't have another baby, Kate. I am forty years old for fuck's sake. I have three kids already. Do you know the risks of pregnancy and labour complications increases drastically after forty. Higher risk of down syndrome. Other chromosomal abnormalities, gestational diabetes, preeclampsia, and even a higher risk of stillbirth. Not to mention the impact on my body. Hormones and pelvic floor muscles. They will never be the same again at this age after four children."

Kate's grip on my knee tightens in a gentle squeeze. "All valid points, Hannah." I can see she wants to say more but holds back.

"I can't have a baby with another man. What will I tell the kids? What will this mean for the memory of their dad? I don't want them to feel like I just forgot about him and moved on. Wiped the slate clean and started again. What? I just replace all the photos of our family with this new one. With Callum not in them. How—How—How can I do that? If I have this baby, I feel like I am letting those three amazing boys in there down. I feel like I'm erasing their dad. My husband. My partner for seventeen years, Kate. Seventeen years."

The tears involuntarily fall, and I can't slow them. I'm sniffling and snorting like a wild boar, but I can't stop. The truth of how I really feel is too much to admit. Because I do love Clark. I think I have known it all along. I know that I can have this baby. I know that all the particulars don't matter. We would figure it out.

But how do I let myself truly fall?

How do I move forward if it means forgetting my past? Forgetting my first love. The father of my children. And how do I ever explain this to my kids when I don't even understand how it would work myself?

Kate pulls me close, hugging me, and I fall apart even more. "You do love him, don't you?"

I nod into her shoulder, sobbing. She holds me by the shoulders and pushes me back so she can look into my eyes.

"Hannah." Her voice is stern but not harsh. "You are allowed to move on! And moving on doesn't mean forgetting. You can honour the memory and life that you had with Callum and the man that he was while still allowing yourself happiness. You keep saying forty like it is the end of your lifespan. You're only halfway there."

I sniff, trying to dry my eyes and stop the tears.

"You have a chance to have a second great love story. Some people never even get the first. Two amazing men. Men that love you and want to be with you. Don't run away from that. The kids...they are resilient. They might love having another male role model in their lives. It doesn't mean that they forget all about their dad. It just means they get a second chance as well."

"You think Clark is going to be okay with us sharing memories? The boys talking about their dad and having old family photos around us."

"If he loves you, then yeah. He needs to love all of you, and that means honouring your past. Loving him doesn't make what you and Callum had any less real or strong. It doesn't take any of that away. And holding those memories of Callum doesn't take away your love in the present for Clark. They can coexist, side by side. One does not have to cancel out the other."

"Do you really believe that? Do you really believe the kids are going to be okay welcoming another man into their lives? A half sibling?"

"You and Callum raised some pretty amazing kids in there. And credit to you for the last three years. Those boys are strong and smart and loving, and I think you need to give them more credit."

I nod again, feeling the tears start to slow. I sniffle back the last of them. This is why I love Kate. She is sarcastic and witty, but when I need her, she pulls all this shit out of nowhere and somehow brings me down to earth.

"Are the boys still seeing the psychologist you saw after Callum?" she asks.

After Callum passed, we all saw one as a family and then individually. The boys were against it at first, feeling embarrassed to talk to someone they don't know about such personal things. But some long serious conversations about the importance of getting help and removing the stigma of talking to someone helped. They got a lot out of it and so did I, especially in learning how best to help them through everything.

"No. We haven't for a while. Maybe I need to book in and get some advice on the best way to tell them about this."

"You're their mum, Hannah. You know what they need. It will all be okay," Kate reassures.

"You think so?"

"You have me and Ben. Sierra and Axel. You have support. Mum and Dad. We're all here for you. You got this. Like you always do."

I let myself smile for the first time since finding out the news, allowing the warm feeling of love and excitement that I had been suppressing rise. I try to look past the guilt and fear and let the realisation that I do love Clark settle around me. While a baby wasn't in my plan for this stage of life, I know that I will be okay. We will all be okay.

Now I just need to find the courage to say the words out loud. I need to tell him.

Then another stark realisation hits me. Callum's family. I need to tell them. They all live close by. They have been a constant in my life from the moment Callum and I got together. His parents still see the kids weekly and I chat to them all the time. I'm close with his sister and her family.

How am I going to tell them? It all feels like too much.

I'm not ready yet. The thought of everything overwhelms me and I feel myself shutting down.

I need to accept the fact that I'm having a baby. No matter how much my mind is conflicted, I can't abort this child. Not at this stage and not with the circumstances.

I need to tell Clark that I'm keeping the baby.

I need to tell him that I feel more for him than I have been able to let myself believe.

Then I need to tell my kids. It's not going to be long before I start to show, and I hate the idea of keeping things from them.

29

Wrecking ball realisations

Clark

I made a list of parts that I will need and then started to make a plan for the car. It's been keeping my mind busy while I wait for the test results and for Hannah to think things over. I can't bear to think about the fact that she could decide to not keep our baby.

Although, why would she bother to make me this appointment?

Why would she care if I believed her or not if she was never planning on keeping them?

My phone vibrates on the roof of the car, and my greasy hands fumble it as I rush to answer the call. "Hi, hi, it's Clark."

"Hi Clark, this is Doctor Ellis. How are you?"

I don't care about pleasantries. Lead with the news, damn it.

I cut straight to the chase. "I'm good, thank you. Have you got the results?"

"Yes. Would you like to know over the phone or would you like to come and collect the report from—"

"No. Now please." I don't mean to sound rude, but I'm dying. Deep down I know that I am the father. I don't know why I need to hear her say the words, but I do.

She lets out a closed lip laugh. "You're a match."

"I'm going to need you to say the words, Doc. Layman's terms."

"Ninety-nine-point-nine percent you are the biological father of this baby."

All the breath leaves my body, and I feel like I'm floating. The biggest smile splits my face, and my shoulders finally relax. I didn't realise I was holding so much tension and anxiety.

I close my eyes and let the feeling wash over me. I'm going to be a father.

"Thank you," I say.

"Would you like me to email you the report?" she asks.

I don't need it. "Yeah sure, great. Thank you."

I hang up and go to call Hannah straight away, but my euphoric feeling dissipates, like a hand waving through smoke at the reality that she has known it was mine all along. And she still didn't want this baby. She might not have changed her mind on that. Then what? Just because the results prove it, because I heard the words or have the report in my hand, it might not change how she feels.

Her actions and words are so at odds. She explained all the reasons she doesn't want this baby. But she handed me that picture and made me the appointment. Why would she want to know for sure? Why would she want me to see our child only to take it away from me? That isn't the Hannah I know.

I think deep down, she does want this baby. She does want me. But she is just scared. She doesn't want to lose Callum in the process.

I lean back on the hood of the car and take a few deep breaths. Then like a wrecking ball, I am hit with another realisation.

Jesus holy fuck!

I'm not infertile. A giant *WHAT IF* slides into my brain. Something I had not even considered.

What if Cherie's baby is mine!

What if that is my baby?

What if I have another child out there? A child I just abandoned.

Shit!

When everything went down with Cherie, I didn't bother with further testing. She cheated. I was told I couldn't have kids. I left. Simple.

Baby must have been the other dudes. Right?

RIGHT!

Only now, apparently, I can have kids. Hannah said it's a change in lifestyle, but what if they got it wrong. What if I could have them all along? I run my hands through my hair, grabbing at it and tugging the short length at the top.

I no longer have Cherie's number saved, but I do remember it. I haven't spoken to her in eighteen months. I have no clue if she is still with the guy. Cory was his name. A guy she met on a girl's night out that turned into the worst and best thing that ever happened to me.

Hannah is the best thing that has ever happened to me. And she is about to make me a father. But first, I need to know if I have another child out there.

I open my messages and type her number in. It takes me half an hour before I actually hit send.

CLARK: Hi Cherie, wondering if I could call you to discuss something. Clark

It feels like I have drunk acid while waiting for a reply. It burns my throat and stomach. I haven't really thought this completely through. How am I going to broach the subject with Cherie?

I keep my mind busy by jumping on Google and searching how to get a paternity test. A heap of at home tests come up. I choose one company and order three of them. I have no clue why but at least I'll have backups. All I have to do is a cheek swab of myself and the child, and send them back to the lap. They send you a report within two days with ninety-nine-point-nine-nine-nine-nine percent accuracy, apparently. Sounds easy to me. Now I just have to get Cherie to agree.

My message was dumb. I should have just laid everything out for her. No, that would have scared her off. If I can talk to her in person, I can reason with her.

Maybe.

I try to go back to working on my car, but I can't help but check my phone every three seconds.

I want to call Hannah. I want to celebrate. To tell her I never doubted her. I want to hug her and rub her belly even though I can't feel or see much there yet. I want to take her shopping for all the things. Most of all, I want to hear her say that she wants this. That she wants us.

I'm scared she won't. I'm scared to death that she doesn't.

I don't know how she is going to react to me reaching out to Cherie, but I'm not going to lie to her about it.

My phone pings, and I trip over my dolly, almost face planting the hard concrete.

CHERIE: Now you want to talk. GO AWAY,
Clark!

Frustrating but expected, considering how we left things. I want to reply, *You're the one that cheated on me spawn of Satan,* but I refrain.

> CLARK: I understand I left pretty abruptly, but I was hurt. I have something I really need to discuss.

Jesus, I sound so formal. Am I applying for a job here? I contemplate just laying it all out in a message again, but I also don't want to tell her about Hannah or the pregnancy.

It's not just my news to share, and Hannah and I haven't discussed it yet. Hell, I still don't even know if Hannah is keeping the baby. I shake that thought from my head. She has to keep the baby.

> CHERIE: You had your chance to speak to me. I tried to explain. You just left. So, NO Clark, you don't get to discuss anything now just cos you decide you are ready.

Ahhh, why is she being so stubborn? She hurt me. She ended the relationship when she gave her number to another man. She drove a knife through it when she replied to that number and started a conversation. And she put the nail in the coffin of the relationship the first time she slept with him.

Did I leave? Yes.

Abruptly? Also yes.

I walked away without letting her explain. There was nothing she could say that would have changed my mind. Nothing she could have done to make me stay. In my mind, she was pregnant with another man's baby.

But would I have stayed if I had known the baby was mine?

No, probably not. I would have been there for the baby, but I would have never forgiven her. Especially that it went on for six months. It wasn't just a drunken mistake. Although I'm not sure I would have forgiven that either.

Hoping I have piqued her interest enough to get her to call me, I hold my phone, staring a hole through it. It feels hot and heavy in my hand. It's almost vibrating.

It pings.

CHERIE: It's easy to blame me for everything. You were working all the time. I never saw you. When you were home, you were exhausted and grumpy. We were supposed to be trying to start a family. I was depressed and lonely. What was I supposed to do?

CLARK: I was stressed and depressed as well, Cherie. But you were supposed to talk to me, not start an affair.

I type the message out but then hit the backspace button. This will just go round in circles. This is why I didn't bother to talk when we ended. I blocked her number and refused to see her.

Maybe I am to blame. Maybe I should have been home more. Been there for her more emotionally. Maybe I worked too much. Was too stressed. Neither of us made positive changes. We never were good at speaking about things like that. She sure as hell didn't mind spending the money all that working made us though.

Nothing will excuse having an affair instead of talking to me. We were both dealing with infertility in our own way. A year of trying with no luck and the reality hitting that we might not get this dream. I used work as an escape to keep my mind busy, and she used another man's dick as her escape.

It's not the same thing. But maybe it is in her eyes.

No matter how it ended, it ended.

Going around in circles over who did who wrong isn't going to change the outcome now. I don't want to look at Cherie and her baby as a roadblock in my way to happiness. She deserves her own happy ending, regardless of how much she hurt me. But I don't feel like I can move forward with Hannah and this baby without knowing with one hundred percent certainty that it isn't my child.

I decide to take the moral high ground.

CLARK: I'm sorry for the way I left. I'm sorry for the way things ended between us.

She doesn't reply, and I decide I'm just going to have to lay it all out. I try to call her, but it just rings out. I try again. Straight to voicemail.

I'm going to have to just explain and hope she understands. I think I know deep down she isn't going to. But I have to try.

I make the executive decision that I'm not going to tell her about Hannah and the baby. I start typing possibly the longest text I have ever written.

CLARK: Cherie, I would have liked to explain this over the phone, but I feel like I will just tell you and hopefully you can understand. I have recently found out I am not infertile. It left me with a lot to think about and the realisation that your baby may be mine. I know I left abruptly and didn't give you a chance to talk to me, so I understand your reluctance now. But I couldn't live with myself if I had a child and I wasn't there for them as a father.

Despite how we ended, I know that you know how much I wanted to be a dad. I just want the chance to check. I don't know if you are still with Cory or how old the baby is now, but I would like the opportunity to do a paternity test to find out for certain. I have bought a few tests online and it's a simple swab test. I can post them to you if you would be willing to check.

I know this is out of the blue and probably not ideal if you are happy and have a family now, but I hope you can understand.

She doesn't reply.
She doesn't answer my calls.

30

Crab croquettes be damned

Hannah

I get a text from Clark. I was expecting it. I know he went for the blood test and he should get the results any day.

> CLARK: Hey, got the results back. Do you want to go for lunch?

I don't need to check my schedule. I know I'm free from twelve-thirty. The last few days I had moved people around and crammed people in to keep busy. Today is meant to be my admin day but I had filled it with clients in the morning and left the afternoon free to try to get my brain to focus on some of the business side of things.

Lunch can't hurt. I can catch up later tonight or over the weekend. I'm dying to talk to Clark. I have been giving him his space to get the results before I tell him any of my revelations about keeping our baby.

HANNAH: I can meet you at one?

CLARK: Sounds good. I'll book Sparrows.

HANNAH: Ohhh yes. I love that place.

CLARK: I know.

I don't bother asking about the results. I know what they would have said. Now that he knows there is no doubt, it feels like a tiny weight lifted. When I say tiny, I do mean tiny. My shoulders still feel weighed down with the fact that I have to tell my children about Clark. I have to tell the rest of my family, my friends and Callum's family that I am about to have another baby to a man most of them don't even know.

All of that is for another day, though.

Today I just want to enjoy telling Clark that he is going to be a father. I want him to get that moment. The moment that he had ripped from him the first time around and the moment I took from him the second.

It's lame but I bought a little tiny onesie. Gosh, I forgot how adorable they are. I took it to a friend who does screen printing, and she put a 'You're going to be a dad' print on it. I wanted to give it to him as a bit of a do-over.

I walk into the little alfresco dining area at 12:58 PM. Clark is already there. He stands when he sees me, giving me a hug and kiss on the forehead as I enter. The moment lingers, his hand cupping the back of my head as he soaks me in, like I have been a missing piece from his body for the last few days.

"How are you?" he asks as he pulls my chair out and shuffles me back in. He sits in the chair to the side of me rather than then opposite.

This is one of my favourite restaurants in town. It has adorable white bench seats with umbrellas outside in a makeshift alfresco area, with astroturf under our feet and plants all along the edges. A one-way road sits in front of it, and beyond that there are clear views of the estuary, where on any given day you will see dolphins jumping out of the crystal water. Their food is to die for—always unique things that you would never think pair but somehow complement each other perfectly. The crab croquettes are my go-to. Although I love that Clark always orders way too many options and we share them all.

"I'm good. You?"

He clears his throat, his face dropping slightly, only for the briefest of moments and then he recomposes himself. His smile is back in place, only it isn't as bright as it normally is.

"Are you okay?" My fingers itch to grab the little crepe paper wrapped gift in my bag and hand it to him. I thought it was a cute way to apologise for my mental breakdown the other day.

I think I always knew I was going to keep this baby. I just...didn't know how to come to terms with it all. Still don't if I am honest. Is it what I would have wanted? Not really, but it's happening. I feel terrible that I took away his moment to find out happily.

"Yeah, I'm okay." His words are genuine but the emotion on his face doesn't match. He is avoiding eye contact, breathing a little heavier, and his hands rub up and down his thighs under the table.

"Clark, what's going on?" I ask, placing a hand over his to stop it from rubbing a hole through his pants.

"I had a thought...after I got the results."

"Okay, what is it?"

"Cherie."

My mouth goes dry. We have never shied away from talking about our past partners. All my adult memories have Callum in them. It's hard to have a conversation without him being in my thoughts.

It never bothered me when Clark spoke about Cherie. He obviously never really talked about what had happened to him and what he went through. I was happy to be that ear for him when he did open up about their relationship, but something about the way he just said her name tells me this is different.

He finally makes eye contact with me, and I give his hand a gentle squeeze to tell him it's okay to continue.

"After I got the results, it dawned on me that I'm not infertile like I thought. And I don't know if it changed. Like you said, my lifestyle is so different now. But..." He turns his hand over and clasps his fingers through mine, holding them tight, like he is afraid if he lets go I will run. "What if that baby was mine." He says the words so fast that I recoil.

I definitely wasn't expecting that.

"You think the baby Cherie had could be yours?" I reiterate.

"I don't know. But there is a chance. I never hung around long enough to ask or see. I don't even know if it's a boy or girl. How old they are now. I—I—"

I suck in a deep breath. If my mouth felt dry before, well now it is filled with dust. I loosen my grip slightly in his hand, but he doesn't let me go.

His eyes flick down to where they are joined. "I sent her a text."

"You what?" I am not a jealous person. Well, I didn't think I was. But the thought that he is texting his ex—the ex that broke his heart—after telling me that he loves me and finding out we are having a baby together, promising me the world... Now what! He is going to go back to her.

My mind is getting away from me. The dust turns to acid. It burns my throat and makes the pit of my stomach feel like it is on fire.

I pull my hand from his and place it in my lap. He reluctantly lets me go. Rubbing his hands over his face, he lets out an audible exhale before his beautiful glassy eyes fall to mine.

"Hannah, it's not what you think. I don't want Cherie. We're done, no matter what. This is purely about the child. If I have another baby out there, one that I just abandoned, it's not fair on them. It's not fair for them to grow up not knowing who their real dad is. This will haunt me forever if I don't find out the truth. I only texted Cherie to ask her if I could send her a paternity test. It's a simple swab of the cheek and we send it back to the lab. Results come in a couple of days."

"And they are accurate?" I decide to swallow my jealousy and anger at this situation. It's most likely the hormones anyway. Okay, maybe it isn't the hormones. They get blamed for everything. I have a right to be pissed off. He begged and pleaded his case and now what? He is suddenly concerned about the possibility of another child.

"Yeah, apparently. Same as the blood test."

He gives me time to process.

I clench my fists together in my lap under the table, trying to hide them from his gaze. "Did she agree?"

"Nope. She basically told me that I had my chance to talk to her and then she didn't reply."

"What are you going to do?"

He clears his throat, averting his gaze, "I'm going to go see her in person. Take the kit myself and try to convince her." His voice is low, mumbled, like his confidence is wavering telling me this. Afraid of how I will react.

I'm not proud of how I handle this entire situation. I was just about to tell him I want this baby. That I love him too.

I stare down at my bag like I have X-ray vision and can see the little turquoise wrapped gift in there. I should give it to him. I know that he is just trying to do the right thing by this child. In one way, he is right. If he is the father, it is not fair for them to grow up not knowing.

But what if he is?

What then?

Everything he said to me means nothing. Will he move back to Sydney? Who will he choose? How will he choose? He can't be in two places at once.

Crab croquettes be damned.

I get up and leave without another word. I don't bother to look back.

Maybe I'm being childish. Maybe I'm acting irrationally. But I can't stop this feeling. A hot poker straight through the gut. I make it to my car, my hands so shaky that I fumble the keys, dropping them on the bitumen. Flustered, I spin around, bending to grab them, but I lock eyes with him instead.

I hadn't realised he was following me; if he had called my name, I didn't hear it. The thoughts in my head are so loud that I hadn't even heard his footsteps behind me. He passes me the keys, and I don't miss how his own hands shake, too.

"Please don't leave like this, Hannah," he pleads, his hand lingering on mine as we both hold the keys.

"Clark, I just need space to process all of this, okay?"

He nods, letting his hand drop to his side, but he leans in and kisses my forehead, whispering, "I love you," before I turn and get into my car. The full emotions unleash as I drive away from him.

I say screw it to my admin and crawl into bed and cry some more. My crying is only broken by the fact that I have to suck it up and go and fetch my kids from school. Put on a smile and be their mum for the rest of the day.

I go about the motions on auto pilot: cook dinner, eat dinner, clean up, bring in the washing, fold and pack the washing, unpack the school bags, clean the lunch boxes, put a new load of washing on, put the dishwasher on, and help the kids with homework.

I crawl into bed at 9:30 PM and the dam breaks again. I have a missed call and a message from Clark.

CLARK: Hannah, I am so sorry. I really didn't want to drop that on you like that, but I had to be honest. I understand you're upset, but it doesn't change how I feel about you.

I love you.

I love our baby.

I want you.

I want our baby.

Please do not make any decisions about our baby until I get home.

I just don't feel like my conscience can rest unless I find out the truth. For the child's sake.

I've booked flights for Sunday. I haven't booked a return, but I am hoping it will be straight away. I hope you understand.

I love you!

Asshole! I throw my phone across the room, then immediately get up and go and get it, checking to make sure it isn't damaged.

I take a few deep breaths and try to calm my irrational pregnancy brain. But no, I am still pissed. I don't know what I expect him to do. I mean, logically I can understand why he needs to know. I can understand his train of thought and the guilt that would stay with him. But I would be lying if I said it doesn't hurt. It feels like he is choosing them already and leaving me to deal with the emotions and stress of this myself.

This is exactly what I was afraid of. He has the freedom to just pack up and leave. To just take off to fulfil his own needs. Settle his own mind and quell his own guilt.

While I...I'm left to deal with everything alone. To face telling everyone alone. To attend appointments alone. To make decisions alone.

I am being dramatic. I know. He will be back. He says he loves me, but what if Cherie's baby is his? How will that change his feelings? Will I be left a widowed, abandoned, single mum of four kids?

The pressure feels like too much. My eyes are heavy and my body is sore. I'm so mad at him. Mad that he didn't think to ask me before he went. That he just made this decision and then booked a flight.

What was I expecting? We aren't dating. We aren't a couple. He doesn't know that I decided to keep the baby. He doesn't know that I feel more for him than I have let on.

The pain and emotion of this feels all too much, and I push my face further into the pillow, letting the tears flow.

Sleep finally comes for me.

I wake with a puffy face and stinging eyes, but I don't have time to worry about any of that. It's time to pull it all together and face another day.

<h1 style="text-align:center">31</h1>

<h1 style="text-align:center">Exactly as expected</h1>

Clark

I've fucked this up. The regret is palpable. I'm sure the people on the plane around me can feel it. I lean my head back on the chair and run my hands over my face.

What am I doing? I have the chance to have a family with an amazing woman. A woman I am madly in love with and a baby that I know is mine. Instead of being there for her like I promised, I've jumped on a plane and am heading across the country to another woman's door. A woman who betrayed and hurt me in the worst possible way. With a baby that most likely isn't mine.

I don't know what makes me think Cherie is going to change her mind on the test just because I rock up at her doorstep with it in hand. But at least then I can say that I tried. I did everything I could have done. Everything I should have done the first time around, when I was too filled with grief and anger that I thought I would combust.

Chances are this child isn't mine and my situation changed due to lifestyle, but I can't live with myself if I didn't find out. If I didn't get to close this chapter. I haven't thought about what I'm going to do if the baby is mine. She lives in a different state. I don't want to be with Cherie, and I have no clue if she is still with Cory or not. I feel nothing for her. But the elated feeling of becoming a father has been overshadowed with the thought that I may already have a child and I just abandoned them.

Maybe I could have handled things better with Hannah, talked it through with her more, instead of dumping it on her and then taking off. I felt like ripping the band-aid off was the best way. The sooner I can put this to bed, the sooner I can move forward. None of this changes the way I feel for Hannah. It's just been under a rain cloud, and I need to clear it up so I can move forward. I don't want to be dealing with this when I have a new baby in my arms and a postnatal wi—

Did I just think that?

Hannah isn't my wife. She has made it abundantly clear she doesn't want to remarry. Hell, I never saw that in my future either. But I'm sure Hannah never saw another baby.

Will this change things?

I can't help but smile at the thought of her being my wife.

I'm getting ahead of myself. She is probably pissed at me right now. She walked out on lunch with little more than a goodbye. I followed. I tried to talk to her, but I'm not twenty something with anger and control issues. When she told me she just wanted some time to process, I respected that. I kissed her on the forehead, told her I loved her, and sent her a text reiterating how I felt.

I waited for the tests I express ordered to arrive, then I jumped on a plane so I can hand deliver it to Cherie and know in good faith that I did everything in my power to find out the truth. If Cherie doesn't agree to test after that, then at least my conscience can rest.

I hope.

Hannah replied that she understands my feelings but doesn't agree. She asked what I'm going to do if the baby is mine, and I didn't have a solid answer for her because I really haven't thought that far ahead.

The plane lands and I call a cab, giving the driver our old address that I have absolutely no idea if Cherie even still lives at. She got the house in the divorce. I didn't care to fight about anything at that time. I was so beaten down that I would have agreed to give her all of it. I just wanted to be as far away from her and the baby I didn't believe I had a chance of having.

What she got in the house, I got in cash from the business sale. What I got with the vintage car, she got in other assets. And so on. It wasn't a nasty or bitter feud. It was fast and sad. I avoided talking to her and had all correspondence go through the lawyer. I didn't show up for any of the meetings. I'm sure Cherie sent messages and tried to call me. I deleted and blocked her number, her emails and her social media. I stayed at a hotel until I took off west.

She never even knew where or when I went.

In hindsight, I probably could have handled that better. I didn't care to hang around and watch her get everything we ever wanted. Watch her belly grow knowing that it was our dream and she betrayed me. Regardless of how I can see the cracks in the relationship clearly now, back then, I thought it was all I ever needed or wanted.

We turn down our street, and I decide to shoot a text to Hannah. I don't know why I feel like I should keep her up to date. Honestly, I miss her like crazy. We may not get to see each other all the time but there hasn't been a day over the last four months where we haven't spoken.

We usually text back and forth all day and spend the nights watching TV on FaceTime together. She calls me on her lunch breaks or between clients just to say, "Hi." I'm craving the sound of her voice right now.

CLARK: I just landed and am headed to our old house. No clue if she still lives there. I'm sorry for the way I left. I feel like I can't give you and our baby all of me with this hanging over my head.

I don't get a reply by the time we pull up to the house. So, I shove my phone back into my pocket and get ready to do this.

I can tell Cherie still lives here when I see our old car in the driveway. My body tenses and I'm instantly hit with the pain I felt when I left. All of it washes back over me, leaving me standing on the driveway like a stunned mullet.

Gripping the handle on my duffel bag so tight that my knuckles turn white, I force my legs to move. My hand lingers over the doorbell for far too long before I force myself to press it. An orchestra of sounds play off in the distance and then I hear footsteps. My heart beats in the same rhythm as the person walking, heavy and loud in my chest. The door swings open, and Cherie is standing there with a baby on her hip.

It's a girl.

She has chubby rosy cheeks, and the small amount of hair she has is pulled up into a little pink bow on her head to keep it from her eyes. She looks just like Cherie. The same deep blue eyes and button nose. I don't see any of myself in her and that gives me a sigh of relief.

My eyes move to Cherie and the relief drains. Her face is not cute and chubby.

No.

It's stern and pissed. Her lips are pursed tightly, and her eyes narrow on me.

"Hi," I manage to get out.

"What the hell are you doing here?"

"You wouldn't answer my calls or reply to my texts."

"Oh, how does that feel, I wonder?" she quips sarcastically.

"Could you blame me?" The words leave before I think, and I mentally berate myself. I didn't come here to fall back into old patterns of arguing back and forth.

It was always like this with Cherie. Fights would drag on for days because neither of us would back down, fuelled on by the others' anger, creating a back and forth with smart-ass comments and insults.

I didn't come here to do that. I didn't even realise we used to do that. Not until I was out of it. It had become so normal for us.

The communication feels so different with Hannah, and I'm mad at myself that I fell back into old patterns with booking this flight instead of talking it over with her first.

"I'm sorry. I didn't come here to argue. I understand you're pissed at me for the way I left. I was heartbroken. I've had the time to reflect, and I can't move on with my life without knowing the truth."

Her eyes narrow even further, and I swear I see one side of her lip curl up. She's angry. "Would it matter now? What would it change?" she asks.

"It could change everything. Don't you want to know? Without doubt. What if Cory thinks he's the father and he isn't? Don't you want her"—I nod towards the little girl, who is twirling Cherie's hair around her chubby little fingers, cooing happily—"to know who her real father is?"

She laughs. "Cory is the father, you said it yourself. You are infertile. The tests showed it."

I swallow hard. I don't want to tell Cherie about Hannah and our baby. I just don't think it's going to help the situation. Maybe I am being selfish. But I want to protect that part of my life and keep it as far away from this as possible.

What will happen if this baby is mine? They are going to have to blend.

I shake the thought from my head. One problem at a time.

This is as much about this little girl in Cherie's arms as it is about me. She deserves to know the truth. What if she grows up thinking that one man is her father only to find out later in life it is another? That doesn't feel right.

I motion towards the little girl in her arms. "What's her name?"

Cherie rolls her eyes at me. "Claire."

"You always loved that name. After your great grandma?"

Her face softens, possibly with the same memories I'm having. Us talking about having kids and planning for the future. What names we like and why.

Our relationship wasn't all bad. There were ups and down like most, but I can see it more clearly now. We weren't right for each other. Planning kids was a band-aid on a bullet hole. I have no doubt the dam would have broken at some point. It was just a matter of when.

Or maybe Cherie is thinking about Claire. About Cory. About their happy little family.

"How old is she?"

Cherie moves Claire to her other hip. "She is nine months old."

"She's gorgeous. Congratulations." The words taste bitter on my lips. In one sense, I'm happy that Cherie got everything she wanted. In another, I'm pissed it was at my expense. She did the dirty, yet she walked away with the family I wanted. I walked away empty and broken.

I try not to dwell on the past. My life has been feeling a lot closer to whole these days.

"So, you and Cory." I don't finish that sentence. I think she knows where I am heading with it. She nods her head. I try not to be pissed that he has most likely moved into the house that Cherie and I bought together. The house we planned on raising kids in. Now she is raising them with the man she cheated on me with.

I can see past Cherie to the entry hall and spot male hats and a jacket on the hooks.

"I'm not doing the test, Clark. Cory is Claire's dad. She loves him and I love him, and I'm not going to bring this up with him because suddenly eighteen months later you had a thought."

"You seem to have missed the plot twist where you were the one that cheated on me, Cherie. All the while you were lying to my face about starting a family. We had been trying for a year. A whole year of talking about our future with kids while you were sleeping with someone else for half of it. We were about to start IVF. What would you have done if I wasn't told I was infertile? Would you have ever owned up and told me about him? Would you have stayed with me and lied for the rest of our lives? Would you have chosen me? Now you say you love Cory. Did you love him back then?" The anger is radiating off me, and I try to compose myself to not scare Claire or have Cherie shut down completely.

She looks at me with just as much anger in her eyes. Claire is starting to fuss, wanting to be put down. Cherie walks out onto the little porch then down onto the front lawn. I follow behind her. She places Claire down on the soft grass and she straight away crawls to a ball, trying to grab it but fumbling with the slippery surface. She crawls to follow after it again, all the while giggling to herself.

Cherie walks close behind her, making sure the ball doesn't roll too far away or off onto the road. "I might have cheated, Clark, but it was you that checked out. I was so desperate to become a mother. We were trying for what felt like forever and each and every month without the positive result you pulled further away. Worked a little later, started a little earlier. Closed yourself in your office. I was so heartbroken and lonely and I needed you.

I never went out with an intention to cheat. I got way too drunk on a girl's night trying to forget the fact that we had just had another negative result. I don't even remember giving him my number, but when he texted me, I replied. He listened to me when you didn't. He was there when you weren't. I didn't love him. Not at first. It was just a way to feel something. I don't know why I agreed to meet him in person. At first it was just someone to talk to. To feel seen and heard. But the loneliness won and I slept with him. We only slept together once. The guilt killed me. It was a mistake, and I told him that. Then I found out I was pregnant. I didn't think there was any chance it could be his. We used protection. But then you told me about your result and my heart sank."

I have never heard her full version of events before. She told me she had cheated and I asked her how long, she said she had been talking to him for six months. That was all I needed to hear. The revelation mixed with the fact that she was pregnant made me sure it couldn't be mine.

I left.

Maybe I should have listened. Would it have changed my mind? Would the outcome have been different?

Probably not.

The bottom line is she still cheated. She betrayed my trust, and I don't think I would have ever been able to forgive her. And the baby wasn't mine. I was so sure of it.

Only now I'm not so sure.

"I was also hurt. I wanted to be a dad more than anything. I had told you that from the moment we got together. You weren't ready to start a family and we waited. We waited till you were ready and we left it too late. That's how it was in my head. I needed to deal with that in my own way, which was to work. To keep busy. I also needed to pay for the IVF, Cherie. That wasn't going to be cheap. I was trying to do what was in the best interest for us, as well as deal with my own sadness of us not falling pregnant."

"So you blamed me. I was barely twenty-one when we met, Clark. I wasn't ready for kids. You said you were okay with waiting," she huffs.

"And I was, until I realised that we may have missed our chance."

"Well, it was never me. It was you," she quips, and the dig stings.

"I know that now. But at the time, I dealt with it the only way I knew how. And that was to throw myself into work." This conversation is going nowhere good. I calm myself and add, "I'm sorry that I pulled away. I should have been there for you."

Her face softens. "I'm sorry I cheated, and I'm sorry I hurt you."

I nod my head in acceptance. "It's in the past now. I was angry at you for a really long time. It's only been recently that that's changed."

"You've met someone?"

I lock eyes with her. She doesn't seem upset or annoyed at the assumption. I wonder if it would be so bad to tell her the truth. I'm not sure I'm ready for that, so I scoff and change the subject.

"So, when did it change? You say Cory meant nothing but here you are. He clearly lives here."

Annoyance flashes back over her features but it is gone the moment Claire grips a hold of my jeans and pulls herself to her feet, using me as a walking stick.

My heart thuds in my chest.

This!

This is what I always wanted. I stare down at the little girl, her tiny fists wrapped in my jeans.

I'm brought back to the moment by Cherie answering my question.

"I don't really know. After you left, I told Cory I was pregnant. Told him about your test and that it had to be his. He never

asked me to confirm it. He was excited to be a dad and we—"
She pauses. I can see it on her face. She is afraid to hurt me.

"It's fine. Tell me."

"We bonded over it and we...we just fell in love, I guess. I'm sorry. I know this is what you always wanted. I'm sorry you don't get to have that. And I'm sorry I hurt you. But I wouldn't take it back. This was how it was always meant to be. I know that might not make sense to you right now but you and I...we just...we weren't right together."

I mean she isn't wrong. I can see it now, too. It pisses me off all the same that now she feels sorry for me. Where was that sympathy when she was texting another man for months on end? Where was that sympathy when she fucked him? Then what? Came home and still slept with me. Told me she loved me while we tried for a baby ourselves.

I grit my teeth to not let the anger overflow again.

Claire has let go of my jeans and plopped back down on the grass. She is staring at a butterfly floating above the bright coloured flowers in the garden bed.

"So you got everything you ever wanted, huh, and now you won't even let me confirm that I'm not her father." I motion to Claire who has crawled after the butterfly and is about to head into the garden bed.

Cherie bends down and scoops her up, placing her back on the grass only for her to crawl straight back there. On the third attempt Claire is too fast, and she crawls right over the limestone edging and into the dirt. She paws at a flower and yanks it right off the stem, then shoves it in her mouth with superhuman speed.

Cherie huffs. "You're going to ruin your dress and get all filthy. Don't eat the flowers, huni." She scopes a finger through Claire's mouth and pulls the flower out, then picks her up and dusts her off. "I have to get her inside and cleaned up. I'm not changing my mind on the test, Clark. Let it go. Cory is her dad."

"Will you just think about it, please? Take this."

I go to pass her the little test that I had bought with me, but she refuses to take it.

"What will it change? I'm happy and in love with Cory. Claire loves him. We are happy. If you are the father, it will tear us apart. And what, you don't even live here anymore. You're not taking my daughter anywhere. Cory is the father and that is that. Go home, Clark. Forget about us!"

She moves back towards the front door, and I want to follow her. I want to shove the test in her hands. I want to scream at her to do the damn test now and let me be free of this. Let me know the answer one way or the other so I can move the fuck on.

The anger radiates off me.

I pull myself back together. I can't let Claire see me angry. I can't let that be her first impression of me. What if I did turn out to be her father, and the first time she met me was filled with anger and frustration? Not to mention I can't physically force them to take the test. What would that look like?

An involuntary low growl rips from my throat, and I crush the little test packet in my hand.

Cherie carries Claire back up to the front door and I let her go. She turns at the threshold. "Go home, Clark," she says one more time before shutting the door on me.

I run a hand through my hair and drag my sorry ass to the closest hotel for the night. I don't know what to do from here, but that went pretty much exactly as I expected.

32

To put it bluntly

Hannah

Kate and I sit rugged up on my couch eating snacks. Clark has been messaging me nonstop, keeping me updated on what he is doing. But I'm finding it hard to reply to him. I'm still mad as hell.

I understand why he wants to know. I understand why he left. I know he has said he loves me, but I would be lying if I said it didn't feel like a rejection. Like he chose her and her baby—a baby he isn't even sure is his—over choosing me and a baby that is.

To put it bluntly, it sucks. The stress of life, the fact that I didn't want this to begin with and he begged and pleaded and promised he would be there, mixed with the pregnancy hormones makes it almost unbearable.

I called Kate the moment I left the restaurant, and she basically has not left my side since. I've done the bare minimum with the kids and house for the last few days, and the guilt eats at me. It weighs heavily on me that this will most likely be my new normal. Once I get further along, my ability to do as much is going to dwindle. And once the baby is here, even more so.

I shove another handful of Maltesers in my mouth.

"He's coming back, Hannah. It will all be okay." Kate grabs my foot and squeezes gently. We are sitting across from each other on the double couch, feet pretty much in the other's laps. Mine are covered in knee high socks that have the middle finger sign all over them in different skin shades. They were a novelty gift from a Christmas party game. They felt fitting for the situation right now. Kate's the polar opposite, with fluffy wool and pink and purple hearts all over them.

"He's already on the plane home. He has been sending me a play by play."

"That's cute. He wants to keep you updated," Kate replies.

"Would have been cuter if he never left." It's snarky and immature, I know. This is the reason I have kept my replies to Clark short and sweet. I don't want to say something I will regret in anger.

I have lived long enough to realise that it isn't going to serve anyone. I need to deal with this feeling of rejection before he gets back. We are about to have a baby together. The last thing I want to do is start off with snarky comments and hostility.

"Did Cherie agree to the test?" Kate asks.

"No. Apparently it's all happy families with Cory and she doesn't want to do the test."

"Cory is the guy she cheated with?" Kate asks.

"Yeah."

"Shit. How does Clark feel about that?"

"I don't know. I haven't asked."

"Hannah." Her face softens and she squeezes my foot again. "I know you are pissed but I feel like he is trying to do the right thing. You have to respect him for that. There are men that wouldn't give a shit. Would just go 'not my problem' and move on. He has enough integrity to want to at least find the truth, for the child's sake."

I look at Kate, playing over what she is saying. I do agree. If I wasn't the one he left, I would probably commend him for trying to do what is right. But I can't help feeling dread.

"I know. It just feels different because I'm the one that stands to lose out. Maybe I am being selfish, but what happens if that little girl is his? She lives on the opposite side of the country. It's not even a short flight. It's five hours and over five hundred dollars a ticket. It's a different goddamn time zone. How is he going to be in two places at once? How is he going to be a father to that little girl and still be here for us? There will come a point where he must choose. He has to choose to either be here or there. Someone is going to lose. As selfish as it sounds, I don't want that to be me or my baby."

Kate considers my views with sympathy on her face. "You've fallen in love with him, Hannah. It's normal to feel those things."

I consider what she is saying. The fear and overwhelming guilt that consumes me at admitting that those feelings for him live in me. It makes me feel sick, but I nod gently.

"Do you think if he hadn't told you he loved you, if it had been the opposite and he had said he didn't want the baby and didn't want to be with you, your decision to keep the baby would have been different?"

I consider her question. It feels heavy because I think I know my answer. However, that wasn't my reality. It's hard to say with certainty that it's the decision I would have made in that situation, when that situation wasn't reality.

"I honestly don't know. The fact is I have made a decision, and I need to accept it now. Whether Clark holds true to his word or not. Regardless of what he feels for me, or I feel for him, we have to do what's best for this baby. And if Clark turns out to have another child in another state to another woman, then I have to accept that everything I feared about this situation is real. I'm going to be raising this baby mostly on my own. I have to start making a plan. Sorting a budget. Just figuring out how I am going to make this all work. Financially and logistically."

"We're all going to be here to help you, Hannah. Whatever it takes, okay?"

Tears prick at my eyes, but not because I'm sad. Because I believe her. I may have lost a lot, but I'm lucky to have the support I do. I know that I will be okay.

We will all be okay.

I grab my phone and open up a Google Doc. My brain is wired this way, but also I have to be organised for my hectic life to function smoothly.

Well as smooth as it can parenting three children solo.

"All right, let's make a list," I say to Kate.

"Ohhh, you know I love lists. But Jesus you heathen, not on your phone. Go and get a notebook."

I laugh as I peel myself off the warm couch to head to my office out in the gym to grab a notebook.

"And pretty pens," Kate yells out after me.

Nodding to myself, I make my way out the door to the backyard to head to my studio. I'm back within a minute with a notebook and a collection of pens.

"Okay, I'm going to start with a list of what I'm going to need. Once I know that, I can start making a budget and then I can figure out how I'm going to pay for all of this."

"Let's get on marketplace. There are always heaps of baby things on there."

"Ohh, good idea."

Kate jumps on Facebook and starts searching marketplace, and I get started on a list. Within the hour, I have a list consisting of everything I will need, from the big items like a cot and pram, right down to the basic clothes I will need to start with.

I've added price estimates next to each item and I've highlighted the things I want to buy new in pink, like the cot mattress and car seat. The items I don't mind getting secondhand are highlighted in purple, like a cot or pram. The items I don't need straight away are in blue, like a high chair. And the items I feel I could live without are in green, like a feeding chair.

Kate has been trolling marketplace and has already sent me over twenty-five messages with different items, including a listing from a lady selling four boxes of baby clothes. One with a complete baby room set up: cot, chest of draws, rug and feeding chair. And another with a side sleeping bassinet—one that connects to your bed—and about eight different pram options.

I go through her messages and favourite the ones I like. I'm not ready to start buying yet and the thought of trying to deal with marketplace at the moment makes my skin crawl.

Once I have the list, I add up the costs. This would be so much easier if Kate let me do this on my phone or computer.

Tomorrow I'll add it to a Google sheet. I can use a formula to pre-calculate everything, then I can make a budget. It's not just the items I need to consider costing for, it's the doctor's appointments and the scans as well.

"Do you feel better having it all written down?" Kate asks as she passes me a hot cup of tea.

"So much better. I always do once I get it all out of my head." She laughs at me before taking a sip of her own tea.

"What are you going to do about Clark?"

"I don't know yet. I suppose I will just talk to him when he gets home. I don't want to be mad at him. I know he is just trying to do the right thing by everyone. It's just shitty timing and a really shitty circumstance."

Kate nods along in understanding. "When are you going to tell the kids?"

"I've been thinking about that nonstop. It's going to have to be soon. I'm already thirteen weeks. I know I'm going to start showing soon and they are going to know." I place a hand on my belly. I can see the smallest of baby bumps forming. But maybe that is because I know it is there.

My belly feels harder though, and I swear I have felt the flutters of the baby already. I can't remember when I felt it the first time with my other three. It feels like a lifetime ago that I was pregnant with them.

"Let me know if you need me here for support when you do."

"Thank you," I say as I grab her hand.

"I better get home but call me if you need me." Kate places her finished cup in the sink. I walk her to the door and hug her good night before crawling into bed.

Right as I am about to doze off, I see my phone light up. I imagine it's just Kate saying goodnight but my heart flutters at the thought that it is Clark. It does that annoying little *patter patter* every time my phone goes off. Normally, I love the feeling. But right now...

I hate it.

I don't want to want him as much as I do. I don't want to have these feelings anymore. It would make this so much easier.

My mind wont still as I try to ignore my phone that has since gone dark again. I angrily grab it on the bedside table. And sure as shit, *patter patter*. *Patter, patter*. That stupid organ goes off on its one tangent.

> CLARK: I'm home. I know it's only been a few days but not speaking to you or hearing your voice... I miss you, Hannah. I'm sorry I went. It was stupid and a giant waste of time. She won't do the test, and I have to let it go. I never wanted you to feel like I wasn't 100% invested in this with you. I'd love to see you and to talk to you when you are ready. I love you.

I slam my head back on the pillow and stare up at the roof. I don't want to be mad at him. I want to be able to enjoy this with him. This is happening. Might as well embrace it. There is no point staying mad at him for something that happened before we even got together. He can't change the fact that Cherie's baby could be his.

As hurt as I am that he went, I also respect him for trying to do the right thing.

> HANNAH: I'm sorry the trip didn't go as planned. I have a scan on Thursday. Do you want to come?

I keep my message short, afraid of what is going to spill from me if I don't. But I do want him there. I still have the tiny onesie to give him.

The reply is almost instant.

> CLARK: Tell me what time and I'm there.
> Thank you.

The 'thank you' in his message breaks my heart. He is thanking me for inviting him to a scan for his own child.

I hate that I have been giving him the cold shoulder for the last few days. I should have been there supporting him through his own heartbreak. This can't be easy for him either.

HANNAH: 1 PM. Come here first if you like. We can have lunch and then go together.

CLARK: I'd love that. See you Thursday. Goodnight.

HANNAH: Goodnight.

I clutch my phone close to my chest. It's stupid but somehow it feels like it brings him closer to me. I let myself sink into this feeling, because I do want him near me.

Always.

I'm in love with him.

33

Die a happy man

Clark

I was afraid it was going to be awkward between Hannah and me. I know she was upset that I went. Upset at me for going or upset at the situation? I don't know.

Chances are Cherie's baby isn't mine. But it niggles at the back of my mind like a worm buried under my skin. I can constantly feel it itching.

The moment I see her though, it all fades away. It dulls.

I let myself in her back gate and head down to her little work studio. I have visited her enough times at her house to know where to go and that it is okay to just go in.

Her kids are at school. I still haven't met them. It needs to happen eventually, and I'm excited to be a part of their lives, but I know Hannah is scared to navigate this and I need to respect her space. And her timing.

Damn, she is beautiful. I can see her through the open doors. She is sitting on a big exercise ball, typing away on her computer.

Her long hair is tied back in a braid, and loose strands hang around her face. She is biting her bottom lip with a look of concentration. I would give anything to replace those teeth with my own. I have missed her so much. The thought that she is pregnant has only made me want her more.

In every possible way.

As if she senses me standing there staring at her, she looks up and spots me. A smile splits her face, and I hope she is feeling the same things I am.

I stride closer to her as she stands, my mind unsure of how to proceed but my body instinctively reaches for her. Wrapping her in my arms, she nuzzles her head into the little curve of my shoulder, the one that feels like it was carved just for her. I grip my hand to the back of her head, pulling her as close as she can get, and let out a deep breath. Her arms wrap around my waist, and we just stand locked onto each other.

I run my hand over the back of her hair, stroking it, and place a kiss to the top of her head. "I'm so sorry, Hannah. If I'm being honest, as much as I want a baby, I don't want Cherie's to be mine. I just wanted to do the right thing. As guilty as that makes me feel, I don't want it to be mine. I want us. I want our baby."

She relaxes into my arms. "I don't want it to be yours either, Clark. But I didn't want to take that moment away from you. I want you to be happy and I know how much you want children."

I squeeze her closer. I feel like I can't get her close enough.

"I have something for you." She folds herself out of my arms and moves back to her desk. She hands me a little wrapped package.

I turn the gift over in my hands. "What is it?"

She chuckles. "Just open it."

I rip open the soft tissue paper and my heart squeezes in my chest. My big hands delicately grip the soft material as I hold it up in front of my face. I can't help but smile. "It's tiny. Are they this tiny?"

"Yeah, they are that tiny."

My heart is racing like crazy. I lay the onesie in my hands. It basically fits across them spread out. "You mean, our baby will fit like this?" I raise them slightly, imagining a baby in the outfit laying in my hands. Their little nappy clad butt in one and their soft head in the other.

Hannah just smiles up at me while I let my imagination run wild. It's not that I haven't seen a baby before. My older brother has two kids. I was in my early twenties when he had them. While I was happy for him and a great uncle, I wasn't overly interested in the baby stage. It scared the shit out of me then. All my friends have had kids. I've been around them. But the baby *baby* stage, when they are this tiny, I've never really been around much.

I can't wait.

"Thank you." I place the little onesie over her desk and move in closer to her. She smells so good.

"You hungry?" Hannah asks, leaning back against her work desk.

"Starving." But not for food. I step closer to her, boxing her in my arms with the desk behind her. I want her so badly, but I know things have been a bit weird between us.

I'm also acutely aware of the fact that I have said *I love you* multiple times without her saying it back. I'll be honest, my ego is slightly bruised. I'm not sure I could handle any more rejection right now.

But I can't help myself. She pulls to me, and my body reacts instantly. I move slowly. She is pregnant. She may not want this at all. And I would be okay with that.

I lean my head down to kiss her neck, and she tilts her head back to give me better access. Her legs open as I grab her around the ass, picking her up and sitting her on her desk. When her legs wrap around my waist, her arms around my neck and her lips claim mine, I know she wants this too. She yanks me closer, and I step between her legs, kissing her like she is the oxygen I breathe.

Fuck, she feels so good. I don't know how I ever lived without her.

In this moment, I know I never want to be without her again.

"We need to be quick," she pants between kisses.

I don't need to be told twice.

Wrapping my hand around her, I move her laptop to the side. I would love to be that guy who sweeps all her shit to the floor in the heat of passion, but I ain't about to go breaking all her stuff. She works too hard for that.

Placing a hand to her chest, I push her back onto the table. Her eyes are bright and she is biting her bottom lip. I can't help myself. Leaning over her, I free her lip with my thumb then let my own teeth replace them. I bite down, enough to give her the pain I know she loves but not to break skin.

She gasps and her legs tighten around me. Breaking free, I yank her tights and underwear off in one motion, leaving her top half dressed. I kneel in front of her, letting my tongue trace up her pussy to her clit. She arches her back off the desk, so I repeat, licking slow, tracing circles around her clit then back down till she is pushing her hips into my face, begging for me.

I move up slightly, gently lifting her shirt to expose her belly. Then I trace my lips up and over the tiny little bump forming there. I place a kiss right where I imagine our baby to be.

I then shake all thoughts of babies from my brain because I do not need to be thinking of my growing child with what I am about to do to her.

Dropping my own shorts and boxers, I free my cock and rub it through her pussy, letting the mixture of her wetness and my saliva coat it. Hannah tries to push down to force me into her. I love how needy she gets, and I love playing with her.

I slide into her slowly and *fuck* it is ecstasy. I slide back out just as slow and watch as her face changes. Her eyes are shut, and she is biting that bottom lip again.

"Eyes on me, baby," I say as I rub my thumb along her bottom lip. Only when she opens her eyes do I enter her again.

She has extinguished all traces of shyness from my being. I want to be the man she wants and needs. In and out of the bedroom.

I grip her hips, pulling her down into me as my thrusts quicken slightly. I'm mindful of being too rough. But she gives little choice, wrapping her legs around me and pulling me deeper with every thrust.

It's hard to maintain any control when she is moaning and writhing under me. I fucking love the way her body moves, and I need to see more of it.

I slow momentarily to pull her up, but I don't pull out of her. I tug her shirt and sports bra up over her head. With one hand over my shoulder, I grip my shirt and yank it over my own head. Her eyes light up and trace the hard lines of abs.

I claim her mouth while I gently lower her back down. Our eyes lock for a moment before mine break to watch her tits bounce in time to my thrusts. She tells me her boobs are her least favourite part of her, but watching them like this...they are hypnotising.

Her hooded eyes move back down to watch where we are joined, and I start rubbing her clit with my fingers.

"Fuck, Clark, harder. I'm so close," she moans breathlessly.

I oblige, hitting it a little harder, one hand still rubbing her clit. I move my other to pinch and play with her nipples. The moment I do, she shuts her eyes, and I can feel she is close.

"Open your eyes, baby. I want to watch you while you come."

She slowly pries them open, trailing them up my body to meet my own. They are so pretty, alight with passion. The way the sun shines through the window, hitting them, has them looking like green sea glass—almost see through.

We fall over the edge together, and I collapse on her chest, feeling her warmth underneath me and the warmth of the sun at my back.

I could die a happy man right here in her arms.

But I have a baby to meet.

34

Clark

"Hannah Grace."

I'm back in these cold, hard plastic chairs. Only now I have her hand in mine and my baby in her belly. I can't wait to see the ultrasound in all its glory.

The little print out Hannah gave me has not left my pocket for the last two weeks. We stand and make our way down the hall, following behind the OB. Neither of us speak, but her hand doesn't leave mine. I'll admit, it feels way too good to be true.

I wait for Hannah to take her seat and then I sit next to her. Dr Ellis gives us a warm welcome and we exchange pleasantries, but I just want to get to the point.

The doctor asks Hannah a few questions. How she has been feeling and if she has felt the baby much. I listen to Hannah answer them all. Then she stands and preps the bed, rolling out a thin sheet of paper over the plastic covered mattress. She advises us that she will be checking for foetal development to make sure there are no abnormalities.

I hadn't thought about the fact that things could go wrong. It has been such a whirlwind, between finding out that this is even possible to heading back east to talk to Cherie. I have been so excited about the baby and seeing it for myself that I kind of missed the entire point of this scan. And that is to check that everything is okay. This scan isn't for us, it's for the baby.

My heart rate picks up, and I try to not let any worry show on my face as I squeeze Hannah's hand a little tighter. The paper crunches as she lays, folding her tights down so the doctor can get to her belly.

"Sorry, Dad, I'm going to need you to move a little," the OB says as she moves the ultrasound machine closer to the bed.

Did she just call me 'Dad'? I can't wait to hear that name fall from my own child's lips. I reluctantly release Hannah's hand and move up higher. I'm standing by her head so I can see the TV they have set up at the foot of the bed. "Sorry," I say, a smile on my face.

"That's okay. I promise I will let you see everything, and I can print a photo for you before you leave."

"Thank you." Hannah looks up at me and smiles. I reach down to swipe a strand of hair from her forehead.

The obstetrician squeezes some gel onto Hannah's lower stomach, giving her a pre warning that it will be cold, then she places the wand over it. A grainy black and white image pops up on the screen, and she starts moving the wand around, tilting it back and forth and side to side. I intently watch the screen. It's just shapes of black and grey at the moment.

Until...

My breath catches and my heart rate spikes. The doctor settles on an image—a grainy grey cone with a black peanut shape in the centre. Inside of that is our baby.

My baby.

Their head looks way too big for their body. Round belly, tiny arms and legs tucked up.

I reach down for Hannah's shoulders and give them a little squeeze. She looks back at me with a warm smile. The doctor moves the wand around a bit more and then clicks a few things on the machine, her face falling slightly.

Hannah notices it too. "What is it? Is everything okay?"

I turn to the doctor, watching her face as she continues to move the wand, then clicks a few more things on the machine.

"Just give me a moment." Her voice is calm, soft.

Too calm, too soft. The voice you use when you need to keep someone else calm. I feel my heart thudding against my chest.

"There's no heartbeat," Hannah says, her eyes boring holes into the screen. I don't miss the way her hand reaches for her chain. She clutches the ring in her hand like it could will a heartbeat.

"What do you mean?" I shoot out before the doctor has a chance to talk.

"Let's not panic yet. I'm just trying to find it." That calm voice again. Soothing.

Thud, thud. Thud, thud.

My own heart feels like it is beating in my throat.

"See that section at the bottom there with HR written." Hannah points to the screen. To the side, there is a heap of writing that makes no sense to me. Underneath is a panel running across the screen, and in the top left-hand corner, the letters HR sit. "That is supposed to show the baby's heart rate. You would see it, the waves. You can hear it too, if they have the sound up." She pauses. "There's no heartbeat." The last word catches in her throat, and she lets out a little sob to set it free.

I turn to the doctor. "Is she right? Is there no heartbeat?"

Dr Ellis's face falls. She lets out a low sigh, tilting her head to the side. "I'm sorry. Your baby is—" She clears her throat. "Your baby's heart has stopped."

"What do you mean *stopped*?"

"Clark, the baby's dead." The way Hannah says it is so blunt. So to the point.

"No. I can see them. They're right there." I all but push the machine and the doctor out the way, moving to the side of Hannah and placing my hand on her little growing belly.

"No." I look at the doctor for reassurance. For anything. But she gently shakes her head at me.

"I'm sorry," she says before wiping the gel off the wand and placing it back in the slot on the machine.

Not again. How can I have this so close in my grasp and lose it again?

I fold over Hannah, placing my head to her belly. I don't care that I'm getting the gel all over my face. I turn my head to the side and rest my ear on her small bump. My eyes sting. Breathing hitched.

"Hannah," I cry out.

She places a hand on top of my head, running her fingers gently through my hair, like she is consoling a small child. I open my wet eyes and stare up at her, my ear still pressed to our baby. Her eyes are filled with tears as well, but none have spilled past her thick lashes. She is holding it together. For her own sake? For my sake? I don't know. Maybe she has just experienced enough loss.

Shit, she has experienced enough loss.

Her husband and now her baby.

I move up, wrapping my arms around her and pulling her to sit. Hannah shifts to face me and wraps her legs around my waist with her arms around my neck. Only it's far different to how we were earlier today. Her head falls to rest on my shoulder, nuzzling into my neck. I feel her hot tears fall as they hit my skin.

I grip the back of her head with one hand and her back with the other, pulling her close to me. I feel her heartbeat mixing with mine. Both erratic, both pounding. But no baby. No baby's heartbeat. Just ours.

I lose track of time, or even consciousness of where we are. She cries into my shoulder as I swallow down my own tears, holding onto her for dear life.

We finally pull apart. Her face is red and blotchy. Her tights still rolled down with gel smeared everywhere. I have no idea how long we were locked together like this. At some point Dr Ellis must have left. The room is quiet and cold, and I just want to go home.

I want to get my hands dirty under the hood of my car and have something else to think about. Gallop out into an open field on my horse, so fast that the wind would whip my hat from my head and leave it for the dirt.

Where my baby will end up.

The dirt.

"What happens now?" I ask as I wipe her tear-streaked face with my thumbs.

"I don't know for certain but depending on how long ago the heart stopped, I imagine I will have to go for a D&C."

"Then what happens?"

"Then we carry on."

What does she mean, we carry on? Like they never existed. Like I didn't just see my tiny baby on the screen—little arms and legs and head. It was right there.

As real as her and I.

"What do you mean, we just carry on. What happens to our baby?"

"I don't know. I've never had a miscarriage before. I don't know. Let's just talk to the OB."

As if on cue, the doctor knocks softly on the door.

"Come in," I call.

She has the same sombre look on her face. "I just wanted to give you some space," she speaks softly as she takes a seat at her desk. She gestures for us to sit as well, and I help Hannah off the bed. She rolls her tights back up and I grip her hand to guide her to the chair, not letting it go as we sit.

"I'm very sorry for your loss."

I nod. But Hannah speaks first. "What happens now?"

"Well from the measurements I just did, I would say the heart stopped at around the twelve-week mark."

"I had a scan just before twelve weeks," Hannah interrupts.

The doctor clicks a few things on her computer and then looks at the screen for a while. "Looking at the measurements we noted at the first scan compared to now, I would say the baby's heart stopped not long after that scan. There wasn't much growth between now and then."

"I thought I felt them move," she sobs.

"You may have. This is your fourth baby, so it is not uncommon for you to feel movement early. Your placenta was posterior so you definitely may have felt the baby move. But not much past the twelve-week mark."

Hannah nods, more tears rolling down her cheeks. I squeeze her hand in comfort, but we both remain silent.

"Due to the fact that it has been at least a week and the baby hasn't passed yet, we will need to book you in for a D&C procedure. It's done locally at the hospital. I will organise a booking date in the next few days. They will put you under general anaesthesia to perform the procedure. I will also print you out some information on the procedure itself."

I'm stunned into silence. Forcing my lips to part, I ask, "What's a D&C?" Hannah mentioned it and now the doctor. I'm imagining it to be something to remove the baby, but how? What happens to my baby?

The doctor goes through the procedure step by step, using as gentle words as she can, but all I hear is that they suck my baby out of her uterus.

She is talking so clinically. Like that isn't a human baby in there.

My baby.

I look at Hannah, wanting her to say something. To say no. To say anything. She is normally so in charge. So fierce. So strong and confident.

I'm still holding her hand, but she is silent. Maybe this loss is bringing the loss of her husband to the forefront of her mind.

I squeeze her hand tighter and take the lead. "Can we keep the baby and have a burial? Name them. It's not just cells and blood to me. I saw them on that screen. I have a photo. That was my baby."

"Absolutely, I understand." The doctor gives me a gentle smile. "Legally there are no requirements to have a burial or a naming until twenty weeks. But it's not uncommon for parents to want to do that for themselves and their baby. We just notify the hospital of your wishes, and they use a slightly different procedure to remove them. Then they can keep the foetus and send you home with it or offer a cremation where they handle everything and you will get the ashes."

I can't believe an hour ago I thought I was headed to see my child. My first time seeing an ultrasound in person. I was going to hear its heartbeat and ask if they could tell yet if they were a boy or a girl.

Now I'm discussing how they are going to cut my child from the woman I love and send me home with a pile of ashes.

Tears prick at my eyes again, but I rein them in. I can see Hannah is one move from tipping over the edge. I need to be strong for her. She has already been through so much.

She doesn't say anything about what her wishes would be for this child and I don't want to ask her here. She looks like if her mouth opens, a gut-wrenching sob will escape and she may never be able to close her lips again.

I wrap an arm over her shoulder and pull her close to my body. She rests her head on my chest just below my shoulder, and I hold her to me like she can't sit upright without me.

"Book it in. We want to do that. Cremation. I want to know the sex before they cremate them, so that we can name them."

"Sure. I will note all that down and make the arrangements today. I will call later this afternoon with a day and time and then the hospital will email you with further details."

"Thank you." I grip Hannah and help her stand. She clings to me, feeling tiny and vulnerable in my arms. She still hasn't spoken. I have no clue if I made the right call about the cremation or wanting to know the sex, but we can discuss it later.

Right now, it's clear she needs me to be her strength. So even though I feel like breaking down myself, I'm going to stand strong for her.

I open the passenger side door of my car and help her in, pulling the buckle across her and locking it into place. I drive us back to her house in silence. Her hand rests on her tiny bump the entire way.

She is already out of the car by the time I make it around to her side to help her. She clutches her bag and fishes her house keys out of them. I take them from her trembling hands and open the door for her. I slide her bag off her shoulder and hang it on the hook by the door. When I turn around, she's gone. I find her sitting on the edge of her bed, her head hung low with both hands clutching at her belly as if she could will our baby back to life.

I close the distance between us and kneel in front of her, placing my hands on her thighs and looking up at her. I don't know what I can say to make her feel better, to take away her pain. I don't even know if she wants me here. Maybe she doesn't. Maybe she just wants space. To be alone.

I slowly remove her shoes and then stand to slide the covers back on her bed. Wrapping her in my arms, I lay her down. I kick off my own shoes and curl up behind her, pulling her into my arms and wrapping her up in me.

She starts sobbing again. "This is all my fault."

"Hannah, no it's not."

"It is. I didn't want this baby. I wished this never happened. I thought about an abortion. I willed this."

The fact that she believes this is her fault tears a hole through me. I can feel it ripping me apart from the inside out.

Gripping her tighter in my arms, I stroke her hair. She relaxes under my touch, and I kiss the top of her head. "Hannah, this isn't your fault. This is just bad luck, that's all. We will get through this."

She sobs uncontrollably in my arms. I run my fingers through her hair and rub her back until eventually she falls asleep.

Checking the time on my watch, I realise that it is almost 2:30 PM. This is when she usually leaves to get the kids.

Fuck.

I don't want to wake her, not when she only just stopped crying. But I can't go and get her kids. They have no idea who I am. I know what school they go to, but they aren't going to get in a car with a complete stranger.

Her sister.

I don't have her number, but I know they are close. She talks about Kate all the time.

Using every ounce of stealth I have, I manoeuvre my body away from hers and slide off the bed. Finding her bag, I pull out her phone. It's locked with a password. This feels insanely wrong, but my only other option is to wake her and I'm not doing that.

I place the phone in front of her face and let the face ID do its thing. Then I head straight to her contacts and hit dial on Kate. It's saved in her favourites so it's a safe bet that it is the right one.

It only rings twice before she answers.

"Hey. How did the scan go?" Her voice is upbeat and happy. She sounds just like Hannah.

I clear my throat. "It's Clark."

"Hi...Clark. Is everything okay?" She sounds sceptical.

"Not really. I—" Before I can finish my sentence, she interrupts me. Shit, I shouldn't have led with that.

"I'm on my way."

"Hannah's okay. I'm here with her, but she fell asleep and her kids will need to be picked up. I don't want to wake her up. We lost the baby."

Kate gasps, and I hear her slap her hand to her mouth. "Ohh, Clark, I'm so sorry. Is Hannah okay?"

"She's..." I don't quite know because besides expressing her guilt, she hasn't said a word. "She's devastated. She blames herself."

"What!"

"I know. I think just because she didn't want the baby at first. She thinks she manifested it or something."

"Oh, my gosh, poor Hannah. Are you okay?"

I don't even know how to answer that question. Because truthfully, I'm not even close to being okay. I rub my hand across the back of my neck. I don't want Hannah's sister to think I'm weak or to worry about me when her focus needs to be on Hannah.

So, I answer as truthfully as I can while still trying to show that I'm strong enough to hold Hannah up through this. "Not right now, but I just need to be here for Hannah. I think this is going to hit her hard after losing Callum."

"Yeah, my heart is broken for you guys. I know she said she didn't want the baby at the start, but she would never have gone through with an abortion. I just know it. She was just scared."

"I think I knew that. Deep down, anyway."

"Listen, stay there with her. I will tell the boys that she isn't feeling well and that they can come have a sleepover tonight. We may swing around later to grab some clothes for them, but I will call to let you know. Just look after my Hannah, please."

"I got her."

"And Clark.

"Yeah?"

"I know she is scared of the feeling, but I know she loves you back."

I pull the phone away from my face so Kate doesn't hear my emotions. "Thanks, Kate."

I hear her sniff. "Okay, I will go get them now. Thank you for calling." Her voice is hoarse and catches on every second word as she tries to hold back her own tears.

I offer her what I can. "I will message you from my phone, to keep you updated on how she is. I got her, I promise."

"Thank you," she says around a sob.

Kate hangs up, and I grab my own phone out of my pocket, adding Kate to my contacts. I shoot her a text.

CLARK: This is my number - Clark.

KATE: Thank you. Look after her please.

CLARK: You have my word.

35

Truly alone

Clark

annah is still out cold a couple of hours later when my phone lights up with a text.

> UNKNOWN NUMBER: Hi Clark, it's Renee, Hannah's Mum. Kate called me. She has the boys, but she is going to bring them home soon to get some clothes. I'm also going to head around to drop some dinner off for her.

A second message pops up straight away.

KATE: Hey Clark, I have the boys. They are fine. I just told them she had a really bad migraine and needed some rest. They are happy to stay the night with me. I promised them pizza and ice cream with unlimited Xbox time. But we are headed home soon to get clothes. I don't want to be a dick, but I know Hannah hasn't introduced you to them yet and I don't think it will be great if you are there. In the politest way possible, can you leave before we get there? You're welcome to go back once we leave. I think she will want you there with her.

I know Hannah is close to her family. I know she told Kate, but I didn't know if she had told her parents about the baby. Or even about me, for that matter.

I don't want to leave her. I don't want her to wake up and find me gone. I want to be the one to console her. To wipe her tears and tell her it's all going to be okay.

I want to meet her boys and introduce myself.

I want to tell Kate that I'm not going anywhere. But I know that Hannah isn't ready for me to meet her kids and I have to respect that. It's the right thing to do.

I place a kiss on Hannah's forehead, tucking her even tighter into the blankets. I fill her water bottle and put it next to her bed. Flicking her phone to silent, I put it on charge so that it doesn't wake her.

Then I reply to everyone.

> CLARK: Thanks, Renee. Hannah is still asleep. Kate has said she is coming around soon so I'm going to head out so the boys don't see me. Hannah wasn't ready for me to meet them yet. Should I wait for you so I can let you in?

She replies instantly.

RENEE: I'm here.

Not quite the circumstances that I wanted to meet her parents under. I feel like a complete dick opening the door for her mum at a house that isn't even mine.

Without a word she moves in, rises to her tip toes and wraps her arms around me in a hug only a mother can give. It makes me want to call my own mum. We are close but she lives in

Queensland and we don't see each other much. We talk on the phone and FaceTime, but I had not told her this news yet.

Renee pulls back, her eyes wet with tears. They mirror Hannah's. She cups my face with her hands. "I'm so sorry," she says.

I fight hard to swallow the emotion boiling inside of me. It's like a dam and with the first crack I know I won't be able to contain it anymore.

I have to keep it together.

"Thank you. Hannah is in bed." I grab the little cooler she placed on the entrance floor as she came in. "I'll take this through to the kitchen and then I will get out your hair."

"Thank you, Clark. It's nice to finally meet you. Hannah has told me so many good things."

Wait, WHAT. She has? Guess that clears up the question of if Hannah told her parents about me.

"It's nice to meet you, too. I wish it was under better circumstances," I say.

"Me, too."

"Would you mind letting me know when the boys and Kate leave? I would really like to come back and be here for her. If that's okay with you?"

"Of course."

"Thank you."

Then I head out.

I'm itching out of my skin awaiting Renee to text me and let me know I can come back. It's been nearly two hours since I left. I went home but I couldn't bring myself to do much more than pace aimlessly around the house.

I feed the animals and have been wearing a hole in my lounge room rug. I thought about getting out there and working on my car, but I want to be ready when she texts me to come back. I don't want to be covered in grease and waste precious time showing when I could be headed back to her.

I glance at my phone every few seconds, checking that it isn't set to silent and that the volume is up so I don't miss anything. I shove it back in my back pocket and pace another lap. Then I feel it vibrate. I almost rip my jean pocket getting it out so fast.

HANNAH: Thank you so much for calling
Kate and for sorting the kids. I'm okay, I
just needed a moment to process it all.
But I'm up now, and I want the kids here.
Kate and Mum just left, and the boys
are staying. Sorry, I know you wanted to
come back.

My stomach drops. It dawns on me just how alone I truly am. I know Hannah is unbelievably strong. I knew she was always going to put her kids first, but I just wish she would let me take care of her.

More than that though, I realise that consoling her and being strong for her was the only thing holding me together. Without it, I feel that dam wall cracking like an egg, water spraying through.

CLARK: Of course, I understand. Take all the time you need. But know that I want to be there for you. Just say the word and I'll be there.

HANNAH: I'm sorry, Clark, I know you are dealing with this loss too. I want to be there for you as well, but I just don't want to put the kids out.

CLARK: You don't have to apologise for putting your kids first. I understand, I'm okay. Call me if you need me. Anytime, day or night. Okay?

HANNAH: Will do, thank you.

I throw my phone across the room. It connects with the wall and bounces down onto the floor.

Damn, I shouldn't have done that.

Running my fingers through my hair, trying to get a grip, I pace over and scoop my phone up. I inspect for damages and find a cracked screen.

Awesome.

What an idiot.

This whole situation is breaking me.

I'm in love with a woman who won't let herself love me back.

I just had everything I have ever dreamed of within my grasp and just like that...puff, it's gone.

I leave the phone ringer on loud in case Hannah changes her mind, then I change into work gear and head out to the shed. If I don't keep my hands and mind busy, I will fall apart. And I don't want to be a mess if she needs me.

I might not be able to fix this situation—I don't even know where to start—but I know how to fix a car. So that's what I will do.

36

Flooded with guilt

Hannah

My head is pounding and my eyes sting from crying so much. The little nap from pure exhaustion and overwhelm did nothing to lessen the guilt and pain I feel. My chest feels heavy. My lungs are struggling to suck in enough oxygen.

My mind runs flashbacks on repeat of the police telling me my husband is gone. Flashbacks of being driven to the hospital, of identifying his body. Flashbacks of his mother and I clutching each other crying, like we needed to be tethered to someone to be able to stay rooted to this earth.

I know it's different. Callum was my husband. The father of my kids. We had lived a whole life together.

This was a baby, just twelve weeks old. We hadn't even breathed the same air yet. It had only been fully formed for a few weeks. Only just developing hearing and a sense of smell and little limbs.

No one can say with certainty that they had a soul. I believe they did.

Did they feel pain when their heart stopped?

Did they know what was happening? Could they hear me talk to them? Did they hear me when I said I didn't want them? When I cried to my sister about how this wasn't what I wanted. When I told Clark that I didn't think I could go through with this.

Did I make their heart stop? Did they give up because they thought they weren't wanted or loved?

My head and heart are flooded with guilt. It leaves a sour taste in my mouth and a sinking in the pit of my stomach.

All the feelings I felt losing Callum rise to the surface, stabbing at my skin from within. But I don't have time to wallow in this. I need to keep moving. For my kids' sake, and for my own.

I know all too well that grieving can consume you. It can swallow you whole if you let it. Suck you under and suffocate you. I can't let it grip me because this time I don't know that I will make it out. It's why I told my kids to stay here and not go with Kate. It's why I told Clark to not come back. I need to keep moving. Stay rooted in my everyday life.

I splash cold water on my face and change into a pair of track-pants and a hoodie. I plaster a smile on my face and head out to greet my kids. My mum and sister just left. Mum dropped dinner for the boys and I. Kate picked them up from school and had them at hers for the afternoon.

I was extremely grateful to Clark for organising that and I hate that he can't be here with me.

A large part of me wants nothing more than to crawl back under the covers and cuddle into his hard warm chest. He held it together today, but I know that this will be killing him. I want to be there for him, too. To offer him the same comfort he offered me. But my children come first. And if I let myself stop, I don't know that I will ever get up again.

I also don't want to put Kate or my parents out. And I don't want my kids to feel like they can't be in their own home.

I know I just lost a baby, but I can't forget about the three kids I already have here. They are my lifeline, my tether to Callum. My reason for pulling myself out of the clutches of depression after their dad passed. They have to be my priority.

I have never lied to my boys. Well, I mean about Santa and the Easter Bunny, yeah. Okay, I may have said the park is closed and that the ride on toys at the shopping centres were out of order a few times when they were little. But for the most part, I have always been open and honest with them. I didn't tell them about Clark as I wasn't sure what it was. I wasn't ready to admit what I felt for him and saw no point in confusing them with it.

Now, not only does the guilt of losing my baby consume me, but the guilt of keeping this hidden from my boys eats at me. I don't know what the right thing to do here is.

They are still so little, at just fourteen, twelve and nine. Are they old enough to handle the fact that I'm dating someone else? Has enough time passed since the loss of their father for them to be okay with this?

Are we dating? Is that what this is? I mean it was where it was going. Clark says he loves me. Does he still feel that way now that I'm no longer pregnant with his child? Do I?

One problem at a time.

I need to decide if I tell my boys the truth about this or if I stick to the migraine story Kate told them. I'm awaiting a call or email from the doctor with a time for the D&C and I'm most likely going to need recovery time for that. I don't want to have to hide in my room in my own house or pretend I'm okay when I'm clearly not. I don't believe that is healthy and whilst I have been strong for my boys, I have never hidden the rollercoaster of emotions I have dealt with after losing Callum.

They saw it all. The real, raw and devastating emotions of it all. I believe them being able to see me like that allowed them the space to show their own emotions as well. It allowed us as a family to heal.

I head out into the kitchen and dining area to find them. I don't know that I'm ready to talk to them about this, but I feel like I have to. They are my family after all.

Liam and Ethan are watching TV in the lounge room, while Noah is doing homework at the kitchen table. His books are open and papers are sprawled out everywhere.

"Hey, boys."

"Hey, Mum. Is your head feeling better?" Noah asks, looking up from his books. Liam barely blinks from the TV, and Ethan comes running over to give me a cuddle.

"My head is still pretty sore, to be honest."

"Nan bought dinner. It's a Shepherd's Pie. We can just heat it up and you can go back to bed if you like," Noah, my oldest, says.

"Actually, there is something I really want to talk to you boys about. If that's okay." I move down towards the lounge room.

Noah's eyes follow me, but he doesn't move. He swivels in his chair to face me as I sit down on the opposite couch to Liam. Ethan is still clinging to me and sits down on the couch next to me.

I take a deep breath and steady myself for this conversation. The truth is, I know in my heart Callum and I have raised good kids. I know that despite all the heartache, I have done my best over the last three years. They are surrounded by family who love them unconditionally and I know that they can handle this.

I've made the right choice in telling them.

It's not that I want them to share in my pain, it's that I want them to know that losses and pain happen in life and it's okay to lean on those you love. It's okay to be vulnerable and to ask for help, even though sometimes I need to get better at that myself. These are my kids, and whilst in one sense I can see how some would think it isn't fair to burden them with this, I want to be able to offer them full disclosure on why I may be struggling emotionally for the next couple of weeks, especially with the D&C coming up.

I get this is a lot to dump on the kids, but I don't want Clark to have to hide in the shadows. He deserves to grieve as well and part of that means being together.

I place an arm around Ethan, hugging him close, and begin.

I keep it PG, of course, but Noah and Liam are old enough to understand the basics. Callum and I were always very honest and open with the kids from the get go.

Ethan barely seems like he is listening, but it is Liam who takes it the hardest. My darling middle child has always been my loose cannon. While Noah is sensible and gentle, Liam is a hurricane. He always feels things the most. When he is happy, he is elated, but when he is angry, he is destructive, and right now he is angry.

Ethan stays by my side. Noah has now moved from the kitchen table to the couch. His face is full of understanding and sadness.

Liam throws the remote onto the couch as he stands. "So you were just going to start a new family, and what, forget all about Dad?"

I stay calm, allowing him to have his say and feel what he needs to. "I will never forget about your father. He was and always will be the love of my life."

"Then what is this new guy Clark to you, Mum?" Noah asks, his voice low and one word away from tipping over into tears.

"He's become someone I care about very much, but how I feel about him would never diminish how I felt about your father."

"Felt?" He says the word like a question. I get the implication. I felt. I said *I felt*. Not I feel.

Tears well in my eyes. Not just for the loss I feel in my stomach, but for the loss I feel for Callum all over again.

Noah stands and follows Liam out of the room, and I turn to Ethan, who seems oblivious to all the tension and heartbreak that just exploded all over the living room walls.

"How do you feel about all this?" I ask him.

"Dad isn't coming back, Mum. No point in waiting around for him."

Well fuck. How is my nine-year-old more cool, calm and collected than me? My nine-year-old, who I thought wasn't following the conversation at all.

"You're right, kiddo. But just because he isn't coming back doesn't mean we love him any less."

"I know that, Mum. No one will replace Dad. But it would be kinda cool to have someone to kick a ball with again. No offence, but you suck at football, and basketball for that matter."

I can't help but laugh. "I don't suck. It's not my fault both your brothers are now taller and stronger than me."

He huffs. "Okay, I'll admit you're not the *worst* at basketball, but you suck at kicking the football."

"I know, it's not my strong suit."

"Can this guy kick a football?"

"You know what, I don't actually know. I'll ask."

"Well, if he can, get him to swap with you for training. You're embarrassing."

"What! I am not. I kick just fine."

Ethan chuckles but leans in to hug me. "Can I go back to watching TV now?"

"Yeah, sure."

I go to knock on Noah's door first. I feel like Liam needs more time to cool down. Noah is lying on his bed with his earphones in, listening to music. I let myself in.

He sits up, slowly pulling one earphone from his ear. "I don't want to talk about it, Mum."

"I know you're angry, so I didn't come in here to push the subject. But I just wanted you to know that no matter what you're feeling, it's okay. I love you and I want to hear your thoughts.

Take all the time you need to process but please come and talk to me when you are ready."

I don't know for sure he can even hear me over his music blaring in one ear, but he slides off the bed and walks towards me. He is taller than me, having Callum's height. He has been taller than me for a few years now.

He wraps his arms around me. "I'm sorry you lost the baby, Mum."

"Thank you," I say, clearing my throat. Through all this, the main factor that has seemed to hurt the kids the most is the fact that I was seeing another man. A man I felt enough for to have a baby with. To hear that Noah understands the loss and can say the words out loud fills me with so much love and pride for my kids.

He releases me all too soon and moves back to his bed. "I don't know if I am ready to meet this guy yet."

"I understand, Noah. Whenever you are ready." I say the words, but I have no clue what Clark and I even are now. Does he still feel the same way about me now that there is no baby tying us together?

I move out of Noah's room to find my middle child, shutting the door behind me as I go. I knock on his door for a second time. I know Liam, and I'm likely to get something thrown at my head if I just enter the bedroom.

"Liam, I know you're mad, but I'm here to talk to you."

I hear a thud on the back of the door, most likely a shoe being thrown at it.

"Go away, Mum."

I slide down to the ground, leaning against the door and sit. I start to regret the fact that I told the kids. I should have just let Kate take them and dealt with this later. I could be relaxing in a warm bath, crying into a bowl of ice cream or binge watching TV to try to help take my mind off the fact that I still have my past baby inside of me.

I sigh, letting out a big breath. I haven't even had a chance to deal with my own feelings on this. I mentally kick myself for being so stubborn. Always in such a rush.

Was I just trying to free my own burden and guilt by dumping it on them or was this really about what was best for them?

Ahhh, the constant mum guilt gnaws at me like a rabid dog to a bone. It's impossible to know if I made the right decision. Was I clouded by grief? I have no idea, but it felt like the right decision at the time.

I should have slept on it. Given myself time to process and think of how best to communicate all this. I should have just allowed Clark and I to deal with this by ourselves, and be there for each other first.

Now, I'm alone, my baby is dead and the three people I love the most are mad at me. My head falls into my hands and I cry. Loud sobs wrack from my body as it shakes uncontrollably.

I know I should be stronger. I know I should go to my room and not let my boys see me like this. It isn't their job to console me. But I can't seem to stop.

Noah comes out first, hearing my cries. He sinks down on the floor next to me, wrapping an arm over my shoulder.

"Are you okay, Mum?" he asks as I let my head fall to his shoulders.

"I feel like I let you all down. I love you kids, but it is lonely without your dad. You kids make me so happy, but it felt nice to have another adult to hang out with. This baby...it wasn't planned. But I was happy about it. Now it just feels like losing your dad all over again."

He sniffs, holding back a tear. "I have noticed you've been happier these last few months."

"You have?" I'm surprised by his perception.

"You started singing again."

"What?"

"You used to sing all the time. You didn't even realise you were doing it. You used to make every task you did into a song."

I look up to him. "I did not."

"You did. You would be folding the washing, and you would be dancing going, 'ohhhh washing, so much washing, why is there so much washing?'"

A laugh spills from my lips. "Oh yeah, I did do that a lot."

"It used to drive us all mad."

"Your dad loved it."

"He used to join in and you two would be dancing and singing the dumbest song about the dumbest task."

"Yeah, I remember that now."

"You stopped doing that. I haven't heard you sing a dumb song in years."

I take a deep breath. He's right.

"I heard you the other day, though. You were making that gross lasagna that none of us ate and you were singing about it while you were making it. That's how we knew it had heaps of vegetables in it. You were literally singing about hiding vegetables in the lasagna."

"That lasagna was good."

"You whizzed up the veggies and added it through the mince. It made the meat look like lumpy green baby shit."

"Language," I say as I playfully slap his arm. He leans into me, chuckling. He laughs just like his dad, and it makes my heart warm.

"I didn't realise I missed your silly jingles until they started again. If that is because of him, if he makes you happy, then I'm okay with it."

"I am happy," I say. "I have been happy," I correct. "You kids...our life makes me happy."

He shrugs. "Have you? You never really do anything but work."

I nudge him with my shoulder. "Yeah, because you guys eat like body builders in bulking mode."

He shrugs. "I don't eat that much."

"I saw you eat a whole loaf of bread plain the other day after school. Like right out of the bag. You didn't even get a plate."

He throws his head back laughing, and it makes me laugh too. The tears have stopped, and we sit together outside Liam's door in hysterics.

Ethan comes down the hallway from the lounge. "What's so funny?" he asks.

"Your brother thinks he doesn't eat that much."

Ethan laughs as well, sinking to the floor on the other side of me.

"Bro, you ate a whole roll of polony the other day," Liam's voice rings out from behind the door, and I realise he must be sitting on the other side listening—a mirror image to us.

"It was a mini roll, and shut up, you know Mum doesn't let us eat polony."

"That stuff is disgusting. That's why I don't buy it. And it is filled with additives."

"It's delicious, Mum," Noah adds.

"Not the way you eat it," Ethan chimes in.

"Yeah, you just peeled the wrapper off and covered it in sauce and ate it like a giant sausage," Liam yells from behind the door.

"Where did you even get it from?" I ask, as I know it wasn't in the house.

"I'm out." Ethan goes to get up to leave, and I grab his arm and pull him back down.

"Spill."

Noah levels a glare at Ethan that could turn him to stone. His eyes go big and he pinches his lips together.

"Shut it, Ethan, or I swear to God I will put bugs in your bed while you sleep!" Liam yells.

"Tell me right now, Ethan," I pry playfully.

Noah shakes his head, staring holes into Ethan.

"We walk to the grocery store down the road from school after you drop us off and buy better snacks for lunch." The words tumble out of his mouth so fast he has to catch his breath afterwards.

Noah face plants his hand to his head. "Why, bro."

"Dick!" Liam yells from behind the door.

"Language," I yell back.

"Sorry," Ethan says sheepishly.

"Is this why you boys never have any pocket money left?" I ask.

"The snacks you buy suck, Mum," Liam yells.

"Language." *These boys will be the death of me.* "And they are healthy snacks designed to fill you up and help you grow. No wonder you come home starving, because you are eating crap."

"Language," I hear from behind the door in a sarcastic tone. I can't help but laugh. There is no mistaking where my kids have picked up their language from.

"Sorry, Mum, but those nut bars you make aren't great," Noah says sheepishly.

"Don't sugar coat it, bro. They taste like straight up dirt," Liam adds.

"Noah, they are filled with lots of healthy fats and protein so that you have all the brain food you need for school. Not just sugar."

"Well they taste like you rolled a turd in dirt," Liam quips.

Ethan spits out a laugh he can no longer hold in, and Noah clamps his lips shut, his shoulders shaking as he tries to contain his own laughter.

"Okay, fine. I will let you buy a couple of snacks you guys like in the next shop, if you promise to stop eating polony and sauce."

"I can't keep that promise, Mum," Noah says from beside me.

"Me either," Liam adds.

"Abso-friggin-lutly NOT!" I'm glad Ethan said frigging and not the other one.

"But I can promise to not be mad at you for hanging out with what's his name if it means you sing your stupid jingles again." I turn to face Noah. The slight smile on his face shows he genuinely means it.

I didn't realise I had been unhappy. I thought I had been doing well. I guess I didn't realise just how starved I had become of affection. Or even just adult connection. My life was full and busy, and I was grateful for it. My kids do make me happy, but I was just going through the daily motions.

"Agreed," Ethan adds as he places his head on my shoulder. I wrap my arm around him, pulling him closer to me.

Then the door moves and we all fall backwards into Liam's room. My head hits the soft carpet with Ethan's head nestled in my shoulder. Noah manages to somewhat right himself, while Liam stands over us, looking down.

"I concur. Polony for all and we will let you keep seeing what's his face."

"His name is Clark," I say, smiling up at him. I turn my head and take in the pure carnage that is his room. God, he must have had a tantrum in here. His pillows are thrown across the room. Shoes lay everywhere and everything that was once on his desk is now on the floor.

I decide not to comment.

"Whatever," he says, still standing over us.

I move to get up and the boys follow. "I'm sorry to have dumped this all on you boys. I wish I could have told you about Clark under better circumstances."

"I'm sorry about..." Liam points to my stomach, not able to say the words. I see his throat work to swallow. His anger comes from a place of sadness. It always has. He took Callum's death the hardest and it manifested as anger a lot of the time.

I step forward and wrap him in my arms. To my surprise, he doesn't try to push me away. Instead, he hugs me back.

"No one and nothing will ever replace what your father was to me, what you boys are to me, but it did feel nice to have another adult to hang out with."

"Noah is right. Your songs are stupid. But I'm okay with listening to them again if it means you are happy."

I smile, because I think that is the kindest thing Liam has ever and probably will ever say to me.

Ethan nods and wraps his arms around the both of us at my waist.

"I love you boys," I say as I reach an arm over to Noah and pull him in. He wraps his arms around us all and we stand in Liam's room wrapped up in a giant family hug.

"I love you too, Mum," Noah says.

"What he said," Liam adds.

"Love you, Mum," Ethan chimes in.

Suddenly, I'm not so alone.

"Now, everyone, get out of my room. I want to play Xbox," Liam says as he unfolds himself from my and his brother's arms.

"Only one hour," I say as I move out of his room.

"Cross my heart," he says as we leave. He leaves his door open and Ethan, Noah and I make our way back to the lounge room. Noah goes back to his homework and Ethan goes back to the TV.

I pull out the Shepherd's Pie Kate made and start dishing everyone up a slice, putting it in the microwave and then delivering it to each of the boys in their respective locations before I plop down at the kitchen table next to Noah to eat.

37

Any time, day or night

Hannah

It isn't until after all the boys have gone to their rooms to go to 'bed' that I go shower and crawl into my own bed.

Grabbing my phone, I check it for the first time since I messaged Clark earlier. I open the message thread of our last conversation.

CLARK: You don't have to apologise for putting your kids first. I understand. I'm okay. Call me if you need me. Anytime, day or night. Okay?

HANNAH: Will do, thank you.

I check the time. It's almost eleven. He did say "anytime day or night". I hit the video call button. It barely gets through one ring before Clark answers. I hear him fumble the phone and a loud clash before his face comes into view. God, he looks good. His short hair is all tousled.

"Just hang on a sec," he says as he moves out of view. His face comes back into the video a second later. "Sorry, I had to wash my hands. I was working on the car." He smiles at me and my whole body relaxes.

"That's okay. I'm sorry it's so late. I've been hanging out with the kids, but they have finally gone to bed and I'm just letting everything sink in now. How are you feeling?"

"Honestly?" He raises his shoulders in a bit of a defeated shrug. "I feel devastated, but I have just been trying to keep busy." He runs his hand over his face, and I see the sadness behind his eyes.

"I'm so sorry, Clark. I know this must be really hard for you as well."

He nods but doesn't say anything. He looks like if he opens his mouth to talk about how he feels, he will collapse into a puddle of tears.

I change the subject. "I told the kids."

His eyes snap up to mine. "About us?"

"Everything. About you, about us, about the baby."

"Shit, Hannah, are you all right? How did they take it?"

"They were pretty upset at first, but we had a really good chat. Apparently, I have been happier lately. Who knew."

He huffs a little laugh. "Do I make you happy?" His tone is playful, teasing.

I meet his eyes and even though it is through a screen, I still feel the connection to him. "Yes."

"You make me really happy, too," he says, more serious now.

We say nothing for the longest time, just staring at each other through the screen. I lay back, sinking into the bed.

"You tired?" he asks.

"I'm exhausted."

"I'll talk to you to sleep while I work."

"Okay," I say as I roll to my side, plugging my phone into the charger, then propping it up on a pillow so I can see without holding it.

He balances the phone off to the side so I can watch. Grabbing a socket set, he starts removing something on the engine that is mounted on a stand. I watch as he places it down and moves to the next one. "These are spark plugs. I'm taking the old ones out and replacing them with new ones."

I'm mesmerised watching his hands work with skilful movements. The way his corded forearms flex as he removes the remaining spark plugs.

"This is a feeler gauge." He picks up a weird looking metal contraption. It is held together in the middle but spins out in a heap of smaller little metal tabs. It looks like the nail colour samples spinners that they give you at the salons. Only instead of sticks with nails on them, they are metal tabs. "Each spark plug must be set to between point eight-six and point nine-one of a millimetre to fire correctly."

I have absolutely no clue what he is talking about, but the low rumble of his voice has me wanting to shut my eyes.

He continues talking me through each task he does while he works.

"This is a torque wrench." He holds up another tool that looks exactly like the one he used to remove the spark plugs. Only he starts to explain how this one is completely different. How it is used to apply a specific amount of rotational force to the plug.

I think the last thing I hear is something about a Newton meter before my eye lids shut for good.

I wake to the sound of a coffee machine starting. My kids wouldn't dare touch my prized possession. Keeping my eyes shut, I sniff. No scent of coffee wafting through the house.

Rolling over, I open my eyes to find my phone has fallen from its pillow prop and is face down next to me, still on charge. I must have fallen asleep listening to the sound of Clark working on his car. He didn't hang up.

I clutch the phone, pulling it off charge and holding it up. I can't see Clark. The phone must be on the bench as I have a shot of his ceiling. He is frothing his milk on his coffee machine now. I can hear the steam bubbling away.

"Morning."

I see his face appear over the top of the screen at hearing my voice. A big smile splits his face. "Morning."

"Wish you could pass me that coffee through the phone."

"I can be there in fifteen and I'll make you one."

God I would love nothing more than that. He picks up the phone, and I see the hope in his eyes. But after everything I lumped on the boys last night, I think I need to give them a little time before I introduce Clark. Noah did flat out say he wasn't ready to meet him.

Clark must notice the hesitation on my face.

"Hannah, I'm joking. I know you aren't ready for the boys to meet me yet. There is no pressure from me."

"It's not that I'm not ready, it's just that I don't know how to go about all this. I just don't know the best way to handle it."

"Well, whenever they're ready, I'm ready."

"Thanks, Clark." I'm interrupted from my thoughts as a second call comes through on my phone. I recognise the number as my doctor's office straight away. "Clark, my doctor is ringing. Can I call you back?"

"Of course, chat soon."

I hang up and answer the call.

My doctor tells me that the hospital has made an appointment for me today. They want to do it sooner rather than later. They are sending me through an email with all the relevant information, but my appointment is for two in the afternoon.

My mind is running wild with everything I need to organise.

I have no clue if they'll keep me overnight. It's a Friday. So, I need to get the kids to school and organise someone to collect them at three. I need to organise them dinner and potentially have someone to watch them for tomorrow as well. I have no idea how painful this procedure is or what the recovery time will be. I suppose the email will explain more.

I open my emails on my phone and read through the information.

Okay, just breathe. Today is just an appointment to confirm there is no heartbeat. A proof of life they call it. Which is stupid because they are not alive, are they? Or did the doctor get it wrong?

A tiny sliver of hope ignites in my chest. But I try to think rationally. The email says it is standard procedure. That the hospital has to do their own ultrasound confirming that the foetus is not alive before they can perform the procedure.

I'm booked in for Saturday at 9 AM for the dilation and curettage procedure. The email outlines everything. It is a day procedure. Under general anaesthetic. I will be released by the afternoon. Recovery time is a few days. May experience cramping and bleeding, blah blah blah. Nothing about the emotional turmoil of them sucking your literal dead baby from your body. No places to call for help if you are struggling with this.

No, "I'm sorry for your loss." Just cold and clinical. A list of to do's.

I give Clark a call back, mindful of the fact that he will be on pins and needles waiting for me. I wonder if the poor guy slept at all. The fact that he was up at 6 AM walking around still clutching his phone, not willing to hang up from the FaceTime call even though I had fallen asleep indicates he might not have.

He is losing a baby, too. I think I'm alone, but he is trying to be there for me despite his own grief.

He also has no family here.

I don't even hear the phone ring before he answers. "Everything okay?"

"Yes and no. I'm booked in at two today for them to confirm there is no heartbeat, then I'm booked for nine tomorrow for the procedure."

"Do you want me there?" I hear the emotion behind the question. He thinks I don't want him there.

A sob racks my body. "Yes."

"What can I do, Hannah? I feel so useless over here, pacing around the house. Tell me what I can do to help you."

A dam in me breaks again. I feel like I haven't stopped crying since I left the doctor's office.

"I'm all right. I'm just exhausted and I have so much to try to organise now. Someone to get the kids from school at three. Kate already left work early yesterday. I'm not sure she will be able to do that again. I will have to call Mum. I have to call and cancel my clients for the day; I don't know when to reschedule them. I don't know the full recovery time. Am I going to need a week, or two? God, I have full books. I'm going to need to go through and reschedule everything. I have to organise dinner for the next few nights, at least for the kids. I was supposed to go shopping yesterday, my house is bare." I'm rambling, barely taking a breath.

"Okay, okay, Hannah, just breathe. Let's just do this one step at a time, all right. Get the kids off to school and then I will head around and we will make a plan. I'm here to help."

"Clark, you're losing this baby, too. I should be there for you as well."

"Letting me help you is what I need. I need to keep busy, and I want to be there for you. I'm not the one that has to deal with the hormones and have an operation. I'm devastated, but I'm okay. Just let me help."

"Okay."

"I will be there at nine."

"Okay."

"Hannah."

"Yeah?"

"I love you."

"I...I..."

"I know."

"Thanks, Clark."

"See you soon."

"Okay."

I go about the motions on autopilot. It's a dance I've done a million times on my own. I have the mornings down to a fine art now, even wallowing in heartbreak.

The kids are on their best behaviour, and I manage to also get out a few phone calls to my morning clients to cancel their appointments. I don't try to tackle rebooking them yet. I will do that when I have recovered. I keep a list of them all, so I know who I have to rebook as a priority.

I get the kids dropped off and am home by 8:50 AM. Clark's truck is in my driveway as I pull up. He pushes off the side of his car where he is propped and follows mine into the garage.

Opening my door as my car rolls to a stop, he doesn't even give me a chance to speak before he is grabbing me and pulling me into him. His strong arms hold me tight and press me to his warm body. I let myself melt into him. I don't want to cry anymore, but having him wrap me up like this feels so safe. It makes me feel like maybe I can fall apart. And If I do, he will catch me.

"I got you," he says as I nuzzle my head into his neck, breathing him in. Woodsy yet slightly sweet. I close my eyes and feel my whole body relax. "Come on, let me take you inside." He peels his body from mine and I internally cry.

I don't want to be away from him. Not even for a minute. I want him to tuck me into bed and hold me like that all day. But I have a list of clients to reschedule, a phone call to my mum to ask for help with the kids over the next few days and shopping to do.

Clark's one hand never leaves my body as he takes the keys and leads me to the garage door. Inside, I sit down at the kitchen table.

"Can I get you anything?" he asks.

"I'm okay. I might just try to get the shopping done online quickly. If I get it done now it can still get delivered this afternoon." I pull out my phone to open the Coles app, but he places his hand over mine.

"I got it sorted."

He leaves my side and heads back out the front door, returning with two armfuls of grocery bags. My anxiety peaks. I'm fussy with my shopping. I like particular brands, and I only let my kids eat certain things. Although, I realised last night that they really don't abide by that at all.

What does it matter if for a few days they eat whatever they want?

Clark places the bags down on the kitchen bench, and I stand to help him unpack.

"When did you have time to do all of this?" I ask.

"I went on the way; it didn't take long. I just got a few things."

"A few things? These bags are overflowing."

"I may have gotten a little carried away. I know you have particular things you like. I tried to remember the brands I have seen in your cupboards. I know you make a lot of stuff yourself, but I got some packet things for the boys."

I start unpacking one of the bags. He has gone all out. There are chips and nut bars and popcorn and goddamn polony. Heaps of snacks to keep the kids occupied but also bags full of apples, oranges, kiwi fruit, a watermelon bigger than my head, bananas, strawberries and blueberries. There is a full bag of meats, steaks, mince, chicken and a lamb roast. Not to mention broccoli, lettuce, carrots and potatoes, too.

These aren't a few things. It's a full weekly shop for a family of five.

Family of five.

The thought makes me smile. Could I have this again? Someone helping with the grocery shopping. Someone to talk to about my day as we unpack groceries. Someone to pour me a glass of wine and make me laugh while we cook dinner together. Someone helping the kids with their homework because I'm useless at math. I spend more time googling answers than actually helping the boys figure it out.

Despite the crushing weight of loss twisting in my stomach, it feels nice to have him here, in my home, helping me with the most mundane tasks.

We unpack the groceries in a comforting silence. Clark mimics my motions as I start to prep the different foods how I like them in the fridge. Washing the apples and pre-cutting the carrots, keeping them in a glass container in water so they stay crunchy.

"Thank you. For all of this."

"No worries. I got ingredients for a few different things. Tell me what the kids like and I can make it. I know you already have a Shepherd's Pie, but I can do lasagna, spaghetti, meatloaf, curry."

"That Shepherd's Pie is gone. Do you not remember how much teenage boys eat?"

He laughs, a big smile crossing his handsome face. "Shit. Well, what else would you like me to make?"

"The kids love spaghetti. It's easy and goes a long way. I can hide a heap of veggies in the sauce."

He moves closer to me. "Sneaky, I like it. I'll do it. You can go rest. Get back in bed or have a bath. Whatever you need." Wrapping an arm around my shoulder, his hand finds the back of my neck and pulls me into him, kissing the top of my head.

"I'm happy to help. Besides, I need to keep busy. Otherwise, all I will do is cry."

He nods but doesn't try to change my mind or argue. I start to pull out the ingredients we need for spaghetti. Clark opens a heap of cupboards, trying to find a pot, then places it on the stove with some water and salt to boil for the pasta, while I start chopping up onions and garlic to sauté.

"You said you don't want to cry anymore," Clark says as he slips behind me and removes the knife from my hands, taking over chopping the onions.

Smiling, I step aside and let him take over, not even mad that he is chopping them like a barbarian. I cook them down and whiz it all up into the sauce anyway, so really it doesn't matter how they look.

I get out a crock pot and start to heat it up. Seeing what I'm doing, Clark comes over and adds some oil to the pot and then chucks the onion and garlic in.

"Where are your spices?"

"Top draw there." I point over to the draw he needs. He moves over to it and pulls out a few things before adding them to the pot with the onion.

I'm usually quite a boring cook. Lots of lean meats and vegetables. So, I have no clue what he adds but it smells damn good.

I start prepping the vegetables while he cooks the onion and garlic for a bit.

I move back over to the stove, trying to open one of the jars of passata that I usually add. Clark notices me struggling and takes the jar from my hands, opening it with zero effort.

I roll my eyes at him, even though it feels nice to have the help. Normally in that situation I would puncture the lip with a knife to remove the pressure.

He hands the jar back to me so he can open the second one and then we pour them both in over the onions. I chuck in a heap of chopped up vegetables—carrot, broccoli, cherry tomatoes, an old parsnip that is dying in the back of my fridge, and half a bag of spinach. I top it up with a little bit of bone broth stock I made and let it boil. Clark adds the pasta to the boiling water, and I bring out a fry pan to start cooking the mince.

We dance around each other like this cooking, and it feels euphoric. Peaceful, safe. Despite the loss, my heart flutters. It's the little things like this that you start to take for granted in a long-term relationship. Well, maybe not take it for granted, but you become used to it. It becomes your normal. When it is pulled out from under your feet, you realise how precious it actually is. Priceless, really.

His fingers brush my hip as I circle to the bin drawer to chuck the mince container away. My hand strokes his back as he starts to stir the mince in the pan. He kisses my shoulder while standing behind me as I start washing up a few of the dishes, the chopping board and knives. My body brushes against him as I stand at the stove checking if the pasta is cooked and giving the sauce a stir, while he cooks the meat.

It's bliss and the only thing missing is the sound of the boys laughing or play fighting around us.

I grab the strainer and go to grab the giant pot. There is enough pasta to feed an army. So it should last two days max in my household.

I chuckle at the thought.

Clark places his hands over mine on the rubber handles. "Let me."

I release the pot, and he carries it to the sink, straining the water. I flick the cold water on to run it over the pasta, and he gives me a sideways look.

"It stops the pasta from over cooking. So it stays Al dente."

"I didn't know that."

He places the pasta in a large container I had set on the kitchen bench, and I move to add the pasta sauce into the blender. He smirks at me again, questioning my methods.

"I blend it all up so they have no idea what vegetables are in it. To them it just looks like tomato sauce. I even add a spoonful of coconut sugar, so it adds a bit of sweetness to it."

He laughs at me but takes the pot of sauce from me and empties it into the blender. I add the coconut sugar and blend it up.

"Sugar is like crack to these kids. Honestly, if you want them to eat something, just add sugar."

"I'll keep that in mind for the future."

He knew it as soon as he said it. The reality of this situation blanketing our happy cooking montage like a storm cloud.

Clark is not here because we are a happy family making dinner for our kids. He is here because my husband is dead and so is our baby. I'm about to go and have that confirmed later this afternoon.

"I'm sorry,"

"Don't be. It is what it is. Just got to get through these next few days."

He nods, wrapping me in his comforting arms again. I place my head on his chest, allowing the steady rhythm of his heartbeat to lull me back to a peaceful state.

We finish blending the sauce and add it to the pasta, then I stir through the cooked mince and place it to the side to cool down before I put it in the fridge.

"I need to call my mum or sister to organise the kids for this afternoon."

He gives me a nervous smile. "I already spoke to them."

"You spoke to my family?"

"I...ahh, got Kate's number from your phone yesterday, so she could get the kids. She gave my number to your mum. We, umm, kind of made a group chat."

My eyes widen. "You made a group chat with my mum and sister?"

He moves awkwardly, running his hand over the back of his neck. "Well, your sister made the group chat. But I'm in it."

"And just what is being said in this group chat of yours?"

His eyes go wide, like he is only just realising now that this may offend me, having people I love all in a group chat talking about me behind my back, discussing how best to help me.

"Kate just said that we could work together to take some of the pressure off you. You know, just while you are healing. Your mum is going to get the kids from school. She will bring them back here to pack a bag and then drop them at Kate's later this afternoon." He pauses, still unsure if they have done the right thing. "Your mum spoke to Noah."

"Hold up, when did she speak to Noah?"

"Umm, last night. He messaged Kate's daughter, Sierra, after you guys had a chat."

"Why?"

"He was worried about you."

"That is the last thing I want. My kids to be worried about me."

"He said Liam took it kind of hard. I think he just wanted to talk to someone about it. Sierra told her mum. Kate told your mum, and your mum spoke to Noah."

I'm shocked. I mean, all my kids are close with Kate and my parents, as well as their cousins. We all live within a short drive of each other, and the kids have grown up with their older cousins. They were around even more when Callum passed. We are a very close family, so I know that the kids often talk to my mum or sister. Noah and Liam have phones. I haven't given in to Ethan yet, but at nine I swear it isn't far away, especially since both his brothers have one.

"So, my whole family has just been conspiring behind my back about what is best for me."

Clark moves closer to me, placing a hand on my hip. "No, it wasn't like that. Kate just made the chat so that she could easily loop everyone in on the plans. She didn't want to bother you with the logistics of it all and just wanted to take some things off your plate while you recover. That's all."

I let out a sigh. I can't be mad at my meddling family, or at Clark for being sucked into their vortex. I'm lucky to have so much help. So many people who care. The emotions bubble in me until my eyes are wet.

"Hannah," Clark says as he pulls me close. "I'm sorry. We all just wanted to help."

"I'm not mad, I'm thankful. Thank you."

"Oh thank God," he says, releasing his own ragged breath, clutching me closer to his chest. "Well, the boys are happy to sleep at Kate's for the weekend so that you can rest and so I can be here."

"Okay, thank you. For all of this." I look up at his beautiful hazel eyes; they are glassy, keeping his own tears at bay. "Are you okay? You lost this baby too."

He shakes his head, biting down on his bottom lip. "I'm not. I'm..." He pauses, trying to think of the right word. "Devastated." He swallows hard. "But I can't change what's happened." He shrugs. "I'm clinging to the silver lining that I can have kids. There's a chance I can still have a baby." He looks down at me hopeful. No, not hopeful. Pleading.

I don't say anything, because what can I say?

Despite the fact that I had got my head around having this baby, aside from the fact that I do feel completely destroyed at losing them, it was never my first choice. It wouldn't be my choice now to try again. But the way he is looking down at me has my heart shattering into a million pieces, tears pooling in my eyes again.

He grips me to his chest, and we stay locked in each other's embrace, silent tears washing over us both.

It also dawns on me that I need to have a conversation with Callum's parents. We are still close. I don't want the kids to feel like they are keeping secrets, and I would hate for them to hear it from one of them and not me.

I decide that it is a problem for future Hannah. Right now, I just focus on the warm body I'm wrapped in. The comforting heart that IS still beating.

38

Clark

Her hair tickles my neck, and my arm is numb, but I don't dare move. Hannah only just fell asleep.

The proof of life went as expected. I don't know why they call it that. I suppose proof of death sounds a bit harsh. We were then given all the details for the D&C procedure for the next day.

The kids stayed at Kate's all weekend. Kate's kids, Sierra and Axel, are twenty and eighteen, so the boys think that they are the coolest thing since sliced bread. They were quite happy living it up there for the weekend.

I have kept Kate and Renee up to date with how Hannah is doing. The procedure went well on Saturday. Well, as good as can be expected. We were having a little boy. Can you imagine Hannah with four boys? Our baby will be cremated, and we will get the ashes within the week.

Hannah and I haven't spoken about names or what we want to do with the ashes but there is no rush to that conversation. For now, I just hold Hannah close.

Her chest rises and falls with steady breathing, mimicking my own as we lay together. It feels good being here. It feels right having her in my arms and being together. I just wish the circumstances were different. I wish my hand was cupped around her growing belly, feeling little kicks. I'm not delusional enough to think Hannah will want to try for another baby; I saw her face when I mentioned the fact that I can have a baby in the future. I know she is crushed about losing this one, but I also know that this wasn't in her plans. She got her head around it and maybe even started to feel excited about it, but she won't want to try again.

A part of me knows that deep in my gut. I cling to her a little tighter. Would this be enough? Will I be happy with this relationship, knowing I can still have children but that I won't? Will I be happy just being a stepdad to her boys?

I'm getting ahead of myself. I haven't even met them yet and I have no idea where Hannah and I stand.

Do I love her? Absolutely? Has she said it back? Resounding *no*! Does she love me? I think so. Does she love me enough to make a proper go at this? I don't know.

It's all questions I want to know and conversations we will have I'm sure, but for now, I just want to hold her. Cling to her. Heal her. Heal myself.

I tune out the pins and needles in my arm and focus on the beautiful lines of her face as she sleeps. Her eyelids flutter a little every now and then. She has the longest eye lashes. They are dark and don't match her hair colour. Does she colour them darker? I know that's a thing. Her full lips are slightly parted and little soft breaths escape.

I drop the heat bag that I was holding to her low belly to help with the cramping. It's since gone cold anyway. Moving my hand just under her shirt to splay across her tiny little bump that is still there, I stroke her soft skin back and forth with my thumb.

This is all I want. Her. If I don't get the baby, this is enough for me. Before I met Hannah, I had come to terms with the fact that I would never have a baby of my own. But if I get her, this life, forever stroking her soft skin and watching her sleep, cooking in the kitchen together and coming home to her and her boys, I will be happy with that. It will be enough. I know that deep within me to be true.

Hannah stirs, waking in my arms. Her lids flutter open as her eyes adjust. It's late afternoon and she has only been asleep for a couple of hours. I haven't moved from her side. If I thought my arm was tingling before, well now I actually can't even feel it. Is it still attached?

She moves her body, rolling over to face me and lifting her head. I take my chance to slide my arm out from under her. It starts to throb with the blood pumping back through it. I rub at it with my other hand. It was worth every second to have her peacefully sleeping in my arms like that.

"How are you feeling?"

"Good, all things considered."

"That's good. Can I get you anything? Your water bottle is next to the bed, but if you're hungry I can make you something."

"I'm good. I might give the kids a call, just to let them know I'm okay."

I don't bother telling her that Kate and Renee have been messaging me nonstop checking in. I have been giving them a running commentary of every detail since the moment they put Hannah under for the procedure.

My family are close, but this is beyond that. It's beautiful, really. The kids are so lucky to grow up surrounded by so much love.

The thought makes me pause. Have they always been this close or was it just due to losing Callum? It's hard to forget the presence he was in this house, especially when his face is hanging on every wall.

There is a photo on Hannah's bedside table of him. She stands with her arms slung over one of her boys' shoulders, the tallest of the kids, so I would say it's Noah. He has a huge smile and his dad's eyes. The youngest one, Ethan, is in Callum's arms—maybe four at the time—with his tongue poking out at the camera. Callum's head is slightly turned, laughing at him. The middle one, Liam, is standing between all of them with a scowl on his face like he really doesn't want to be there but has been forced to participate.

It's a beautiful photo. Hannah looks gorgeous in a yellow sundress with pink flowers and thin straps. More than that, she looks so happy. A smile that touches her eyes, making them sparkle. She looks like she is on the verge of laughter.

The photo doesn't make me jealous. Not of what she had with Callum, or of the family and happiness she had. It doesn't make me sad or angry seeing her so happy with another man. I know she loved Callum with everything she had. Instead, it makes me feel hopeful.

Hopeful that one day I can make her smile like that. Hopeful that one day I can show her happiness like that. Hopeful that one day I might know what it's like to have a family like that. That loves me so fiercely.

Her past is her past and I never want to replace it. I don't want to erase it. I don't want her to feel like she has to forget him to have me.

I just hope she knows that.

Hannah gingerly moves to sit up and I wrap an arm around her waist, helping her the rest of the way. She grabs her phone, and I move off the bed to step out and give her privacy so she can call them. I head to the kitchen to make her a cup of tea and reheat her heat bag.

She comes walking out a few minutes later, and I slide the steaming teacup across the bench as she takes a seat on the stool. "Here."

"Thanks."

I walk around the kitchen island bench, wrapping my arms around her and placing the reheated bag over her belly. "How are the boys?"

"They're good. Actually having a lot of fun. Sierra and Axel took them to Perth today. They went to Level Up, bowling and did an escape room."

"That sounds fun."

"Kate will drop them back Sunday arvo so they can relax a bit before the school week."

"Think you will be all right by then?"

The doctor said recovery time is only a few days. I'm well aware that he was talking about physical recovery. Mental recovery is an entirely different beast. I know because I don't really feel okay. The weight of the loss feels heavy on my shoulders, but I feel like if I crack, who will hold her?

Hannah needs me and being there for her is exactly what I need.

"Yeah, I reckon I will be fine. I mean, I'm sore and crampy now but that's to be expected. I may just have to get Mum or Dad to take the kids to school on Monday, but after that I think I will be fine."

I want to tell her I can do it. I can be here Sunday. I can help to entertain them, cook dinner, get them to school and help with homework.

I don't say any of that, though.

The boys know about me now, so that is a step. I just need to be patient. Let her process all of this and do it in her own time.

39

Waves of insecurity

Hannah

The last month has gone by so fast. The boys have been great. My family, even better. My mum and dad have been around almost every day since the Monday after the procedure.

My mum has cleaned and cooked and done washing, and Dad has mowed my lawns. He also started rearranging things in my already immaculately organised shed. I think he was unsure of how he could help, so this allowed him to be here and keep busy. I still haven't told Callum's family yet. Still deciding on the best way to broach the conversation.

Clark has been amazing. I went back to work on the Wednesday after the procedure and he has been here every day. As soon as I'm back from dropping the kids off, he is here, waiting with a coffee and most mornings a breakfast bagel. He helps my dad in the shed, literally just moving things from one shelf to another. He helps my mum cook and fold laundry. He randomly brings groceries and snacks for the kids and even bought them a new video game for their Xbox. He takes off every now and then to do his own work and look after his animals, and he always leaves when I leave to get the kids. We fall asleep talking to each other on the phone every night.

It feels good having him here. It feels better than good, actually. However, I can't help the heavy cloud that stays over us. We have yet to have a serious conversation about all this.

We received the ashes for our baby. I offered to split them so he could take some home with him, but he said he didn't want to split him. He wanted him to stay whole. So, he sits in a sealed bag in a jar on a shelf in the living area next to Callum.

A small part of me hopes they found each other in whatever afterlife is out there. I know the type of man Callum was and he would be looking after him, I have no doubt.

I know we need to have a few serious conversations, but I just don't know where to start. We have both been successfully avoiding the subject. A little bit of avoidance to live in bliss for a while. But I know that isn't healthy long term. We need to talk about it eventually.

What do we do with our baby's ashes? Do they stay in the jar, or do we want to scatter them somewhere? What do we name him? What is our relationship without him? Where is this going? What do we both want?

I've been too scared to voice any of these out loud. Afraid to burst this perfect bubble. Before the pregnancy, it was honestly perfect between Clark and me. I would have been happy to ride that wave forever. No expectations. No pressure. Just great company when we needed it and even better sex. But everything has changed now, and I don't think we can go back to what it was. I just don't know what our future looks like.

I know Clark wants a baby. Now that he knows he can have one, will it be enough to just have me and the boys? Is he going to decide it isn't enough and leave?

Then there is still the underlying issue of Cherie that I know plays in his mind. Is her baby his? Now he doesn't have a tie to me, will he go back and try harder with her?

I pull into my driveway and like clockwork, Clark is waiting by his car with coffee and breakfast bagels. I can't help but smile.

"Morning." His smile is bright, and he looks so damn fine.

"Morning."

He leans over and kisses my forehead; it heats my entire body. We make our way inside and sit at the kitchen bench, opening our bagels and sipping our coffee in comfortable silence.

"You got a busy day today?" he asks, swallowing a mouthful of bacon and egg bagel.

"I've got two clients booked after lunch before I have to go get the kids. Then I was just going to try to catch up on paperwork. I have a heap of social media content I need to make. I also have to send a few bank statements through to the accountant so that she can start the BAS for this quarter."

"So yeah, busy then."

I can't help but laugh. "Always. What about you?" I know Clark has money. I don't think he is loaded *loaded*, but he seems to have enough to not really have to work a lot.

I'm also aware he has been booking the work he does around me and my schedule, so that he can be here as much as possible. He seems to work really early in the morning or late in the afternoon.

"I had a job this morning, just a routine service. Then I have a rebuild I am working on for a client that will take a while. I have been doing that at night."

"What about your car? How's that coming along?"

"Good, slowly, but I enjoy working on it."

He is sitting next to me at the kitchen bench. As we chat, his hand absentmindedly strokes my thigh. I don't think he is intending it to be a turn on. It's just a sweet gesture. A way for him to connect with me, and let me know he is here.

To be honest, sex has been the last thing on my mind. His touch and embrace have been a strength for me—a comfort. This is the first time since the loss that his touch has lit me up again.

Clark is a gentleman, so I know he will never make the first move, especially given what we have been through. When I want sex again, it will have to be initiated by me. Me letting him know I'm ready. Am I?

I feel good. Physically, anyway. The loss is still heavy in my heart, but I'm fully recovered from the procedure.

Mentally? Well, we are all a little messed up from life's curve balls, aren't we? I'm doing the best I can, given the circumstances. Pleasure and distraction are exactly what I think I need right now. And it sounds so much more fun than paperwork.

Clark is oblivious to my internal thought process or the way my body is heating. He sips his coffee and finishes his breakfast. His free hand now rests heavy on my thigh as his thumb strokes back and forth.

I move from the stool, chucking my coffee cup and bagel wrapping in the trash. He turns in his stool to follow me when I walk back, stopping in front of him. His legs part and he wraps his arms around me, pulling me in. I mould myself to his body. Hard and warm. It feels safe there. Calming.

Raising my head from his shoulder where it has pretty much lived for the last month, I stare up at him. His kaleidoscope eyes dance with yellows, greens and blues.

Then I kiss him, soft and slow. My hands roam his back and the strong muscles that line it. His hands hover on my hips. He kisses me back and I can tell neither of us want to stop. It breathes life back into me. The feel of his lips, warm but soft on mine. His hands roaming my body. How I lived without this for so many years, I do not know.

With my intention clear, Clark stands, gripping my ass as he pulls me up and into his arms. My legs wrap around his waist, and he starts moving towards my bedroom, his lips never leaving my body. They kiss my lips, my neck, my collarbone. Gently laying me down on the bed, he crawls on top of me. His arms support most of his body weight so he isn't crushing me.

Moving to the side, his hands find the bottom of my shirt, and slowly he pulls it up. His lips kiss the skin the shirt leaves behind, all the way up to my sports bra, which conveniently is a zip front. I rise slightly so that he can remove my shirt completely and then lay back down.

He kisses my neck as his fingers toy with the little gold zip, slowly peeling it down to expose my chest. His tongue dances around my nipple, trailing over them softly. He sucks my nipple into his mouth, gently biting down with his teeth. The effect is like lightning straight down between my legs. The sensation makes my skin rise with goosebumps. I arch into him, trying to calm the part of me that is desperate for him to be inside me already.

Clark pulls his shirt up over his head with one hand. I eye the hard lines of his body quickly before he is back on top of me. His lips find mine again, while his hands work their way down to my tights.

Damn it, why do I have to wear such tight clothing that is so hard to get out of fast?

He slides the soft material down over my hips and ass, then moves himself to get them the rest of the way down. My G-string joins them on the floor next to my discarded top.

A quiet wave of insecurity rolls over me, catching me off guard. Laying here naked in front of him, it's hard not to think of all the ways your body changes with kids and pregnancy. Even in those early days. It may be nothing that physically he would notice, but it's a feeling. I know it's there. My stomach feels different. My boobs feel different. I've just had a bunch of people I don't know poking around down there while I was out cold. It's a strange feeling trying to shift your mindset from mother and caregiver to partner and lover.

I want this. My body craves it.

Instinctively, I lean into his touch, wanting more, like a magnetic pull. My head is a mess. The feeling of his mouth on my nipple makes my body feel alight. But...my mind starts to think about how they were supposed to feed my baby that no longer grows inside of me.

His hand traces over my stomach and the feeling makes goosebumps rise and heat flood lower. But...my head starts thinking about how that was meant to be swelling with my growing baby.

His fingers trace lower, finding my clit and rubbing in soft teasing circles. I push into him wanting more. The feeling makes me pant with need. My body aches to have him inside of me. I'm hungry for it. But...the conflict in my mind starts remembering that just a month ago, our baby was sucked right from there and now lives in a pile of ashes in a box.

Clark has always read me well, paying attention to my body's cues. He pulls back, staring down at me. His hand leaves me and I all but cry out wanting it back.

"Hey, we don't need to do this," he says gently, his face inches from my own.

"I'm just in my head, that's all."

"Do you want to talk about it? Or do you want me to take you out of it?" His voice is low and husky, but he waits for my reply before his mouth finds my skin again.

"Please, I don't want to think about anything except how good this feels."

He lets out a slow chuckle that warms my skin as his hands find my body again. "Yes, ma'am." His fingers trail back down to my clit and start working me over in firm circles before sliding further down and into me.

My body arches into him, wanting more. He slides a finger back out before adding a second. I rock my hips into his hand, shutting my mind off and focusing on nothing but the pleasure coursing through me. The heat that ignites low in my stomach. The tingling on my skin and the ache between my thighs. My hands find his denim shorts and undo the button one handed, sliding the zip down.

He removes his fingers from me and the feeling leaves me empty. It's only for a moment while he removes his shorts and boxers.

Moving back over me, his hard cock teases my entrance. I push into him, and he grips the base of his cock, letting the tip slide in.

"Ohh fuck," I groan.

"You missed me, baby? Cos *fuck* I missed you."

"So much, please," I pant.

His smile turns sinful as he slides into me painstakingly slow. I feel every inch, making my eyes roll into the back of my head and my back arch. Clark moves slowly, sliding in and out in steady strokes. I hungrily claw at him, trying to get him to move faster and deeper.

"I fucking missed you. You feel so good." His eyes close briefly, lost to his own pleasure. I give in to the slower pace, letting my body follow his rhythm.

He keeps his eyes or lips on me the entire time—kissing me, sucking my ear lobe, teasing my nipples—until I feel that heat build deep inside of me. I clutch his shoulders, pulling him closer as his thrusts quicken but only slightly.

His body moulds into mine as I let go, heat working its way through me. My eyes roll into the back of my head, and he slows his pace again, letting me ride the waves of my orgasm.

"OH.MY.GOD," I pant. Clark simply chuckles as he continues to draw in and out of me in slow, deep strokes, making my sensitive body come alive again.

"Hannah," he says between kissing my neck and collarbone.

"Yeah?" I pant breathlessly.

"I'm so close to coming inside that sweet pussy of yours. But..." He pauses to place another kiss on me, and I know exactly what he is asking.

"Oh shit, ummm. Can you pull out before you come."

His pace quickens again as he leans up. He grips my thighs and yanks them up higher, angling my hips. His grip stays fixed on my thighs as he starts thrusting into me again.

"Fuuck!" he all but growls. His grip tightens and I swear I will have bruises there in the morning.

I don't care. I don't want him to let go. Not ever. I want to tattoo his fingerprints there so that it will always remind me of how good this feels.

"Let me come on those pretty little tits of yours," he says between thrusts, and I have to admit, I fucking love dominating Clark. I know this is his way of asking permission, and holy hell it turns me on when he talks dirty like this.

I give him a nod because that is all my body can manage at this point. His thumb finds my clit and rubs until I'm panting through another orgasm.

His eyes stay on me while I float back down to earth, his pace not wavering while he waits for me to finish. Then he pulls out and shifts to the side, stroking his cock in his hand as he releases himself all over my tits. His cum is warm and sticky as it hits my chest and runs over my skin. His breathing settles as he runs his knuckles through his cum, swirling it over my nipples before bringing it up to my lips. I lick my lip, tasting him on my tongue. And I really don't know why that movement is so damn hot.

I swear I should be too old for stuff like this. But he makes me feel like I'm experiencing sex for the first time again.

He scoops me up and carries me through to the shower, standing me up but supporting my weight as I find control over my legs again. He gets the water temperature just right before helping me in and washing his cum off me with my body wash and a loofa.

"I have to say, I love this aftercare almost as much as I love the sex. Are you going to wash my hair as well?" I playfully jab at him.

He chuckles and pulls me closer. "I would do anything you wanted of me, washing hair included."

"No honestly, don't touch my hair. I have a set routine, and I do not want you to fuck with it." I playfully swat his hands from my body.

"Then teach me." He hands me the shampoo.

I side eye him but decide to go with it, squeezing some of the shampoo into his hands. He starts rubbing it through my hair, massaging it into my scalp.

Okay shit, no direction needed. I lean my head back further into his hands as he works the shampoo into my scalp. He turns me to help me rinse it out before he goes for the conditioner.

"No, see, I shampoo twice," I say as I take the conditioner bottle from him and squeeze shampoo back in his hand.

"Okay, why?"

"You know what, I don't actually know. Just something my hairdresser told me to do, and I've done ever since."

"Well, who am I to go against your hairdresser?" He starts massaging my scalp for a second time and OH.MY.GOD I'm considering telling him I do it three times because it feels so damn good. That will probably completely dry my hair out. I don't want to mess with the system I have been using for the last fifteen years.

He rinses the shampoo out for the second time.

"What now?" Clark asks, staring at the three other bottles sitting on my shower shelf.

"That one." I point to my purple conditioner. I only use it every third or fourth shampoo.

He squeezes the conditioner into his hand, brows rising at the colour of it. "Why is it purple?"

"It's to stop my blonde going brassy. The purple counteracts some of the yellowish colour that blondes get," I explain.

"Ahh, I see." He starts massaging the conditioner into my scalp and if I thought the shampooing felt good, then this is to die for.

The last time I had any form of pamper was when Clark took me on the night away and booked me the spa day. Before that, it was at least three years since I had anyone else even touch me.

I should have been better with self-care. But it was hard to not feel guilty at doing things for myself when my boys had lost their father. I had been living on autopilot for those years, pouring every ounce of love and energy I had into my kids because I'm all they have left. I made it to the hairdresser once every six months and did pretty much everything else myself at home when I had the chance.

I breathe deeply, leaning into his touch. Tension melts from my body. Maybe, just maybe, I can take my foot off the pedal. Let someone else drive. Even just for a little while.

I lean back further, and the back of my body touches his front as his hands work through my hair. Clark leans down close to my ear. "You keep pushing back into me like that with your body all slippery from this conditioner, and I'm going to take you again. Right here."

I feel his cock twitch against my ass. I purposely push back a little further, baiting him. I shift my hips from side to side, letting my slippery skin slide across his cock.

His hands leave my hair. One grips my hip, while the other wraps around my throat. He uses his hand at my hip to pull me back into him, angling my ass up so his cock meets my pussy. His hand around my throat gently squeezes and pulls me down, angling me even more. Then, in one smooth motion, he thrusts his hard cock into my already aching wet pussy.

All signs of the sweet, slow and controlled Clark who just made love to me on the bed are gone. Instead, replaced with a savage who fucks me like I am the oxygen he needs to breath.

And I fucking love it!

His grip on my hip doesn't waiver but the one around my throat loosens. His hand stays there and every now and then he tightens his grip to slightly block my airflow, just a little and never for long. The effect on my body is instant. Every time his grip tightens, my pussy reacts, clenching around him and sending me closer to another orgasm that I don't believe is possible to have.

His hips move hard and fast, and he leans over my back, biting into the flesh at my shoulder as his grip tightens around my throat again. The pain tips me over the edge and that third orgasm I didn't believe possible rolls through me. My legs are barely able to hold my weight as the waves of pleasure wash over me with the water.

Clark follows me with a few more hard thrusts before pulling out and gripping his cock to come over my ass. He gives it a playful little slap before rubbing his cum all over me.

"You look good covered in my cum, baby."

"Well now you're going to have to clean me all over again."

"I will happily spend the rest of my life cleaning you."

The weight of his words rests heavy on me. I don't know if he means it the way I interpret or if it was more light-hearted.

I thought I was going to be spending the rest of my life with Callum. Then for a long time I couldn't imagine ever feeling things for anyone else. Couldn't imagine bringing anyone else into my kids' life.

Suddenly, I'm imagining all these things and more.

With Clark.

"I love you, Clark." I've been terrified to say the words out loud. Terrified to even think about them. Terrified if I let myself love Clark that I would lose Callum. If I bring him into the kids' life, they will lose Callum.

These last few weeks have made me realise just how madly in love with Clark I actually am. How much I want this.

I stand with my back to him as he rubs body wash over me. He pulls me close to him and places his head down into the crook of my neck. I feel him smile.

"I'm sorry it's taken me so long to say it. I was just scared to voice it out loud. I realise now that loving you doesn't diminish the love I had for Callum. It's not more or less, it's just different. You are different. I'm different now, too. And it's equally as powerful. I'm madly in love with you, Clark."

"I'm madly in love with you too, Hannah."

I want to say more. To initiate the hard conversations that we need to have. How we are going to make this work. But I just can't bring myself to do it now. I sense the same from him.

For now, I just want to live in this love bubble that we have created. Warm and blissful. Avoiding real life issues.

At least just for today.

40

With everything I am

Hannah

I move through to Clark's bedroom to use the bathroom. We have been out riding for the afternoon, but now I need to get ready to grab the kids from school and take them to football training.

It's been a week since I told him I love him and we have been living in denial of all the realistic issues we are about to face. Instead, absorbing the feeling of love and euphoric orgasms. It almost makes me think we can go back to the way it was.

Although, having that taste of him in my house most days, cooking together, the way he always has a coffee ready for me when I come here, or brings me one when he comes to mine after I drop the kids at school. How much he helps around the house when he spends the day at mine. I've loved having him around so much. It gave me a taste of what it can be like, and I want it all.

I want to wake up in his arms and have him join me at footy training and kick the ball with the kids. I want to have him lie in bed next to me while I read instead of holding a phone with him on the other end. I want him back in my shed pottering around. I have no clue what he and my dad were even doing in there. It looks exactly the same to me. The clangs and bangs reminded me of what domestic life felt like, before everything went to shit.

And I want that back. I want what is to come. What I can become with him by my side. I want Clark.

I know it isn't the same. I'm not trying to replace what I lost in Callum. They are so different. I'm a different person now, too. The very fibre of my being was changed for good the day Callum passed. And every day since.

I head out of the bathroom, stopping at Clark's dresser where he placed the little onesie I bought him with the 'I'm going to be a dad' printed on it.

He kept it. I don't know why I thought he wouldn't. He wants kids of his own. Now he knows it's a possibility, is he holding hope we can try again?

The weight of real life crashes down. The balls fall in slow motion, smashing to the ground in pieces of broken glass around me.

Clark appears at the door, and I now realise I'm holding the little onesie, staring at it. His eyes find mine and I know he sees the broken pieces as well. His face falls slightly and then he composes himself.

"You kept this?"

"Hoping one day I get to do up those little buttons around a baby."

"Clark, I…"

He pushes off the door frame and closes the distance in two strides. "Hannah, I know you don't want to try again. You never wanted a baby, I know that. I'm not going to try to convince you to change your mind. I love you and I want to be part of your family. I want to make it my own. I want to meet your boys and be a father figure to them. I want you, Hannah."

"Will that be enough for you?"

He doesn't hesitate. "Yes."

"Do you mean that?"

Again, not a moment of hesitation. "With everything I am."

I sigh. I don't want to be the one to take that dream from him. But I'm so conflicted. "There is a part of me that wants it back, you know. It wasn't what I wanted to begin with, but I got my head around it and I was happy. And while I am devastated we lost our baby, there is also a small part of me that feels kind of relieved." I let the weight of my words settle around us, watching his face grimace with pain at my truth. But he says nothing. "I'm sorry. I feel horrible for even thinking that."

"You never have to apologise to me for how you feel, Hannah."

"I know you wanted this baby so badly. And I did too once the shock had settled. But I don't know which part of me is winning. The part that wants the baby back or the part that is relieved. I've been scared to tell you, just in case it means you didn't want this anymore. If I can't give you what you want."

"You are what I want. Hannah, I don't want a baby if it isn't with you. Being with you...I've realised just how wrong everything else in my life has been up until this point. I want us."

"You want this now, but what happens in five years, ten? Are you going to resent me? Clark, your clock isn't ticking. Well, it is, it just seems to be going backwards." I laugh. "You are hot enough to find a younger woman. Someone who wants kids and marriage and all of that. Someone you can build a life from scratch with. You're such a good man. You would make such a good father."

He steps closer to me, cupping my face with his hands. "I've built a life from scratch already. I've dated younger already. Look how that worked out for me. I don't want to settle for anyone else. And I don't want a baby if it means I don't get you."

"I just don't want you to regret it. I can't guarantee that I will want to try again," I whisper up at him.

"As long as I get you for life. Forever."

My eyes open a little wider. "Are you asking me to marry you?"

He laughs at me, leaning down to place a kiss on my forehead. "Abso-fucking-lutely NOT, Hannah. You think I would propose like that?"

"What, are you going to ask my father for permission first?" I tease.

His gaze turns serious. "No, you don't belong to your father. But those three boys…" He pauses, his eyes boring holes into me. "They do belong to you, and I feel like they need to be happy with me in their life before you will ever be able to give me the answer I want."

"Is that what you want? To marry me?" I hadn't ever thought it would be something I would do again.

"Is it on the table?" Clark asks, his thumb stroking my cheek.

I pause, thinking it over. If you had asked me six months ago, it would have been a resounding NO. But now, I think it would be nice to be Clark's wife.

"It's on the table," I whisper.

His smile grows and he wraps a hand around the back of my neck, pulling me into his lips as he kisses me. "I think I would like that. Calling you 'my wife'."

"Okay, slow it down there, cowboy. One step at a time."

"What's the next step then?"

"Well, you've met my parents."

"You want to meet my parents? I'll call them right now. They already know all about you."

"You told your parents about me?"

"I think I told them I was in love with you on the drive home from the first weekend I met you."

I laugh, but he pulls his phone from his pocket and hits dial.

"What! I thought you were joking about calling them now."

Clark just shakes his head at me, putting the phone on speaker as his mum answers.

Panic washes over me, but the moment he says he is here with me, and her warm voice chimes my name, the nerves dissipate. His dad joins the call, and I realise Clark must have been giving them daily updates because it feels like they know everything about our relationship. Which I'm not mad about. It is sweet and I realise just how invested he is in this. While I have been holding back, fighting my feelings, he has been all in from the beginning, waiting patiently for me to catch up.

We talk for the next fifteen minutes before his parents have to head off, and we end the call.

"What's next, Hannah? Cos I'm here with my highlighter about to start crossing things off this list."

"Next I have to go and get the kids before I get stuck at the back of the pick-up line. Then I need to talk to Callum's parents. I don't want them to find out through anyone else. Then, I think we organise a time for you to meet the kids."

"Tell me when and where and I'll be there."

I leave smiling from ear to ear. Did I really just meet that man's parents over FaceTime, promise him a future with marriage and line up a date for him to meet the kids?

Yep, and I'm not even mad about it.

41

This is sparta

Clark

"Clark, you look fine. My boys are not going to care about the colour of your shirt."

I know this, but first impressions and all. "I think the blue one is better."

"Clark, seriously, that one is fine."

I pull the white tee over my head and chuck on literally the same shirt but in blue. It's nothing fancy, just a plain tee. A staple. I let out a breath and start fiddling with my hair in the mirror. I always keep it pretty short—skin fade at the sides and short on top. It's much easier when working in the heat and with greasy car parts. There isn't much need to do anything with it, but thankful with my age it's still thick and without a single grey.

Okay, I lied, there have been a couple. My hair isn't dark, so they blend in, making it appear more of a sandy blond than brown.

I run my hands through the top strands to move it around. Hannah stands at the bathroom door, shaking her head at me. It's been a few weeks since Hannah told me she loves me, and I still can't wipe the smile from my face. There is a part of me that is still devastated at what we lost but the fact that I still have her...that's all I need.

I had been open with my feelings for her early, but I knew she wasn't ready to voice hers. I knew she needed more time to work through her complicated feelings about losing Callum. She had a lot on her plate. A whole life with him, and his family to consider in all of this as well.

I know it was hard for her to tell them about me. But they took it well. They all just wanted to still be in the kids and her life. I'm okay with that. The more love and support she and the kids have the better, in my opinion.

I just wanted to be included in that.

She was always going to put her kids first. The fact that she is such an amazing, dedicated mum to those kids only makes me love her more. I would have given her all the time she needed. There was a huge part of me that thought after we lost the baby, she would realise this wasn't what she wanted and leave. Push me away.

I'm still terrified of that if, I'm honest.

Which is why I want to make an effort to meet her kids. If they don't like me, she is going to choose them. And rightly so. If the boys don't want me around, I'm most likely going to be back where I started. With Pam the savage goat, my dog Banjo and a couple of horses.

"All right, I've got to go pick them up from school. I'll see you at my house in around an hour."

"I'll be there."

"Don't be so nervous. It will be fine." She places a gentle kiss on my cheek and turns to leave. I grab at her and pull her body against mine. I will never get enough of her.

"See you soon." I cup her face and kiss her. Her body moulds into mine and I don't want to let her go.

She giggles against my neck as I hold her.

"I have to go." She pries herself from my arms, and I playfully slap her ass as she walks away. She glares at me, feigning annoyance, but I don't miss how she sways her hips a little more as she walks out the room.

Tease.

"I liked the white better," she throws the offhanded comment back over her shoulder as she leaves, and I know she is just doing it to stir me up. The blue looks good.

Doesn't it?

Ahhh, shit. I pull the blue off and chuck the white back on, then go back to moving my hair around on my head.

I pull up at her place at 3:30 PM. I really didn't want to get here before them and be lurking out the front when they got home. However, my anxiety wouldn't let me wait any longer.

I grab the three bags off my passenger seat and head to the door. Then I turn around and walk back to the car, ready to chuck the bags back in. These were a dumb idea. What was I thinking? They aren't little kids anymore. And I'm showing up with what? Homemade gift bags. I'm such a dick.

They are going to think I'm trying to buy their attention.

I didn't tell Hannah I was going to do these goodie bags. It was my idea and a dumb one at that. I had bought them a few little things that I knew they liked, just from what Hannah had told me about them and what I've noticed around the house. Nothing overly expensive. I wanted it to be more personal.

Ethan is into Minecraft and loves to read, so I got him a 'Diary of a Minecraft zombie' book I saw at the shops. Then a giant packet of Zappos. I know Hannah is going to kill me over the sweets but...worth it if the kids like me. I also got him a packet of Cheezles—I know they are his favourite chips—and a few Hot Wheels cars. I don't know if he is too old for them at nine, but I remember loving them as a kid. I would be lying if I said I didn't love hunting through them all to find the good ones even as an adult.

I almost squealed in the aisle like a child when I found the exact car I'm fixing up—a Ford GT 500 Shelby. I then went to about seven different shops to find more so I could give one to all the boys. I may have grabbed one for myself as well. I probably could have bought them online, but I was worried they wouldn't arrive in time. Spending an entire day driving from town to town to visit every Kmart, Target and Big W was worth it. I hope.

Liam, I got the same: Hot Wheels car, Sour Worms, Maltesers, a giant tin of Milo and a mug. Hannah says he is currently obsessed with Milo. I found a mug that had 'have a nice day' written on it and when you lift it up to take a drink, it had a middle finger sign on the bottom of the cup.

I could not stop laughing. It seemed fitting from what Hannah has told me about Liam's personality. I know I don't have kids of my own, but I know enough to realise that was wildly inappropriate for a twelve-year-old, so I passed on that one. I ended up going so far down the rabbit hole of novelty mugs that I psyched myself out too much and ended up with a pretty boring looking one from Kmart.

Hannah told me Noah loves toasties, and I know the kid can eat. I found a microwave toastie maker. It's just a silicone sandwich grill thing that you put the toastie into and then put it in the microwave. I'm still a fan of the OG method but four-teen-year-old me would have loved this. He also has the Hot Wheels car, and the weirdest flavour of spicy chips that I had to go to a speciality candy store to get. Hannah had mentioned that Noah loves the weird spicy flavours, so while on my adventure though different shops I tracked some down, and I added in a packet of Sour Straps.

However, now I feel entirely stupid rocking up to meet them with a bag full of novelty items.

The decision is taken from my hands as Hannah's car pulls up into her driveway before I get a chance to chuck them back in the car. Caught red headed holding three gift bags next to my car on their driveway, like a giant weirdo.

Exactly what I was trying to avoid.

I should have waited longer to come here. Or texted Hannah to make sure she was home. The garage opens and she drives in. I don't want to crowd them all as they get out of the car, so I wait by mine until they have exited.

Liam heads straight inside, without so much as a second glance. Noah waits by the car with his backpack on, but Ethan follows Hannah as she strides over to me and kisses my cheek.

"Hey," she says.

"Hey."

I glance down at Ethan standing at his mum's side. "Hi, I'm Clark." I extend my hand out to him to shake.

He completely ignores it and points to the goodie bags in my other hand. "Hi. Is one of those for me?"

He's nine so no hard feelings on leaving me hanging on the handshake. I love how to the point he is.

"Sure is." There is no way out of it now, so I swallow the anxiety and hand him his gift bag. Hannah eyes me quizzically while Ethan starts opening his bag right there on the driveway.

"COOL!" he squeals as he pulls out the Minecraft book. "Mum, did you see this?" He continues to empty the remainder of the bag on the driveway. "Can I eat these now?"

Hannah looks up at me with pursed lips.

"Sorry," I get out with a slight shrug. I knew she would be pissed about the lollies, but I have kids to win over. I'm not playing fair.

"Yeah sure, bud," she answers.

He wastes no time ripping into the Zappos and opening the Hot Wheels.

"Thanks, Clark," he manages to get out around a mouthful of chewy lollies.

"No problem."

Noah has now made his way over and I reach out a hand to shake. At the age of fourteen he is probably more acutely aware of the entire situation than Ethan is. He is taller than Hannah and looks like his dad the most. From what I can tell from pictures of Callum, anyway.

"Hi Noah, I'm Clark."

He removes his hand from the shake, and it finds its way to the straps of his backpack. He pulls at the excess length used to tighten the straps. "Hi."

"This one is for you." I pass his bag over and he takes a hold of the straps. "It's just silly little things, but I hope you like them," I sheepishly add, feeling awkward as all hell.

That is until I lock eyes on Hannah. She has a huge smile on her face, and her eyes are glassy. She is watching the entire interaction with wonder, and it makes my heart beat a little faster in my chest.

"Thanks." Noah peaks into his bag, spotting the spicy chips. "Dude, I love these. Where did you find them?"

"A lolly shop in the city."

"You went to the city to get a packet of chips?" Hannah chimes in.

"Yeah, I was trying to find a specific Hot Wheels."

"That's your car," she states, motioning towards the packet that Noah has pulled out of the bag. Ethan is watching from the floor as he reads his Minecraft book and devours a whole packet of Zappos.

"Yeah, I found one in Kmart down here. Then I drove to Perth, stopping at every shopping centre on the way till I found more of them."

Noah gives me a look that clearly shows the difference in the times we grew up in. "Why didn't you just do it online?" he asks.

"I was worried it wasn't going to arrive in time. So, I just spent a day driving."

"Don't you work?"

"Yeah, but for myself. I'm a mechanic."

"Oh yeah, Mum did mention that."

"Why are you driving that if you have a cool car like this?" Ethan asks as he pops up, holding the mustang in his hand, swirling it around like he is driving it through the air.

"Well, it isn't exactly running just yet. I'm fixing it up and rebuilding the engine."

"Nice," Noah adds. "Liam will love that. He loves cars."

"Good to know."

"Come on, let's go inside." Hannah starts towards the garage again, and Ethan shoves his goodies and the empty wrappers back into his gift bag.

"Is Liam all right?" I ask Hannah once we are out of earshot of the other two.

"He always seems to feel the most but isn't the best at showing it. He holds a lot close to his chest. He just needs some time to ease into it."

I grab Ethan's backpack from the boot of the car that Hannah has opened, and she shuts the garage door as we make our way inside. The kids have all but disappeared as we make our way to the kitchen. I put the backpack on the kitchen table.

"Are there things that need to come out of here?" I see two empty lunch boxes sitting in the sink, assuming they are Noah and Liams that they have already taken out. I also spot the blue folder bags sitting on the kitchen table. Homework bags, I presume.

"Yeah, lunch boxes and homework bags."

I unzip the bag as Hannah starts washing the other lunch boxes in the sink. I pull out the lunch box bag and unzip it, before scraping the leftover food into the bin and then handing the box to Hannah at the sink. Moving to pull out the homework bag that matches the two already on the kitchen table, I then zip the bag up and take it to the front door. I know they keep them under the bench seat by the front door. I place Ethans next to his brothers.

Back in the kitchen, I grab a tea towel and start drying the lunch boxes that Hannah has washed. "Should I go to Liam or just let him come to me in his own time?"

"Oh, Liam," she sighs. "He is my tricky one for sure. He has a harder time with showing how he really feels. He's not upset you're here. Just give him time and space."

"I can do that."

Noah comes back into the lounge room after changing out of his uniform and sits at the kitchen table to do his homework.

Ethan also reappears and plops down onto the couch, flicking on the TV, as Hannah and I prepare dinner.

It's barely 4 PM. Hannah says on the nights where they have no sport they eat early and then the boy's snack for the rest of the night. We have had this dinner planned for a while, so I already bought around steaks to cook and snacks for a movie after.

"Do you want me to cook the steaks on the barbeque?" I ask as I help Hannah with the salad. Noah's ears prick up, and I see him turn his head to watch the interaction between the two of us.

Hannah shifts nervously. "Umm, we don't have a barbeque anymore." She avoids my gaze and carries on washing the lettuce to put into the salad bowl.

"We smashed it with hammers," Ethan yells from the couch, barely breaking his connection with the TV. My eyes find Hannahs, but she keeps staring at the dish soap and watching the little rainbow colours dance in the bubbles, like it is the most fascinating thing she has ever seen.

"What did the barbeque do to deserve that?" I say in gest.

Noah eyes me, breaking from his homework completely to join the conversation. "Mum couldn't get it to work properly."

"No, Dad forgot to clean it after he used it last, remember. It was so caked with dried food, all dusty and dirty because we hadn't used it in so long." Ethan has now moved from the couch to the kitchen table next to Noah.

"Yeah, then Mum spent like two hours rage cleaning it," Noah laughs.

"Then when she tried to light it, the gas had run out," Ethan adds.

"Ohh yeah, we all drove and got a new gas bottle, and Mum couldn't figure out how to change it. Then remember Liam burnt his hand trying to light it for her."

Hannah puts down the lettuce. "That was the final straw. The burn wasn't bad, but I just snapped in frustration."

"You more than snapped, Mum. You lost the actual plot. You kicked the whole thing over," Ethan says.

"Yeah, remember, you totally went 'THIS IS SPARTA' on it," Noah spits out around fits of laughter. Hannah cracks a smile now, and I can't help but join in on the laughter. I can just picture her kicking the thing over.

"It cracked when it landed and then you stormed off to the shed and came back with a hammer and started laying into it."

"Yeah, wasn't my finest parenting moment, let's be honest."

"It was the best," Ethan adds as he jumps up, mimicking swinging a hammer. "Noah went and got more hammers, and we all started smashing it until it was completely bent out of shape."

"Please tell me you turned off the gas and disconnected it before you went all Sparta on it?" I ask.

"No, I really don't think we did," she replies sheepishly.

I palm my face with my hand, stifling a laugh. "So, we have no barbeque." The *we* just slips out but Hannah doesn't seem to notice.

"Well, it went to the tip almost three years ago now, so no. No barbeque," Hannah says as she moves the washed lettuce to the chopping board.

"I miss barbeques," Noah says, putting his head back down to his homework.

Ethan starts moving back towards the lounge. "Me too. We haven't had a good steak in years."

"Hey, I cook steak for us all the time."

"Yeah, you aren't great at it, Mum." Noah doesn't even break concentration with his work.

"I'm offended. I make great steak."

"Mmmhum, sure, Mum," Noah continues.

I smirk, watching the exchange between them all. All except Liam.

"Well lucky for you boys, I am an excellent steak cooker, and I'm even better with a barbeque."

"Well, that would be great, but as we have established we don't have a BBQ." Ethan is now slumped back on the couch, pointing the remote at the TV to change the channel.

"Let's go get one." All three of their heads snap to me at the same time. "It's barely four-thirty, and Bunnings is open till seven. Let's go get a barbeque."

"Are you being serious?" Noah's face is full of hope as he places his pen down and turns towards me.

"Yeah." I look to Hannah to gauge her reaction. Have I overstepped? I'm not trying to buy their affection, but a barbeque? I can give them that. "It's kind of a sin that you don't have a barbeque in Australia," I add.

"I agree. Can we, Mum?" Ethan is now at her side, looking up at her with pleading eyes. I know she isn't going to say no to that.

"Let me just talk to Clark for a second. Okay, boys?"

Shit, I've overstepped.

"That's a no," Ethan comments as he mopes back towards the couch.

Hannah moves to walk towards her room, and I follow. I can't believe I've messed this up already. I wasn't thinking.

"I'm sorry, did I overstep? I just—"

"It's fine, Clark, I'm not upset, It's a really sweet gesture." Hannah avoids my eyes and looks down at the ground. "I just don't really have the spare funds to buy a barbeque right now. Noah has a school camp trip to Canberra next month that is costing me like two grand. Plus, the Winter Basketball comps start soon, and between the three of them playing, I will be up for just over a grand in registration fees. That's not even their uniforms. I-I-I can't go buy a barbeque. I wish you spoke to me first, because now their hopes are up."

I wrap my arms around her. "I'm sorry. I should have thought before I spoke. But I wasn't meaning you would pay for it, Hannah."

"I don't like the idea of you buying us things like that. I mean little goodie bags for the kids are fine, it was a sweet idea, but a barbeque? They can be expensive."

"It's what happens in a partnership, isn't it? Money is shared. What's mine is yours."

She swallows hard. "We're at that stage, are we? Sharing money."

"I'm meeting your kids, Hannah. It's not lost on me how serious that is for you. Especially with what you all have been through. So yeah, I'm at that stage. I'm all in here. I thought I made that clear. Now will you please let me buy you and the boys a barbeque and cook you all a proper steak?" I hug her close and place a kiss on the top of her head. "If that's okay with you?" I add.

I can see she is apprehensive. She has always been adamant about paying her own way when we do things together. I have never pushed the topic because I never wanted her to feel like she wasn't independent or capable. I know she is both those things. I would be lying if I said it didn't go against the provider in me. I internally cringe every time she pulls out her wallet or asks to split dinner.

"I think we have no choice now. The boys are excited for barbeque steak. I hope you are as good a cook as you've made out, because as you can tell, they will be brutal."

"I think I'll manage," I say as I wink at her.

Hannah pulls the door open, and three boys come tumbling into the room.

"You guys were listening to that?" Hannah asks, staring at them as they recover.

"We're going to go get a barbeque!" Ethan is basically jumping up and down. Noah is smiling from ear to ear, and Liam just stands deadpan, but I swear I see the hint of hope in his eyes.

"Mum said yes, let's go," Ethan squeals.

I move to grab my keys and wallet from the hallway table as the boys all follow me like little ducks in a row out the front door to the car.

42

I'm not going anywhere

Clark

We pile into the car, and I pull out of the driveway to head to Bunnings. The boys are playing a game of rock paper scissors to see who gets to choose the music. Liam wins and throws his phone to the front of the car, asking Hannah to connect to the Bluetooth. She fiddles with the screen's settings then passes it back to him.

Noah moans as a pop/rock song comes through the radio. Hannah and I side eye each other at the playful banter coming from the back seat.

"Are they like this all the time?"

"Pretty much. Constant competition and banter. Wait until the fights start, then you know we're really having fun."

We pull up at Bunnings and make our way inside to the barbeque section. The boys split up and start calling out to us to show us their favourites.

Noah has stopped at a six burner barbeque. "This one is cool."

"It's twelve hundred dollars. Absolutely not. Look, this little one is perfect, and it's only two hundred." Hannah moves in front of a small two burner barbeque.

"It's tiny and you have three boys. If I want to cook five steaks at a time, we need a bigger hot plate than that."

Hannah grips my arm. "Clark, you are not spending twelve hundred dollars on a barbeque. Do you understand me?" Her words are stern and her grip on my arm is tight, but I know her well enough by now to know where I can push.

I'm not trying to overstep or use her love for her boys against her, but I want to be able to do this for them. I have the means and the money, so why can't I?

I take her hand from my arm and hold it in mine. "Hannah." I stare down at her softly. "Please let me do this. I have the money, and I want to spend it on a barbeque. Please just let me give you and the boys this."

Her eyes don't leave mine. I see her internal struggle with letting someone take care of her. To spend money on her when she has worked so hard to do everything on her own for so long. Her eyes are glassy, like she is fighting back tears, but she nods at me.

I lean in and kiss her, closed mouth, just touching her lips gently with my own, mindful that her boys are watching the interaction. I'm not sure how affectionate I can be in front of them. Normally I crave her, itch to touch her skin, but she hasn't initiated any form of affection in front of her kids so I will wait for her to lead that.

"Show me what you want, boys." I turn to face them. Ethan calls me and says he found the perfect one. We all follow him around to the next aisle, where all the inbuilt barbeques stand.

"This one, I reckon." He stands proudly in front of a six burner barbeque built into a bench top, complete with a sink, a cupboard and draws. It all stands on casters for easy moving.

"Look, Mum, it even comes with a cover to stop it getting dirty like last time," he adds.

"That was your dads fault he didn't clean it properly," she quips. Her head snaps to me to gauge my reaction. I see her regret it as soon as the words leave her mouth. I have no issue with her remembering Callum or talking about him. I've told her as much, especially with the boys. I smile at her and her tension eases.

"I like this one," I say as I drape an arm over her shoulder.

"I like it too," Noah adds.

I look at Liam. His eyes meet mine for the first time and he nods his approval.

Hannah moves closer and her eyes go wide when she sees the price tag. I quickly rip it from the display and shove it into my jeans pocket to stop her stressing over it.

"All right, let's go find it on the shelf. And we better get some gas bottles and barbeque utensils while we are at it."

"I'll grab a trolley." Noah heads off to the trade section to locate a large enough trolley as Liam starts hunting the shelves for the flat pack version.

"Here," he shouts from the opposite end of the isle that Ethan, Hannah and I look at.

We make our way down, as Noah heads back with the trolley.

"You boys grab that end and I'll grab this end. Ethan, can you steady the trolley while we load it up."

They collectively nod and we start lifting the boxes. Hannah stands back, watching us work together. We load everything up and make our way to the counter to pay.

Hannah leans in close next to me so the boys can't hear her words. "That's almost a three grand barbeque and we barely have room for it out the back. Plus, you now have to build it all. We will be eating dinner at ten o'clock." Her words are harsh, but her tone is playful. She shakes her head at me but there is a smile that reaches her eyes on her face.

"It will be fine. We have four of us to build it. And I've seen your outdoor area. My internal measurements say it will fit perfectly."

"Your internal measurements? What the hell is that?"

"I can't explain it. I can look at the space and know the measurements. It's a blue-collar worker thing."

"What do you mean?"

"Years of working with my hands and building things. I can't explain it, but you just start to know the measurements of things. Like a chef starts to be able to gauge the measurements they are using just by looking at them."

"You're a mechanic, what are you measuring all the time?"

"Just trust me, okay? I promise I will feed you before seven."

"Mum gets hangry if she doesn't eat every couple of hours." Ethan pops up, obviously hearing the entire exchange.

"I know, I've seen it. I'm glad she carries that trail mix around with her everywhere."

The boys start laughing.

"You are all laughing at me but every single one of you has come crawling to me at some point asking for some because you're hungry. Next time, I will make you suffer."

I playfully nudge her. "I secretly love that mix."

"I know. I catch you snacking on it all the time."

"Eww, you like her bird seed too," Noah mummers.

"It tastes like dirt," Ethan adds.

"Firstly, it's a very healthy snack, and secondly, you think anything that isn't chocolate or lollies tastes like dirt."

Ethan shrugs in agreement as we get to the front of the line.

"I can't watch this; it's too much money," Hannah proclaims as she walks through the checkout to wait for us outside. The boys help me shift the boxes so we can scan them all at the self-checkout and I pay.

Half an hour later, we have everything laid out in the outdoor area to start building. Conveniently my time with Hannah's dad reorganising the shed has me now knowing where everything sits. So, finding the tools I need won't be hard. However, I'm acutely aware that using her late husband's tools may not sit right with her. Rearranging everything had been her dad's idea; I just followed his lead. I didn't overthink the implications too much.

Callum never really got to use this space, but she still kept it for him. Maybe for herself? For the boys? Or maybe because she isn't ready to let go of them yet.

I pull her aside as the boys start arguing over where to lay the items, grabbing containers to put the different bags of screws into. Noah has the instructions already laid out and is reading everything word for word.

"We need a screwdriver and pillars for the first bit," he yells. Liam jumps up to head to the shed.

"Is it okay for me to use his tools? I don't want to just assume. I'm happy to quickly head home and grab my stuff."

"No, of course not. It's the boys' tools now and I think it's great that they can learn how to use them all. I mean, I am pretty good with a flat pack but beyond that, I'm useless. Thank God for Dad over the last few years."

"Okay, I got it."

I follow Liam into the shed where he is hunting for a screwdriver. I'm aware that I haven't spoken to him at all yet. His gift bag still sits untouched on the kitchen bench. So, I don't want to make him uncomfortable.

"If we use this impact driver, it will cut the time in half. And save your hands." I grab the little Milwaukee container that I had seen in here with the impact driver in it, then move to grab the batteries off the charger.

"Isn't that a drill?" He looks at me, holding a Philips head screwdriver in his hand. I can already see it's the wrong size for the screws I saw in the packet.

I pull down the other container that has the hammer drill in it that I saw previously. "This one here is the drill. See this." I show him the little pictures that line the top of the drill and the rotating mechanism that sets them. "This is the drill setting. You use this for drilling into wood, metal, plastic." I turn the setting to the hammer. "This is the hammer drill. This is for drilling into brick or concrete." He watches me intently. "Then this," I turn the setting to the screw, "is for screws. So, where you have pre-drilled holes or you tighten up a screw. It allows you to adjust the torque so you don't over screw it."

"So why aren't we using that one for the screws?"

"The impact driver is purely just for screws. It's lighter and smaller so you can get it into tighter places. It is easier to use than the drill for projects like this. But we can try them both if you want. See what you like better."

He nods. I place the drill back into its slot in the case and hand him the impact driver case while I grab a set of pliers. "We will also need the bit set," I say to him.

"What's that?" he asks, confused.

"The attachments that we put into the drill to be able to screw." He nods in understanding as I motion towards the shelf where it sits.

Then we head back out to the patio.

Noah is smart and organised. I'm impressed with how he has already opened and laid out the items we need for step one. Ethan is eagerly following his instructions and Hannah is back in the kitchen finishing the salad. She smiles at me as I walk past the door, and I can't help but feel a small amount of pride.

This is going well so far. I mean, maybe I did buy them with a ridiculously expensive barbeque, but I don't regret it. In fact, I'd do it again. In a heartbeat. I would have paid triple that, quadruple, to see that smile on her face.

"This is perfect, Noah."

He beams with pride as Liam and I place the tools down. I open the cases.

"What do you want to try first?" I ask Liam as the other two watch on.

"The drill."

"Okay, get it out."

He grabs the drill, and I pass him the battery to insert. "Like this?" he asks as he tries to slide it into place.

"Yep, exactly."

"Remember Dad showing you this," Noah adds. He doesn't look at me while he says it, and I don't take it personally. The boys would have been six, nine and eleven when their dad passed, so I imagine Callum would have shown them some things like this.

"I can't remember," Liam says, his eyes flicking to the ground.

"That's okay. We will figure it out. Noah, do you know how to use the impact driver?" He nods. "Okay, you can use that one."

"Can I have a turn?" Ethan asks.

"Of course. Come here, I'll show you both." He shifts next to Liam who has now put the battery on and is awaiting the next step. Noah connects his own battery to the impact driver.

"This is the bit set, so we just need to find the right fit and then I'll show you how to put it in."

"So, we check it against these screws?" Liam asks.

"Yep, exactly."

The boys start testing different bits against the screws. My internal measurement system is in overdrive wanting to grab the one that I know will fit, but I sit back and let them do it.

"Here, this one," Ethan calls. He shows me and sure enough, it is the exact one I had been eyeing.

"That one is perfect." I show them how to open the chuck and place the bit into it, then tighten it back up. Liam does it with ease, and I just check to make sure it is tight enough.

Noah finds his own bit, and I show him how the impact driver doesn't have a chuck and how the bit just clicks in. Moving back to Liam, I show him how to make sure he has the settings changed to screw. He turns it and then shows me.

"Perfect." I then explain how to turn the torque down, telling him that because the holes are already predrilled and the wood is soft it won't need to be high.

"Do I need to do that on this one?" Noah asks.

"Yep, but this one is slightly different. See these little buttons down here at the handle?"

"Yeah."

"These are the modes. Mode two here should be good for general screws, like what we are doing."

Conveniently, I have the exact same Milwaukee tools in my shed, so I know the brand. I know the modes and settings like the back of my hand. Callum obviously had good taste. In tools and women.

I mentally kick myself for even thinking about my girlfriend's dead husband. Fuck this is weird. But there is nowhere else I would rather be.

It's strange, but I feel at home. It already feels like a family to me. I glance up over the boys as they fiddle with the drills and spot Hannah. She is watching us adoringly from inside, her face bright and a smile covering her lips. I wonder if she feels the same.

With the tools set, I grab the instructions.

"The wheels are first," Noah says as moves the items we need closer.

"So, these wheels that turn all ways like this are called casters." The boys nod and I show them how to place them onto the first panel that will become the base.

Liam places the screw on the end of the bit, and it falls straight off.

"Don't forget the washer. Then put it like this." I put the washer on and then place the tip of the screw through the predrilled holes in the caster plate, pushing it slightly so it bites into the wood. Taking my hand away, the screw stays upright.

"What's that do?" Ethan asks, pointing at the washer.

"It spreads out the force of the screw head so that it doesn't bite through the wood or damage whatever you are screwing into. It can also help the screw stay tight over time."

He nods, and I motion to Liam to bring the drill down to the screw. "You want to hold it straight up so that you don't screw it in crooked and you want to push a little bit. These should go in easily, so let the drill do the work."

"Should I go?"

"I'm going to hold this bit here, okay." I place my hand down on the caster plate. "Normally you would do this with your other hand to stop it spinning if the screw grabs, but I'm going to do it just in case. I don't want it to spin and hurt your hand."

The last thing I want is for one of them to get hurt. Hannah would never forgive me.

I hold the caster steady, and he squeezes the trigger. The drill starts to work. The other two boys watch on as Liam's face lights up with excitement and pride as the screw tightens to the washer and the caster plate.

"You don't want to do them up too tight, not to begin with anyway. You need the caster to be able to move slightly so you can line up the other holes. Once all the screws are in and you make sure it's nice and straight, then you go and tighten them all up."

"Okay, so should I loosen that off?"

"Yep. See that little button there at the side? Push that in."

"Like this." He pushes the button through.

"Yep, now that's in reverse. You do the same thing, and the screw will come out." He places the bit back on the screw. "Just loosen it off a little."

He squeezes the trigger and loosens the screw slightly.

"Okay, let's do the rest."

He grabs the next screw and washer and puts it in place.

"Can I do this one?" Noah grabs a second caster and moves to the other side where the four holes are.

"Yep, same process. Just let me hold the caster, okay?"

"I can do it." I don't want to argue with him or falter his confidence but if he doesn't hold that caster hard enough and the screw grabs, it's going to hurt if his hand is in the way. Noah at fourteen has decent sized hands, so he should be okay. He has the impact driver, which is significantly lighter than the drill.

"Just make sure you hold tight."

"I got it."

I watch carefully as he follows the same process Liam and I have just done. He places one hand over the caster to hold it still and holds the driver with his other.

"The driver is going to work a bit faster, so squeeze slowly till you get the hang of it." He nods and does it perfectly. Slow and steady. He has good control over the tool, and I'm quietly impressed.

Ethan is dying for a turn, so I give him the impact driver and hold it with him for a few screws, then give him more range to have a go. He also smashes it, and the four casters are on in no time at all.

"You guys don't even need me here," I joke.

Both Noah and Liam's heads snap up, and they look at me. Fuck, they have already lost their dad, and I make a joke about them not needing me here to help. I didn't mean it like that, but it hits me that they might actually be enjoying this as much as I am.

"Don't worry, I'm not going anywhere. Your mum needs her steak." I see Liam's shoulders relax, and Noah moves to the instructions to look for the next step.

"This is fun," Ethan quips, spinning the casters around, oblivious to everything else.

The next step is the sides and the draw slides, and we work well together. Noah calls out instructions and Ethan runs to grab the pieces from the piles they already prepared. Liam doesn't let go of the drill. He is surprisingly good with it, not needing much more instruction.

I quickly get demoted to holder of panels, fetcher of items, and explaining things as we go, while also making sure they read the instructions correctly. Every now and then I give them little tips of the trade that will make things smoother or easier.

Hannah pops out and proceeds to sit on the outdoor setting, watching us work. It takes us about two hours to finish, what with me showing and explaining things as we go.

We pack everything away and the boys help me wheel it into the space I had in mind. As expected, it fits perfectly.

"Okay, your internal measurements are spot on. It's like it was made for that spot."

It sits against the wall just to the left of the sliding door and butts right up to the enclosed side wall of the patio. The rest is open, so this is the perfect spot to keep it out of the elements.

"I will have to put an exhaust fan in the roof here but that's easy enough to do later. Tonight won't hurt." I'm aware that Callum had passed not long after this house was built. He never got a chance to build the extra things like an outdoor barbeque or perfectly arrange his shed. I don't want to overstep but it feels nice to be able to help Hannah with these things, especially for the kids.

"It does look good there," Hannah says. We all stand back and admire our handiwork.

"Looks good, boys. Well done," I say, feeling like a real dad.

"What now?" Ethan asks.

"Now we eat. I'm bloody starving," Hannah says.

"It's only just past six. I'll burn the hot plate in."

"Thanks." She leans up to her tippy toes and kisses me, and my heart skips a beat.

I can't describe how good it feels to be here. For her to let me into this family. To be trusted enough with power tools and her kids.

I can't wipe the smile from my face and as I look at the kids, it appears that neither can they.

43

Couldn't feel more right

Clark

"Can you pass me that wrench?" Two seconds later, it is in my hands. I tighten up the bolts and then move to the next section. "You want to do it?"

I hand the wrench to Liam, and he moves into my spot and copies what I did. He is good with his hands and loves working on the car.

It's been four months since we built that barbeque together. I'm not going to lie and say it has all been smooth sailing. Ethan's maturity has helped. He's easygoing and adaptable. Him and I have bonded over the animals while I have shown him the ropes. Even Pam likes him. He loves how much space we have out here at my place to kick the football. We even started building a treehouse together, with plans to add a flying fox. We haven't told Hannah that part yet. I can't say it will be entirely to code. But it will be lots of fun.

Liam has been another story entirely. I thought building the barbeque together was our bridge. It seemed to be for the other two. But after that day, he pulled away, completely ignoring me whenever we were in each other's company.

Hannah seemed to think that it was guilt. That he felt guilty for allowing me to show him things a father should. Guess it was the same guilt she wrestled with. I noticed every time she felt it because she would reach for her ring that hangs around her neck.

I trusted her guidance and gave him space. But I knew that the car was my way in with him. The first day the boys came to my place, I showed them her. Ethan had been ecstatic, wanting to sit in it and pretend to drive it while asking a million questions. Noah had been excited in his own quiet way, but Liam had refused to join us altogether.

Later that night, I had seen him make his way out the house and into the shed. I found him running his fingers over the block that sits on a stand. I didn't speak to him, and he never even knew I saw him. I left him to be in there, but I laid breadcrumbs and made sure to leave the door open for him to join me, hoping that he would come to me when he was ready.

One night about a month ago, while everyone else had headed to bed, I made my way to the shed to work on the car. He joined me half an hour later, not saying a word. He had shadowed me, watching with intent. We didn't speak about anything of importance, but we worked on that car side by side for over an hour together. I didn't explain things like I did with the barbeque that day. I literally just handed him a tool and said do this, and he did.

After that night, it became a regular occurrence. When the house grew quiet and Hannah got into bed to read, Noah watched TV in his room, Ethan slept, and Liam and I would make our way to the shed and work in quiet understanding for an hour or two.

Slowly I started explaining more and slowly he started asking more questions. Soon enough I had him singing the lyrics to AC/DC and playing the air guitar while I showed him the ins and outs of fixing this car. I know he kept his cards close to his chest, but with every turn of a bolt the conversation had drifted to a more serious nature.

I know I will never replace his father and I'm not trying to. But I also know we are on our way to our own relationship. And that's all I could ask for.

I don't know how I ever lived without this woman and these boys. Liam's love for this car—him and I spending time together fixing her up. Ethan floating around, loving just being wherever his brothers are and drawing plans for his treehouse. Noah's quiet admiration for nature and the animals. Hannah's intoxicating laugh wafting through my house. The easy way we have fallen into a rhythm of domestic life together is out of my wildest dreams.

When Hannah and I talked about the kids coming here, she had made me promise that the guns would stay far away and locked in the safe. I mean they always were anyway. She didn't want the boys around them, especially at this age, and I respected that.

We then all went to Ikea to buy things to make rooms for them at my place, and now we move between two houses. Hannah loves her place near the beach. It's new and custom built for her, the boys and her work. She has her gym there and it's a beautiful house. She loves it out here as well. It's just out of the hustle and bustle of the town but close enough to not be driving for hours if you run out of milk. She loves the animals and the kids do, too. Especially Noah. He loves riding the horses, and I've been looking at getting more so we can all ride together.

Right now, Hannah is at her house finishing up with clients. I grabbed the boys from school, which meant she could work a little later. I have constantly told her that she doesn't have to work more, or at all for that matter. I have more than enough money, but she loves her job and her clients. She loves the business she has built, and she enjoys the work.

Although, if I'm serious about spending the rest of my life with her and these three boys, I imagine I may have to pick up the work slightly to cover day to day things. I suppose it's good for the boys to see a good work ethic as well.

And I am serious. About a life with Hannah.

I know it's early but as you get older, time seems to move quicker. You know what you want. And I want this. Her and these boys.

Forever.

I want to ask Hannah to marry me.

With Cherie, I went down the traditional path of asking her father. However, I know Hannah, and I have spent a bit of time with her dad. These kids are her world and If I'm going to ask anyone for permission, it has to be them. Not her dad.

I've been thinking about it a lot and now is as good a time as any.

"I wanted to ask you guys something," I finally work up the nerve to say.

Noah looks up from his homework books that he has spread out on a desk. I bought it for him to place in the garage. Liam glances up from the block that he is working on, and Ethan pops his head up from the book that he is reading while lounged in the front seat of the car.

"I'm just going to come right out and say it, okay, but I want you guys to know that you can be honest. Don't sugar coat it. I'm happy for the blunt truth of how you feel about this." They all stare at me in anticipation, waiting for me to elaborate. "I want to ask your mum to marry me."

Liam's eyes narrow on me. I expected him to react the hardest. To maybe storm out. To not want to talk about it. But he is the first to speak.

"Are you asking for our permission?"

I nod. "Yeah. You boys mean everything to your mum, and she means everything to me. I know we are still getting to know each other but you guys mean a lot to me, too. I wanted to know how you would feel about it."

"Does she even want to get married again?" Noah asks.

"I know when we first met, she said it wasn't something she thought she would ever consider. But we've talked about it since, and she is open to remarrying. But how you boys feel about it will be a big part of her decision. And I want you to be honest with me about your feelings."

"She still wears her wedding ring from Dad on her necklace." Liam places the wrench he was using on the side bench.

"I know, and she never has to take that off if she doesn't want to. She loved your dad very much, still does. I know that. I know that her wearing that ring is a way to remember what they had. I'm not trying to replace him, or what he was to you guys. But I want to be here for the future. I don't want you guys or your mum to forget the memories you had with him. But I'd like to be able to make new ones with you all." I pause, feeling emotional and honestly a little awkward pouring my heart out to these kids. "If that's okay?" I add.

The boys all look at me, saying nothing for the longest time, and I regret asking. *Idiot.* We were making such good progress. We all got along so well, and I had to ruin it with this shit—

"Fine, but if you die, I get this car." Liam grabs the wrench and goes back to what he was working on.

"I ain't planning on dying."

"No one ever does," Liam quips. His eyes stay fixed on me, but sadness swirls within them.

"You're right. And I'm sorry that you boys have had to go through so much loss. I can't control death, but I can control what I do with my life, and I want to be in yours. In your mums." None of them speak but all their eyes follow me. Shit, this is heavy. A bit too heavy. Maybe this was the wrong move to talk to them about it. I decide to lighten the mood. "Whether your mum and I marry or not, I want to be around for the long haul. So how about this. When you get your license, this car is yours."

The bolt Liam was about to start fastening slips from his fingers and clatters to the floor, the sound echoing off the tin walls of the shed. "Really?" His eyes snap to mine.

"Yep. I mean, in all honesty, you've done more work on her in the last month than I have in the whole time I have had her. So yeah, you keep working on it like this and she's yours." A look of pure elation lights Liam's face.

"Hey, I'm the oldest, what do I get?" Noah interjects.

"What do you want?" I joke.

"A horse of my own."

"I was planning on buying more anyway so we all had one. Done deal."

"I don't want a horse." Liam pops his head back up from the block. He has picked up the bolt and is back to screwing it into place.

"You already get the car," Ethan chimes in, his head popping out the window.

"I want a quad bike, then I can ride with you guys instead of being on a horse," Liam says, barely looking up from what he is working on. He doesn't like riding the horses.

"They can be dangerous," I add.

"More dangerous than a horse," he quips.

"You have a point. Fine, as long as your mum is on board with all of this. I'll get a quad bike. And more horses." I look at Ethan. "This isn't me buying your permission, we will do this anyway, but since I'm giving out gifts like a genie, what do you want?"

He shrugs his shoulders. "This is pretty cool as it is."

"Mum is never going to agree to quad bikes anyway," Noah says, going back to his homework.

"Well, I get this car no matter what, right?" Liam asks over his shoulder.

"Boys, can I ask your mum to marry me or not?" My tone is playful, enjoying this banter between us. It feels natural and easy, and I love their sense of humour.

"Yep," Liam is the first to answer.

"Sure," Ethan adds.

"I'm cool with it," Noah says.

I can't wipe the smile from my face.

"Okay, we need a plan. I need your boys' help with ring shopping."

"I will make a list of good stores to visit in Perth. I'll check the maps and plan for the best order to visit them for efficiency," Noah says.

"I'll come up with an excuse as to why we all need to go without her. Noah, can you check that calendar thing Mum is always on about and see when we are all free."

"You have the same app, Liam."

"I know, but I don't know how to use it."

"You should have listened when Mum explained it."

"Bro, just check the dates."

"Will there be snacks?" Ethan steps out of the car, joining in on the excitement.

"You can be the chief snack purchaser. We will go to the shops," I add.

Noah has his phone out, and Liam and Ethan move closer to him, staring around him to view something on the app they were talking about. I tentatively move in, not wanting to intrude but also curious.

Hannah has mentioned the family app she has. She has all the kids' schedules in there and it allows them all access. Well, Ethan doesn't have a phone, but Liam and Noah have it. They can also send messages to each other and it has a tracking on it, so she can see where they are.

"Here, in two weekends. It will be school holidays, and we won't have sports over the weekend." Noah points to a space on the app that isn't as heavily coloured. Then he clicks on a pink section on Saturday and it pops up with 'Hair Appointment'. "This is perfect. Mum has a hair appointment on that Saturday," Noah says.

"Is there football on that day? We could go to a game in the city and then go to the shops after," Liam adds.

"I'll check." I bring up the AFL app, grateful for some involvement. I have a look at the schedule. I'm from Sydney so I'm a Swans fan, but I love the sport and will watch any game.

"There is a game on Saturday. Eagles Vs Collingwood. I'll try to get us tickets." The boys squeal in excitement. I know Callum was an Eagles fan, but I don't know if the boys have been to a game since he passed. "Right, we need to do some recon on styles she likes. Let's not make it obvious but ask some questions."

We spend the rest of the afternoon talking about ways I can propose and diamond shapes we think she would like. Noah starts compiling a list of the best ring shops to visit, and I manage to get some tickets for the game from a friend who is an Eagles member.

It couldn't feel more right. Although now I have to explain to Hannah why her kids are asking for a quad bike and horses and how I just promised a twelve-year-old a car.

44

Take me to Disneyland

Hannah

Clark's stubble tickles my neck. His warm body rests against the back of mine, arms wrapped around me. This has fast become my favourite place in the world. Lying in bed together. He didn't have to sneak in after the kids went to sleep and he didn't have to sneak out before the sun rose. Not that I minded that at all. It did add a level of excitement.

But this?

This is what I want. Me in his arms. Him in my life. In my kids' lives.

We all had dinner together, and he cooked for us on the barbeque. The boys still tease me about how much better Clark's meat cooking skills are to mine. Then we made popcorn and watched the Minecraft movie.

The boys have since left us alone, heading off to their rooms to do their own thing, joking together about how apparently people were letting chickens loose in the movie theatres during the chicken jockey scene.

Clark and I finished cleaning up before getting into bed ourselves, making love between these sheets and him holding me in his arms afterwards.

This!

It is perfection.

I can't believe that I had been scared to let this type of love in again. Clark has made such an effort with the kids. It took some time for Liam to ease into it, but they have all bonded. Clark fits effortlessly into their playful banter and is not put off by their constant bickering or the level of chaos.

We've basically been inseparable. It feels like Clark has been in our lives forever with how easily this has become our new normal.

Clark's breath is warm and steady on my neck, and I let myself relax further into him. "Hannah, I want to ask you something." His voice is low and soft in my ear.

"Mmmm," I hum, not wanting to open my eyes, lost in the afterglow of orgasms.

"Will you let me take you on a holiday?"

My eyes flutter open. Who doesn't want a holiday? "We can go on a holiday, Clark. We could go back down south and relive the weekend we met." I wriggle back into him slightly and feel him twitch against me.

His hands tighten on my hips. "Stop that. I don't have the energy to go again. And that's not quite what I had in mind."

I chuckle but don't stop pushing back on him. "What did you have in mind?"

"I was thinking overseas."

I shift in the bed to face him. "I don't have a passport, and it's so hard to coordinate with the kids. I can't just leave them to go overseas on a holiday. And my work."

My mind starts mentally calculating the logistics of it all. The cost of a passport and the timeframe to get them. The kids' schedules and the cost of flights from Australia to literally anywhere else in the world is insane.

"Hannah, I want to take the kids. All of us."

"I mean, I could probably afford Bali. We all need passports which are crazy expensive and take up to six weeks—"

"I want to cover it. Passports, flights, everything. And I was thinking more like...Paris."

"PARIS!" I jolt upright. "No, I am not letting you pay for that."

"I know you like to pay your own way, and I know you hate the idea of relying on someone else, but I am here for the long haul, Hannah, and I have the means. Let me spoil you. And the kids."

My face softens. I love this man so much, but it is hard to let go of all the armour I have had to wear over the last three years.

"I love that you want to do this for us, but I'm terrified to let you."

"Why?"

"In case it doesn't last."

"It's going to last."

"You don't know that. You don't control death, or time." My face falls thinking about it. No one ever thinks the worst would actually happen to them. No one ever goes into a relationship thinking it will end. You go in hopeful. Positive. Praying for the best. But I have lived through the worst.

Clark's face is full of sympathy as he sits up. His hands cup my face, and I feel tears start to spill.

"Clark, you don't know what it was like to have been so secure and safe in something for so many years, only to have the rug ripped out from under you. Suddenly I was alone. Single income. The only person to deal with everything. It all fell on me. But I have found my groove with it, and I am terrified to go back to relying on someone in case it all goes away again."

He kisses my cheek and the tears that lace it. "I know, Hannah. I know you have lived through the worst case. And I can't promise you that I will outlive you. You're right, I can't control time or death. But I can control what I do while I am here. And I want to give you all of me. All my time, all my energy, all my love, all my money. All of me. I want to give it to you and those kids.

If you let me. I want to spend the time I do have loving you and this family."

I nod, more tears involuntarily spilling from my eyes. He wipes them with his thumb and pulls me in for a kiss. I melt into his touch. It feels right.

My heart wants to say yes. To spread my arms out and fall knowing he will catch me. My head has to think about it practically. It has to be prepared for the worst case. I have to have a plan. If all this goes to shit, I can't have myself be one hundred percent reliant on him.

I have my house, my car, and a successful business that I know can provide for us. We have been dividing our time between the two houses. Clark has offered to pay some form of rent or add to the utilities, but I haven't let him. Although I haven't missed the way he will leave cash conveniently lying around the house. I'll find notes randomly in my wallet. Or he will show up with armfuls of groceries to restock the fridges. He'll jump in first with his card to pay whenever we are out doing things.

Would letting Clark take us to Paris be the worst thing?

"I've always wanted to go to Paris."

"I know, that's why I suggested it. Plus, there is a Disneyland there for the kids."

"Screw the boys, I want to go to Disneyland."

He laughs. "Thought you would like that. We can get you a Mickey shirt and ears if you like."

"And fairy floss."

"And fairy floss," he acknowledges, kissing my wet cheeks.

"The kids are going to flip out at this."

"I can't wait to tell them."

"We should plan something cool, like…" My mind swirls with excitement. "Can we get matching family shirts?"

He chokes on a laugh. "You might have a hard time getting Liam in a matching family shirt but I'm in."

"I'll deal with him." I laugh, knowing full well he is never going to agree to wearing matching shirts.

"When are you thinking?" I ask, mentally scanning over our schedule for the next year.

"As soon as logistically possible. We can start the process for passports now and start looking at flights and accommodation."

I open my phone to look at my calendar to start searching for a date. "It's going to be expensive, Clark. Passports alone are going to be close to fifteen hundred. Then flights for all of us. They are easily going to be between fifteen hundred and two grand per flight."

"Hannah, it's fine. I got it."

I sigh. "Just how rich are you?" We've talked about money. I know he sold his businesses for just under four million. I know he owns his house and car and has no other debt. I know that he doesn't really have to work and does it because he loves the trade, but we haven't actually talked figures.

"Not rich *rich*, but I suppose I have a lot."

"You don't want to tell me?" I'm not offended. Money can be a sore point for a lot of people, and I know he always felt like Cherie was more into the money than him.

"No, it's not that. I'd add you to the bank account tomorrow. I just get awkward talking about it." He grabs his phone, opens up a banking app, then passes his phone over to me.

"Jesus Christ. That is a lot of zeros."

He lets out an awkward chuckle. "It's just money."

"That's something that someone with money says."

His face softens. "You're right, but I didn't come from money. My family wasn't well off. I opened my first mechanic business when I was twenty-one. I sublet a shed at another business, and I worked my ass off."

"I know that. But you said you sold that for just under four million, right? Then almost half went to Cherie. How did that figure triple?"

"Crypto," he huffs under his breath. The word is barely audible.

"Crypto," I repeat.

He nods. "Yeah, I bought the house, car and stuff I needed to run a smaller scale business, then I put a decent amount aside in savings. I had a lot of time on my hands and one of my mates back home was making money day trading. I started researching it and playing around with it. Turns out I was pretty good."

"How are you pretty good at it? Isn't it like gambling? Just guess work."

"Not really. I mean, there is an element of luck, but it's more like investing in shares. Some I leave in with different coins to grow and others I buy low and sell high. A lot of it comes down to research and good timing."

"I see."

"I keep the money in that account and I don't really touch it. The interest I earn a month on that account alone would cover this trip. Then I have this account." He points to the screen at an account with a couple grand in it. "This is my normal account. I get paid my jobs in this one and this is what I use for day-to-day stuff and any bills. Then I have a few different crypto accounts that I play around with. I keep about a mil in them collectively so that I have quick access when I want to buy coins. I take anything over that out and add it to the savings account, and I guess it just grew."

"That's insane." I know absolutely nothing about crypto. To me it sounded exactly like gambling, but Callum and I had never been one for shares either. We had a few friends who had made money with different investments like that.

Callum was an electrician, and he worked really hard. I had stopped working at a physiotherapy clinic when I fell pregnant with Noah and I never went back. I was still at home with Noah when I fell pregnant with Liam, then again at home with Liam when I had Ethan. I didn't start my business until Ethan was in school.

We had been on one income for so many years that we just got used to living with less. I loved that I was able to be home with my boys. Them losing their father made that decision even more solidified. I was glad I had that time with them. While it had been tight at times, we always got by.

"Okay, so you can afford to fly us all first class around the world and back three times over."

"I could probably afford to buy a jet and fly you."

"Jesus, we will be fine in economy. It kills me to say yes to something like this. I like to be able to pay my own way."

"I know, but you don't have to now. I know you work hard, and I know you love your work. I'm not saying you ever have to stop, if you don't want to, but let me help. What good is all this money if I can't use it to spoil the people I love."

"Okay."

"Okay?" he repeats excitedly. "You'll let me take you guys on a trip?"

"Yes, Clark, we can go on a family trip." The word family just slips out, but it feels nice thinking of him being included in that. It makes me smile. His eyes meet mine and I hand his phone back. "I mean, I'll show you my bank account, but it's pretty lame."

He laughs again, wrapping his arms around me in a bear hug and tackling me to the bed. His large body weighs me down, warming me up from the inside out.

"You never have to use your bank account again if you don't want to." His face is inches from mine. He places a kiss on my forehead, then my lips. "I meant what I said. I'll add you to mine tomorrow if you want."

"No, don't do that. It's fine the way it is. But Paris does sound nice. Let's do it."

45

Clark

*C*heers erupt from the stands and the rows shake as people jump from their chairs. Ethan jumps up onto his, tipping his soda all over the floor while swinging his scarf in the air. Noah is standing and clapping, and Liam has his hands to his mouth making a megaphone, screaming, "YEAH BOYS."

We are in a sea of blue and gold. I had to go and buy a shirt. The game is close and the boy's team, the Eagles, just took the lead with a tricky goal from the corner pocket. We are deep into the last quarter with only four minutes and twenty-two seconds on the clock.

The crowd starts to chant, "LETS GO EAGLES, LETS GO. LETS GO EAGLES LETS GO."

The clock stops as they take the ball back to the centre for the ball up.

Everyone takes their seat, and silence descends around the stadium. The only sound to be heard is the soft patter of the residual raindrops that fall around us. The umpire bounces the ball and time slows as we watch the boys desperately try to keep control of the slippery ball.

It feels like the whole crowd is holding their breath.

The time sounds and everyone jumps to their feet in roars.

Eagles win.

The boys are ecstatic, jumping up and down. We high five each other and a few random people that sit behind and in front of us, staying standing to sing the team song.

It has been a fantastic day so far. Hannah had a hair appointment and the boys and I planned this day as a cover to buy a ring for her. We made our way up for the lunch time game and ate hot dogs while we cheered for our team. Well, the boys team. I'm still a loyal Swans supporter, but hey, I'll wear the shirt for them. It's going to be interesting when they play each other. But if I have learnt anything about these three amazing kids, it's that they love the banter. And they can give as good as they take.

Something tells me it will be fun.

We make our way out of the stadium and head to the car to drive over to our first stop. Noah has made a list of five jewellers in the city and first up is Solid Gold. The list also includes Tiffany and Co and the Perth Mint, and some independent stores as well.

I should have been nervous to take three boisterous boys into a fine jewellery store, especially since they are jacked up on soft drinks and junk food, riding the high of a win. I'm also well aware that in Eagles guernsey and jeans, we don't exactly fit the aesthetics of fine jewellery stores.

I should have planned ahead and bought a change of clothes for all of us.

Too late now.

I wonder if I should give the boys a little pep talk, like I hear Hannah do sometimes. She will quiet them all down in the car on the way to somewhere and explain the rules and expectations for them behaviour wise.

It always seems to work to calm them slightly.

Slightly being the key word here.

I decide against the pep talk. That's encroaching on dad territory and despite how much I love hanging out with them, I don't want them to feel like I'm trying to replace their father.

I'm just going to wing it and hope for the best. We enter Solid Gold first and the boys split, roaming the cabinets, looking at different rings. We kind of meet in the middle and collectively decide that nothing here jumped out at us. While they are beautiful, they were, I suppose, traditional in a way—plain bands with large sparkling diamonds in multiple different cuts. Nothing screamed unique enough for Hannah. Which is exactly what she is to me.

We pile into the car and head to Tiffany. I had in my head due to the movies that this would be the place. All girls want a Tiffany ring. Right? But it was the same as Solid Gold. The rings were stunning and sparkly, but nothing that screamed Hannah to me. The boys agreed.

We made our way to a few more, having no luck. It wasn't until the second last store that we struck gold.

Literally.

It was a small boutique, an independent jeweller. The rings were all unique and beautiful, like nothing I had ever seen before. Lots of different colours, with pink diamonds, blue diamonds. I didn't even know they existed. Sapphires and rubies. The rings were exquisite and each of us said 'WOW' more times than I could count.

Then I saw it.

I knew the moment its pretty blueish green hue reflected under the lights, catching my eyes. Everything about it is perfect.

"This one." I point to the ring through the glass display, and the shop assistant moves over to it. The boys collectively shift closer to me.

"OH MY GOSH." Awe paints Noah's voice.

"That's lit." I have no idea what that means but I think Liam likes it.

"That's so pretty," Ethan adds in approval.

"Can I have a closer look at that one please?"

"Sure." The lady heads to the back room and returns with a black tray lined with velvet. Putting on a white cotton glove, she opens the cabinet and gently places the ring on the black material. "Follow me."

We all follow her to a table where she places the tray down. There are only two chairs, so I stay standing and motion to the boys to sit. Ethan and Noah take a chair while Liam stays by my side.

"Can we pick it up?" I ask.

"Of course." The lady places a card next to the ring. It has all the specifications listed.

I pick up the tiny band between my thumb and forefinger, moving it around so it catches the light. It has two main stones in the centre. It looks like they wrap around the finger, joining in the middle. They are slightly different shapes—one larger and one sleeker.

"The stones are both sapphires."

"I thought sapphires were dark blue?" Noah asks.

"Sapphires are amazing. They can actually be any colour. The colour depends on the presence of secondary chemical elements in its composition."

"That's dope," Liam exclaims.

"This stone," the lady points to the larger one. It is darker blue in colour but still not as dark as I would have imagined sapphires. I too thought they were only dark blue, "is a one point two carat pear cut sapphire. And this one," she points to the second stone that is more a light teal colour, reminding me of Hannah's green eyes, "is a one carat marquise cut. Then it has four marquise diamonds and ten brilliant cuts."

The main gems sit just touching with the smaller diamonds sitting in between. To me, the pear represents me, connecting to the delicate slimmer greenish marquise cut. Then the four marquise diamonds sitting around represent Hannah's three boys and one for the boy we lost.

I've never seen anything quite like it. The two different colours and cuts coming together to make a perfect ring, with the addition of the clear sparkly diamonds framing them.

I love it.

"I think your mum will love this." I don't tell the boys my full reasoning.

I pass the ring to Noah for him to have a closer look. "I agree. It's perfect."

Ethan now leans in as well. Noah passes it along to Ethan and his eyes go wide. "Mum is gonna flip."

I can't help but laugh.

Ethan passes the ring to Liam, who inspects it closer than the other two. He doesn't say anything, but his head is nodding slightly. I don't think he even realises he is doing it.

"Do you know her size?" Liam asks.

The boys look to me, but I was prepared for this.

"I tested the rings on her necklace around my finger. Her wedding band fits just above my knuckle on my pinky." The boys nod in understanding, but the lady gives me a quizzical look. I don't bother explaining.

She moves to retrieve a suitcase. Upon opening it, I see it's for sizing. It is lined with rings with letters next to them. She pulls one from its snug position in the tray and hands it to me.

I place it on my pinky finger. "Nope, too big."

She takes it back and passes me a different one.

"This one is right."

"Okay, was the ring still on the chain when you tried it?"

"Yes, she was asleep, so I had to do it carefully."

She nods and the boys stay silent, watching on. Liam is still holding the ring, mesmerised by it.

"Can you give me an idea of the thickness of the chain?" The woman motions over to a wall where necklaces hang, and I point out one that looks similar. "Okay, so we want to go up a size to account for the chain width when you tried it on." She places the size up on my pinky. "What do you think of this size?"

"That looks about right."

"Have you seen the price of this thing?" Noah interrupts, picking up the little card that holds all the information.

"Hooolllleeeyy," Liam exclaims, while Ethan's eyes go wide.

"Your mum is worth it. What do you think, guys? Is this the one?"

Ethan nods enthusiastically.

Liam hums a, "Mmmhum, definitely."

Noah steps closer to me. "I think Mum is going to love it."

That's all the acknowledgement I need.

The ring needs to be resized, which the sales assistant advises is going to take about a week. I pay and we excitedly load up into the car to head home, talking about ways I can propose. The kids have no idea that I'm planning to do it in Paris. They have no idea that Hannah and I have been planning a trip.

Although we need to tell them soon because we have to get their passports organised. I don't know if Hannah is planning on surprising them or if she is just going to tell them outright. But I will leave that up to her. Either way, I am buzzing with electricity as we make our way home.

"Do we have to call you dad if Mum says yes," Ethan innocently asks from the back seat.

The question shocks me. I wasn't expecting it.

I have wanted nothing more than to become a father. To be called Dad. But I would never expect these boys to call me that, especially if it wasn't what they wanted.

"That's up to you guys. You don't have to call me that."

"What should we call you then?" Liam and Noah are silent as Ethan asks his questions.

"I don't know, bud. I'm happy with Clark but if you want to call me Dad, I'm happy with that too. I think you guys should choose what you want to call me."

"One of my mates calls his stepdad Bonus Dad," Noah adds.

Liam scrunches his nose up. "That's lame."

Ethan slaps a hand out to back hand him from across the seat. "I like it."

"It's kind of wordy. Like, can you imagine having to say, 'hey Bonus Dad' every single time you want something," Noah offers.

"I'm not saying that in public either," Liam quips.

I let them talk it out, not offering any input, but internally, I'm screaming 'Yesssss.' I love the sound of Bonus Dad. To me it doesn't take anything away from Callum but means that they view me in that same category.

My heart beats in little irregular palpitations while they hash it out.

"If you two losers choose that, I'm just saying BD."

"I love that," Ethan calls.

Me too, bud. Me too.

"That's way easier," Noah adds.

"I'm good with BD," I finally add, deciding to join the conversation. I'll know what it means and that's enough for me.

"Deal," Liam chimes.

"It's settled," Noah adds.

"Do we start now, or only if Mum says yes?" Ethan asks.

I look at Noah who is in the passenger seat. "Damn I hope she says yes."

"I think she will," Noah replies, holding my gaze.

"She will." Coming from Liam, who is the most blunt and honest of all three of them, means a lot.

"I hope so, too. And I'm going to start now. BD," Ethan chimes.

"I like it," I say as I twist my arm around the seat, making a fist. Ethan fist bumps me, and I swell with a tiny bit of pride.

BD. I love it.

I hate what Hannah and her boys have had to go through for me to have this. If I'm honest, if I could take it all back for her and these kids, if I could make it so that Callum never left, I would.

In a heartbeat.

Even if it meant that I never got to meet her, never got to have her. Never got to feel this kind of love, this kind of family, I still would. I'd take it all back for her to never have had to feel that pain of loss. But I can't do that. And I thank the universe that we did meet and that I get to have her now.

Get to know these boys. Get to have them call me BD. Get to have this type of family. This kind of love.

46

It's just different

Hannah

"Get on your own side." Liam elbows Noah off the arm rest they are fighting over. A small amount of his hot chocolate spills from a little hole on his takeaway lid, landing right on his new crisp white jumper that he bought especially for this trip.

"Liam you ass, look at what you did." He flicks the tray leaver on the back of the seat in front of him and pulls it down, placing his drink on it.

As if on cue, the flight attendant pops up out of nowhere. "Sorry, sir, but you need to put the tray up. We are about to take off."

Noah makes a slight huff, but thankfully the attendant has already moved on.

"Hold this." He shoves the drink at Ethan and then elbows Liam back, hard, shoving him back off the arm rest. "There are two there."

"Yeah, but your arm is too fat. It's touching me," Liam snaps.

"Liam, why don't you and Ethan quickly swap seats," I helpfully chime in from across the aisle. The boys wanted to all sit together in one row, so Clark and I are across the aisle from them. Clark is in the aisle seat, and I'm in the middle.

"Cos Ethan cracked the shits and wanted the window seat, remember Mum." Liam gives me an eye roll.

"Liam, do you want to sit next to your mum and I will sit there? Her arms are tiny, look." Clark's hand wraps around my wrist and he raises my arm up.

I let it flop, making a face at Liam. He is being a bit of a dick, if I'm being honest. I can say that about my own kids. Can't I?

"Noooo," they chime at me.

"Boys, we haven't even taken off yet and we are already fighting." I turn my head to Clark and sigh. "This is going to be rough."

He lifts his arm, and I move my head forward so he can sling it over my shoulder and relax my head back on him. He tilts his own head and places a kiss to the top of mine.

"They'll be fine." Men always say that. And it usually is fine because the mum makes it fine. I internally laugh to myself.

Clark is great with the boys. Sometimes having that masculine energy around them is exactly what they need.

"Noah, pass me your jumper and I'll try to get that out before it stains," Clark says as he removes his arm from around my head to grab something out of his backpack. "Liam, I also bought these." He hands him a small 'O' ring with little smooth metal-coloured tabs on them. "Thought we would have the time to confirm the colours."

"Ohh sweet." Liam takes the ring and starts flicking through it as Noah passes the jumper over to Clark.

"Ethan, guess what else I found," Clark calls over the other boys.

"What?" Ethan's head turns from the window to look at Clark as he pulls sweets from his bag.

"The Lego lollies."

Ethan squeals, and Clark throws them across the aisle for him to catch.

"Where were they? We went everywhere the other day trying to find them," I ask as Ethan rips into the bag and starts pulling out little blocks and linking them together before shoving them all in his mouth.

"Kmart," Clark answers as he tips a bit of water onto the small hot chocolate mark on Noah's jumper.

"You're going to make that worse." I gently nudge Clark as the water starts to spread the tiny dark mark, making it even larger.

"Shit," he huffs.

I take the jumper, grateful for his distractions as Liam is now fixated on the little metal tabs, not caring who is resting their arm where. Ethan is happily staring out the window, chewing away. Noah puts his headphones in and starts tapping away on his phone.

I pull out a small packet of baby wipes that I never got out of the habit of carrying since the kids were babies. I now always have a small packet in my handbag. A packet also resides in my car for quick clean ups.

These boys are so damn messy.

I start scrubbing at the stain with the wipe and it starts to fade. Lucky it was only a tiny bit, and we got to it fast enough.

"I still think we should stick with the original. Wimbledon White with a blue centre stripe."

Clark nods like he understands exactly what Liam is on about. Those two have bonded over the car. Every spare moment Liam has been out there working on it with Clark.

I can't explain the feeling of seeing these boys with him. Seeing them so happy again and having someone else to spend time with them. Sometimes I'm so busy that I don't get the time to just be with them. To join them in the things they love like I used to when Callum was still around.

It's been nice to have that again.

The boys start to settle into their own things. The fight over the arm rests is completely forgotten now. It will probably be three point two seconds until the next disagreement.

We ended up just telling the boys about the trip. I needed to get their passports organised, so it was just easier. We all sat around the dinner table, and I told them that we wanted to plan a trip to France. They were ecstatic. Well, Noah and Ethan were. Liam asked what the weather would be like and if there were beaches.

We had to get organised fairly fast after that as we wanted to catch the end of summer in Europe. I hadn't worried about taking the kids out of school. But the school had given them assignments that they can complete centred around the holiday so they didn't fall behind.

We decided on flying from Perth to Singapore, staying a few nights at Sentosa Island and exploring Singapore. Then flying from Singapore to London and staying a week there before heading to Paris. We'll stay for a week, then head to Barcelona for the beaches.

It seemed like a waste to come so far and not try to see more. But we also didn't want to spend the whole time travelling and only getting a day or two in each place.

For the trip home, we decided to go to Thailand and stay for a few days and then head back to Perth. The flights were brutal to do in one shot so breaking them up with a few days somewhere made sense. Especially when managing three teenage boys' emotions.

We spent nights sitting at the dinner table planning the trip. Noah, the organiser, was so helpful, researching places to stay and things to do. He has even made an itinerary for each day so we can cram the most into it.

I have never been overseas and neither have the boys. So excitement levels are high. I can't believe how life changes in the blink of an eye. Five years ago, I would have never thought I would be doing anything else. My life felt content. Full. Three kids and a husband I adored.

Three years ago, I couldn't see a way out of the dark shadows that encased me. Left widowed with three children, I never imagined I would ever find love again. I didn't want to.

Then I met Clark, and the whirlwind that followed was intense passion and overflowing love. I never imagined I would be able to feel these things again. I never imagined I would be able to give my kids this kind of family again. It feels so surreal.

Guilt still gnaws at me from time to time. Sometimes it feels like I'm cheating on Callum. Like I'm doing something wrong by letting myself receive this kind of love and for giving it back.

I knew Callum. I knew him better than anyone else. I know that he would want this for me. He would want me to be happy. He would want the boys to have this. And if it can't be with him, I know that he would have liked Clark.

That feels strange to think. My late husband and my boyfriend in a room together. But I know that Callum would shake Clark's hand and say, "Thank you." I know that because, if it was me, if I was the one who passed, it would have broken me to see my family hurt. To see them lonely and in so much pain. I would want them to be happy. If the shoe was on the other foot and I had been the one to go, I would be looking down on my family smiling if they found this kind of love again.

Tears sting at the back of my eyes, threatening to spill. I try to blink them away, but a traitor sneaks past my lashes and makes it way down my cheek. I move to wipe it before anyone sees, but Clark is already there, watching me fondly.

His body turns towards me, blocking me from the boys so they don't see me cry. He gently runs the pad of his thumb across my cheek, wiping the tear away. Then he wraps an arm around me, pulling me into the nook of his shoulder, the part where my head fits almost too perfectly, like he sculpts that little divot right below his collarbone just for me.

"You okay?" His voice is soft, meant only for my ears. I feel his breath brush the top of my head.

"I'm really happy. These are happy tears."

"I'm really happy, too."

"Thank you, and not just for this trip that is wildly over the top." I laugh, the tears drying. "But for everything. For not letting me push you away, for loving me, for loving the boys. Everything."

"I got you, always. Thank you for letting me. For loving me back. For giving me this family."

I settle into his arms and close my eyes. I don't know what this feeling is called. Bliss, peace, love, home, contentment.

I know I've felt it before. But it's not the same.

It's not more or less.

It's just...

Different.

Finally, I let myself sink into that feeling, allowing myself to accept this as my family. To accept it all. I'm allowed to move on, guilt-free.

I deserve to be loved. To feel love. To accept love.

47

Can we keep him

Clark

I'm sweaty in places I didn't know you could sweat. I swear even my knees are sweating. It's not the heat. The weather is perfect here. Sunny and twenty-eight degrees celsius. Not a breeze in sight.

We have just been to the top of the Eiffel Tower after waiting in line for what seemed like days among the crowd. Up the glass lifts, the view was already spectacular. We then made it to level one and waited in line again to head to the top. We had marvelled at the three sixty degree views. Looking out over the city from that height was a surreal feeling. I had to admit, it was worth the crowds and the wait. And the slightly nauseating feeling that was swirling in my gut at being so far away from having my feet on solid ground.

The boys wanted me to do this at the top, but I knew it would be too crowded. I wanted something slightly more private.

I know Hannah would want the same. I don't want everyone listening in or clapping.

Plus, what if she says no?

The thought grips me around the throat and feels like it is choking the air from my lungs, but I breathe through it.

We make our way back down and across to the large perfectly manicured rectangle lawn that sits across the street.

Shit, this is it.

This is what we had planned. I place my hand in my pocket, wrapping my fingers around the little box that has resided in there all day. I give it a squeeze to reassure my brain that it is still there.

We have adjoining rooms at our hotel—Hannah and I staying in one room and the boys staying in the other. The boys and I had come up with a plan before we left home. They then spent the last few nights locked in their room apparently creating what I needed, away from Hannah's eyes.

I wanted the boys to be involved. I wanted a beautiful backdrop, but I didn't want it to be too public.

We had come and visited the tower at night, and it was spectacular. Part of me now regrets that I didn't do it under the sparkling lights against a milky sky. But I wanted the video. I wanted the memento to keep forever, and I thought this was the best way.

I lead us to a spot on the grass that will allow us to get the tower in the background. "Let's get a photo here."

The boys, who have been complaining at the sheer volume of photos Hannah has been making them pose for, obediently comply.

They know this is the plan.

"I'll ask someone if they can take it for us," I advise. There are enough people around to have someone get the shot without it being too crowded to make this awkward.

A couple who looks like a mother and daughter are close by, and I approach, feeling a little embarrassed. But I need someone else to take the video otherwise she will see on the front of the screen as we try to get the shot.

I politely ask them if they would mind getting a picture for us and they agree. Noah pulls Hannah over to a spot that allows us to get the view of the tower in the background, and the other boys follow, standing behind her.

"It's recording, not a photo. Please just keep going and don't react to anything. Pretend you're taking pics and getting the right angles. Is that okay?" I speak quietly so that Hannah can't hear, but she is far enough away now.

The lady raises her eyebrows at me as she smirks, but she nods and says, "Okay." The pair move back slightly and keep the camera on us as they move around.

The boys shuffle behind Hannah, and I drape my arm over her shoulder. The boys came up with this plan and I loved the idea.

"Why don't you guys come next to us?" Hannah says, trying to grab Liam and move him next to her.

"Nah, we're good here."

"But they won't even be able to see you behind us." Hannah reaches for Liam again.

"Let's just take the photo, Mum. We're right here."

She huffs but faces forward and smiles.

"Did you get it?" Hannah asks the lady.

"Almost," the woman yells back. "I'll just get a couple more from a different angle." She kneels and aims the camera up to try to get the full tower in the background, playing the perfect part.

I hear the boys shuffling around behind us, but I keep my arm firm on Hannah, making sure she stays facing forward.

"What are you boys doing?" she asks as they giggle and carry on.

I turn my head to make sure the boys are done. Noah is shoving something back into his pocket and Liam has his arms behind his back. Ethan has the biggest cheeky grin across his face.

Noah nods at me.

"Okay, I think we got it," I say as I move towards the pair holding my phone.

"That is going to be the worst photo ever," Hannah laughs as I take the phone from the lady.

"I think it turned out amazing. Take a look." The lady who looks like the mother eyes me with a smirk as I pass the phone to Hannah.

She opens the photo app. "There's only a video here. What are you guys up to?"

I reach over her and click on the video. It starts to play with no sound. A clear image of me walks away from the camera and wraps an arm around her. Liam runs behind us, doing a star jump and a pose to the camera mid-air. Noah walks to him and nudges him playfully, while Ethan copies his brother and runs and jumps. Hannah twists but I turn her back to the front.

We stand and smile like we are posing for a photo, all in our mandatory matching holiday T-shirts that Hannah had made for us. Then the boys remove paper from their back pockets. Hannah tries to turn again and in unison they all place their hands behind their backs. She shakes her head but faces the camera again.

"What is going on?" She looks up from the phone in her hand. All of us, including the two ladies, are watching. She looks back down to watch the video again.

It plays out, the boys removing their hands from behind their backs and holding up signs above their heads. Those little shits. My eyes sting, holding back my emotions as I read the signs. A sign that now appears to be as much for me as it is for Hannah.

Hannah's eyes are fixated on the video. She's smiling, but I can see how glassy they have become.

The boys start cracking up laughing and shoving each other around, obviously happy with how their signs have affected both Hannah and me. They were supposed to write *WILL* on one piece of paper, *YOU* on another and *MARRY ME* on the last.

I turn to the boys and Noah shrugs. Ethan laughs, and Liam just nods at me. I tune back into the video.

The words are smaller, but you can make it out.

Noah's sign says: WILL YOU MAKE HIM OUR BONUS DAD!

Ethan's says: SAY YES!

Liam's says: WE WANT TO KEEP HIM.

I wasn't going to drop to one knee. I know Hannah would hate a big scene, but it feels appropriate now, as technically I haven't actually asked her since the boys have changed my sign idea. I mean, if I'm honest, I do like theirs better.

My hand wraps around the little box in my pocket and I pull it out. Dropping down to one knee, I open the lid. "Hannah, I'm so in love with you and these crazy boys. Will you marry me?"

"Bonus Dad." The words are barely more than a whisper as they fall from her lips. "That's what BD means, isn't it?" Tears spill from her eyes now. The boys had taken to calling me that. Hannah had questioned it, but the boys and I had told her it was an inside joke.

I stand, placing a kiss to her forehead. "I know this is a lot, especially with the kids."

"You organised all this?"

"The boys and I, yeah. They helped me pick the ring as well."

Her eyes flutter down to the ring sitting in the box. The sparkling-coloured sapphires and diamonds glinting in the sun are stark against the black lining. Her eyes widen, like she didn't really take it in before. "Holy shit."

"Do you like it?"

"Clark, that thing is huge."

I laugh. I think that's a yes to liking the ring. But is it a yes to marrying me?

The mother and daughter duo hover off to the side, giving us space but clearly too invested in the outcome to leave.

I run my hand through my hair, nerves eating at me. The boys excitedly hover around us.

Hannah's fingers skim over the delicate jewels. "I love you too, Clark," she says as she leans up and kisses me. I pass the ring from between us and Noah grabs it. My arms wrap around Hannah as she buries her head in the crook of my neck and whispers, "Yes," around her tears.

"Was that a yes, Mum?" Liam asks. "We can't hear you."

She nods her head but doesn't remove it from my shoulder. I grip her tighter. Hannah reaches an arm out and blindly searches for one of her kids. It lands on Noah, and she pulls him into us.

Ethan weasels his way in between us, wrapping his arms around his mum. I peel an arm from Hannah and find Liam. Placing a hand on his shoulder, I pull him into us as well, wrapping my arm around them all.

Hannah's sobs quieten as we stand locked in a family hug.

"Okay, this is getting weird now." Liam is the first to pull away. Hannah and I laugh.

Noah hands the ring box to his mum. "Did we choose good?"

"Yeah, put it on already," Ethan adds.

"I hope you have good travel insurance cos that thing costs more than our car," Liam adds.

Hannah's eyes shoot to me, and I fold my lips together, scratching the back of my head awkwardly. "It wasn't that much," I add sheepishly.

"WHAT, it was..." I cut Liam off with a gentle shoulder nudge and he looks at me, raising his eyebrows. "It wasn't that much," he quickly repeats.

I take the box from Hannah's hand, removing the ring. It feels tiny in my fingers. Bringing her hand up, I ask, "May I?" I place the ring in front of her finger. She nods and I slide it on, mentally high-fiving myself for nailing the size.

"It feels strange to have a ring on this finger again," she admits. "But I love it, and you."

48

Bag of goodies

Hannah

The rest of the time in Paris was amazing, filled with food, shopping and sightseeing. And the highlight, of course: Disneyland.

We are now in Barcelona. We rented a three-bedroom apartment through Airbnb. It is a five-minute walk to Playa de Bogatell, and is in an apartment complex that has a pool. It's perfect. I thought I loved Paris, but something about the slightly warmer weather here, the people, the beaches, the food, and all that Spain has to offer has me head over hills in love.

Quite honestly, I never want to leave.

The only thing I don't love is the coffee. It has been impossible to order a latte the way I like it, even with learning some of the language. We had an app that helped us translate to Spanish, but we have fast realised that in Barcelona they speak a slightly different dialect called Catalan. Regardless, we have tried our best. But no matter how well I try to say, "Café con leche, por favor," the coffee is never right for how I have it back home. And nowhere has hazelnut syrup. Clark is fine because he likes his coffee black and strong anyway, which seems to be the standard around here.

The boys have loved Barcelona as well and we have spent the days exploring or relaxing by the pool or on the beach. We did a day trip to Costa Brava to kayak and snorkel through caves. This was possibly my highlight. The crystal-clear water making way to large cave mouths was breathtaking.

We hired bikes and ventured out into the city to visit Park Güell and the Sagrada Familia. Right now, it is siesta. A part of the day I have grown to love more than the tapes. A lot of shops shut down, and the streets clear out. We have all taken to napping. I don't know how we are going to kick this habit when we get home and have to get back to normal life.

The city is alive at night. It doesn't get dark till past nine, which is the strangest thing to us. Families head out to dinner at 9:30 PM and it is not uncommon to see children playing or out with their parents at ten at night.

We all stay up late, enjoying the night life and the beautiful city, and then sleep in and explore, or relax on the beach, then enjoy a siesta in the afternoon.

The boys are in their rooms napping. My body is pulled close to Clark's with his heavy arm draped over me. I'm in nothing but a bikini with a white cotton sarong wrapped around my waist.

Drying saltwater leaves little white marks along my skin that is still warm from the aftereffects of the sun. That and the heat radiating off Clark's bare upper body next to me.

We lay on our side facing each other. Clark's eyes are closed but I can tell he isn't asleep. His fingers absentmindedly skim across my back, stroking back and forth. The feeling sends tingles down my spine all the way to my core. He moves up to the string of my bikini, toying with them, before his hand flattens out and smooths the skin underneath where they are tied at my back. Finding the string again, he gently pulls to unravel them. They fall open as his fingers move up and down my now goosebump lined back, around to the side of my ribs. Turning his hands, his knuckles run over my skin just under the triangle of my bikini.

I feel the tops of his fingers trail the underside of my breasts, making my nipples harden. His eyes are now open and focused on the little pieces of material that cover them. He sees the effect he is having on me. My body gives me away.

A lazy smile crosses his face. My hands itch to touch him. Tracing my own finger over his firm chest, I swirl the light patch of hair in the centre, down smooth, hard abs, and stop at a line of hair that disappears under his shorts. I know exactly where it leads.

His fingers find my nipples, and he slightly pinches and rolls them. I can't help but arch my back, pushing my chest further into his big hands. A moan slips from my lips. He chuckles, clearly loving the effect he is having on me.

His hands explore my upper body before he brings them up around the back of my neck. Finding the tie there, he pulls at the string, releasing it and slowly pulling the material away from my body, leaving my chest exposed to him. His mouth finds my nipple, and he flicks his tongue over it before sucking it into his mouth and gently nipping.

A moan I can't seem to keep in escapes again.

"You better be quiet or I will put something in that pretty mouth of yours." His voice is low and guttural. The words have an instant effect on me. My body tenses and wetness pools between my thighs.

Shy Clark is endearing and sweet, but fuck me if I don't love the way this man has come out of his shell in the bedroom. He has learnt how much I love him to take control, and he has no issues stepping into that role. It drives me wild.

I clench my thighs, running my tongue over the top of my teeth, a ragged breath on my lips. I want to obey but I also love pushing him. I want to see what he does.

So when he deftly undoes the tie of my sarong, letting it fall open and slides his hands under my bikini bottoms, finding me wet and waiting, his fingers spreading my wetness around before sliding them into me, I make sure I moan a little louder.

It's not even exaggerated though. The feeling of his thick fingers entering me while he nips and then licks over my nipples has me ready to combust.

I try to grind on his hand, but he pulls his fingers from me.

"I warned you," he rasps as he rises to kneel before me.

I think he is going to lower his shorts and choke me with his cock. My mouth waters for it. But instead, he moves off the bed and heads to his suitcase, pulling a little black velvet bag from it.

"What else have you been hiding in that suitcase of yours?" I lean up on my elbow, intrigued. This man surprises me. Going from asking permission and looking shocked when I asked him to wrap his hands around my throat, to now pulling out a... Is that a ball gag? Oh, my gosh, security must have had a field day when they scanned his suitcase.

"Ohh shit." I close my mouth and pinch my lips together. This is something I have never done.

His eyes are dark as he moves back towards me. Tossing the bag on the bed next to me, he raises an eyebrow as he holds up the strap with the gag, as if asking permission.

I nod. Why the fuck not?

"Turn around," he orders as he flicks the lock on our bedroom door, ensuring no wandering kids can enter.

I shift up to my knees and turn my back to him. He gently sweeps my hair from my shoulders, and the gag appears in front of my face.

"Open."

I do as he says, and he places the rubber ball in my mouth, securing it behind my head. My jaw is forced open wide, and I'm not going to lie, it is not comfortable. But my body is humming with anticipation, my pussy is throbbing, and every nerve ending feels alive with electricity.

I breathe through my nose, testing it out. Okay, it's easy enough, but it is impossible to swallow, and saliva quickly pools in my mouth.

His stubble scratches at my neck, and I feel his breath warm on my skin before he kisses up my neck from behind. "Tap me twice if it gets too much," he whispers in my ear.

I nod again and he roughly pushes me face first into the mattress. Gripping my hips, he yanks them up to meet his as he kneels behind me. My breathing is ragged, and I try to swallow as I prop myself up slightly onto my elbows.

His tongue licks a line from my ass all the way down to my pussy as his fingers find my clit. He slides in and out of me, before licking up and down between my ass and pussy. I'm suddenly glad for the gag because I want to scream. My body is wired, and I want something more inside of me.

His tongue teases me over and over again as his fingers on my clit bring me to the edge before backing off. His pace changes from hard and fast while I squirm under him, only to ease off at the perfect or completely frustratingly imperfect time.

I feel like I'm riding a wave. Up up up over and down down down again. Getting right to the peak only for the tide to change as he slows his rhythm.

He knows exactly what he is doing, the bastard. But I fucking love it. I want to swat his hand away and take over on my clit so I can come. But I know if I do that, he will tie my hands up and *mmm*, do I want that?

I decide to just embrace it. For now!

His hand leaves my clit, and he slides a finger deep inside of me, moving it front and back, hitting my walls and making me squirm. He adds a second thick finger, then a third. *Fuck.* My back arches and I push back into him. He pulls them from me altogether and I moan around the gag. It is nothing more than a muffled cry.

I'm not empty for long though. There is no warning before his hard cock slams into my soaked pussy. My arms give out, and my head sinks into the soft mattress. His pace is fast and hard, and my body shakes as I ride that wave up again.

"Fuck, baby," he moans softly, folding his body over mine to find my ear before straightening back up. Gripping my hips, he pulls me back onto him to meet each thrust. I pant around the gag, drool coating it as his pace slows.

His hand leaves my hip and runs a line down my spine all the way to my ass. He toys with me. He presses slightly but doesn't enter. He keeps his finger there, applying slight pressure. The feeling mixed with his slow steady strokes has me almost ready to implode.

He leans down over me again, finding my ear and sucking the lobe. "I still want to fuck you here." His finger presses harder on the *here,* and I relax into it as it enters me slightly.

I moan around the gag. I want him everywhere. It's been forever since I've done anal, but I remember enjoying it, especially when this turned on.

I turn my head, making eye contact with him and nod, giving him the approval he is looking for.

His eyes darken and they flick back down to my ass. His pace doesn't falter, sliding in and out of me. He looks like a God. His broad chest flexes as he thrusts and his arms tense as his hands grip my hips.

He slows before letting spit slip from his perfect lips to hit my ass. His finger finds its way back there and he moves the wetness around, sliding his finger back in and out. Only a little bit at first. Each stroke pushes it further and further inside of me.

The feeling of both holes being filled is euphoric. My body screams and I pant around the gag.

"Do it," I try to say, but it comes out as nothing more than muffled sounds.

"What's that, baby? I can't hear you," Clark whispers in my ear.

"Fuck my ass," I try to say, but again, nothing but muffled cries.

He lets out a chuckle before leaning over me again. "Are you begging, baby? Cos it sounds a lot like you are begging for me to fuck you here." He pushes his finger deeper on the *here*.

My body reacts before my brain has a chance to catch up; my head is nodding fast. Fuck I have never wanted to come so badly. I want him everywhere.

His cock still slides in and out of my soaked pussy, the added pressure in my ass making me drenched. He adds a second finger and the feeling has me sucking in a breath, gasping.

The stretch, the burn. It's not painful but it's a feeling I can't describe. My body is pulsing. Pressure gives way to bliss once my body adjusts. I turn my head, locking eyes on Clark's as he moves his fingers and cock in and out of me in unison.

"You want my cock here, Hannah." His voice is low and husky.

I nod again and he doesn't miss a beat. He pulls everything from me, but I don't have time to think of how empty I feel. He grips my hips and flips me over.

I land on my back. He grips my thighs, yanking me down into him and shoving a pillow under my hips, propping me up and angling me how he wants. Then he pulls lube from his magic bag of goodies. Gripping his cock, he covers his length in it, before he pushes his cock slowly into my ass. I gasp around the gag, eyes shutting at the pressure.

"Eyes on me, baby. I want to watch your face while I fuck your ass with my cock and your pussy with my fingers."

I snap my eyes open, finding his as he slowly pushes deeper into me. His fingers find my clit, and he rubs over the bud. The pressure in my ass moves to pleasure.

"That's it, baby. Relax for me." The praise has my body tingling, relaxing and allowing him deeper. "Good girl. I'm almost in," he husks. The words have me blushing despite the fact that he has me gagged and his cock in my ass.

His eyes stay fixed to mine as he pushes fully inside of me. My body relaxes around him.

"Fuuck yess," he groans quietly, before sliding back out and in again. Slowly at first. "You okay?" His face turns serious as he eyes me. I nod and claw at his chest, pulling him closer, wanting him to move. He smirks and starts thrusting in and out of me a little faster.

His fingers find my pussy, and he pushes two inside of me, curling them up. They move in sync with his cock as he fucks me in both places.

My body convulses under him, and I find my clit with my fingers. Every nerve in my body hums. The feeling is so overwhelming. I swear it's mere seconds before I'm screaming around the gag and biting down on the rubber. I claw at Clark's shoulders and back as he leans over me, his body weight solid. Unclipping the gag behind my head with one hand, he quickly moves it out and replaces it with his mouth, swallowing my cries as I come in what feels like the most intense orgasm I have ever had. My body pulses. Dark spots dance across my vision. My heart and head are pounding.

He doesn't slow his pace as he fucks my ass. A few more hard and fast strokes later, he is collapsing over me in ecstasy.

"Fucking hell," he mutters, letting his body rest on me. "Eres perfecta," he whispers in my ear.

I think he just told me I was perfect. How long had he been practising that one?

I want to say, "You too", in Spanish but I have no idea how, so I settle on, "Ditto."

"Let me get you cleaned up so we can do that all again."

I chuckle as he pulls out of me and scoops me into his arms, carrying me to our adjoining bathroom. Clark holds true to his word, only this time he fucks my pussy while he holds me up against the cool tiles of the shower.

I could get used to this lifestyle.

49

To hold forever

Hannah

I completely surrender to the feeling, losing control and letting him lead. Clark dips me back and my hair tumbles down behind me, long loose waves cascading to the floor. I tilt my head back and his mouth finds my neck, placing a gentle kiss there.

I hear cheering and clapping but I don't care to turn and see the crowd. It isn't large, just our closest friends and family. It's intimate and exactly how we wanted it. Being a second wedding for us both, we weren't overly concerned with having anything large. But a chance to get dressed up like this again was almost too good to pass up.

We didn't rush it, taking about a year to plan and book things in. The year has been as close to perfect as you could get. We have continued to live between the two houses, finding a balance and a love between both the beach and the bush—having the best of both worlds. The boys have loved having Clark around. Clark and Liam finished the car. The boys drove to the winery in it today.

Clark and I will head back to the resort in it later tonight. We decided to stay at the same resort where we met. Well, technically we met on the side of the road, but I wasn't about to have my wedding there. It didn't feel right having it at the resort either, as that was where Olivia and Rowan were married. Even though both Olivia and I said it doesn't matter, it still just felt wrong to use the same spot as one of my best friends.

Plus, every time I have ever driven past this place, I have thought it would be a beautiful setting for a wedding. We head down south a lot, and it is just off Caves Road. Cobblestone steps lead down to a path, and multiple large, wooded sleeper rails form arches that finish at a pond's edge. Lush green vines snake and twirl up around and over them with bursts or fragrant pink roses and delicate sprays of pure white, pea-shaped flowers against lime green foliage.

It was the most beautiful setting to walk down. The train of my simple dress followed behind me. Seeing Clark in a suit, standing there with my three boys, their faces glowing with joy beside him, made my heart melt into a puddle on the floor.

The large cellar has been converted to our reception area. A few circle tables surround a centre dance floor. Rustic wooden floorboards and floor to ceiling wrap around windows that look out to the vineyard.

The place is stunning.

All our closest friends are present. Clark's family have flown over from Queensland and all mine are here. Callum's, too. I know that seems weird, my dead husband's family at my new husband's wedding. But they are still a constant in our lives. They wanted to be here, and I wanted them here as well.

I know that Callum has Ari, our little baby boy. We finally were able to have that conversation and give him a name he deserved. He sits next to Callum in our home, matching urns with matching rings resting atop them. It felt right giving him my ring to forever hold.

I know they are both watching, smiling. I know Callum would want this for me. So, I allow myself to have it.

Clark pulls me back up into his arms and we do a few more spins before others head onto the dance floor and join us.

The night disappears into a swirl of dancing, toasting and chatting before we are given the final call at 11 PM. Most of the guests are staying at Driftwood Estate. We organised a bus that has pulled up to collect everyone. Clark and I have a driver who is driving us back in his Mustang.

We decided to keep the wedding kid friendly, so the place was filled with children dancing and laughing and eventually a game of spotlight was held out around the vineyard by some of the older kids.

My mum and dad take the boys—who insist they don't need anyone watching them—onto the bus to make sure they get to their room safely. They have their own suite in an adjoining room to us.

So, we at least had some semblance of privacy. If such a thing exists with three children.

The bus leaves and our driver takes us back to the resort. Clark and I sit side by side in each other's arms in the tiny back bucket seat. His hand rests on my thigh through the split in my dress and he gently strokes his thumb back and forth.

I have been dying to have him to myself all weekend. Between the kids and all our family and friends, the last-minute planning and the busy morning today, I feel like I have barely seen him.

We beat the bus by quite a stretch. Knowing that my parents will take care of getting the boys to their room, we decide to sneak off before they arrive back.

"Want to go for a walk along the beach?" Clark asks. The night is sublime. It's late but it is warm and still. Not a cloud in the sky. Stars dance overhead, with the soft glow of the moon enough to light a path.

"Relive the last time we were here?" I ask.

He smiles at me. "If that's the plan, give me a minute." He leads me to a bench seat just by the path and I sit down. He has his jacket folded over his arm, his sleeves rolled up his thick forearms.

He wraps the jacket over my shoulders. It's not cold and I don't need it, but the gesture makes my heart flutter all the same.

He disappears back into the resort, and I lean back against the bench, watching the stars dance and reliving memories of the night in my mind. The smile on Clark's face as I walked down the aisle. The way my three boys looked so grown up standing next to him as his best men. Dancing with each of my children.

Clark comes walking back towards me not long after he left with long, fast strides. He looks to die for. Black pants and crisp white shirt tight over his broad chest. His undone tie draped around his neck. He is carrying a blanket and a pillow.

"Smart," I say.

He comes up in front of me and drops to a knee. Taking my foot in his hand, he skilfully undoes the strap of my shoe before sliding it off, repeating the process with the other one before kicking off his own.

We walk hand in hand down the beach path, and find a secluded spot up by the dunes far enough away from the resort. Clark lays the blankct on the sand and places the pillow down. He sits with his legs out, leaning back on his arms. I drop the jacket from around my shoulders and bunch my dress up to straddle him, sitting on his lap.

He brings his hands to my face and pulls me in for a kiss. "My wife," he says as he breaks the kiss. "I have been dying to say that."

I chuckle into his neck as his fingers run along the top of my arms, sliding the chiffon sleeves of my dress off the curve of my shoulder. A soft breeze caresses my skin where my backless dress leaves me exposed. It makes me shiver.

His warm hand follows the breeze as they splay over my lower back, pulling me closer into him. Gently, he grips a fistful of hair and pulls my head back, angling my neck up to his mouth. He trails kisses down to my collarbone and then along to my other shoulder. Using his teeth to grip the second sleeve, he slides it down, hands never leaving my body.

I grind into him, loving the feel of the night sky above us, the gentle laps of the waves behind us and the soft cool sand below us.

Finding my mouth with his, Clark deepens the kiss and it turns feverish. Hot and hard. Hands pulling at each other's hair and clothes until we are naked. He pulls a condom out of his pants pocket as I straddle him. His hard cock teases my wet pussy.

"I came prepared this time." His smile is devilish as he starts to rip the packet. "Didn't want to make a mess on your dress."

Callum had a vasectomy after Ethan, so I have not been on contraception for over nine years. I really didn't want to go back on anything, which Clark supported. Since realising he can have children, we have been using condoms or strategically timed pull outs.

We've talked about it and while Clark has expressed how much he does want a baby still, he has said he wants us more. Me and the boys. That it is enough for him. He doesn't need to try again. I haven't known where I am at with it completely.

Until now.

I shake my head at him. His eyes find mine in a silent question. I grip his cock around the base and sink onto him. He tosses the condom packet to the side, gripping my hips. I grind into him, and he pulls me deeper. We move together, deep and slow, basking in the moonlight's energy.

Clark's large arm snakes around my waist and he flips me, guiding me slowly to my back on the blanket. I find the pillow with my head. Gripping my thighs, he pulls them apart and slides back into me. My head sinks further back into the pillow as he moves. His skin is illuminated by the soft glow of the moon.

I meet every thrust before he leans over me, my legs wrapping around his hips, pulling him into me deeper. He kisses me hard and fast. Both of us are breathless, panting into each other's mouths as our hips move, chasing the release.

His arms wrap around my upper body, pulling me into his chest, locking me to him as he moves. Our breaths become ragged as we get closer. I can feel his body tensing.

"You sure," he whispers in my ear. His breath is warm and the feeling on my skin only sends me closer to the edge.

I nod against him, tugging at his short hair, pulling him back to me.

His resolve lets go. His thrusts become harder, faster, deeper and more frantic. His body clings to mine as much as mine clings to him. Sweat drips from his skin, mixing with my own. His mouth is hot and heavy, taking my breath with each of his own sharp inhales as we both crash.

Pleasure courses through our veins, and my body shakes with the release. Clark collapses down onto me, slick with sweat.

He kisses my cheek. "I love you, my wife."

I chuckle into his neck again. "I love you too, my husband."

I never thought I would say those words again, especially to another man. But I'm glad I get to.

50

I don't want to be rude here

Clark

I feel my phone vibrate in my pocket. Wiping my hands on the rag by the bonnet, I pull it out, expecting it to be Hannah telling me she is finished work.

We have been living between the two places. I have my work and equipment here and all the animals. It made sense to keep the place. Plus, I added quad bikes and extra horses for the boys.

The boys love it here. They often set up a tent in the backyard pretending to camp. They love bringing their friends out here, too. We set up huge bonfires and have camp out nights with all our friends.

Us dads have taken to making ghost walk trails. We go and hide in different places around the bush, even going so far as to climb trees and make spooky noises as one of us leads the kids along the walk, only to jump out and scare them along the way.

They have been some of the best nights of my life, surrounded by family and friends, cooking barbeques and sitting by a giant bonfire, while playing Spotlight and the hilariously scary bush walks.

Trail rides on the horses and making tracks with the bikes to ride along has also been a blast. I've finished renovating the place, having the extra motivation with Hannah helps. I loved having her input on the things I had no clue about.

I love that our kids—yeah, I'm calling them ours—get to have the best of both worlds. I work here during the day while Hannah is at work, or I head out to clients' houses to do work on their cars. I've picked up a bit more work to account for the extra mouths, but I make sure I'm around for all the important things.

I check my phone and my heart stops.

WHAT THE FUCK!

It's been almost two years since I heard from her. It had always played on a loop in the back of my mind. I didn't hound her for an answer because I knew she wasn't going to give me. It would have solved nothing.

I click on the message, intrigue winning out.

CHERIE: Clark, it's Cherie. I wasn't sure you would still have my number. I probably should call but I wasn't sure you would answer after how we left things, so I thought I would text. Can I call you?

My mind races. There would only be one reason she wants to talk. I would think so, anyway. Can't imagine she is just ringing after two years for a general chit chat.

I don't waste any time.

I hit dial on her number instantly. She answers before it even rings.

"Hi." Her voice is soft and low.

"Cherie, hi." I try to hide the urgency in my own. I don't want to lead with "what's up" or "get to the fucking point" so I suck in a breath and patiently wait for her to explain the reason for her message.

"How are you?"

"Cherie, I don't want to be rude here, but what's up?"

"Always straight to the point, aren't we, Clark." She is met with silence, so she continues. "Claire was bitten by a dog at a park."

"Shit, Cherie, is she okay?" I ask.

"She's okay now, but she did need stitches. Because of her age they put her under. Apparently it's easier because when they are so little, they can move too much, and since it was on her face they were worried about scarring."

"I'm so sorry. I hope you're all okay." No one wants a child to be hurt, but I can't help but wonder what this has to do with me. I don't voice that, though.

"Thanks. I think Cory and I are more affected than her. She is back to herself already. Still loves our dog. It was awful though."

"Poor thing. I'm glad she is all right.

"The owner was horrified, but we didn't want the dog put down because of it. I think Claire grabbed its ear or something. But it should have been on a leash around the kids."

"It sounds awful. I'm sorry." I don't know what else to say. It is awful, but it also has nothing to do with me. But I don't ask questions.

Just let Cherie continue.

"Well, when she went in for the surgery, I panicked. What if something went wrong? What if an accident happened that was more serious, and she needed an organ or blood, or I don't know. It just made me realise that we need to know if Cory really is her father. I bought a new test online, and we did it with Cory and Claire. It was a match. So, you're not her father, Clark."

I let out the breath I didn't realise I had been holding. I think in the back of my mind I knew this had something to do with that.

"Thanks. I appreciate you letting me know and despite every-thing, I am glad that Cory is her father." And I mean that. It all worked out for the best.

"Thanks, Clark. Believe it or not, I am sorry for what I did. I should never have hurt you like that."

"It was for the best. I'm pretty happy with my life right now." I'm not trying to rub it in or be harsh, but I have never been happier. I don't say as much to her though.

"I'm glad."

"I'm glad Claire is all right. I don't think that is something any parent wants to go through."

"Thank you. She will be fine. Okay, well I guess that's all I wanted to tell you."

"I appreciate it. Bye, Cherie."

"Bye, Clark."

I hang up and go to dial Hannah straight away to tell her. I can't hide the relief I feel. The huge weight lifted from my shoulders. It felt like the last missing piece of the puzzle being replaced. This thing that was always left dangling over my head, playing in the back of my mind like an itch that no matter how hard I scratched it never goes away. Dull but I can feel it.

I let out a deep breath. Hannah will be with a client right now. I'll tell her when I see her this afternoon. It will be better in person anyway. She is supposed to finish up at two and I was going to head around. We would then both go get the kids and head to football training together.

The time drags but eventually Hannah texts that she is finished. It's 1:45 PM. The smile doesn't leave my face as I make my way around to her place, ready to tell her the news.

51

Beautifully blended

Hannah

My hands are shaking as I hold the packet, clumsy fingers struggling to grip the slippery plastic. Finally, I get it open and place the contents on the bathroom sink.

I know Clark is waiting for my call to come around and we should probably do this together. I don't want to get his hopes up. I know he has said he is happy, and we are all he needs, but I know how much he wants this. If I tell him I'm late for my period, I know there will be a light of hope that will ignite deep within him. I know because I can feel it there within me.

With my age, chances are now I actually am perimenopausal and in fact not pregnant.

I try to push the fact that I'm now almost forty-two out of my mind. We haven't been actively trying. We haven't been tracking ovulation or forcing sex at certain times. We definitely haven't been trying not to though. We have just been enjoying ourselves. Not worrying about what happens.

We put the thought out there that if it is meant to be, it will be, and we will be happy either way.

But now I'm three days late.

I grip the little test and head into the toilet.

I know the instructions say to wait a certain amount of time before checking, but I didn't even read them. They are still folded up on the box. And honestly, I'm too impatient for that shit. I don't think I have ever waited the allocated time for any test I've done for the kids in the past.

I pull up the stick and clip the lid back on the tip, watching as the liquid starts to move across the white pad, turning it a yellowish colour. I watch as a distinctive pink line shows up instantly. My heart thuds in my chest as a second pink line comes up directly next to it, indicating that I am in fact pregnant.

Shit.

Anxiety floods me. The realism of it hitting me hard. But I want this.

I shut my practical brain down for a moment. The one that panics about money and people dying too young and the fact that I'm considered geriatric in the world of pregnancy. The added complications that could arise. The fact that I could miscarriage again. I shut it all down and allow myself to feel the excitement.

It's there.

A smile lights my face. I'm madly in love. I found love a second time. Some never even get to experience this kind of love once. I have three amazing boys and am about to bring a fourth child into this crazy, beautiful, blended family.

The warmth spreads across my chest. I grab my phone to call Clark.

I pause. This will be better in person. I want to see his face when I show him the test. I text him instead that I'm finished and to head around. He is opening the door no more than fifteen minutes later.

I take a deep breath and grip the test, heading from the kitchen table where I had sat tapping my feet for the last fifteen minutes.

"Hey," he says, chucking his keys into the bowl on the hallway table. "Guess what?" He looks so excited. He closes the distance between us and cups my face in his hands, placing a kiss to my forehead and then my lips.

I lean into him, wrapping my arms around him, still gripping the test. He didn't even notice it.

"What is it?" I ask.

He pulls back slightly, and I keep my arms around him to hide it.

"I'm not her father." His eyes are fixed on mine. "Cherie called." He goes on to explain the whole thing, never breaking contact with me.

I'm relieved for him, and for us. I know this was a weight on him. Truth be told, it always played in the back of my mind as well. A ticking time bomb of *what ifs*. What if one day a daughter he didn't know suddenly showed up?

"That's horrible for Claire and Cherie, but it's good to finally have answers. I know it was weighing on you." He kisses me again. "You might not be Claire's dad, but you are a dad."

"I know." He nods. "The boys are everything to me. I love them so much."

"Well." I release my arms from around his neck and hold out the test in front of him. "We might be adding another one to the mix."

His eyes glow. "What? For real?" His voice breaks as he takes the little test from me and clutches it in his hands. "Oh, my God, Hannah. Really?"

"Yeah, I was late, so I tested just now. It is obviously very early, but I'll make a doctor's appointment."

Clark crashes into me, wrapping me in his arms and picking me up clean off the ground. My feet dangle in the air and his head finds the nook of my neck as he nuzzles into me, breathing me in.

He spins me around in the dining room, clutching me almost as hard as he clutches the little test in his hand.

Epilogue: Completely perfect

Clark

I walk into the bedroom to find Hannah sitting on the bed, her face streaked with tears. The kids and I have been out all day in Perth to sort out a secret mission. We told Hannah that we were going to Timezone and lunch for the day. Well, we did go to Timezone, see a movie and go bowling, but we had other motives as well.

They stand at the threshold of the bedroom door, wanting to know what has happened but not wanting to rush in and crowd their mum.

I move to the side of the bed, kneeling in front of her and taking her hand in mine. "What's wrong, baby?"

Her eyes slowly find mine. They are bloodshot, with tears still spilling over her lashes. "Clark, I am so sorry. I don't know what happened."

"Talk to me. Tell me what's going on."

"I've lost it."

My face pales and I feel the energy behind me shift. "Lost what?"

"My ring, Clark. I've lost my ring. I always take it off when I do weights because the band rubs on the bar and the jeweller told me I would wear it out. It also feels horrible when I lift heavy. So, I always take it off. I did a workout early this morning and I always put it on my desk." Hannah never wanted a wedding band. She said her one ring was more than enough and felt it didn't need anything else. "I got distracted and..." She looks to the kids behind me. A blush creeps up my neck thinking about the distraction she is talking about.

She had woken at 5:30 AM to go workout. I had gone in there at precisely 5:45 AM and fucked her on the weight bench, and her desk, and against the wall.

But we don't say that around the kids.

She continues, "It must have gotten knocked to the floor." My mind thinks back to how I hungrily laid her on her desk and ate her out like she was breakfast.

I laugh.

"Clark, this isn't funny. I forgot about it and started working. I only just realised it wasn't on my finger and now I can't find it anywhere. It's gone." She brings both her hands to her mouth and a sob wracks her body.

SHIT! I hadn't thought about this. About how upset she would get if she realised it was missing. Fuck, fuck, fuck. I didn't think this plan all the way through.

I turn my head to the boys and nod. Noah is holding Sophia. She is only two, our baby girl among all the boys. She is spoiled beyond measure. She lives in one of our arms at all times, never having to walk or fetch her own snacks or really do anything herself.

Between all of us boys and Hannah, she is treated like a pint-sized princess, clicking her fingers and having someone fall at her feet to help her with whatever she needs. We're probably setting her up for failure in the real world, but in this house, she is our princess, and she is doted on.

Noah passes Sophia to Liam and grabs the box out of his pocket. With a sheepish smile, he passes it to me. I stay kneeling in front of Hannah as she watches the whole exchange, curiosity on her red blotchy face.

"I'm sorry," I say as I open the box in front of her. His eyes go wide with shock, before she wipes at her tears with the back of her hands. "I must admit, I maybe didn't think this plan all the way through. But I wanted to add a stone for Sophia."

Hannah delicately runs her fingers over the ring, eyeing the new marquise pink diamond that has been added to her ring. It sits high up in between the larger pear and marquise stones, joining the two of them together.

"The ring is complete now."

"OHH MYY GOD," she breathes out. "That is so beautiful."

Relief washes over me. I had organised this with the jeweller a long time ago. It took a while to source the pink argyle diamond because the mine here in Australia is now closed. Pink argyle diamonds are rare and expensive, especially in the size and shape I wanted.

But it was worth the time, effort and the money.

We had lined this day up and the jeweller had everything ready to go to get the stone added in the one day. She said it would be a push, but she managed to get it done. I knew Hannah would notice if it was gone longer than a day.

My hope was, I would distract her, nab the ring, and she would get too busy to worry about it during the day and we would be home before she really had a chance to think too much about it. Only the jeweller took longer than anticipated and we are home way later than planned.

"I'm sorry, Hannah. I didn't mean to upset you. I took it from your desk this morning."

She slaps me on the arm playfully.

"Sorry, Mum," the boys sing in unison. Sophia pushes out of Liam's arms to run to her mum.

Hannah picks her up and cuddles her. "You little turds. The lot of you."

"But how much do you love it?" Liam asks, coming in closer, eyeing the ring that Hannah has now put securely back on her ring finger.

"It's perfect. I love it. Thank you."

She is right.

It is perfect.

All of it is perfect.

Read on for a snippet of Return to Sender...

1: Love is only a feeling

Scarlett

I can feel his presence, his energy. Feel his eyes boring holes into me. It is so real that I swear I can hear his voice, as it fumbles over the syllables that form my name. The hairs on my neck stand up, pin prickles tickling my skin from within. Goosebumps roaming my arms. I don't have to see him to know he is here. I can just tell.

I know that sounds so hocus pocus. But I believe when two people suffer a trauma together, they connect in a way that cannot be explained. Almost like their souls become intertwined. They become intune with the other's presence, feelings and emotions without a word being spoken.

Bonded...

Although, it had always felt like this for us. From the moment I first laid eyes on him.

I remember the moment, the pull, as we drove down the driveway to our new home. I was just eleven years old. We had moved town for a job my mum had taken.

We had locked eyes for the longest time, as my mum had turned the car into our new driveway. His image was burnt into my mind like a hot branding iron to skin.

His eyes were the most amazing shade of green I had ever seen. Even from a distance they shone bright, like green emeralds in the sun. He was climbing a tree that was in his front yard.

"The neighborhood looks nice," my mum had said as she put the car in park and turned the engine off. She had turned to face me with a soft smile. "I wonder if he goes to your new school," mum continued, once she had noticed what or rather who I was looking at.

She was trying to make small talk to lighten the mood, I had been crying the entire drive. I remember feeling nothing but misery. I didn't want to move towns, leave my school. my friends, the only home I had ever known.

Yet despite my every protest and reasoning, here we were. Pulling up to our new house. In a new town, where I was to start a new school tomorrow.

In reality it was only an hour away from our previous home town. My mum had been offered a promotion within her aged care facility. It meant more money. But it also meant a transfer to a bigger facility, in a different town.

I knew that being a single mum who's partner had split at the mention of a baby being on the way, she had to make sacrifices. More money and less hours meant more time together. Just the two of us, the way it had always been. But to me, we might as well have been moving to another universe.

I looked out the window and across at the house next door. The lawn was perfectly manicured in strips of light and dark grass.

There were flower beds that lined the house with explosions of colorful flowers pouring out of them. A large tree in the middle of the yard. I looked up at the boy now sitting on a branch in the tree that rose high out the ground.

His piercing eyes were staring straight back at me. We were locked onto each other for what felt like a lifetime.

I was shaken from my daze and his hypnotizing eyes by yelling coming from the house.

"Vin," a deep dark grumble. "Vin," lounger, more frantic. "VIN," almost a roar.

He jumped off the branch landing on the ground and ran to his front door. A man stood in the doorway. He was tall and wide, taking up most of the entrance space.

The boy stopped briefly and looked back at me, a shiver coursing down my spine. Then he squeezed past the man and ran into the house. I sat in the car staring at the front door thinking about the question my mum had asked.

Would I see the boy at school tomorrow? The boy with the long wavy caramel hair. The boy that looked way too tall and gangly to be my age. The boy with the emerald green eyes.

If only I had known then what I know now.

So here I stand, water drops sprinkling my skin. The sprays from Niagara falls are raining down around me. Skin goose bumped and pin prickled. I can feel the earth shift. Like my world is about to be flipped on its axis. I have been living upside down for years. Right at this moment I can feel it, I know it is about to change...again.

Acknowledgements

I wasn't going to write any acknowledgements. Honestly, in all my years of reading, I can hand on heart tell you I have never read a single one. Sorry to all you amazing authors. But then I realised something. The acknowledgements aren't necessarily for all readers. They are for all the amazing people who helped you on your path here. A chance for them to see their name in a book and to hear the words "thank you" and "I appreciate you," because that matters.

So here goes.

Firstly my husband... Well, what can I say? I do a shit tonne of complaining but you fund my entire existence and make my life infinitely better in every way. Whilst I like to believe I could survive without you, because I am a strong independent woman, I don't ever want to find out if that's true. Without you, I don't believe I would have the confidence, inspiration, drive and well, the funds. You work so hard for our family, but always make time for us and for that I am eternally grateful. I know your hyperactive brain can't chill enough to read any of my stories, but you have listened to every plot outline. You have given ideas and feedback on how to make these stories better and make everything align and work. You never bat an eyelid when I ask you to help me with things, like building a book wall, making PR boxes or putting on costumes for social media. You are every book boyfriend rolled into one and I adore you.

My family, including my in-laws. You guys always show up. You have always supported everything I've done. Worked in stores, helped with social media, helped with the kids so I can follow this dream. Never asking for anything in return. I am so lucky to have such amazing support and encouragement from you. I love you all, thank you.

To my incredible friends. My sisters are included in this because you two are my best friends. There are too many to name but I know you know who you are. A few of us were talking over a few too many cocktails the other night about the definition of a woo girl. We all agreed that a woo girl is someone who shows up for their friends, who cheers them on fiercely no matter what they are doing. If that is the definition, then you are all the epitome of woo girls. I also have to include the guys in our circle who are just as loyal and supportive. You all have encouraged and supported every single crazy idea I've done, most of you for twenty plus years. Every business, every idea, every path I've taken. You have all shown up time and time again, cheering me on and helping in any and every way. Friends like you all are so rare. I love you all so much.

Jay, thanks for being my unofficial PA even though you are so busy with your own thriving business and life. You drop what you are doing and come and help me, coming to almost every event with me. You listen to every plot I have, give feedback, read unhinged books with me and never judge when I fall for the morally black anti-hero of the story. One day I will take us both to an international book event. We will meet Tate James and ask Corvin King to growl and call us good girls haha.

To my new bookish friends I've made on this journey, the readers, authors and owners of book stores. I can not believe how incredible this community is. Everyone sharing ideas and tips and hyping each other up along the way. Every one who stops and talks to me at events and buys a book, shares my content and messages me to chat. The authors I laugh with at events and book stores who take a chance on stocking my stories. It truly is an amazing community and I am so thankful I get to be a part of it. Thank you.

This book would not be what it is without the lovely women who beta read it for me. Yvi, Jessica, Nicola and Jaime-lee. It is anxiety inducing to put your work out into the world. You were the first people to read this story and you gave me such valuable feedback. It helped elevate this story to what it is now. Thank you.

Chloe, my editor, I am so glad I found you. Your insight and knowledge helped round this story out and I am so happy with how it turned out. Thank you for all the kind words and hype you have given me and this story.

Iryna, when I randomly messaged you and asked you to commission some art for my books, you dived straight in. You didn't baulk at my weird request or when I sent you images half naked to draw. You encapsulated my vision so perfectly and your artwork continues to be a stand out in the book. Thank you, you are so very talented.

I think that's it for now. Thank you everyone who picks up my stories. I appreciate you so much. I hope you love them.

Nicole x

About the author

Hi, I'm Nicole Bazley.

Okay, okay, I am going to be completely honest here. Nicole Bazley is a pen name. She is an alter ego created to gain the confidence to publish my first book. It's not that I don't think my stories are worthy. I do. It's just a daunting experience putting it out there. One I've held myself back from for many many years. Ten to be exact!

While the name isn't technically my real name, it embodies me in so many ways. Nicole is me! She is the creative author who has so many love stories to tell. This name means something to me on a deep level.

A little about me.

I love the beach, my family, being outdoors and staying active. I have always been a book lover and will read almost anything. My favourite authors are Jodie Picoult and Lee Child. I could read the Jack Reacher stories on repeat till the day I died.

I have always loved to write. Poems, songs and little stories, this is my first time putting my work out there.

I would say, I write contemporary romance stories that will have you free falling.

I hope you love them as much as I love writing them.

Nicole x

Let's stay connected!

Website – www.nicolebazley.com

Email – nicolebazleyauthor@gmail.com

Facebook - @niolebazleyauthor

Tiktok - @nicole.bazley.aut

Instagram - @nicolebazleyauthor